A Blessing for Miriam

A Blessing for Miriam

JERRY S. EICHER

HARVEST HOUSE PUBLISHERS
EUGENE, OREGON

Cover by Garborg Design Works, Savage, Minnesota

A BLESSING FOR MIRIAM
Copyright © 2015 Jerry S. Eicher
Published by Harvest House Publishers
Eugene, Oregon 97402
www.harvesthousepublishers.com

Library of Congress Cataloging-in-Publication Data
   Eicher, Jerry S.
   A blessing for Miriam / Jerry S. Eicher.
      pages cm. — (Land of promise ; book 2)
   ISBN 978-0-7369-5881-3 (pbk.)
   ISBN 978-0-7369-5882-0 (eBook)
   1. Amish—Fiction. I. Title.
   PS3605.I34B57 2015
   813'.6—dc23

2014021856

Printed in the United States of America

15 16 17 18 19 20 21 22 23 / LB-CD / 10 9 8 7 6 5 4 3 2 1

Chapter One

The flickering flames from the kerosene lamp danced on the bedroom wall as Miriam Yoder opened the letter from her *mamm*. She carefully pressed the fold creases out on the bed quilt. A letter from Possum Valley was an anticipated and blessed event, so Miriam had waited until they'd finished the supper dishes in Aunt Fannie's kitchen before she allowed herself this luxury. She focused on *Mamm*'s handwriting.

My dearest Miriam,

Greetings from home. We do so miss you, and think often of your life on the plains of Oklahoma. I hope all is going well with your school-teaching job and, of course, your relationship with young Wayne Yutzy. You'll have to bring him home sometime soon. We all look forward to meeting him, although from your description and Shirley's report when she arrived back in Possum Valley, there's no doubt in our minds that

5

we will fully approve of the young man. Your life is such a blessing to us and those around you, and also to the Lord, I'm sure.

We're all doing well health-wise, and for this we're thankful. Beyond that, I wish I had only light and cheerful news to share, but I don't. Our hearts ache for Shirley. I fear she's taken a turn for the worse. After baby Anna was born and Shirley came back to Possum Valley, we so hoped she'd be different. For a time it was so. Shirley seemed to have learned and grown from her time in Oklahoma. Why she decided to come back, I never could understand. The lessons in humility and virtuous living were exactly what she needed, but the *gut* lessons didn't last long.

Now it's early spring here, when life is all fresh and blooming outside, but my heart is anything but glad. I tremble to tell you this, Miriam, but Shirley went out with Jonas Beachy two nights last week, and that wasn't even on the weekend. You know how we feel about Jonas. A Mennonite boy would be bad enough, but Jonas is worse than either the Mennonites or the *Englisha* because his family left our community years ago. That church his dad runs now is awful strange— if one can believe the rumors. I tell myself that the children of others in the community have done worse in their *rumspringa* time than Shirley. I also comfort myself that she's only eighteen. Maybe she'll grow out of this phase. Maybe my hopes were too high after you and the two oldest boys turned out so well. I know one cannot expect the same thing from all of one's children.

Miriam laid the letter aside and sat up on the bed. The letter still had another page, but she needed to catch her breath. The news of Shirley's fresh disobedience wasn't too much of a shock. There had been hints in *Mamm's* letters since late last fall. What disturbed Miriam the most was the line that she herself had "turned out so well."

Mamm and *Daett* still didn't know about her secret. Miriam had never told them the whole truth about what Mr. Bland had left her in his will. They knew that the *Englisha* man she used to work for had given her his farm at his passing, but that was all. They didn't know about the money…the two million dollars.

Why had she kept the money hidden? She'd always been the *gut* girl at home. Even her *rumspringa* time had been a mild experiment in a few gatherings among the Possum Valley Amish youth. Why had she kept this secret from *Mamm* and *Daett*? Was she afraid *Daett* wouldn't bless her because of how he felt about money, let alone large sums of it?

Miriam pushed the dark-blue drapes aside from the bedroom window and looked over the spread of Uncle William's commercial greenhouse. In the daylight hours the place bustled with business. Wayne Yutzy, the handsome young man she was promised to, worked there. It had been back in September when he'd asked her to marry him and she'd accepted. When she then told him of her inheritance from Mr. Bland, he'd taken it in stride, much to her relief. She hadn't been able to bear carrying the secret alone any longer.

Miriam let the drapes flutter from her hand. What was the real reason she'd never told *Mamm* and *Daett* about the two million dollars? The answer to that wasn't too difficult: *Daett's* strong feelings about the unrighteousness of money and what the possession of it did to people. "The heart must never be set on riches," *Daett* said often. "The Lord gives no grace to those who love money."

But the money hadn't tainted Miriam like *Daett* claimed money always did. She hadn't spent it on material goods. That must mean something, didn't it? The money was sitting in the bank in

Sugarcreek, Ohio, far away from Oklahoma. And the Lord had showered grace upon her life—much more than she deserved. Look how she'd been accepted in the Oklahoma community. She'd even been asked to teach school for this term, and the students' parents were singing her praises at school gatherings.

Miriam had so much she was thankful for—the Lord, first of all, and Wayne after that. Wayne had loved her before he knew about the millions, and he still loved her afterward. Wayne wasn't like Ivan Mast back in Possum Valley. There *Daett* had been right about what money did to a person. Ivan had been sweet on her in their teenage years, and she'd anticipated he would ask her home from a hymn singing someday.

Ivan had given every indication he would, and she hadn't detected any change in his smiles…until the Sunday evening he took the beautiful Laura Swartz home. The Swartz family had moved back to Possum Valley from the community here in Oklahoma, but Miriam hadn't paid the new family much attention. How could she have been so blind? And how could her heart have become entangled with a man who would drop her at a whim? On top of that, he had sought to renew their relationship after Mr. Bland left her his farm. Ivan had arrived at the Yoder home with professions of renewed love and affection.

How could the man think she wouldn't see through that? To make matters worse, he'd done so *while* still dating Laura! Ivan claimed the inherited farm made little difference, but that wasn't true. Miriam rejected his advances. Soon after that, she traveled to the Oklahoma community with Shirley to help Aunt Fannie with her baby's arrival. Both Miriam and Shirley needed this fresh start. Shirley was trying to fight the temptation to be with Jonas Beachy, and Miriam was trying to recover from Ivan's betrayal.

The Lord had blessed the move, and soon after their arrival baby Jonathon had been born to Aunt Fannie and Uncle William.

The baby was now a happy, chubby boy. Even now Miriam could hear his cooing downstairs. He was, no doubt, ready for bed. Miriam smiled at the sound. Babies were surely one of the Lord's great blessings to the world. They came as a reminder of all that was sweet and innocent. Would she and Wayne have children? Miriam's neck and face flushed at the thought. She shouldn't think of such things, even though she was promised to Wayne. But she did love the man, and he would make a *wunderbah* father—if the Lord chose to give them children. Miriam knew married life wasn't always smooth, but she was confident the Lord would continue to supply grace for whatever might lie ahead of them after their wedding. Hadn't He done so up until now?

Miriam flopped on the bed. Why did she think of trouble that might lie ahead? Had the letter from *Mamm* affected her? Miriam sighed. *Yah*, in part, though her heart had already been troubled about something else. Esther Swartz from Possum Valley had appeared in the Oklahoma community this past month. She was Laura's older sister, and all the memories of how Ivan had betrayed Miriam came alive again. She had no reason to dislike Esther. She seemed like a kind and compassionate person—even if she was Laura's sister and just as beautiful.

And Miriam shouldn't blame Laura for the problems back home anyway. That trouble was with Ivan Mast. The Swartz girls had a *gut* reputation in Possum Valley, and Esther had come to Oklahoma to care for her elderly grandmother, Mabel. Who could fault a girl on such an errand? Aunt Fannie had said tonight at the supper table, "The Swartz family sure is appreciating what Esther does for her grandmother. I guess the Lord sends the help we all need when we need it."

The Lord would also help her, Miriam assured herself, because she needed help. She knew that Esther had a past with Wayne from when her family lived here before their move to Possum Valley. She could also tell from the way Esther acted that she still had feelings for him. Miriam hated thinking such thoughts, so she told herself that she was mistaken. Esther might smile in Wayne's direction, but she sent smiles to all the unmarried men.

Miriam played with the edges of the letter as her thoughts whirled. She hadn't dared bring up the subject with Wayne. She wanted to ask him why he was clearly returning Esther's shy smiles, but Wayne would think he was promised to a jealous woman. He'd claim he was fond of Esther like everyone else. She could hear him say the words even now. And why shouldn't she believe him? The Oklahoma Amish community was known for its friendliness. Wayne's love for her was a sealed matter, and she should trust him. He had begun to speak lately of their plans for the future, including what they would do with her two million dollars. Nothing was sure yet, but Wayne had his eye on a farm north of the community where they raised cattle. He'd even driven her past the place once so she could see for herself.

"With the two million," Wayne had told her, "we can start up after the wedding without the crushing debt load many young couples are under. Give the farm in Possum Valley to your parents," Wayne had decreed with a grin. "You want to stay here anyway."

And she did! His generosity warmed her heart. But what if Wayne's feelings for her were now influenced by his plans? Hadn't Ivan's affections turned because of her inheritance? What if Wayne wanted to return Esther's attentions, but he couldn't bring himself to give up the hope of owning a huge cattle farm? Miriam groaned out loud. "What a horrible thought! Wayne wouldn't do something like that. He loves me for my own sake," she said out loud. Then she waited, as if expecting the bare walls to answer. There was only silence. To ease her mind, she would speak with Aunt Fannie tonight—even if that included the revelation of her secret money.

Miriam left *Mamm*'s letter on the quilt and quietly walked downstairs. Aunt Fannie and Uncle William were in the living room. There was no sign of baby Jonathon except for his blanket, which lay askew in front of the stove. Aunt Fannie glanced up with a weary look on her face.

"Did you get the little fellow off to bed?" Miriam asked with a smile.

Aunt Fannie smiled back. "*Yah*, he's settled in for the night. Does your *mamm*'s letter say anything about baby Anna?"

Miriam frowned. "I haven't gotten that far. I..." She let the thought hang.

Concern crossed Aunt Fannie's face. "Is something wrong at home?"

Miriam took a deep breath. "Nothing more than the usual. Shirley's out with Jonas Beachy again. Could we...?" Miriam motioned toward the kitchen with her head.

"Sure." Aunt Fannie rose at once.

Uncle William wrinkled his face. "You mean I don't get in on the juicy news?"

Aunt Fannie paused to squeeze his arm. "I'll keep you up-to-date, dear—if you need to know."

Uncle William laughed. "That's what I was afraid of."

"Ignore him." Aunt Fannie took Miriam's arm and led her toward the kitchen. "He's only teasing."

Miriam gave Uncle William a quick, conciliatory smile over her shoulder just in case he was offended, but his attention had already returned to the weekly *Budget*. She knew he did care. The love and concern from both of them warmed her heart. How blessed she was to have such a mature and caring family at her beck and call when *Mamm* and *Daett* weren't around.

Aunt Fannie motioned toward a kitchen chair. "Sit and tell me what's troubling you."

Miriam groaned a little. "That may take a while, and it's already late."

"We have all night—if it's that serious." Aunt Fannie studied Miriam's face. "Was there awful news in the letter?"

Miriam shook her head. "It's me. I think I'm the root of the problem…maybe…at least a little…but I don't know for sure."

"You're not making much sense, dear." Aunt Fannie stroked Miriam's hand. "Has something happened at school?"

Miriam tried again. "I know this is going to sound crazy, but I…I have a secret. In fact…" Miriam half rose from the chair, "perhaps I should get the bank statement for you so you can see what's going on for yourself."

Aunt Fannie patted Miriam's arm. "You're still not making sense. Are you saying you have money problems? I'm not sure I can believe that. Your salary from the school is plenty, and you don't spend hardly anything—at least not that I can see. I mean, you're never in town, and you're a decent girl with *gut* spending habits."

Miriam looked away. "I'm not a decent girl. I have a huge secret that even *Mamm* and *Daett* don't know about."

Aunt Fannie's eyes widened. "Miriam? Really? Have you and Wayne been indecent?" Aunt Fannie stood. "I think I'd better get Uncle William."

"It's not that!" Miriam said quickly. She took in a huge breath and blurted, "I have two million dollars in my bank account."

Aunt Fannie froze. "Now I *am* getting Uncle William."

Her footsteps faded as Miriam buried her face in her hands. The confession in front of Uncle William wouldn't be quite as painful now that she'd told her aunt. Hopefully they would speak words that would ease her struggle.

Chapter Two

———◆◆◆———

M iriam sat on the kitchen chair listening to the low murmur of her uncle and aunt as they talked in the living room. Nervously, she clenched and unclenched her hands. Did Uncle William have harsh things to say that Aunt Fannie didn't want him to repeat? Did he believe the news? Likely it was the latter. Uncle William would only speak grace into her life.

Miriam looked up when she heard footsteps approach the kitchen. Aunt Fannie entered first, followed by Uncle William. Their faces were grave as they sat down on the chairs on either side of her.

Uncle William cleared his throat. "Miriam, what you've told Fannie is…well…quite a surprise, to say the least. Two million dollars? Is that right? Will you tell us about it—starting at the beginning?"

Miriam tried to keep the tremble out of her voice. "I've mentioned that I worked for Mr. Amos Bland for two years or so. I was his caretaker—cooking, cleaning, and the like. You know when he died that he left me his farm. But what very few people know is that Mr. Bland also left me two million dollars."

"And you've kept this a secret until now?" Uncle William asked.

"*Yah*. The only person I've told is Wayne. I thought it best to not tell anyone in the family at the time knowing how *Daett* feels about earthly riches." Miriam squirmed in her chair. "And I've mentioned how Ivan Mast acted when he found out I'd inherited a productive, working farm. Imagine what would have happened if he'd known about the money too."

"Okay, I see. So why are you telling us now?" Uncle William regarded Miriam steadily.

Aunt Fannie interrupted before Miriam could answer. "You really have two million dollars?"

"Would you like to see proof?" Miriam started to stand.

Aunt Fannie waved her back down. "Of course not. I believe you. It's just so…well, such a shock."

Uncle William raised his eyebrows. "Well, if you don't mind, I'd like to see this proof."

Miriam got up and walked up the stairs. Aunt Fannie sputtered something behind her, which she couldn't understand. Once in her bedroom, Miriam found the latest bank statement in a dresser drawer. With it clutched in her hand, she made her way back downstairs. Surely Uncle William believed her, Miriam told herself. He just wanted to see the proof for himself. A man would want to see proof. Still, she had a sinking feeling in her stomach. *Daett* had always said money bred distrust and dishonesty. Perhaps Uncle William felt the same way.

Uncle William and Aunt Fannie looked up as Miriam entered the kitchen. She handed the statement to Uncle William and slipped into her chair.

He stared at the page for a few moments and then let out a long breath. "Well, you do seem to own close to two million dollars."

"That's an awful lot of money." Aunt Fannie's voice was filled with awe.

"Well, I inherited two million dollars", Miriam admitted uncomfortably. "I withdrew some when I wasn't sure the money was real. According to the lawyer, compounded interest will increase the funds substantially. To simplify matters, I just think of it as two million."

"That sounds reasonable" Uncle William said. "So, you haven't told anyone among us except Wayne?"

Miriam nodded.

"What did Wayne say?" Aunt Fannie's awe still lingered in her voice.

Miriam felt a smile leap across her face. "Wayne loved me before, and he still loves me now. That's what I like about him. He's so…so unlike Ivan."

Uncle William nodded. "That was a rotten deal…what Ivan did. But I hope he saw his mistake. He was married last fall, wasn't he?"

Miriam let her gaze fall to the table. "*Yah.*" She wasn't sure about the lesson part. Ivan wasn't a man to learn things easily. Look how he'd refused for the longest time to take her no as her answer. Likely he'd married Laura without repentance for his actions toward her.

Uncle William gave Miriam a penetrating look. "I wish you'd told your *mamm* and *daett* about the money. Keeping secrets is never a *gut* idea, Miriam."

"*Yah*, I know," Miriam said, her head hanging low.

"Don't be too hard on the girl," Aunt Fannie said, reaching for Miriam's hand.

Uncle William continued. "Well, what's done is done. I think you made a wise decision in telling Wayne. It wouldn't be right to be his promised one and hold such a secret."

"I'm sure you're right," Miriam agreed.

Uncle William continued. "I advise you to write home at once with this news, and allow your parents to offer their input. They may have *gut* instructions that only parents can give. In the meantime, you can pray that the Lord gives you protection from the evils of money. It's not a small matter to have access to such a large amount of cash. You seem to have handled things well so far—except keeping it a secret. But one never knows. Temptation is always lying close to the door. Money can make it even easier to leave the faith or doubt the provision that only the Lord can provide."

"I won't leave the faith!" Miriam exclaimed. "I've never thought of such a thing. And I will pray now as I've been praying up to this point."

Uncle William smiled and got to his feet. "Then I'll get back to my *Budget*. May the Lord bless you for sharing this with us. May He also give you and Wayne wisdom on this matter. You will need it, believe me."

Aunt Fannie touched Miriam's arm again once Uncle William left. "I hope that helps, dear. I'd follow everything William advised."

"*Yah*, but I still have a problem," Miriam whispered.

Aunt Fannie sat up straight. "You have more secrets?"

"Not secrets—fears," Miriam corrected.

"Fears? Fears about what?" Aunt Miriam asked.

"Do you think I have anything to worry about regarding Wayne's affections for Esther Swartz? I think she's sweet on him. And I worry that…"

Aunt Fannie snorted. "Wayne dotes over you every time I see the two of you together. And Esther? She's in Wayne's past. And to speak the truth, it was Esther, not Wayne, who pursued that relationship."

"*Yah*, I've heard that." Miriam kept her gaze on the kitchen wall. "Then I must be imagining things." She hoped her voice carried more conviction than she felt.

Aunt Fannie wasn't convinced. "What makes you so skeptical?"

Miriam took a deep breath. "Okay, it's like this. I see Esther smile at Wayne all the time, although I admit Esther also smiles at the other unmarried men too. But Wayne smiles back at her! I worry that maybe he's in love with her. Perhaps he doesn't want to leave me because of the money. Esther's quite beautiful, and I'm so plain."

Aunt Fannie reached over to stroke Miriam's arm. "I really think you're imagining things. Wayne's sister, Joy, has always been *gut* friends with Esther. Wayne probably looks at Esther as his sister. And by the way, you're not 'so plain.'"

Miriam wrinkled her nose. "But it's not the same as being beautiful like Esther."

Aunt Fannie clucked her tongue. "I never thought I'd see the day when you'd be worried about such things."

Miriam felt heat rise up her neck. "I know it's wrong, and that beauty is vain, but I also know that Ivan never asked me on a date because he was attracted to more beautiful girls. And Esther is Laura's sister."

Aunt Fannie clucked her tongue again. "You must forget about Ivan and Laura, Miriam. Would you want things to be any different? Look what you would have missed if you'd married Ivan—the community here in Oklahoma and meeting Wayne. Isn't Wayne of much deeper character than Ivan ever was?"

Miriam nodded.

Aunt Fannie continued. "Besides, Laura seems a much better fit for Ivan, don't you think? That's, after all, why he married her."

Miriam forced a smile. "I guess you're right. I just needed to hear someone say it."

Aunt Fannie peered into Miriam's face. "There now. Don't things look much better now that you have them out in the open? You should never have carried these secrets around by yourself. It's a wonder you're not a total nervous wreck. And with Esther showing up, why, it makes perfect sense that you'd think the same thing might happen all over again."

"I feel kind of foolish." Miriam hid her face in her hands. "You don't have to tell Uncle William, do you? He might tell Wayne."

Aunt Fannie frowned slightly. "I keep no secrets from the man, and you should file that concept in your mind. Don't ever keep things from your husband. The Lord didn't make marriage for secrets. Your Uncle William will know better than to pass this on to anyone else."

"Okay." Miriam managed a smile.

"Now you forget about Ivan and Esther." Aunt Fannie wrapped her arms around Miriam for a tight hug.

"Thanks for the comfort," Miriam said. "I know I partly accepted Wayne's attentions at first because of the great hurt Ivan had left in my heart. But I do love Wayne now. I'm sure his feelings haven't been affected by the money."

"That's the spirit." Aunt Fannie patted Miriam on the arm. "Now, the best thing for you is a *gut* night's sleep. No more thinking about money or Esther Swartz. You are Wayne's promised one, so until your wedding spend your time building a strong foundation with the man. The Lord will bless both of you greatly. I know William approves of the match, and so do I. You are a perfect couple."

Miriam laughed. "That's a stretch, but thanks. I feel so much better now. I don't know why I didn't tell you all this a long time ago."

"We live and learn." Aunt Fannie rose to her feet. "I'd better follow my own advice and get some sleep."

Miriam listened to Aunt Fannie's footsteps fade before she stood to blow out the kerosene lamp on the kitchen counter. Her lamp was still burning upstairs, and she knew the way to the stairs in the dark. With only the slightest touch of her fingers on the wall, Miriam found the stair door and went up the steps. The soft glow under her bedroom door welcomed her. She knew she shouldn't have left the lamp lit while she was gone, but with all the stress this evening the small error was understandable. Now Uncle William and Aunt Fannie knew of her big secret, and the world seemed much the same. They took the news like Wayne had—as if it didn't really matter other than for the dangers involved. Money was of this world, and it didn't make life any better as the *Englisha* mistakenly thought.

She would tell Wayne about the first part of the conversations she had tonight with Uncle William and Aunt Fannie. That would be her contribution to gradually adapting to the "no secrets in marriage" concept.

Picking up *Mamm*'s letter from the quilt, Miriam seated herself on the bed. She scanned the rest of the words. There was mostly news about the two farms that *Daett* ran with Lee and Mark. The roof had sprung a leak in Mr. Bland's haymow. Thankfully *Daett* had discovered the problem before much hay was spoiled. Miriam read on, but *Mamm* seemed to have lost her enthusiasm after the sad news of Shirley's transgressions.

Miriam prepared for bed and dropped to her knees by her bed to pray.

> Oh, dear Lord, help *Mamm* and *Daett* at home while they deal with Shirley. And forgive my transgressions and secrets. I'm trying to find my way in life and don't always do the best. Give Uncle William and Aunt Fannie a special blessing for their kindness tonight. Thank You for Wayne and his love. I also pray for Esther Swartz. Bless her for coming all the way out here to help her grandmother. Give Esther the extra grace she needs for the demands older people can make sometimes. Amen.

Miriam got up and slipped under the covers. She quickly fell asleep.

Chapter Three

———◆◆———

A week later, the late-Friday-afternoon sun hung low on the horizon as Miriam stood by the schoolyard fence. Wayne Yutzy's buggy had appeared in the distance moments ago. She could have stayed inside, and should have, Miriam told herself. It wasn't *gut* for her to appear too eager. But she was Wayne's promised one, and she wanted to wait for him where he would see her right away.

Thoughts of Esther Swartz drifted through Miriam's mind, but since her talk with Aunt Fannie, she'd vowed there would be no more jealousy. Wayne loved her, not Esther. Besides, Wayne was coming to pick her up for a buggy ride in just a few minutes. Wayne had asked for this extra time together. He had something special planned—if she didn't miss her guess. There had been a twinkle in his eyes when he came up to the house after work and asked, "Are you busy Friday around five?"

Her smile had come easy enough. "You know I'm always busy."

He had returned the tease. "That's what I like about you. What about a little buggy ride after your schoolwork is done?"

She'd allowed her eagerness to show. "I would love that."

Wayne had left with a quick grin over his shoulder. When Aunt Fannie heard about Wayne's plans, she extended a supper invitation for afterward. These extra hours together would be a great way to start the weekend, Miriam decided.

Wayne's buggy came to a stop in front of her, and Miriam ran forward and pulled herself up onto the seat.

"*Gut* evening, Wayne!" she greeted.

He returned her greeting with a warm smile. "Did I arrive too early?"

Miriam settled herself on the buggy seat. "No, the timing is perfect. I finished the last of the students' papers only moments ago."

"I saw you waiting," Wayne teased.

Miriam felt hot blood rising up her neck, and she laughed self-consciously. "Why should I wait inside when the weather's so nice?"

Wayne chuckled. "That's Oklahoma for you. Here we have splendid weather and splendid people."

Miriam played along. "You don't have to convince me."

Wayne grinned. "Just making sure. You never know when folks from Possum Valley will bolt back home again."

Miriam sobered. "Surely you don't think I'm like my sister Shirley? She had reasons to return home that I don't have."

Wayne laughed. "Not a moment's doubt. I'm just teasing."

Miriam smiled even as she let out a small sigh. "Sorry. That's a sensitive subject right now. *Mamm* wrote me that Shirley's hanging out with Jonas Beachy again. Shirley should know better than that."

Wayne reached for Miriam's hand. "I'm the one who should apologize. That was careless of me. Does your *Mamm* think Shirley will get over him?"

"We hope and pray she will." She sighed. "Let's not think about her troubles right now." Miriam forced herself to brighten up. "Where are we going?"

The twinkle was back in Wayne's eyes. "Ahhh, to a very special place. Not too far."

"Am I supposed to guess?" Miriam asked, but she already knew. There was only one place close that was special to them as a dating couple.

Wayne grasped the reins with both hands. "You can try."

Miriam leaned against his shoulder. "You're taking me back to where we were promised…down by the creek."

Wayne nodded. "I hope you don't object. I know it's not been that long, but I wanted to go there again to remember…and to rejoice in our future together. And the weather's just like it was last fall. Isn't that *wunderbah*?"

"Oh, Wayne!" Miriam tried to breathe evenly. "How did you know I needed this?"

"I didn't." He turned right at the stop sign. "It's been six months or so…sort of an anniversary, I thought."

Miriam's words came out in a rush. "You're a *wunderbah* man. I'm so blessed."

Wayne laughed. "I'm glad you feel so, but I'm the one who's blessed. The Lord has done a great work in our lives, Miriam. I can never be thankful enough for the moment you appeared in the community."

Miriam clung to his arm. She wasn't about to bring her awful fears about Esther into this precious moment.

Wayne glanced at her with a question on his face.

Miriam spoke up quickly. "I have to tell you something. I told Uncle William and Aunt Fannie about the money the other evening. I hope you don't mind."

A smile played on Wayne's face as he pulled the buggy to a stop. "Sure, that's fine. But let's think about us now, Miriam. And what lies ahead—if the Lord grants us a long life together."

Miriam nodded and waited while Wayne climbed out of the buggy with the tie rope. He returned after tying the horse to a tree and offered his hand to help her down.

She extended her hand to his strong arm as her foot reached for the buggy step. With deftness she leaped down to stand beside him. "Thanks, Wayne. That's so sweet of you."

He waved off the compliment. "Come. Our special occasion was right down here. Hopefully the winter storms didn't wash everything away."

Miriam followed him down the slight bank with the help of his offered hand again. They ended up beside a rushing brook, the quick flow of the water a soft noise around them.

Wayne's voice added to the charm of the moment. "The log's gone…where we sat last time."

Miriam leaned on Wayne's arm. Silence fell and neither of them moved. Here she'd told Wayne about the money, and here she'd kissed him for the first time. There hadn't been many kisses since. Wayne was a man of principle, and the Oklahoma community had a stricter *Ordnung* for dating couples than Possum Valley. But she could use a hug this afternoon. He didn't have to kiss her. She'd understand if…

Wayne's hand reached for hers. "Let's walk downstream a bit."

They wouldn't get far before the overgrowth stopped them, Miriam thought. But she allowed Wayne to lead the way. Perhaps he was looking for another log where they could sit and talk and think about the past and maybe the future—their hopes, and dreams, and, perhaps, a date for their wedding.

Wayne paused in front of a low-hanging branch. His laugh was dry. "No logs. I guess we'll just have to stand."

Miriam's fingers tightened around his hand.

Wayne smiled down at her. "We should have come back here sooner. This place has so many *gut* memories. I should get that *Englisha* artist in town to do a painting of this spot."

"*Yah*, it does hold special memories." Miriam looked up to hold his gaze for a moment. "And we have the future…if the Lord wills it."

Wayne's arm slipped around Miriam's shoulders and pulled her close. "That's another thing we should talk about."

"*Yah?*" She looked up again, her face expectant.

"Well…" He held the word out for a long moment. "We've been moving along at a rapid clip with our relationship, so perhaps we should speak of a wedding date."

"Oh, Wayne!" Miriam grinned and leaned against his shoulder. "I so hoped you would say that!"

"You did?" Wayne's voice caught. "So you think this fall would be okay? That's not too soon for you?"

She pulled away to regard his face. "Not too soon at all. I can't wait!"

He laughed softly. "This was much easier than I'd imagined."

"That's what I like about you." She touched his hand. "You're so confident, and yet underneath you're so kind."

Wayne smiled and lowered his head to look into her eyes. "So late October then?"

Miriam couldn't keep the eagerness out of her voice. "That sounds *gut* to me. I'll have to write *Mamm* to be sure the date will work for them. They do have to plan the wedding back in Possum Valley. But I'll go home in early May after my teaching job is done. We can begin the major planning then."

His face fell. "I'll miss you all those months, but I understand. The time will fly though. And then we'll be together on the farm."

Miriam smiled. "You know I look forward to that day. So let me ask *Mamm*. October shouldn't be too soon for her at all."

Wayne found Miriam's hand again. "The Lord has been in our relationship from the beginning."

"*Yah*, He has," Miriam whispered. Memories of the first time she'd seen Wayne's face filled her mind. She looked up at him. "You made quite an impression on me when I arrived in Oklahoma with Shirley."

He smiled down at her. "You mean when you arrived with Mr. Whitehorse? I thought you were a vision of heaven when you stepped out of the car."

"Wayne," she scolded, "don't say such things."

He grinned. "You're a beautiful girl, Miriam. I want you to be my *frau*—and soon."

"Oh, Wayne!" She wanted to wrap her arms around him. It seemed like years since Wayne had really hugged her, and her heart ached for the comfort. But she couldn't reach for him first. It wouldn't be right.

His free hand touched her face. "I love you, Miriam. Don't ever doubt that. I will always love you with all my heart. Only the Lord will be first before you. I'm so glad you're okay with a fall wedding date. I know most couples date for longer than a year, but it's like I know you so well, and..." Wayne's voice trailed off.

Miriam caught her breath. His fingers warmed her entire body. She decided she could wait a while longer for the comfort of his arms. October would come soon enough, helped along by the rush of wedding plans. Already she could see the letter she'd write to *Mamm*. It would be full of questions of where, what, when, and how everything would be done. *Mamm* would be thrilled. Miriam was sure of that. *Mamm* had given her approval, and nothing would change now.

Wayne interrupted her thoughts. "I should meet your parents, you know. What if they don't approve of me?"

Miriam laughed. "You don't have to doubt them, Wayne. *Mamm* already told me she approves."

He didn't appear convinced. "But they haven't met me yet."

Miriam looked up into his eyes. "Shirley had a lot of *gut* things to say about you when she got back, and there's my opinion, of course. *Mamm* and *Daett* trust me."

Wayne reached out, and Miriam stepped into his arms. He held her tight and whispered into her *kapp*, "This is a great honor, indeed."

Miriam said nothing as she cuddled into him. She wanted this moment to never end.

Chapter Four

———◆◆◆———

Later that evening, Miriam and Aunt Fannie were putting supper on the table as the low rumble of Uncle William and Wayne's voices drifted in from the living room. A plate in Miriam's hands almost slid from her grasp. She caught it before it crashed to the floor.

"Slow down!" Aunt Fannie's order came in a whisper. "What has gotten into you, child?"

Miriam caught her breath. She could barely say what she was feeling: *Excitement! Exhilaration! Euphoria!* She was going to marry Wayne! And soon. She turned to Aunt Fannie. "Wayne and I drove to the creek after school. It was wonderful."

"I see." Aunt Fannie didn't move as she waited for more information.

Miriam set the plate on the table and stepped closer to her aunt. "Wayne wants a late-October wedding. Tonight I'm going to write *Mamm* to see if it will suit."

A delighted smile crept across Aunt Fannie's face. "So that's what all the excitement is about."

"Do you think it's too soon?" Miriam asked. "You seemed to hesitate."

Aunt Fannie laughed. "No, I'm not surprised at all. And remember how little your fears about Esther the other evening had to do with reality. I'm excited for you!"

Miriam let out a breath. "Thanks for hearing me out the other night. It was *gut* to speak of them, even if they were unfounded."

Aunt Fannie looked wise as she shared, "The two of us speaking in private was better than you bringing it up with Wayne. I hope you didn't mention your fears regarding Esther to him."

"No, I didn't say a word about her."

Aunt Fannie resumed supper preparations. "*Gut!* The less said about her the better. Our people trust in promises given, and Wayne has given his to you twice now. You ought to thank the Lord each day for such a decent, prospective husband."

"Oh, I do!" Miriam said dreamily.

Moments later Aunt Fannie motioned toward the living room. "Call them. We're ready."

Both men looked up when she appeared in the doorway.

"Supper ready?" Uncle William boomed before Miriam could speak.

"*Yah,*" Miriam said with a smile.

Wayne sent her a quick smile, and Miriam beat a quick retreat, taking her seat at the kitchen table. Aunt Fannie smiled as the men filed in. Baby Jonathon was in Uncle William's arms.

Wayne settled into his seat with a pleased look on his face.

Her intended's nearness rushed over Miriam.

Uncle William set baby Jonathon on his blanket beside the kitchen stove. He took his seat and cleared his throat. "We're so happy to have the two of you here tonight. Right now you're my favorite couple in the community." Uncle William chuckled. "Of course, Miriam's my niece by marriage, and Wayne's my hired hand as well as my nephew, so maybe that has something to do with it."

"We'd still be thrilled," Aunt Fannie countered. "The whole community is so happy with what the Lord is doing in your lives."

Miriam hid her face behind her hands, and everyone laughed. The young woman from Possum Valley wasn't used to such plain talk about love.

"I agree with that," Uncle William continued. "Let's pray now." They all bowed their heads and Uncle William led out.

> Our gracious and merciful heavenly Father, blessed be Your name. Great is Your lovingkindness toward us. Each morning Your grace is poured out fresh into our lives, for which we express our feeble and inadequate praise. Bless now this evening and the food that Fannie and Miriam have prepared. Be with us as we spend the rest of the evening together. Give us a peaceful sleep tonight. Amen.

"Amen," Wayne echoed.

Miriam kept silent, as did Aunt Fannie. Amish women didn't participate in public expressions of worship, for which Miriam was grateful. She didn't know how the men could speak of the Lord's ways in front of other people. She had a hard enough time talking to God when she was alone. Thankfully, she could look forward to life under Wayne's direction. He would lead out as a godly man should and supply what she lacked. Hadn't Wayne already given her direction on how the two million dollars should be handled? She could trust him with her whole heart.

Wayne gave her a warm smile as if sensing her thoughts.

Miriam returned the smile. She looked toward Aunt Fannie as she passed around the food.

"So what's the latest news on the happy couple?" Uncle William's voice filled the kitchen as he dipped out some potato salad.

Miriam drew in a quick breath but said nothing. This was Wayne's place to comment.

"Plans, I guess." Wayne chuckled. "*Gut* ones. Miriam is agree-able to an October wedding—if it works out with her folks. But, of course, this is to be kept under wraps until we know for sure."

"Of course." Uncle William didn't hesitate. "I won't tell a soul. Not even the bishop will hear a whisper from me!"

Everyone laughed.

Miriam's hand trembled as she dipped mashed potatoes onto her plate. She didn't know Bishop Wengerd from the Oklahoma community that well. She only saw him at the Sunday services. The bishop was a young man with a wife and two young children. But he wouldn't be the one Wayne and she would need to visit to request a wedding announcement. Wayne would have to make the trip out to Possum Valley because that's where Miriam's fam-ily lived. Wayne and Miriam would visit Bishop Wagler together. Because Bishop Wagler didn't know Wayne, the young man would likely bring along a letter of recommendation from Bishop Weng-erd. That would expedite things and take care of any character questions—if Bishop Wagler had any.

Aunt Fannie whispered to Wayne, "I'm so thankful you're tak-ing such good care of Miriam."

"I'm more than glad to," Wayne whispered back with a smile.

Miriam allowed the joy of their conversation to fill her heart. Moments later her *daett*'s face drifted through her thoughts. A chill ran up her back. *Daett* would have to be told soon about the money she'd inherited. He wouldn't be happy, that was for sure. She wasn't sure which he'd be unhappiest about—that she had money or that she'd kept it a secret. Uncle William had advised her to write to her parents, but she hadn't yet. Maybe Wayne could give her further advice. Or maybe they could tell her parents when Wayne visited Possum Valley? Although not quite as courageous, that seemed like the easiest way to handle it.

"How is this marriage stuff going to work out?" Uncle William asked. "Miriam's teaching school, which doesn't let out until the first of May. And she's from Possum Valley."

"William!" Aunt Fannie scolded. "Miriam lives here now."

Uncle William gave his *frau* a fake glare. "You know what I mean. Tradition says Miriam has to marry in Possum Valley."

Wayne didn't miss a beat. "We've talked about that, and the details have to be worked out, of course—with the Lord's help. And if the October time doesn't work with Miriam's parents, then we can wait until it will work."

"That's well spoken." Uncle William nodded his approval. "I like that attitude."

And so did she, Miriam decided. Should she say so? Miriam gathered her courage but her voice still squeaked when she said, "I like that in a man—in *my* man."

Uncle William hooted with laughter. "Now that's doubly well spoken. I would say you're getting what you're looking for in a *frau*, Wayne."

Now Wayne turned bright red.

Miriam was glad Uncle William said what he did. Already she felt like Wayne's *frau*.

"Stop teasing them," Aunt Fannie said. "They're a sweet couple."

Uncle William looked ready to say something else, but he must have thought better of it.

The silence that followed was broken only by Wayne's fork scraping his plate.

Aunt Fannie broke the quiet by leaping to her feet. "The pies! I almost forgot them!"

"Can't forget the pies!" Uncle William declared with a grin.

Aunt Fannie waved the hot pies over the table so the delightful smell wafted through the air before she set them down. "There! Everyone fall to. I'm sure they're delicious, if I do say so myself."

"Did Miriam bake them?" Wayne eyed the offered delicacies.

Aunt Fannie smiled. "Well, she certainly could have. But I made these. Miriam's too busy with school—and taking off for parts unknown with her man."

Miriam turned red again, but Wayne laughed.

The two men both took large pieces and drove their forks into the flaky crust and abundant filling. Miriam cut a smaller portion out of a piece and gave the other half to Aunt Fannie. They leaned toward each other to whisper like coconspirators, "Gotta watch the weight."

The men seemed not to notice their giggles as Wayne asked William about the weather forecast for the next week.

Uncle William pronounced with great certainty, "I expect business at the greenhouse to take off if the rains don't hinder things. People are beginning to move about."

Miriam hadn't noticed the weather because she was preoccupied with school and Wayne. Uncle William usually knew how to call things right when it came to his business though.

Uncle William turned to Miriam. "Maybe you can help out a few hours after school? That is, if I can keep you away from young Wayne here and get some work out of you. We can't have idle chit-chat going on, you know."

Miriam didn't hesitate. "For you the answer is always yes—even if I'm busy with school activities."

"Are you sure?" Aunt Fannie sounded concerned. "You mustn't overdo yourself, Miriam."

"I'll be more than glad to help," Miriam assured them both.

Uncle William grinned.

Miriam stood and began to clear the table, but Aunt Fannie waved her off. "Go out and spend a few minutes with Wayne before he has to leave. I know he's wanting to get home and rest, what with the slave labor that's needed next week."

Wayne chuckled as he stood up. "I don't know about the slave labor, but I should be going."

Wayne and Miriam stopped to put on coats before they stepped out the front door into the cool of the night.

Wayne took Miriam's hands in his. "It's been a nice evening and a wonderful afternoon. Thanks."

"I'm the one who should say thanks." Miriam stepped closer to look up into his face.

They stayed that way for a long moment before Wayne's hands found her shoulders and pulled her close.

Miriam's thoughts raced. She would get her kiss tonight after all! Her thoughts ceased as Wayne's face came closer and she lost herself in the moment.

Chapter Five

Shirley Yoder hung on to the bag of fast-food with one hand and the door grip with the other.

Jonas Beachy glanced over at her with a grin as he crested the hill and then brought his fancy convertible to a stop with a squeal of tires.

The young woman drew in a long breath and took in the view of Possum Valley. She could make out the well-ordered Amish farms by the lights from gas lanterns hanging in windows even though the bright twinkle of stars shone overhead. Behind them lay the small town of Berlin, Ohio.

"I guess we could have eaten somewhere much nicer than Burger King." Jonas chuckled. He opened his car door so the interior light turned on and then reached over to dig a Whopper and fries from the bag Shirley held.

That they'd gone to Burger King was a surprise to Shirley. Jonas usually took her to nice, sit-down restaurants. Why was tonight different? What was he up to?

"You're awfully quiet," Jonas teased. "Burger King not up to your standards?"

Shirley took out a chicken sandwich. "No, I like Burger King fine. It's just not where we usually go."

"For fast food, I usually like Subway. Tonight I just wanted something different."

A stab of pain ran through Shirley. Was that how Jonas looked at her? As something different? The poor Amish girl who was a nobody? With his money, he probably had his choice of women. Why had he picked her tonight?

Since returning from Oklahoma several months ago, Shirley had gone out with Jonas a few times. She never knew if or when he'd call again. Did he like her for real or was she just some kind of Amish amusement for him? And was she okay with that? Yes, she was. Dating Jonas was an opportunity she just couldn't pass up. She decided she'd not feel guilty about seeing him like she had last fall. She was, after all, into *rumspringa*, and Jonas fit into that scenario well. She didn't want to let him go.

Jonas gazed down at the valley. He pointed toward the light illuminating an Amish farmhouse. "I wonder who lives there?"

Shirley looked quickly and then unwrapped her sandwich. "I don't know," she replied. "It could be the Stolls, but Possum Valley is a big place. It could be someone else."

Jonas's voice was low. "I've often wondered how life would have turned out if my parents had stayed Amish."

Shirley looked over at him. "You're not thinking of going back to being Amish? Is that why you keep seeing me?"

Jonas laughed. "I don't think so...I mean the going Amish part. I see you because I like you."

A soft sigh escaped Shirley's lips. "I like you too. But I'm only on my *rumspringa*. I'm not committed to your world."

His grin filled his face again. "Not yet anyway. But maybe someday?"

"You mean leave the Amish and join your church?" She gasped. "I could never do that."

Jonas shrugged. "You also told me we weren't made for each other last fall. Remember? It was on a night like this. We were out near Apple Creek…and we kissed."

Shirley tried to take a deep breath. That evening had been so special. And that kiss had been their first and only kiss—so far. Was that why Jonas had brought her here tonight? Did he want their relationship to return to where it was headed last fall, before she'd left him for Oklahoma?

"It doesn't bother me that you're Amish," Jonas said.

"I'm glad," Shirley said. "But we both know…" She let the words go unsaid, knowing he'd understand what she wouldn't say. We are worlds apart. One of us would have to give up a lot. Do we love each other enough for that?

"I understand." Jonas nodded. "But I still like being with you."

Jonas played her well, Shirley thought. That was why she was drawn to him despite her continual resolutions to never see him again. Her mind told her this relationship could never work, but her heart told her she could love Jonas…for now. And there was the fact that Jonas's *daett* was one of the richest men in the county. She was ashamed to admit that part of her attraction had to do with their money. Jonas deserved a *frau* who loved him for himself, not for what he possessed and might someday inherit.

Jonas reached for her hand. "You've never really told me what happened out in Oklahoma."

Shirley held her untouched sandwich and didn't move. Jonas had accepted her return without explanation so far. Why bring it up now? Was he really interested?

"You don't have to answer if you don't want to." His voice was kind.

Tears sprang to Shirley's eyes. "Oh, it was lots of things, I guess. Mostly turmoil with myself. Trying to figure out where I belonged. It didn't seem to be in Oklahoma."

"You're not eating." He motioned toward her sandwich.

Shirley looked down at her food. "I'm...I'm just thinking about things, that's all."

He said nothing more as she took a bite and chewed slowly. The sandwich was delicious. She didn't often get a chance to eat in *Englisha* restaurants, even places like Burger King. For one thing, there simply wasn't abundant money in the Yoder household. And *Mamm* had said nothing about Shirley getting an outside job since she'd returned from Oklahoma. *Mamm* clearly wanted to keep her around the house. And now they didn't desperately need the extra money with the income from Miriam's farm. Plus neither *Mamm* nor *Daett* wanted her to have money to spend on her own...too much independence, Shirley figured.

"This is a nice place to think." Jonas finished his sandwich. "And to talk...once you've finished your sandwich. If you want to."

So Jonas was intent on conversation. Could that mean he was serious about their relationship? Maybe that would explain the quick trip to Burger King and their drive to this quiet, romantic spot. A shiver ran through Shirley. Could she become Jonas's *frau* someday? Could they say the sacred wedding vows together? *Daett* and *Mamm* and the others wouldn't come to the wedding. That much she knew.

"I can talk and eat." Shirley gave him a warm smile. "My voice is a little dry, that's all."

In the dim light, Jonas motioned toward the cup holder that held their Pepsis. "Drink then."

"I will." Shirley took a long sip through the straw.

Already Jonas ordered her around, and she wasn't sure she liked that. But she'd obeyed, which showed how deeply ingrained her response to a command was. Did Jonas's church share the Amish view about women and their relationships with men, especially after marriage?

"What do you want to talk about?" Shirley ventured, her curiosity eager for satisfaction.

Jonas took another sip from his Pepsi. "It's been a long time since you came back from Oklahoma, but you've never really told me why you came back."

Shirley hesitated. Why not just be upfront about it? "The truth is, I don't think they liked me much out in Oklahoma."

"Didn't like you?" Jonas looked like he didn't believe her.

"Well…" Shirley searched for the right words. "Not like I'm used to being liked. They ignored me, and Miriam received all the attention."

"That's strange. Did you do something to set them against you?"

"No, of course not!" Heat flared in her face, but she didn't care.

"Then why?" Jonas probed. "Did some man turn down your attentions?"

Now she could feel her face getting flushed. Shirley gathered her wits together. "Maybe I don't want to answer that."

Jonas gave a dry laugh. "I think that's my answer right there."

"I didn't like him anyway. Not like I like you." Shirley almost regretted the words as soon as they escaped her mouth. She went on. "I was trying hard to fit in with what and how I was supposed to be, but nothing was working. I felt so out of place."

"It sounds like you're just finding your way like all of us have to do," Jonas said wisely. "And I like the part about you not liking him the way you like me."

"You shouldn't have heard that." Shirley looked away. "Pretend I didn't say it, okay?"

Jonas laughed. "I don't think so."

Shirley didn't move as his hand reached over and his fingers entwined with hers. Was this the start of a new chapter in their relationship? Or at least a return to what they used to have? Her heart pounded at the thought. On the one hand she wanted this badly—Jonas's love and attention. On the other hand, if she kept on with this she would lose so much that she treasured—the Amish community, their satisfying way of life, and *Mamm* and *Daett*'s approval.

Jonas continued. "Let's go to my house. I want you to talk to my parents."

Shirley sat up straight. "About what?"

He smiled. "Call it a whim. Will you come?" Jonas squeezed her hand. "Please?"

Shirley's laugh was strained before she said, "If you ask like that, how can I say no?"

He chuckled. "You do want to come, don't you? I mean, we Beachys aren't horrible people you must avoid. You must know that. If we were, why would you go out with me?"

"It's my *rumspringa*." Shirley grasped at her last straw.

Jonas raised his eyebrows. "Come on, Shirley. Let's be honest. This is more than *rumspringa*. For me you'd consider leaving the Amish, wouldn't you?"

Shirley drew in a sharp breath. "I have thought about that—in my daydreams, I guess. Especially since I came back from Oklahoma. But when I'm not daydreaming—when I'm facing reality—I don't think it will ever happen."

"Then let me do all I can to persuade you." Jonas settled in as if he'd prepared a long speech. "I know there's the issue of my church, but I hope to convince you that we're a much better choice. All of us believe in the Bible and in following God's will. Maybe not the same way the Amish do—or think they do—but we're walking in the light we have, Shirley. I've been hoping I can take you to one of our worship services. I think you'd like it." Jonas paused for breath.

Shirley reached over and touched his arm. "Okay. I'll go to your house. But we'd better get moving before it gets too late." Jonas's face lit up, and Shirley knew she would've agreed to go long ago if he'd only kissed her again.

Chapter Six

◆◆◆

Twenty minutes later the immense Beachy home cut a stark profile against the starry heavens. Though she'd been here before, Shirley leaned forward for a better view as Jonas drove up the long driveway. She took a deep breath as he pulled to a stop in front of huge garage doors. *Mamm* and *Daett* wouldn't approve of this visit, but they didn't have to know. This was her *rumspringa*, and that was that!

"Here we are," Jonas quipped as he hopped out of the car and came around to her side to open her door.

As she followed Jonas to the entryway, she tried to imagine living in a house like this. If she and Jonas continued their relationship, could it be that she'd live here—or in a house like this? Using her beauty was her only ticket to success, especially in this *Englisha* world. Did she want this life? The question throbbed inside her as Jonas held open the front door. The rich mahogany shone in the bright light from the ornate fixture perched high above them.

Jonas motioned with his hand. "You first."

She *did* belong here! Shirley told herself. Jonas surely thought so. Her place of birth shouldn't determine her station in life, should it?

The hall opened in front of her, and Shirley kept her step steady. The last thing she wanted now was to project insecurity. Thankfully she'd left her *kapp* in the convertible. She'd taken it off soon after Jonas picked her up. Her long hair was down. Shirley brushed lose strands from her forehead. The Amish dress she had on couldn't be avoided, but at least she could fit in a bit better by letting her hair down. The Goodwill store in Berlin had lots of pretty *Englisha* dresses she would love to buy, but she didn't have money for such things.

Jonas led the way through the kitchen. High ceilings arched above them. Shirley recalled the place as large, but this was even bigger than she'd remembered. She tried to calm the beating of her heart as they entered a massive living room. Shirley kept close to Jonas and pasted a bright smile on her face when he stopped in front of his parents.

"Mom, Dad, we thought we'd stop by." Jonas glanced toward Shirley. "You remember Shirley Yoder?"

"Hi," Shirley managed to squeak out. Her voice sounded shrill, but whose wouldn't in such a situation?

"Of course we remember Shirley," Jonas's mom, Mary, said. His dad rose from his chair and added, "It's good to see you again, Shirley."

Jonas led Shirley to the couch where the two sat down.

"Jonas has been telling us all about you," Mary continued with a warm smile. "You were gone for a while, and I think he missed you."

"Mom!" Jonas said, his face and neck turning red.

"*Yah.*" Shirley kept her voice steady. "That was last fall. My sister Miriam and I left for Oklahoma to help with the birth of our aunt's baby. We stayed a while, and then I came back when my newest sister, Anna, was born. Miriam is still in Oklahoma. She's teaching school now."

"Oh." Mary appeared interested. "That's a worthy endeavor. I once thought about teaching school, but it was not to be."

Shirley smiled but she didn't want to talk about Miriam. What would her sister think if she knew where she was right now? A shudder passed through her body.

"I'm sure Jonas has told you that Raymond and I were both raised Amish." Mary glanced at her husband. "We try to remember our roots."

"That we do." Raymond nodded. "So, Shirley, are you going back to Oklahoma anytime soon?"

"I don't think so." Shirley clutched her hands on her lap. "*Mamm* keeps me busy around the house."

The truth was that both of her parents would be overjoyed if she chose to return to her aunt's house, but Shirley wasn't about to say that.

"How is the spiritual life among the Oklahoma Amish?" Raymond asked.

Shirley wasn't sure how to answer, but she got out some information. "Okay, I guess. They do some things differently out there than we do here. They frown at *rumspringa*, for one thing."

Raymond chuckled. "That may be a good thing. Not much spiritual growth comes out of flirting with the world."

Jonas muttered, "Dad, please."

But Raymond didn't hesitate. "Being Amish isn't all that it's cooked up to be, so I can understand people wanting to leave. But there's a better way to do it than letting young people go wild and spend time in sin."

"But *rumspringa* isn't sinning, Raymond," Mary spoke up. She patted her husband on the arm. "You remember that, Raymond, don't you?"

"Most of it comes mighty close." Raymond frowned. "Look at what goes on in our own community most weekend nights."

Shirley swallowed with difficulty. Her voice might not work

well, but she had to speak up. "I'm not really on *rumspringa* the way most of our young people do it. I only go out with Jonas, which I hope isn't sinning."

"There you go, Raymond." Mary's smile was strained but triumphant. "Jonas knows what he's doing."

Solemn silence descended on the room and was deepened by the high ceilings.

"I hope so," Raymond finally said. "I didn't mean to offend you, Shirley, but this is a matter of principle for me. Even if some young people do *rumspringa* and dating right, many of them don't."

Jonas's hand found hers, and Shirley didn't pull it away.

Jonas stood, pulling gently, and Shirley followed. "We're going to go upstairs. Come on, Shirley."

Mary stood. "I'll get some lemonade from the kitchen, Jonas. You can take it up with you if you want."

Jonas looked like lemonade was the last thing he wanted at the moment, but he waited until his mother returned with a pitcher and two glasses. "Shall I make some popcorn for you?"

"Don't bother, Mom." Jonas took the pitcher with both hands. "We'll be okay."

Mary rushed on in spite of her son's protest. "I'll make some right away and bring it up. You make sure Shirley's comfortable and that she feels welcome in our home. She's a really nice girl."

Jonas gave his mom a little smile.

Raymond nodded. "I didn't mean to make you uncomfortable, Shirley. I hope you know that."

"It's okay." Shirley pulled herself out of her stupor and took the two glasses Jonas's mom was holding. "It was nice to see you again."

Mary gave her a cheery smile, and Shirley returned it. Neither Jonas nor his *mamm* were responsible for his *daett's* comments. Likely they came from Raymond's position as a preacher in his church. Weren't preachers supposed to test all things to see if they were true? At least that's what the Amish thought.

Jonas moved toward the grand staircase, and Shirley followed. Arriving on the second floor, he opened the door to his bedroom and set the pitcher of lemonade on the dresser. He turned to face her. "I'm sorry, Shirley. I had no idea my dad would grill you like that. I know you're doing nothing wrong. I wouldn't have brought you here if I'd known he'd say what he did."

Shirley shrugged. "It's okay. I know that not all of our young people behave themselves while on *rumspringa*. Your *daett* had a point."

"It still wasn't necessary to bring it up with you." Jonas paced the floor.

"It's okay…really." Shirley took a seat on the bed. "I think this just confirms what we both already know. We come from two different worlds that don't mix well."

Jonas frowned and stopped pacing. He shut the door and then sat down next to Shirley. "My dad objects only to the *rumspringa* part. Would you consider changing that?" Jonas regarded Shirley with expectation.

"What do you mean?"

"Let's consider the idea of you coming to our church. Dad would approve of that."

"But…b-but…" Shirley's voice caught. "But I'm not ready for that. And my parents…"

"Of course." Jonas focused on the far wall. "It was just an idea. I do wish that you and I…" Jonas's voice trailed off too. After a long pause, he went on. "I just want to know you more, Shirley. I want to see if…if we should be together. Since that first day I saw you in Berlin by your buggy I've known you're the most beautiful girl I'll ever meet."

"Is that all?" Shirley hesitated. "Do you like me just because I'm *gut* looking?"

Jonas's grin returned. "You are that—and so much more! There has to be some way we can make a go of things."

A knock came on the door, and Mary entered without waiting for an invitation. Shirley liked that about Mary. It spoke of a sound relationship with her children, even though it might seem a little intrusive at times.

"Popcorn." Mary set the brimming bowl on the dresser. Her gaze took in the empty glasses and the full pitcher of lemonade. Mary hesitated. "I hope you enjoy your stay this evening, Shirley. I know Jonas enjoys your company."

Shirley smiled and said thank you.

Mary turned and left, closing the door.

Jonas jumped up and filled the lemonade glasses and popcorn bowls. He motioned for Shirley to follow him.

She stood and walked to the dresser. Picking up a bowl and a glass, she followed Jonas onto a balcony that overlooked the rolling lawn beside the house. She'd been here once before, and the sight still took her breath away. The great expanse of stars swept across the sky, and she could just make out the rolling hills extending into the distance. Jonas's form filled her peripheral vision. They leaned against the rail and ate their popcorn in companionable silence. Jonas must have decided his effort to push a visit to his church wouldn't succeed and had backed off. That's wise of him, Shirley decided. After all, they were both young and had many years ahead of them.

There was no sense in rushing into anything. Her heart reached out to him, but it also had roots at home with *Mamm* and *Daett* and her community. She would need time to sort this all out. Maybe Jonas's *daett* thought she was interested in Jonas because of their wealth. The thought stung because there was some truth to the accusation. If only *Daett* didn't have such strict ideas about money, she thought. Then she wouldn't feel the lack of it so strongly.

Shirley focused on her lemonade and took a small sip. Jonas set his glass on the balcony deck and slipped his arm around her waist.

That she could handle. She leaned against him instead of the rail. Now, if Jonas would kiss her…this evening would be complete.

"I'm glad you're with me tonight, Shirley." Jonas's voice seemed to fill the darkness with joy.

"I don't regret that we came here," Shirley tried to sound brave and sure.

"Dad didn't mean anything by what he said," Jonas said again, almost as if he was trying to convince himself too.

"I know."

Moments later Jonas's arm slipped away, and he picked up his lemonade. "I guess I'd better get you home."

It was clear there would be no kiss tonight. Shirley hid her disappointment as she turned toward him. "I guess it is kind of late."

"Maybe next time will go better." Jonas sounded hopeful. "There *will* be a next time, won't there?"

"*Yah*, if you wish it," Shirley said, squeezing his hand as they went back into the house. Inside she wanted to shout with joy. This was the first time he'd mentioned seeing her again.

Chapter Seven

———◆•◆———

Ivan Mast drove south of Berlin, Ohio, on State Route 39. He kept one buggy wheel on the shoulder of the busy road when he could. Even then the traffic backed up momentarily on the uphill runs. Dusk had fallen an hour ago. There was no danger of an accident, Ivan told himself. His buggy had flashers on both sides, low headlights on the front, and the traditional slow-moving vehicle triangle and red lights in the back. Still, when three cars wouldn't pass his buggy, Ivan pulled into Kline Lumber's parking lot to allow them more room. His gesture would be appreciated, he was sure.

Ivan held the reins firmly as his horse, Billy, pawed the gravel. Both of them were impatient to get home. Ivan still had horse stalls to clean tonight, and Billy was surely anticipating his box of oats. Laura, Ivan's *frau*, had sent him into Berlin to shop after he got home from his job at the Beachy's furniture shop. He'd wanted to wait until tomorrow, but Laura said she needed Alka-Seltzer tablets tonight for her severe cold. It seemed to Ivan that the woman was susceptible to every bug that passed through Possum Valley.

Pregnancies were supposed to prevent such things, but not with Laura. Why the Lord had chosen to make Laura's pregnancy such a difficult time, Ivan couldn't imagine. But His ways were beyond question. Perhaps beautiful women had to suffer more to make up for what they enjoyed in other areas.

Ivan watched car headlights bounce on 39 and smiled. Laura had conceived soon after their wedding back in November. He would be a *daett* before long. The joy...and responsibility...already occupied his thoughts.

No time to think of that now, though. Ivan looked both ways before he let the reins out, and Billy plunged forward again. His hoofbeats on the road soon settled into a steady rhythm, and Ivan let his thoughts drift again. Laura was excited about one thing this week. Another letter had arrived from her sister Esther in Oklahoma. Esther had returned to the Oklahoma Amish community to care for the Swartz family's ailing grandmother, Mabel.

Laura had wanted to read him the whole letter, but Ivan had waved his hand for silence once enough of the details emerged. Esther had resumed her interest in a young man in the community and felt she was close to a conquest of his attentions. The young man's name was Wayne Yutzy, a handsome fellow by Esther's account. They would soon date, Esther was certain. Laura had giggled as she reread that portion of the letter.

Esther was capable of plenty of charm, that was for sure, Ivan thought. She easily matched her sister in beauty and charm. The two had their pick of any of the unmarried Amish men in Possum Valley they set their hearts on. Esther was the eldest, but she'd not accepted a date since the family had moved back to Ohio from Oklahoma. Apparently this Wayne situation explained why. Esther had left her heart in the West—no doubt with this Wayne fellow.

Laura had chosen Ivan out of all the Amish districts' eligible men. This was a great honor, and one he was grateful for. Laura was a catch, there was no question about that. He adored her many virtues more each day. Now that she was with child, his affections for her increased. Why else would he be on this inconvenient trip into town this late in the day? For Laura's comfort, of course. Still, there were chores that awaited him at home.

Ivan glanced behind him as another thought niggled at his brain. Why was Laura so interested in her sister's conquest in Oklahoma? There was the sister thing of course, but he was sure it went deeper than that. Perhaps all the way back to why Laura had chosen him in the first place. He'd never have dared to ask her home after a Sunday evening hymn singing if Laura hadn't made it abundantly clear with bright smiles that she was interested in him.

And that was after he'd had his heart set on Miriam Yoder for several years. The attention he'd paid to Miriam had been no secret in the community, he was sure. In retrospect, it seemed like Laura had liked the challenge of pitting her charm against that of another girl. Miriam hadn't stood a chance, even with her deeper character and personal maturity.

He had nothing to be ashamed of, Ivan told himself. He'd married the woman he'd wanted. *Yah*, there had been the *kafuffle* over the farm Miriam had inherited from that *Englisha* man. Ivan had attempted to resume a relationship with Miriam after he'd found out. Miriam believed his affections were tainted by her farm ownership, which hadn't been entirely untrue. Sure, he'd thought about what a farm, free and clear of debt, could do for him, but in the end he'd put all that aside.

His main mistake had been dating Laura while he spoke of love with Miriam. That had been the height of foolishness. Laura could easily have dumped him when she found out, and she would have been in the right. Instead, Laura had risen to the challenge and closed the deal with him rather quickly.

Ivan winced when he considered that Laura must know this

Wayne fellow was now dating Miriam. She had to know. Such things weren't secret in the Ohio and Oklahoma Amish communities because of their strong ties to each other. For one thing, *he* knew about it, and it seemed like most folks in his community knew. Sure, he was aware partly because he still had some interest in Miriam's whereabouts. Such was usually the case with former sweethearts, wasn't it? They lingered in a man's mind. But if he was honest, Miriam outranked both of the Swartz girls in character. In looks—now that was another matter.

Esther followed in her sister Laura's footsteps, Ivan told himself. When she set her cap for a fellow, she would land him for sure. Ivan didn't like that—the idea that Miriam might lose out again to a Schwartz. But what could he do about it? Should he order Laura to tell Esther to back off? Laura wouldn't listen. She enjoyed conquest too much. And who said Esther would listen even if Laura passed on the message? Any explanation of the wrongness of what Esther was doing would bring up questions about his involvement with Miriam and Laura's actions during their courtship. She'd used kisses and other female wiles to win his heart, even knowing he had strong feelings for someone else.

Ivan glanced over his shoulder at the cars lining up behind him. He pulled aside again. No, he wouldn't broach that subject with Laura. Not in a hundred years.

Ivan waited, his gaze on the cars as they drove past. Billy didn't paw the ground this time. That last hill must have taken some of the fire out of him. Moments later all the cars had passed, so Ivan continued on. He had best leave the subject of Esther alone. There were too many angles he didn't wish to explore. What if Laura should ask him if he had regrets that he wasn't the possessor of Miriam Yoder's farm? Miriam's *daett*, Eli, currently tended the place for her. The word in the community was that Eli now owned the place but had promised to return it to Miriam once she married.

Ivan frowned. The farm could have been his place now instead of the rental where he lived with Laura. No, he wouldn't be able to lie if Laura asked him. Even a moment's hesitation on his part would send her into hysterics. Why Laura couldn't believe she'd won his heart fair and square or that he considered the wedding vows unbreakable was beyond him.

Ivan cheered up as a new thought crossed his mind. Perhaps Laura and Esther were both wrong. This Wayne man might be impervious to Esther's charms. Ivan stared over the darkened fields of Possum Valley, and his brow knitted. It was true that marriage wasn't marriage until the vows were said, but Miriam had dated this Wayne fellow for some time now. Shouldn't that carry some weight? It would serve Esther right to lose out to Miriam.

Ivan sighed as the headlights of another car broke over the hill ahead of him. He needed to get home. Hopefully Laura had the letter out of sight when he returned so they could talk of something else. If not, he'd steer the conversation to safer ground. Laura didn't need any enlightenment on how he felt. And she wouldn't ask if he kept his mouth shut about Esther's devious plans.

A car raced past, shaking the buggy. Obviously a guy in a hurry. It sure looked to Ivan like it was Jonas Beachy's fancy convertible. Jonas was his boss's son, although in reality Jonas was his boss at the furniture shop. Raymond Beachy rarely showed his face around there anymore. Jonas must be headed out to Berlin…or Wooster, more likely. The boy had plenty of money and could go where he wished, unlike Ivan. He pushed the bitter thought away. He had Laura's love and beauty to comfort him and that was enough. A man couldn't have everything. Still his gaze lingered on the fancy convertible.

Ivan stiffened as the car's taillights suddenly blossomed and the vehicle braked hard. He heard the screech of tires skidding on pavement as a thunderous thump boomed through the air. The headlights, now on high beams, pointed off the road and illuminated a herd of deer near the brow of a knoll.

His heart racing, Ivan sped up Billy. Jonas might need assistance—and quickly. The boy had been going pretty fast. When Ivan was within a dozen feet of the crash site, he pulled off the road and onto the shoulder. His flashing lights normally served their purpose well, but they seemed inadequate now. They'd have to do until the police arrived. Already another vehicle ahead had pulled to the side with flashers blinking. Ivan saw the driver pull out his cell and assumed he was calling 911. Help would be on its way.

Quickly climbing out of the buggy, Ivan hurried toward the convertible. A huge deer lay partially in the road obviously in the throes of death. Approaching the convertible on the driver's side, Ivan breathed a sigh of relief to see Jonas appeared unscathed. He already had his car door open and was leaning in to help a woman who occupied the passenger seat.

"May I help?" Ivan asked as he stared into the convertible. Both air bags had deployed, and there was blood on the seat and on Jonas's shirt.

Jonas's face showed surprise when he looked up. "Ivan! Has anyone called 911? Shirley's hurt!"

Ivan held up his hands. "I'll check to be sure someone has." He looked for cross traffic before he dashed across the road to the nearest parked vehicle. They were lined up in both directions now as everyone wondered what had happened and whether help was needed.

Ivan stopped at the first car's window. "Did you call 911?" he asked.

A woman answered anxiously, "Yes, sir. Help is on the way. Is anyone hurt?"

Ivan nodded and thanked her for calling for help. When he returned to the convertible, a man and a few women had gathered around it. Already sirens blared from the direction of Berlin. Ivan hung back as a blanket was thrown over the shoulders of the injured woman and cloths were put against the deepest gashes. She was bleeding severely from wounds on her head and shoulders. Jonas had said her name was Shirley. Could it be Shirley Yoder, Miriam's sister? Ivan shuddered at the thought. He'd heard that Jonas had gone out with Shirley a few times.

Ivan retreated as an ambulance pulled up. He'd best get out of here before he was blocked in. Jonas and his passenger were now in capable hands. Ivan could do nothing more for them. He climbed into the buggy and guided Billy off the road shoulder, moving slowly until he was clear of the ambulance and the police cars that had arrived. Already a man in uniform was directing traffic around the accident.

Ivan was back on the road, still shaken by the accident and considering if the passenger was Miriam's sister. It was well known that Shirley was on her *rumspringa*. Ivan knew Eli Yoder wouldn't take it well if his daughter had taken up with the likes of Jonas Beachy.

Chapter Eight

———◆◆◆———

Shirley clung to the side of the gurney as the ambulance sped through the night. She tried to move her head to glance at the attendant on one side of her, but she couldn't.

"Hold still, dear," a voice ordered above the chatter of a radio.

The pain from her head and face seemed to burn through her whole body. Shirley whimpered as the memory of the accident replayed in her mind. The line of deer seemed to appear suddenly on the road ahead of them. The next scene she remembered was a glimpse of brown coming over the hood and then a sudden explosion of white hitting her in the face, followed by a swerving motion she figured was Jonas slamming on the brakes and steering sideways. She vaguely remembered something hitting her head and face over and over, but she was so dazed that she wasn't sure what had happened.

Shirley groaned. Why had this happened? Was this the Lord's punishment on her? Shirley tried to move her hand up to her head, but it wouldn't move.

A voice gently said, "No, ma'am. Don't move. You've been in an accident and are hurt."

Shirley already realized that, but how bad was she? She wanted to ask, but no words would come. Was she all right? She shivered as pain overwhelmed her again. She remembered seeing blood around her, and the truth crept in. Her head must be injured badly. The more she thought about, the surer she was. There had been a lot of blood. And her face hurt. Much more than superficial cuts and bruises would. She tried to shift on the gurney.

"Hold still, dear," the voice ordered again. "I've given you something to dull the pain and help you relax. You're in an ambulance on the way to the hospital."

Shirley tightened her fingers on the thin rail and allowed her mind to drift. A numbing haze seemed to be wafting around her. She felt the pain ease, but the the calm was punctured with another question. Have *Mamm* and *Daett* heard about the accident yet? *Daett* already had strong objections to her relationship with Jonas. Now he would have a lot to say when he learned she was in the hospital. And this ride in the ambulance would have to be paid by someone, to say nothing of doctor and hospital bills. They had no insurance, but perhaps Jonas did. But really, Jonas wasn't responsible for deer ambling onto the road. How did people pay for things caused by accidents?

At least Jonas had held her hand while they waited for help. She'd noticed that he didn't leave her side until she was loaded into the ambulance. Shirley groaned and felt someone squeeze her arm gently.

"We're almost there. Please hold still."

Noise chattered from somewhere above her head. This time she realized that information was being passed back and forth, probably via a radio. The attendant next to her leaned into her line of sight. "Shirley, your parents have been notified by the police. A state trooper will bring them to the hospital."

Shirley held perfectly still. Was she supposed to be happy about this? *Mamm* and *Daett's* presence wasn't the most comforting thought right now. This night had turned into a nightmare—and after such a pleasant evening with Jonas. She tried to turn her head, but cried out from the increased pain.

"Dear!" The paramedic placed gentle hands on both sides of Shirley's head. "You must hold still."

Tears welled up in her eyes. Was there more to her injuries than she realized? What else would provoke such a vigilant reaction from the paramedic? What if the doctors couldn't fix her up? What then?

She felt the ambulance slow as the siren wail ceased. Shirley breathed a sigh of relief. The awful ride was ending. They must have arrived at the hospital. She'd have some answers soon. What if her face would heal but she'd be scarred for life? Could she survive if her beauty was gone? Would anyone like her? Would Jonas still be interested? If she was scarred up, what man would want to stay around?

Shirley forced her mind to stop as the ambulance halted, the back doors opened, and paramedics rolled her gurney out of the ambulance. They went through some doors and bright lights assaulted her eyes. The rush of people talking and machines humming droned in her ears. Doors swished around her, and silence replaced the droning. The lights didn't dim though. Soft voices spoke and kind faces peered down at her. Shirley began to tremble. Even *Mamm* and *Daett* would be a welcomed sight at the moment.

The ambulance paramedic appeared again by Shirley's side and squeezed her hand. "Good luck, girl. You're going into surgery now."

Shirley could only nod her thanks, and the paramedic seemed to understand.

The gurney moved again, and Shirley noticed ceiling lights passing by. She closed her eyes. *Oh, please, God, let this end!* But she realized this night was far from over. She was no longer in charge and might not be for a long time. Perhaps never again. Tears escaped her eyes, and then the gurney stopped, she felt pressure on her arms, and sleep came.

◆◆◆

Shirley awakened in what seemed like moments later. All was quiet. Where was she? What had happened? She tried to focus. There'd been an accident. She'd been taken to the hospital. An awful ambulance ride. The swish of doors. Bright lights. And then...nothing.

Shirley shifted and realized she was on a bed. *Mamm's* face appeared in front of her. "Don't move, Shirley. Don't move unless you have to."

She was tired of being told to not move. "Tell me, *Mamm*. How bad is it?"

Mamm didn't answer right away. "You're in what they call the recovery room. You've had surgery, and now you need to rest."

"Who's here?" Shirley tried to sit up, but *Mamm* pushed down gently on her shoulder.

Shirley had caught a brief glimpse of *Daett* seated on a chair beside her bed. He hadn't said a word. His lecture would probably have to wait until they got home. But she wanted to get it over with right now, even though the world seemed to be swirling around dizzily.

When no one said anything more, Shirley whispered. "I'd rather be chewed out now rather than later, *Daett*. Let's get the lecture over with."

"No one's chewing anyone out." *Mamm* stroked her arm. "You need to sleep now."

"*Daett* will have his say," Shirley insisted. "I know you don't approve of Jonas. But I couldn't help myself."

In the silence that followed, she sensed *Daett* rising and coming closer.

He spoke in hushed tones. "*Yah*, this is what comes from following the world, Shirley. How many times have I warned you on how the Lord looks at these things? We sow to the flesh, and we reap to the flesh. The Lord will not be mocked. If we disobey, He will stand by His word. You can be thankful this wasn't a serious injury. You could have been lamed or blinded or even killed in such an accident."

"Not serious?" Shirley whispered. Her hands reached up to touch her face and encountered bandages. "Unless I miss my guess, I'll be scarred from this, won't I?"

There was a brief silence before *Daett* said, "Life is not about how a person appears. This is another lesson you will do well to learn."

Shirley ignored her *daett* and reached for *Mamm*'s hand. "How bad will the scars be? I know something happened to my face."

"Hush now." *Mamm*'s fingers tightened in hers. "The doctors aren't saying much—at least the ones we've spoken with. They'll be in soon. I'm sure they'll tell us more. They may not know until the bandages can be removed."

Daett's voice rose in volume. "Of all the things to think about at this moment, Shirley, it shouldn't be your looks. What does that matter? Your soul is what's important. Inward beauty transcends outer beauty. You should know that. 'Favour is deceitful, and beauty is vain: but a woman that feareth the Lord, she shall be praised.'" *Daett* paused for a moment. "You should be thinking of repentance, Shirley. I believe this is a warning from the Lord. This is the result of lusting after *Englisha* cars and *Englisha* ways that are not right for our people. Humble yourself, Shirley, and seek forgiveness for the path you've taken these past few months."

Tears stung Shirley's eyes, and even *Mamm*'s hand in hers didn't provide much comfort. *Daett* was right. She should repent. Only she couldn't. She couldn't repent from the way she felt about Jonas. She couldn't be like Miriam, which was really what *Daett* was wanting.

Daett must have taken her silence as encouragement because he continued. "We love you, Shirley, your *mamm* and I. But we can't approve of the way you've been conducting your life of late. And now when this warning from the Lord also knocks on your door, you must take it seriously. Open the door of your heart, Shirley. Let the Lord's Spirit…"

"That's enough now." *Mamm*'s quiet voice stopped *Daett*'s. "Shirley must rest now."

Shirley couldn't see *Daett*'s face through her tears, but he must have agreed with *Mamm* because his form faded from sight. Her hand tightened on *Mamm*'s. "Tell me, *Mamm*. How bad is it?"

"I'm not sure." *Mamm* hesitated. "There are bandages over most of your face. You were in surgery for a few hours."

They both knew that meant it couldn't be good.

Another question formed in Shirley's mind. "Where's Jonas? Is he all right?"

Mamm glanced in *Daett*'s direction before she answered. "Jonas came in with his parents earlier while you were in surgery. He's bruised and sore but all right. We asked them to leave."

"It was best that way," *Daett* spoke up. "That part of your life is over."

"But it wasn't Jonas's fault," Shirley choked out. "The deer ran across the road in front of the car. He couldn't stop in time."

Daett didn't look at all sympathetic. "We will stand with you, and we're all the family you need." He reached over to his hat sitting on a table. "I have errands. The cows must be tended to. *Mamm* will stay with you until you're released."

"How will you get home? I was told a trooper would bring you here."

Daett looked away. "Jonas had someone stay to take us home.

One of their church people, I think. They'll drive *Mamm* and you home too."

You won't let me see Jonas? Shirley managed to strangle the cry before it could be heard. Protests wouldn't help right now.

Daett stopped by Shirley's bedside for a moment, but he didn't say anything more.

Shirley decided she must appear properly contrite under the bandages. Perhaps she'd feel repentant eventually. If she was indeed permanently scarred, maybe she would be able to straighten up her life. Besides, if she was no longer *gut* looking, Jonas wouldn't want a relationship with her. *Daett* was correct on that part. It was over.

Shirley clung to *Mamm*'s hand. She cried softly.

Mamm stroked her daughter's hair.

"*Mamm*, I don't think I can handle looking…looking, well, looking not pretty. I don't think I've been vain, *Mamm*, but looks were all I had. Will the Lord ask me to go through life ugly? Isn't that too much to ask of any girl? And especially of me? I have no other redeeming qualities—not like Miriam. How will I find a boyfriend? And what about Jonas?" Shirley's questions ended in racking sobs.

"Perhaps this will help develop character in you that has value in the Lord's eyes."

Mamm meant to comfort, but her words didn't. *Mamm* was on *Daett*'s side. What Shirley wanted was assurance that things would return to normal. She wanted to walk out of here the same Shirley she'd been when Jonas picked her up at home.

"The Lord knows what's best," *Mamm* comforted again.

Tears burned in Shirley's eyes.

Chapter Nine

Ivan looked up at the overcast, Saturday-morning sky as he walked in from his early morning chores. There would be rain soon—*yah*, and it fit his present gray mood just fine. It was his day off, and he'd looked forward to working outside in the sunshine. His job indoors at Beachy's furniture had given him a pale complexion and made him weary in heart. Now it looked like he'd be in the barn all day—or the house. He wasn't sure which was the right choice. Laura would have something for him to do if he stayed inside. She sure was grouchy with her morning sickness. That mood had been on full display last night when he'd returned home. So much so that he hadn't talked much—and neither had she. He'd gone to bed without telling her about the accident.

Ivan pushed open the mud-room door of the small house and entered to kick off his boots. He stuck his head through the kitchen doorway and said a forced, "*Gut* morning."

Laura stood at the stove and didn't turn around. "You already said that."

Ivan came all the way inside and grumbled, "There's nothing wrong with two *gut* mornings, is there?"

Laura didn't answer as she plopped the egg plate down on the table. "Breakfast is ready."

"That's *gut*," he said as he sat down.

Laura glared at him. "Did you see the weather outside?"

He shrugged. "It's going to rain, so I'll work inside."

Her face brightened a little. "Then maybe there is something *gut* about the morning. You can fix that shelf in the basement I'll need for my summer canning. And you can add a few extra shelves while you're at it. No woman has too many shelves for her canning."

Ivan didn't say anything as he stared at the plate with two eggs. "You know I like three eggs. There are only two. One for you and one for me."

Laura's face darkened again. "Three eggs aren't *gut* for you."

Ivan took a deep breath and held in his negativity. "At least there's plenty of oatmeal."

A smile played on Laura's face. "You need to think of your health now that a *bobbli* is on its way."

He choked back a response and bowed his head in silent prayer. Laura still had her head bowed when he lifted his.

She finally looked up. "You didn't pray very long."

Ivan pulled his one egg on his plate and avoided her gaze.

Laura still looked at him. "You need to pray our prayers out loud like my *daett* used to. I like to hear them at mealtimes and during devotions. With the *bobbli* coming, it's something you need to do." Laura touched his arm. "I thought I'd help, so I bought a prayer book. It's on the desk in the living room."

Ivan blinked. "I'm not ready for that yet. And some Amish men never pray aloud."

Laura's fingers tightened on his arm. "But you will, won't you? I want our children to grow up like I did—with their *daett's* voice leading out in spiritual matters. It's important to me."

Ivan didn't look at her. Laura had said enough on the subject, and it was time to speak of something else. In the end he'd give in, but for now he'd put up a display of resistance.

"There was an accident on the way home last night," he said.

Laura wasn't distracted. "You shouldn't change the subject just because you don't like it."

Ivan ignored her. "I think Shirley Yoder was with Jonas Beachy, and they wrecked on 39."

"Eli Yoder's daughter?" Laura leaned forward.

"*Yah*, I think so."

"How bad was the accident?" The single egg still lay on Laura's plate.

Ivan shrugged. "I'm not a doctor, but a deer went through the windshield. Shirley's head and face looked cut up. There was a lot of blood."

"And you didn't tell me this last night when you got home?" Rebuke was in her voice.

"I had other things on my mind," Ivan said. "You didn't have much to say last night either, you know."

"But this was your boss, Ivan. And Shirley is Miriam's sister. She meant something to you…at one time, anyway."

"Miriam Yoder means nothing to me now."

Laura gave him a long glare before continuing. "Tell me about the accident. How did it happen?"

"Right after Jonas passed me, going pretty fast, a line of deer chose to cross 39. When Jonas saw the deer, he must have braked and swerved, but he still hit one."

"If Shirley was hurt, it might bring Miriam home for a while," Laura mused.

"Could be," Ivan allowed.

A smile spread across Laura's face. "This might be Esther's chance to get Wayne. With Miriam gone for more than a week Esther could state her affections for Wayne without interference."

His spoon stopped halfway to the sugar bowl. "The two of you are shameless."

Laura giggled. "It worked for me, and I don't see you complaining." She glanced at the swell of her stomach. "You don't have regrets, do you?"

Ivan didn't hesitate. "Of course not. But still—"

"Then don't complain," she said, cutting him off. "Miriam's not married to Wayne, and it's probably her farm that's drawing him into her net anyway. That girl couldn't get a decent man to date her until she had bait to offer. I say Esther is doing Wayne a great favor. He'll see it eventually, just like you did. And aren't you glad, Ivan?"

"*Yah*, of course," he repeated.

Laura reached for Ivan's arm and squeezed it. "I'm glad you didn't fall for Miriam's farm. I do love you, and our child is a blessing from the Lord. How could it be otherwise? He won't be tainted by the things of this world."

He swallowed quickly. "Are you saying the *bobbli*'s a boy?"

Her face glowed. "I don't know, Ivan. I'm just making my point that Esther is doing the right thing. We should help her where we can."

Protest died in his throat. What could he say? She'd only turn his objections around somehow.

"I'm glad you agree with me." Laura smiled as she pulled her hand back and started on her egg.

Ivan gulped the last of his oatmeal. Let Laura think she'd won the argument. He rose and walked to the kitchen window. Outside the clouds had opened up with a deluge. He would have to work in the basement on Laura's shelves. He'd tinker in the barn after the rain had let up—if it ever did.

Laura's voice called to him. "I'm finished eating and ready to give thanks again."

He returned to the table and bowed his head. Silence filled the room. How he'd ever get the words of prayer out of this mouth, he wasn't sure. Maybe he should begin trying sooner rather than later. Postponement wouldn't help, and Laura had purchased the prayer book. She was trying to help, and he should be grateful. He opened his mouth and managed to get a few words out. "Dear Lord in heaven, forgive us our sins and help us live righteous lives. Thank You for the food we've eaten, and Laura for her hard work in preparing it. Amen." Ivan waited a long time before he lifted his head.

Laura appeared pleased as she led the way into the living room.

Ivan picked up the Bible on the desk before he joined Laura on the couch. Laura had wanted to place two hickory rockers in the living room right after the wedding, but he'd put his foot down. Rockers were for old people—or maybe for couples with children. With their child now on the way, he figured the rockers would soon appear. He'd cope, Ivan decided as he opened the Bible. He read from the marked place where he'd stopped yesterday morning—Ephesians, chapter five, verse six: "Let no man deceive you with vain words…" He listened to the sound of his own voice and glanced at Laura. She seemed to be listening as well. Why was he hesitant to speak aloud prayers to the Lord? Likely because it involved speech with the Almighty, Ivan told himself. That was something he needed to get over now that he was a married man and the head of his own household.

Ivan closed the Bible and reached for the prayer book Laura had purchased. Without a sideways glance at Laura, he knelt and waited for her to join him. Then he read the words of the first prayer: "Now he who without thanks and prayer, from morning sleep arises. And he who can forget God's praises, how sorrowfully he begins the day…" Ivan continued until the end. It was a long prayer, and he said every word with care. He liked speaking prayer aloud, now that he'd begun. This was how things were supposed to be. He was the head of his family, and soon there would be children. And Laura had led him to do this. He ought to thank the Lord especially for her. He had a wife who was not only beautiful, but spiritual enough to guide him to what he needed.

Ivan stood and closed the book.

Laura got up also and took his hand. "That was so *wunderbah*, Ivan. I knew you could do it."

"Thanks for the encouragement," he said quietly. "Now for your shelves."

She glowed. "Make them strong, Ivan. Just like our home will be with the Lord's help."

He looked away. "*Yah*, I will." Her praise was unwarranted. Laura deserved more credit than he did, but why say so? He'd savor this bright moment on this dark-and-dreary morning. Hopefully Miriam would be able to hold on to this Wayne Yutzy of hers. He wished her all of life's happiness and joy. But he wasn't about to mention that to Laura.

Chapter Ten

Miriam listened as Wayne told the story at the kitchen table with great expression. "We were in the barn that evening for our chores, and Joy had this bunch of little kittens who were just beginning to stagger about. They'd already learned that we give them fresh milk during chore time, so they're out waiting with their mother for their treat. Of course, they can't sit still—and even more so with the sleepy spring flies buzzing around. At first they only snapped at them, but soon they got to swatting with their little paws, followed by tumbles over each other. Esther and Joy couldn't stop giggling, and I had to join in myself. It was that funny."

Miriam looked away from Wayne's face as the story continued on. Wayne was here for lunch, and somehow the subject of kittens had come up. Wayne had jumped in with this story, but at the mention of Esther's name, Miriam flinched. At least Esther had only been on the sidelines. Miriam tried to put the image of Esther and Wayne laughing over kittens out of her mind. There was no reason she should be jealous. She had vowed she wouldn't be.

"They are the cutest things, I must admit," Wayne concluded.

There were chuckles all around the table. Even Uncle William seemed to have enjoyed the tale.

Moments later a knock came from the front door and silence fell in the kitchen, except for Uncle William. He started to get up, muttering, "I wonder who that is in the middle of the day?"

Aunt Fannie motioned for him to sit. "I'll get the door." She rose and disappeared into the living room.

Whoever had arrived couldn't be a big deal. Not much happened in Oklahoma on Saturdays. Everyone moved slower as they got their work done and prepared for Sunday services. Today, even the *Englisha* had slowed down, as business in the nursery had been light all morning. Miriam had helped out a few hours and then returned to the house to work in the kitchen. The row of pecan pies on the counter was a testament to her morning's labor. They looked delicious, but she hadn't dared taste one. She noticed Wayne's gaze drift toward the waiting pies too.

"I hope they're *gut*." Miriam wrinkled up her nose. "I had to rush."

"I know they'll be *gut*!" Uncle William declared without hesitation.

"You can be sure of that," Wayne echoed William's sentiment.

Miriam stared at the line of pies. "Looks can be deceiving, you know."

"They weren't with you," Wayne teased.

Miriam gave Wayne a grateful smile. She'd written *Mamm* this week about the proposed wedding in October. She was sure *Mamm* wouldn't turn her down, so the matter was settled. She was Wayne's promised one, and she would soon be a married woman. She took a deep breath and thought of Wayne's kiss the other Friday night. Wayne wasn't plentiful with his kisses, but he would be once they were married. She was sure of that.

Wayne nudged Miriam under the table. "What are you thinking?"

Heat rushed into Miriam's face.

Thankfully Aunt Fannie saved the moment when she reappeared at the kitchen doorway. "It's for you, Miriam, and it sounds serious. You're to call home at once."

Miriam jumped to her feet. The flaming in her face turning icy cold. "Why? Is something wrong?"

"I don't know." Aunt Fannie appeared worried. "Young Leroy found the message down at the phone shack that had been left early this morning. There weren't any details."

"This morning?" Uncle William sounded puzzled. "And no one found it before now?"

Aunt Fannie gave him a sharp glance. "Well, it's not like the community's hopping with activity on a Saturday morning." Aunt Fannie wrung her hands for a moment. "Go call back, Miriam, and leave a message if no one answers the phone in Possum Valley."

"I'll do that." Miriam was at the kitchen doorway. "And don't wait for me on the pecan pie."

"Should someone go with Miriam?" Aunt Fannie suggested.

"I'll go." Wayne was already on his feet.

Miriam spoke over her shoulder. "You don't have to. I'll go alone."

Before Wayne could protest, she'd rushed out the door. Leroy lingered on the steps and greeted her with a warm smile.

"Hi, Leroy." Miriam smiled back. "Thanks for bringing the message up."

"You're welcome." He trailed after her on the walk down the road. When she gave him a quick glance, he shrugged.

"I'm going that way," he explained.

That was true, Miriam figured, but she noticed he waited outside the phone shack while she stood inside and dialed the number.

News from Possum Valley was a big deal, and Leroy didn't intend to return home until he was up-to-date. She couldn't blame him. He was a normal, curious boy.

Miriam tensed as the rings sounded in the receiver. The answering machine was set for six rings, the same as the one by the Bylers' in Oklahoma. That gave anyone who was near time for a dash to the phone. The shack was a quarter mile down the road from her parents' place, but someone else might hear.

"Come on answer!" Miriam whispered as ring four passed. She was ready to hang up when the phone clicked.

"Hello," a female voice sounded hesitant.

The words came out in a rush. "This is Miriam Yoder. I'm calling from Oklahoma."

"Oh, *yah*, Miriam. This is Betsy Mast. I was walking past and didn't know whether I should answer."

"I'm glad you did." Miriam took a deep breath. "Do you know why my parents would want to contact me?"

There was a long pause. "Maybe about your sister Shirley's accident last night."

"What accident?" A chill ran down Miriam's back.

Betsy cleared her throat. "We haven't heard much, but the man who was driving her hit a deer."

"Jonas, no doubt." Miriam tried to breathe. "How bad is it?"

"I don't know." Betsy hesitated. "They took her to the hospital. That's all I know."

Miriam thought for a moment. "Would it be too much to ask if you'd go up to my parents' place and ask them to call me in an hour? I'll be at the same number they called me at before."

"Sure." Betsy's voice was kind. "I wasn't going that way, but I have the time."

"Thank you so much." Miriam hung up the phone. She waited a few seconds before she stepped out of the phone shack.

Leroy met her with an expectant gaze.

Miriam told him, "The car my sister Shirley was riding in last night hit a deer. I haven't talked to my parents yet, so I don't know how bad it is."

"A deer," Leroy muttered and turned to go. A deer wasn't much in Oklahoma, and how much damage could a deer do?

To Miriam, Leroy's attitude was clear, and hopefully he was right. But why had her parents called instead of written? A phone call wasn't warranted for a mere fender bender. And Betsy had said Shirley was taken to the hospital. That could mean anything from a few scratches to…Miriam gasped as possibilities expanded in her mind.

As she made her way back to the house, Miriam wished she'd said thirty minutes instead of an hour. She could have waited at the phone shack for that long. But that would leave Aunt Fannie and Uncle William up in the air. Better to give them the little information she had.

Aunt Fannie met her at the front door with a concerned look. "Serious, is it?"

"I don't know." Miriam swallowed the lump in her throat. "Shirley was involved in an accident last night and was taken to the hospital. I sent someone to tell *Mamm* I'd be back at the phone booth in an hour. After that I should know more."

Aunt Fannie gave Miriam a quick hug. "It'll be okay, I'm sure. Shirley makes it through these things in one piece. Who was she with?"

Miriam met her aunt's look. "I didn't ask, but I suppose Jonas Beachy. Who else?"

"Maybe the Lord is speaking to her," Aunt Fannie ventured. "I know Shirley was encouraged to live a godly life while she was out here last year."

Uncle William stuck his head out of the kitchen doorway. "Would someone fill me in on the news?"

Wayne joined them. "I want to know too."

They were both dears, Miriam thought as she repeated the details of what she knew.

"Maybe you should plan a visit home," Uncle William suggested when she finished.

Miriam drew in a sharp breath. "Then you think something serious has happened?"

"Not necessarily." Uncle William gave a quick laugh. "But I thought you might need an excuse to get away from us."

"Don't tease her," Aunt Fannie scolded. "Not at a time like this."

Uncle William sobered. "Sorry, but you still might consider a trip home, what with the wedding and all. You could use the time to plan things, even if Shirley's condition doesn't warrant a trip all by itself."

"That does sound like a good idea," Aunt Fannie said.

Miriam's mind spun. "I'd have to take off from teaching school for at least a week—and more likely two. I couldn't do that. It wouldn't be fair to a substitute."

Wayne spoke up. "Sarah Mullet, the young woman who taught last term, might substitute. Sarah had her baby around Christmas. This is about the time she might want to get out of the house for a while, isn't it?"

"Don't talk like that!" Aunt Fannie scolded him. "But maybe that would work. I'd even offer to babysit Lester for Sarah. I hold him sometimes at the church services, and he's a little darling."

Miriam took a long breath. "I think we'd best slow down. We don't know how bad the accident is. And you can't do this for me anyway. It's not right."

"You'd be doing it for me too." Wayne had a slight grin. "I want our wedding to go off without a hitch."

"There you go." Aunt Fannie was all matter-of-fact now. "The issue's settled even before you talk with your *mamm*."

Miriam still hesitated. Visions of her schoolhouse and students filled her mind. "I don't know. I like my teaching job, and unless Shirley's really hurt…"

"Spoken like a true schoolteacher." Uncle William nodded his approval and looked to Wayne. "Now the two of us have to get back to work. Uncle William looked back at Miriam. "I hope Shirley's okay, but regardless, I think you should visit Possum Valley, Miriam."

"Same here," Wayne said.

A horrible thought crossed Miriam's mind as the two men left the room. Did Wayne want her out of the way so he could be with Esther unhindered?

Aunt Fannie's hand pressed on Miriam's shoulder. "Shirley will make it, okay. Don't look so worried."

"I hope so," Miriam managed. She didn't dare let on about her wicked thoughts about Wayne and Esther.

"Sit down and eat a piece of pie." Aunt Fannie's voice was insistent. "It will strengthen you for whatever lies ahead. I'll send William over tonight to speak with Sarah Mullet. That will make a better impression than if you go yourself."

Aunt Fannie cut a small piece of pie, and Miriam sat down to eat. The sweet pastry stuck to her throat, but she managed to swallow with a little difficulty. Aunt Fannie's sympathetic eye was on her the whole time.

"That's better now." Aunt Fannie patted Miriam's shoulder when she finished. "Why don't you help with the dishes until it's time to leave for the phone shack?"

Miriam nodded and the two women worked in silence. They still had several plates left to wash when Aunt Fannie motioned with her hand. "You'd better go now. It's almost time."

Miriam tried to walk slowly but ended up in a run. Great concern for Shirley had washed over her. Miriam prayed while she waited for the phone to ring. "Dear Lord, help us all. I don't know how bad things are or what You're trying to tell Shirley, but help her bear the message and find You in all of this. Let the news be *gut*…"

Miriam jumped when the phone rang. She grabbed the receiver. "Hello, *Mamm?*"

"*Yah*, Miriam." *Mamm*'s voice trembled. "I'm afraid I don't have *gut* news to share. You'd best come home for a few days, if you can."

"What happened, *Mamm?*" Miriam clutched the receiver until her fingers hurt.

"Betsy said she told you about the accident last night, so you know that." *Mamm*'s voice paused. "Shirley's at the hospital, but she's not doing well—in her spirit, that is. Her head and face are in pretty bad shape too. The deer's hooves went through the wind-shield on Shirley's side. The doctors have done what they could, but they say there will likely be a lot of scarring and even more surgery later. I'm sure you can imagine how Shirley will feel about that. Can you come home for a few days? I know that's a lot to ask with your teaching job, but Shirley needs you right now—even if she doesn't realize it."

"Yah, *Mamm*, it's already planned."

"*Gut*…"

Miriam listened as *Mamm* continued with more details of the accident and the aftermath.

Chapter Eleven

———— ◦•◦ ————

The familiar Ohio countryside drifted past the Greyhound bus window as Miriam wrapped her shawl tightly over her shoulders. The next stop was New Philadelphia where *Mamm,* and perhaps *Daett*, would pick her up after the long bus trip in from Oklahoma. She looked forward to seeing her parents again, though the first precious moments would probably be overshadowed by Shirley and her injuries.

Wayne had gone along for the trip into Coalgate to see her off. His smile had been warm as usual. Miriam even got the impression he wanted to sneak around the corner for a quick goodbye kiss. That hadn't been possible with Aunt Fannie and Mr. Whitehorse along. But the thought had warmed her heart for the past two days on the bus. The glow had lingered until she'd reached Ohio. It had dimmed in the past few hours.

Possum Valley was northwest of the bus stop, and the vicinity brought back memories of Ivan and Laura. Laura was Laura Mast now, and Miriam had no regrets about that. The memories were the problem. If one man—Ivan—had rejected her, why couldn't it happen again? This time with Wayne and Laura's sister, Esther?

Miriam sighed. It was tragic that Shirley was in this accident, but perhaps some *gut* could come out of it. Maybe Shirley would learn to live a more godly life. And for good measure, maybe Miriam would deal with some of her memories of Ivan before her wedding in October. What an embarrassment it would be if she brought Wayne to Possum Valley to marry and all she could do was think about her past—and Ivan.

Miriam peered through the window as the bus cruised through downtown New Philadelphia. Moments later it lurched to a stop. Right away Miriam caught sight of *Mamm* standing by herself beside the car of their neighbor, Mrs. Faulkner. Her family didn't hire *Englisha* drivers unless they had to. *Daett* had strict convictions about such things, although Mrs. Faulkner was glad to help out when she could. Miriam grabbed her carry-on and joined two other passengers in the aisle as they made their way slowly off the vehicle. The bus driver waited at the bottom of the steps and then led them to the outside luggage compartment. Miriam paused to send a quick wave and smile toward *Mamm*.

Mamm's face stayed sober as she waved back.

Miriam retrieved her large suitcase and headed across the parking lot.

Ahead of her, *Mamm* opened her arms for a long hug and whispered, "Welcome home. It's so *gut* to see you again."

"And you too." Miriam held on to *Mamm* for a long moment.

"Welcome back to Possum Valley!" Mrs. Faulkner's cheerful voice greeted her from the driver's seat.

"It's *gut* to be back." Miriam tried to sound equally cheerful. She whispered to *Mamm*, "How is Shirley?"

"We'll talk about that later." *Mamm* motioned toward the car's trunk. "We have to get back. I helped Naomi prepare lunch for the men before I left, but baby Anna's been fussy all day. The school-children will be home soon too."

"Shirley's home then?" Miriam guessed as she lifted her suit-case into the trunk that Mrs. Faulkner had popped open from the driver's seat.

"*Yah*, they let people go early nowadays."

After stowing her luggage, Miriam and her mother got into the backseat, shut the doors, and buckled up.

"I'm awfully sorry to hear about your sister," Mrs. Faulkner said, as she guided the car out into the street.

"So how is Shirley?" Miriam tried again.

Mamm looked out the window. "Shirley's more troubled than anything. Health-wise she'll be fine."

"Accidents can be so traumatic," Mrs. Faulkner offered in sympathy.

They rode in silence out of New Philadelphia and through the town of Dover. Miriam glanced over at *Mamm*. She knew Mrs. Faulkner was used to quiet Amish people, but the truth was that under normal circumstances there would be plenty of conversation going on right now. There was her wedding, and Wayne, and Shirley's true condition to speak of, all of which *Mamm* apparently preferred to discuss in private.

"Did you have a *gut* trip?" *Mamm* finally asked as Mrs. Faulkner drove up Highway 39 toward Sugarcreek.

Miriam smiled. "It was okay—as far as Greyhound travel goes, I guess."

"Glad it was you and not me," Mrs. Faulkner put in. "I don't like buses. They smell funny."

Miriam gave a small laugh. She said to *Mamm*, "Aunt Fannie and Uncle William send their greetings. And Wayne does to. He saw me off at the bus station in Coalgate."

A trace of a smile played on *Mamm*'s face. "He sounds decent

enough, but then we wouldn't expect anything else from someone you like."

"Oh, my!" Mrs. Faulkner exclaimed. "Do I hear that special
note in someone's voice?"

Miriam's heart warmed as she answered. "*Yah!* I've been seeing
Wayne Yutzy for some time."

"That's wonderful!" Mrs. Faulkner hadn't lost her enthusiasm.
"Any wedding plans in the air yet?"

Miriam chuckled, and Mrs. Faulkner joined in. She knew the
Amish habit of secrecy when it came to weddings.

"Well, distance makes the heart grow fonder," Mrs. Faulkner
said. "At least that's what they say. So this Wayne fellow will be all
the happier to see you when you return."

Miriam smiled. "I sure hope he will be."

Mrs. Faulkner continued. "Your sister will be just fine. I heard
that Beachy boy has seen to it that she has the best doctors. And you
know the Beachys have plenty of money, so everything will be the
best it can be." Mrs. Faulkner slowed down to pull into the Yoder
driveway. "I have it from one of the first responders. The Beachy
boy called his dad from the crash site, and they told the ambulance
where to take your sister. Nothing but the best for those Beachys."

Miriam glanced at *Mamm*. "Is this true?"

Mamm shrugged her shoulders. "I wouldn't know. *Daett* did say
all the hospital bills have been paid by someone."

Mrs. Faulkner continued undaunted. "Our children often do
the strangest things, even the best of them, so don't feel too badly."
She came to a stop beside the Yoder house.

"I suppose so." *Mamm* smiled tiredly. "What do I owe you?"

"Just the usual." Mrs. Faulkner fluttered her hand about. "You
know I'm always glad to help your family."

"Thanks for the ride," Miriam told Mrs. Faulkner while *Mamm*
wrote out a check. Miriam got out and retrieved her suitcases. She
waited at the end of the walk for *Mamm*. The sights and smells

of home washed over her—the old barn with its sagging windows, the white house under the trees where she'd been born and grown up, the wafting scents of plants and animals. All of it seemed unchanged since last July. She was the one who had changed, and in ways she couldn't put her finger on.

She looked around again. She would bring Wayne here before too many months had passed, and they would say the vows in this house.

After Mrs. Faulkner pulled out of the driveway, *Mamm* joined Miriam.

"So much has changed since I left, and yet nothing really has," Miriam said. "I can't get my mind around it."

"You've grown up," *Mamm* allowed, but she was obviously distracted. "Come, Miriam. You must see Shirley now. She needs your encouragement."

Miriam followed *Mamm* toward the house. She knew she must be strong even though she felt weak inside. Shirley had left Oklahoma last fall when she should have stayed where the Lord had put her to work on her problems. Here in Possum Valley, she'd managed to make things worse for herself. But none of that was what Shirley would want to hear right now. Miriam decided she needed to offer Shirley the same compassion she'd received. Had not the Lord sent her Wayne's attention when she hadn't deserved it?

Miriam took the front steps with care. Under normal conditions, Naomi and Shirley would both be out on the porch by now, but the front door hadn't even opened.

Miriam was held back by *Mamm*'s hand. "Don't act shocked when you see her. Remember, her face is covered in bandages."

Miriam nodded.

They both walked up the porch steps together. They entered the home, and Naomi peered out of the kitchen doorway with baby Anna in her arms.

"Hi!" Naomi gave Miriam a little wave.

Miriam wanted to rush over for her first peek at her new baby sister, but she quickly noticed Shirley lying on the couch in the living room. Bandages covered most of her face, and there was a look of dismay in her eyes. Miriam hurried to her side and knelt, taking her hand.

Shirley jerked her hand back. "I'm not a little *bobbli* you need to fuss over."

"You don't have to snap at her," *Mamm* protested. "Miriam's come all the way from Oklahoma to see you."

I wish she hadn't, Shirley's hardened eyes said, though Miriam noticed they almost brimmed with tears at the same time.

"I'm so very sorry about the accident." Miriam took Shirley's hand again, and this time her younger sister didn't pull away.

"So am I." Shirley's voice was bitter. "I'll have scars across my face for the rest of my life."

"You can be thankful you have life at all." *Mamm*'s voice was clipped. "And your attitude is disgraceful, Shirley. A *gut*-natured woman is what the Lord values. How your face looks doesn't matter at all."

"That's not true from where I sit," Shirley protested.

Mamm let the comment go.

"We understand." Miriam stroked Shirley's hand. "And *Mamm* also understands. But maybe things aren't as bad as you think."

"Sure they are," Shirley complained. "I know that scars are scars, and the best doctors can do is make them less obvious. That's what they said, Miriam. From now on I'll always be the 'Shirley who was in a car accident on her *rumspringa* and made ugly.' Jonas is gone too. He won't want to see me when I'm like this."

That's a *gut* thing, Miriam thought, but she kept it to herself.

Mamm grimaced and disappeared into the kitchen. Naomi also vanished with baby Anna. Clearly Shirley had gotten on both of their nerves since she'd arrived home from the hospital, and Miriam could see why.

"You really must get yourself together," Miriam tried to keep her voice soft. "Look at the blessings we do have…like a new sister in the house."

Shirley's tears trickled down her cheeks. "That's easy for you to say. And what's a baby but another mouth to feed, which we can't afford? All the while, you seem to get blessings dropped on your head all day long. You get a farm from Mr. Bland. We go visit Oklahoma, and everyone loves you. The perfect man snaps you right up. Of course you've got nothing to complain about. *I'm* the one who can't do anything right. Look at me!" Shirley waved her hand across her face. "Miss Scarface. That's what I'll be. No man worth his salt will ever love me."

"The Lord will lead you as always," Miriam ventured.

Shirley wasn't convinced. "At least you came home to see me. That's nice."

"I wanted to." Miriam's voice caught. She had to tell the whole truth. "And while I'm here, I hope to plan my wedding for October. Maybe you can help?"

Shirley hesitated. "I heard about the wedding. And I'm glad you came for some reason besides me. I've never been worth much anyway. I can't keep even one of my *gut* intentions or promises. I'm a failure. At least now I'll look it."

"Don't say that!" Miriam pulled Shirley into a tight hug. "You're not a failure. God loves you, and I love you."

Shirley didn't resist, and she clung to Miriam for a long time.

Chapter Twelve

Miriam had been home for a week, trying her best to bring Shirley out of her doldrums to no avail. That was painfully obvious as *Daett* finished the Sunday morning prayers, and Shirley fled upstairs. Miriam had suspected Shirley wouldn't want to go with the family to the church service, but she hadn't expected the moment to be quite this dramatic.

Daett's lips were set in a straight line. "That girl!" But he said nothing more, and *Mamm* made no move to follow Shirley up the stairs. They had decided to leave things be for the moment. Shirley would survive on her own for the day. *Daett* wasn't about to dignify Shirley's behavior by allowing one of the family to stay home with her.

Miriam would have volunteered but with an ulterior motive. She simply wasn't up to facing Ivan and Laura as a married couple. But, she decided, she'd have to do it eventually, so why not today? Ivan was in her past, and *Daett* was right that Shirley didn't need support for her childish actions. Sure, the wounds on Shirley's face hadn't healed and were still under bandages, but Shirley should face things as they were—just like Miriam needed to face Ivan. All of the family had accepted that Shirley would bear reminders of that fateful evening with Jonas for the rest of her life.

"I'm leaving," Lee, the eldest of the brothers announced. "Who's going with me?"

Mark, the second oldest of the boys, glanced at Miriam. Clearly Shirley usually was the third passenger in the men's single buggy. Apparently the horse Miriam usually used, Mindy, hadn't been driven on Sundays since she'd left.

"I'll go with the surrey," Miriam offered. She'd noticed Naomi's eyes gleam at the possibility of driving with her brothers.

"No, you won't," *Daett* announced. "Naomi will come with us."

Daett was a great stickler for order, and the youngest didn't take the place of the older. Lee and Mark shrugged as they went out the door.

"Sorry," Miriam whispered to Naomi before she followed them. She almost said *maybe next Sunday*, but that would mean she thought Shirley would be staying home again. That was an option *Daett* wouldn't tolerate for another Sunday. Hopefully Shirley would figure that out by then and find the grace to accept the inevitable.

Miriam walked outside and waited beside the buggy with Mark while Lee went to get his horse, Sandy.

Mark grinned at her. "So, you haven't told me what this Wayne fellow is like."

Miriam felt a blush fill her face.

Mark's grin grew wider. "Must be really something."

"You could say so," Miriam managed.

"Will the wedding be this fall?"

Even though Mark was family, she wasn't about to tell him the date—not yet. He couldn't have helped but notice the wedding plans she and *Mamm* had been working on at the kitchen table all week. Plus, he and Lee had been required to clean the upper level of the barn of spider webs on Saturday—a preamble to wedding preparations. That wouldn't suffice for the wedding—a more thorough cleaning lay ahead, but Mark had surely put two and two together.

Miriam gave him a wry look. "We'll have to see, I guess."

Lee appeared before Mark could reply, and they helped him hitch Sandy to the buggy. Moments later Miriam was seated between the two young men. Lee drove toward Bishop Wagler's place, where the services would be held.

Bishop Wagler would be the person Wayne and she would visit to have their wedding announcement made public. A thrill ran up Miriam's back. Since she'd been in Possum Valley for a few days, things had finally begun to feel real about the wedding. She really would be marrying Wayne. Just like Ivan had found his lifelong love with Laura, she would find hers with Wayne.

"Spring's about here, I reckon," Lee said as he lifted the storm front and Miriam leaned back on the seat so Mark could secure the snap on the roof of the buggy.

"I asked Miriam whether she's going to wed this fall," Mark responded.

Lee laughed as he drove the buggy out of the driveway and onto the road. "And you expected her to tell you?"

Mark made a face. "She's my sister, so why wouldn't she?"

"Maybe because she doesn't want to." Lee clicked his tongue and Sandy sped up.

"I think I have the right to know," Mark said. "I'm her brother."

Miriam ignored both brothers as she stared down Route 39 toward where she'd been told the accident had occurred. She could almost imagine the dark evening and the deer as it flew into the car's windshield.

"Why can't I know about the wedding?" Mark's voice rose a little higher this time.

"Okay." Miriam smiled as she gave in. "It's in October as it stands now. I'm here partly to plan it with *Mamm* and, of course, to encourage Shirley."

Lee snorted. "Does Shirley know about the wedding?"

"*Yah*." Miriam kept her voice quiet. "But she also knows I didn't come just to plan the wedding."

"The world doesn't turn on Shirley's axis," Lee muttered. "It's high time she learned this."

"Don't be too hard on her." Miriam rushed to her sister's defense. "She tries. I was with her in Oklahoma, and Shirley really does want what's best."

"Apparently not badly enough." Lee didn't sound mollified. "Why else would the Lord have to smite her like this?"

"Lee!" Miriam turned to face him. "That's so wrong. Shirley has a *gut* heart."

"Even a hard-boiled egg has a heart of gold," Mark said, sarcasm in his voice.

Miriam whirled on him. "Not you too? You boys are the limit. No wonder Shirley's in the dumps."

"Don't blame us," Lee objected. "I didn't go out with Jonas Beachy after *Daett* told me not to."

"So you're the perfect saint in your *rumspringa*?" Miriam gave him a glare.

Mark muffled a laugh, and Lee kept his eyes on the road.

"See!" Miriam drove the point home. "You should have a little compassion."

Silence hung in the air as they approached Bishop Wagler's place and joined a long line of horses and buggies. The only sound was the chorus of hooves on pavement.

"It's such a beautiful sight," Miriam leaned out of the buggy for a better view. Possum Valley with all its people."

"You must get lonely all by yourself out there in the big, wild West," Mark said.

Before Miriam could correct him, Lee teased, "Pull your head back, Miriam. I don't want people to think my sister has been affected by all that loneliness."

"I'm not lonely in Oklahoma." Miriam sat up straight on the buggy seat. "There are just less people, that's all. And I'm not 'affected.'"

Lee grinned as he turned in the driveway and pulled to a stop. Miriam climbed down at the end of the sidewalk to join the other women as they approached the washroom. She shook hands with a few of them and exchanged "*gut* mornings."

"You're surely not back to stay?" Deacon Hochstetler's *frau*, Leona, commented.

"No." Miriam shook her head. "Just visiting Shirley after her accident. They have a substitute teacher for me in Oklahoma."

Leona's face registered surprise. "For long enough to make the trip? They must really like you."

Miriam turned away before Leona could see the look of pleasure on her face. She hadn't thought of it that way, but Leona was right. She must be held in high esteem by the Oklahoma community for them to hold the position two weeks for her. How things had changed from her standing here. Here Shirley had always been the seemingly blessed one.

"Please help Shirley, dear Lord," Miriam whispered quickly. "She's home all alone and must really be hurting."

"What was that?" Leona glanced her way.

Miriam moved closer before she answered. "I was just thinking of Shirley at home alone today. She wouldn't come to the service."

"Is she still that bad off?" Leona was all sympathetic.

Miriam sighed. "I wish that were the only reason, but Shirley's face is going to be scarred from the wounds, and she's not accepting it very well."

"Oh, the poor thing. I can't imagine how difficult that would be." Leona's face showed her concern before she moved on to greet the other women.

Miriam left her shawl in the washroom and tried to keep a low profile. Pride was an awful thing, and she didn't want Leona's praise to swell her head. All teachers were loved, Miriam told herself. Maybe Wayne would keep her high esteem in mind as he faced Esther Swartz's charms today.

Miriam pushed thoughts of Esther away. She could do nothing about what was happening in Oklahoma, and this would be an excellent time to practice her virtues—scarce though they seemed to be when it came to Esther. She would have patience with Wayne…even if he was tempted by Esther's smiles. The woman had *gut* looks, there was no question about that. Esther and Shirley were on the same level when it came to physical beauty. Why then had Shirley's been taken from her, while Esther and Laura got to keep theirs? Now Miriam was the one with the bitter thoughts—and she'd just prayed that Shirley wouldn't be overwhelmed by hers.

"Please help me too, dear Lord," Miriam added in another whisper. A moment later she repeated the prayer when she walked in with the other unmarried women and caught sight of Ivan seated among the married men. He had grown a nice beard since she'd seen him last. He was more handsome than ever. No wonder she'd fallen for the man! And also no wonder Laura had made such an effort to capture his heart. Miriam didn't have beauty on her side, and character didn't always trump looks. She knew that by personal experience.

Miriam took her seat on a backless bench as thoughts continued to rush through her mind. This was exactly why she hadn't wanted to see Ivan until she was safely married to Wayne. He was a reminder of her deficiencies and of her inability to keep a man's attention. But Wayne wasn't Ivan, Miriam reminded herself. Wayne was a perfect gentleman when she told him about the money, and he wasn't affected by it at all—like Ivan had been.

Miriam breathed deeply as the songs began. She caught Ivan's eyes on her soon afterward and managed a decent smile in return.

He nodded and smiled back. All was forgiven, Miriam told herself. She didn't hold any bitterness against him, and he obviously felt the same. The past was the past, and there was no reason things should repeat themselves. She was going to trust Wayne. He might smile at Esther today, as she had smiled at Ivan, and Wayne's reasons would be just as pure as hers. His heart was knit to hers in love, and nothing would change that.

The songs continued, and the ministers soon came back from their meeting upstairs to begin their sermons. Miriam tried to focus as Bishop Wagler got up to speak, but all she could see in the bishop's face were the expressions he would have when Wayne came and they asked to be married in October. The bishop would be sober-faced like he was right now, but there would also be a twinkle in his eye. The bishop would be so pleased when he read the letter Wayne would bring from Bishop Wengerd in Oklahoma. The letter would attest to Wayne's sterling character and *gut* standing in the Oklahoma Amish community and church. After Shirley's wild troubles, Bishop Wagler would be glad that the first of Eli Yoder's girls had settled down so well.

And in October the bishop would preside as Wayne and she exchanged the sacred wedding vows. His face would be even more sober and the twinkle would be gone because marriage vows were a most serious matter. One could never undo them once they were said. And she would never want to—and neither would Wayne. A soft smile drifted across Miriam's face. She could imagine how scared her *yahs* would sound in answer to the bishop's questions. But she would still be married, scared or not.

Miriam sat up straight as she caught Ivan's eyes on her again. He'd wonder why she was smiling at the bishop. Well, he'd think what he wanted. She hadn't been left out in the cold when Ivan had picked Laura over her. She would soon be married to a man of much better character than Ivan Mast possessed.

Chapter Thirteen

On Friday evening of the following week, the late-afternoon sun filled the kitchen as Shirley prepared supper for the family. With Miriam now on her way back to Oklahoma and Shirley up and around, fixing supper had fallen to her. She'd decided she would go out tonight with Lee and Mark even with her face the way it was. She couldn't stand a moment more in this house with the constant sympathetic looks from *Mamm* and the rest of the family. Well, all except *Daett*. They tried to cheer her up with empty words like "looks aren't everything," but such statements were like slaps across the face. Better to be out with the *rumspringa* crowd, she thought. At least they would speak the truth. Likely, they'd groan out loud at her condition. *Yah*, she'd feel the full pain of those groans, but at least they were evidence of what she already knew. Her hopes for a happy life with a *gut* husband who would think she was beautiful were over.

She didn't trust Jonas to speak the truth either. He hadn't seen her yet with the bandages off, although he'd stopped by again this week. She was glad he felt responsible for her—enough to make sure that the hospital bills were paid and to drop by. She refused to see him though. The Beachy family had seen to it that she was given the best of medical care. She had an appointment with a plastic surgeon next week, but there was only so much that could be done. She was scarred now and would always be. There was no reason to pretend otherwise. And Jonas would never care for her like he had before. It wasn't possible. The truth was plain enough in his eyes. And she didn't blame him one bit. From the beginning she'd been drawn to his money and he'd loved her beauty.

Shirley rattled the pots and pans in the lower cupboard as she pulled out the one she wanted. Naomi would be in soon to help with the vegetables. Shirley would rather have worked alone, which wasn't possible if she wanted to have supper on the table in time.

As she banged the pot down on the counter, Shirley thought of this coming Sunday. She would have to attend the church service. *Daett* would make sure of that. And then all those people who knew her so well would see her face and say more empty words. "It's not that bad, Shirley, cheer up." "The Lord must have been looking out for you, Shirley." To that she'd want to reply, "Really? Why didn't He protect my face then?" The unspoken reply would be because she was being punished for her rebellion.

Well, she decided, she wouldn't go to the services. No matter what *Daett* said. He couldn't make her go. What could he do? Carry her out to the buggy like she was a *bobbli*? Shirley gave a wild laugh at the thought. What a sight that would be.

Naomi cleared her throat at the kitchen doorway. "Are you okay, Shirley?"

"*Yah*." The lie slipped out of her mouth easily.

"You sounded…weird." Naomi came in slowly. "All that banging and slamming…and that laugh."

"I'm fine." Shirley set her face into neutral lines. "I'm perfectly fine. I was just thinking of going out tonight."

"With Jonas?" Incredulity filled Naomi's voice. "Will he have you again?"

"I see you know the truth. No, I'm sure he won't." Shirley grabbed the potato masher with vigor.

"Well, whether it's Jonas or someone else, I hope someone says the right thing to you. You snap at everyone. You just aren't yourself anymore. Frankly, you've become a terror to the whole family."

Shirley mashed the boiled potatoes with both hands on the masher. "Like I could care. I have to live with these awful scars, and you have to live with me. Get used to it."

Naomi turned to look out the window at the sound of a car approaching on the gravel driveway. "There's Jonas now. Maybe he can say the right thing."

"Jonas?" Shirley froze. "Send him away, Naomi."

"I'll do no such thing." Naomi didn't move. "I'm having nothing further to do with this. Someone else can answer the door."

Tears stung in Shirley's eyes as she made a dash for the upstairs door. One of her siblings could deal with Jonas. Maybe *Daett* would if he noticed Jonas's presence from where he was finishing chores in the barn. *Mamm* was in the basement, so she wouldn't even notice Jonas's arrival.

From her room upstairs, Shirley peeked past the dark drapes. Jonas came up the sidewalk with his head bowed. He looked burdened about something. She couldn't imagine what. He still had everything going for him. Why Jonas kept up his visits was beyond her.

Shirley glanced downward as the cellar door opened to the outside, and *Mamm* came out to meet Jonas. So *Mamm* had noticed his arrival. She had a warm smile on her face as she shook Jonas's hand.

Mamm motioned toward the house and Jonas nodded. Moments later *Mamm* disappeared under the porch roof while Jonas still stood in the yard. What *Mamm* intended was obvious enough. She planned to fetch her down to speak with the young man. Apparently Naomi hadn't been the only one to wish they could reach out for Jonas's help. Shirley froze with her hand on the drapes. She didn't want to talk to him ever again. The conversation would go nowhere and increase the pain in her heart.

Shirley pulled back as Jonas's gaze crept along the upper level of the house and past her window. If he noticed her presence, he gave no sign of it. He looked down again, and Shirley stepped away from the window. She might as well tell *Mamm* about her plans for tonight. Wasn't the general *rumspringa* crowd better than Jonas Beachy—at least from her parents' point of view? At least they were still Amish.

A quick knock came on the bedroom door.

Shirley said nothing.

A moment later the knob turned, and *Mamm* appeared. Her glance took in the window and the open drapes. "I see you noticed Jonas arrived."

Shirley still said nothing.

"You need to come down and see him." *Mamm*'s voice was firm. "You owe him that much. He's been paying your medical bills, after all."

"He's the one who hit the deer." The words exploded out of Shirley's mouth.

"That wasn't Jonas's fault," *Mamm* chided. "You know that."

Shirley tried to calm herself. "I'm not seeing him. Not like this." Her hand crept to her face.

"Shirley, you can't stay in your room and hide from him forever." *Mamm* reached out for her hand. "Come. He's waiting for you."

When Shirley resisted, Mamm sighed and said, "All right, then. I'm bringing Jonas up here." *Mamm* turned to go.

Shirley rushed to her side. "Please don't, *Mamm*. Let me deal with this my way. I'll go out. I won't hide. In fact, I'll go out tonight. I'll meet Amish friends and…" Shirley's voice trailed off.

"You plan to go out with Lee and Mark?" *Mamm's* hand was on the knob.

"If they won't take me, I'll go myself." Shirley put on her best stubborn look.

Mamm hesitated. "I guess Amish friends would be better than Jonas, but still…" *Mamm* thought for a moment. "Jonas won't go away, so you will have to deal with him. Come talk to the man, and then you can go out with Lee and Mark."

Shirley took a deep breath. *Mamm* had agreed to her going out tonight. She could hardly believe it. Her parents didn't usually do that. But she would have to speak with Jonas if she wanted to stay on *Mamm's gut* side. And perhaps this was for the best. The ties with Jonas would have to be formally severed once and for all.

As they went downstairs together and approached the front door, a sudden dread filled Shirley. Jonas, the man she had loved. The man who had kissed her and traced her pretty face with his gentle fingers. She would die when he saw and recoiled from what was left of her beauty. Her feet reluctantly moved ahead.

Mamm seemed to understand and held the door open. "I'll wait for you in here."

Shirley turned her face away as she went out the door.

Jonas heard the door open and came toward her.

"Shirley, I'm so glad you'll speak to me. I'm so sorry about all this."

He was beside her now, his voice in her ear.

She could manage no response other than to cry softly.

His hand touched her arm. "Shirley, look at me. You're still beautiful."

Shirley lifted her face toward him and choked up. No words would come out.

"I'm so sorry," he repeated.

Shirley took a deep breath. "Well, now you see my face. I'm a monster now."

His gaze traced her face and followed each scar. "No, Shirley. You're not that. But the insurance company will continue to see that you get the best doctors. They'll take care of you. You'll see."

Shirley laughed bitterly. "Like that will do much *gut*. I am what I am."

His hand found hers. "There's nothing I can say to make this easier or better for you, is there?"

She shook her head. "I should never have tried to live in your world, Jonas. I guess the Lord is punishing me for my sins."

He pulled in his breath. "You must not say that, Shirley. God isn't like that."

She couldn't keep the words back. "Then the devil did this, Jonas? I'd rather believe I'm in the Lord's hands than the devil's."

He seemed at a loss for words.

She whispered the next words. "I thank you, Jonas, for everything. For your concern, for your help with the bills, for your help with the doctors. I know this wasn't your fault." She squeezed his hand. "And for the times we had together. I'll always cherish those moments. But we can't go on like we were before. You know that."

"But, Shirley…" He gripped her hand.

"I should have stayed in Oklahoma, Jonas. That's where I belonged, but I didn't. I ran…and now I've run into trouble I can't fix. I'll never convince myself otherwise. I'm ugly now, and I'll always be. You don't want an ugly girlfriend."

Any protest died on his lips.

She reached up to touch his face. "Don't look at me anymore, Jonas. Just leave. Perhaps you'll remember me the way I was before this nightmare."

Jonas was silent as he stared at her.

"Go, Jonas." She touched his arm. "Please."

"I'll see that you're taken care of," he said.

Shirley nodded and wiped her tears away.

Jonas reached over and kissed her on the cheek. Then he turned and walked back to his car.

Shirley watched him drive away, and then turned and walked slowly up the porch steps.

Mamm met Shirley at the doorway and wrapped her in a hug. "How did it go?"

"He's not coming back."

"It's for the best." *Mamm* held Shirley at arm's length. "And you're still beautiful to us."

"To you, maybe. But to everyone else I'm ugly. No one will ever love me again."

Mamm wisely kept silent.

"I'll finish supper now," Shirley said dully, moving toward the kitchen.

"I'm going to help." *Mamm*'s voice was firm. "I need to be with my Shirley tonight."

Chapter Fourteen

L ater that evening, after supper, Shirley sat between Lee and
Mark as they took the buggy west toward Berlin. After that
final meeting with Jonas, it was good to get away for a while. Even
Daett had raised no objections to her going with her brothers.
Maybe *Mamm* had said something to him in private.

"Where are we going tonight?" Mark asked. "Not that it matters that much."

Lee gave a grunt like he didn't care either. He turned the buggy
north.

"Let's see if there's a gathering in the field behind Millers." Mark
leaned forward on the buggy seat.

Lee grunted again. "They had the gathering there last week. No
one does anything twice around here."

"We ought to check just the same," Mark insisted.

Lee didn't say anything, but minutes later he pulled in behind
the Miller farmhouse, south of Berlin. A glow drifted above the
barn roof. Shadowy cars and a few buggies appeared in the distance.

"I guess you were right," Lee allowed.

Mark glanced at Shirley. "Are you ready for this?"

"Why wouldn't I be?" she snapped.

Lee laughed. "You'll see."

The buggy bounced to a stop, and her brothers leaped out. Lee tied Sandy to a fence post, and the two brothers headed for the barn. Shirley followed several steps behind. A few hay wagons had been pulled out of the barn, and lanterns hung on the racks.

Shirley kept her face hidden behind one hand as she surveyed the young people. It was difficult to tell for sure who was *Englisha* and who was Amish. She knew some Amish youth would change into *Englisha* clothing for their *rumspringa* weekends. Drinks Shirley assumed were sodas sat around on the wagon beds, along with an assortment of snacks. Lee and Mark headed straight for the offered food, but Shirley hung back, not wanting to draw attention to herself.

"How are you doing?" a male voice asked in Pennsylvania Dutch.

Shirley jumped. "Okay, I guess. I just got here."

"There's plenty to eat and drink. Help yourself."

The young man's face was in the shadows, which meant that hers was also well hidden. She would go no closer, Shirley decided.

"You want to go get something?" He motioned with his hand toward the wagons. "They ought to have some music up soon. A little rock 'n roll and a little country. Some nights they even have a few gospel songs."

"No, I'll stay here." Shirley didn't move. "You can go on though."

"Sure you don't want to come?" the stranger coaxed with a pleasant laugh.

"I think I'll go over there." Shirley pointed vaguely toward a group of young folks still in the background.

"Suit yourself," he said and laughed again as he wandered off.

Shirley drifted towards the group she'd pointed out. She had to make a move in that direction at least, even though the man was now lost in the crowd. Who was he anyway? It could have been anyone from the surrounding counties. There were hundreds of Amish young folks in the area, and then there were all the *Englisha* youth who joined in for the fun.

Shirley caught sight of Lee with a drink in his hand. Her brother loved sodas, which *Daett* didn't allow on the Yoder farm. She peered at him again. That looked like more than just a soda. She'd look the other way, though. What Lee did here was his own business. He wouldn't arrive home drunk, of that she was sure. Neither would Mark. Fear of *Daett* would see to that. She was the only one of the family so far who had dared defy *Daett*, and look how she'd ended up.

Shirley kept away from the lantern lights as she stepped near two girls who were in an animated conversation. "I told you," one of them was saying. "I told you how many times already? The man's not *gut* for you."

"But I love him, and he's so cute and…"

"That's because you have no sense, Millie. No sense at all. You're like young horses that can't stay out of the oat bin. Look at where that gets them."

"I could eat him alive, that's for sure." A giggle followed. "I'm going to marry him. I've already decided that."

"Oh, Millie! Will you never learn?"

Shirley moved on with the girl's exasperated protests in her ear. No, Millie probably wouldn't learn. *She's too much like me*, Shirley thought bitterly. At least she had the sense to cut ties with Jonas when things became too impossible. Perhaps she had more sense than she gave herself credit for.

A male voice stopped her again. "A *gut* evening, isn't it?"

"*Yah*, it is," Shirley allowed. Did she have some flag up that drew attention to her? It certainly wasn't her face. She made sure that marred object stayed in the shadows.

Music began near one of the wagons and drowned out his

response. Because she didn't respond, he repeated louder, "I said you must be new here."

"How did you guess?" Shirley also raised her voice.

His laugh sounded soft. "You're wandering around the edges, testing the waters."

"It's that obvious?" Shirley ducked her head as the lights from a car swept across the field. Over by the wagons the volume of the music increased.

"No, I'm just observant." His smile was obvious even in the darkness. "Want to grab something to eat?"

Shirley shook her head and raised her voice. "Not tonight. Thanks, though." He certainly must be observant, Shirley thought, if he noticed me with all the shadows around here.

"How about if I get you something, and we can move back a little further and talk?" he asked. The man didn't wait for an answer before he moved toward the wagons.

Shirley wondered if she should fade away before he returned, but she remained rooted to the spot.

He soon returned with his arms full. "Here we go!" His voice was muffled. "Take some of these off my hands, won't you?"

Shirley took a few of what looked like bags of pretzels and potato chips.

"And drinks!" he hollered in her ear.

Shirley drew back her hand but the cold drink was already between her fingers. She gripped the offered object before it crashed to the ground. Nothing *gut* would come from such a clumsy move.

Shirley held up the drink to get a look at it.

His chuckle could still be heard above the racket. "Root beer," he told her.

"That it is," Shirley replied, her voice drowned out. She wasn't used to trying to converse in the midst of such noise. Visions of sitting in a quiet restaurant with Jonas filled her mind. With it came a pain like a vise was tightened around her heart. She must forget those nights. This was the world she'd been born into.

"It's quieter back there." His voice was raised so she could hear him. He motioned toward the back of the crowd.

Shirley followed him. Harmless root beer meant he had no evil intentions. With all that was being offered, no wonder *Daett* frowned on these gatherings.

He paused to tilt his head and laughed. "There. This is better. Quieter back here. And here we even have hay bales set up to sit on."

Shirley looked around. They were still in the shadows. Several more bales of hay dotted the area, although they were all empty.

"There will be more people joining us before long," he said. "Couples like to be alone and talk. Can't do that over there."

A protest rose to her lips, but Shirley squelched it.

"Are you a farm girl?" He opened a bag of chips and shrugged when she didn't answer. "You seem used to sitting on hay bales."

"You're a good guesser," she finally said, trying to keep sarcasm out of her voice. She hadn't expected this conversation to occur with a man on her first night at a *rumspringa* gathering.

His laugh was soft. "Isn't that what's interesting about nights like this—learning to know people? And such a nice girl like you."

"You don't have to turn on the charm for me." This time her voice had an edge. "You'll regret it."

He glanced at her profile. "You're a strange one, you know."

"I didn't ask you to come back here. You can leave if you want to. You'll want to soon enough anyway." She expected him to get up and leave but he didn't move.

"Did I say something wrong?" he asked.

Shirley gathered herself together. "No. I appreciate the food, but it's better if we just call it a night and each go on our way. You'll meet someone else—a nice, pretty girl, I'm sure."

He still didn't move. "Something's troubling you. What is it?"

"Nothing's troubling me," Shirley shot back. "You've been kind enough, but I'm afraid I'm just not very good company tonight."

"What's your name?" The question came quickly.

Shirley laughed with an edge of bitterness. "It doesn't matter. 'Girl' is *gut* enough, isn't it?"

"You're definitely troubled about something," he stated before taking a swig of root beer.

She should get up and leave, Shirley thought. But she stayed. He hadn't seen her face yet. When he did, he would do the leaving. Why prolong the agony? Now desire rose inside of her. She wanted the cold, hard truth, didn't she? She actually wanted to hear him voice the words that would cut like fire. She needed to hear them. To put herself where she belonged. Isolated. Alone.

"Come!" She pulled on his hand.

He didn't draw back.

"Come and I'll show you what's troubling me."

Shirley chose just the right spot. They would be alone but the lights of the lanterns still reached them. She turned and let the beams fall full on her face. She let him see the truth. She shouted to be heard. "This—this is what's troubling me." She pointed to her face.

He said nothing, his face impassive.

"Now, do you want to leave?" Shirley's words were clipped.

He took her arm and led her back to where they'd been. Only then did he speak. "I can see what you mean. The destruction of such beauty must be an awful thing. The scars look fresh. It must have happened recently."

His voice was at least kind, Shirley noted. It lessened the sear of pain at his acknowledgment that her beauty had been destroyed.

He continued. "I'm sorry something like that happened to you, but I'm also glad you showed me. You have great courage."

Tears stung her eyes. "Now you see why this is the first time I'm here. I used to have better things to do. Fancy restaurants and good times with a nice-looking man who had money and thought I was beautiful. Note that I said *was*."

"I see." He sounded pensive. "A fallen Amish princess. But you landed well…or don't you know that?"

It was the kindest thing he could have said, Shirley thought.

"Now," he continued, "are you ready to tell me who you are?"

"Shirley Yoder," she choked out. "Eli Yoder's daughter from this county."

"Glen Weaver," he said. "From up in Wayne County.

Chapter Fifteen

———◆◆———

Miriam awoke with a start on Saturday morning. The sun was up and illuminating the familiar Oklahoma countryside. The scene stretched all the way to the horizon outside the upstairs bedroom window of Uncle William and Aunt Fannie's house. She was back home from the trip to Possum Valley, and she'd overslept. Throwing the covers back, Miriam got up and dressed quickly. Mr. Whitehorse and his *frau* had picked her up at the bus station in Coalgate after midnight, but that was still no reason to oversleep. She had a full workload of papers to correct at the schoolhouse, to say nothing of a hoped-for chance meeting with Wayne. She wanted to hug him and reassure herself that all was well between them. Of course it would be, she reminded herself. Her nerves were stretched from the long trip back and the sleep she'd lost on the Greyhound bus. One smile from Wayne would drive all her doubts away.

Rushing down the stairs, Miriam found Aunt Fannie busy in the kitchen with the breakfast dishes.

"You don't have to break your neck coming down the stairs!" Aunt Fannie exclaimed with a smile. "You have the right to sleep in this morning."

"I did sleep in…" Miriam found a kitchen chair and rubbed her head. "Everything seems a little hazy."

Aunt Fannie laughed. "My head would feel horrible after a long trip in those Greyhound buses. Maybe you can catch a ride with a van-load traveling to Possum Valley when you head back after the school year ends."

Miriam groaned. "I don't even want to think about that long trip again, Greyhound or otherwise."

Setting a steaming tray of bacon, eggs, and toast in front of Miriam, Aunt Fannie said, "I kept things warm. I didn't want to ask too many questions at two o'clock in the morning when you came in, so start talking. Fill me in on the news while you eat."

Miriam smiled. "You didn't have to make breakfast. I could have fasted this headache away."

"You're doing nothing of the sort." Aunt Fannie pulled up a chair. "I know you have all your schoolwork to plan for next week, and I'm sure Wayne will be by to see you soon. He's working today in the greenhouse."

"He is?" Miriam caught her breath.

Aunt Fannie's face sobered. "If Wayne doesn't talk with you, then speak with him. You need to. What you told me before you left, Miriam, well…well, you'd best talk with Wayne."

Miriam clutched the edge of table with both hands. "What do you mean? Has something happened?"

Aunt Fannie shrugged. "I never thought the day would come when I'd say this, and I told William it might be all my imagination, which I hope it is, but still…"

Miriam reached for her aunt's arm. "Tell me, please! I have to know. I've been worried sick all the way home—and even before that. It's true, isn't it? What I feared is true?"

"What's true?" Aunt Fannie didn't meet her gaze. "Maybe we're not talking about the same thing."

"Oh, *yah*, we are. Wayne and Esther Swartz. You saw them together while I was gone, didn't you? Talking and…"

"Miriam, don't imagine things." Aunt Fannie stopped her. "Wayne's true to you, I know he is. William told me the same thing. It's just…I'm not used to how some girls act anymore. Esther's a little outgoing, that's all. But eat. Your food's getting cold."

"Eat?" Miriam exclaimed. "How can I eat now?"

Aunt Fannie got up from her chair.

"What were they doing?" Miriam's gaze followed her.

"Nothing much."

"Don't hide this from me, please," Miriam begged. "The truth will hurt, but I have to know."

Aunt Fannie returned to her chair. "Smiles, mostly. And they disappeared outside together after the hymn singing. I don't think Wayne took her home. He wouldn't do that. And Wayne's buggy was still there when William and I left the hymn singing a half-hour later."

Miriam's head spun. "How bad was it? The smiles? Did everyone notice?"

Aunt Fannie looked away. "Wayne seemed to like her smiles, and he gave plenty back."

"Then others also noticed?" There was little question in Miriam's voice.

"William didn't."

Miriam didn't move, and her food remained untouched.

Aunt Fannie continued. "Of course, men wouldn't. William's blind as a bat when it comes to such things. Plus he likes Wayne. Of course, I do too. I thought with all my heart he was true to you. I still think he probably is."

"Oh, dear Lord, how can I take this?" Miriam laid her head in her hands and moaned. "So my fears weren't just about nothing.

Wayne likes Esther's attentions. He couldn't resist them while I was gone."

"At least he resists them when you're here," Aunt Fannie consoled, trying to sound cheerful.

Miriam moaned again. "If this is true…Oh, I can't think about it. And our wedding is planned for this fall. I sat up with *Mamm* most of two nights to get the details down."

"Your wedding is the least of your worries right now." Aunt Fannie touched her hand. "And maybe there's nothing to it."

"I've lost a man once," Miriam groaned. "Wasn't I just reminded of that back in Possum Valley? I might as well throw my heart out into the road and let every passerby drive over it."

Aunt Fannie wrapped Miriam in a tight hug. "You must never say that. And we mustn't imagine too much until you've spoken with Wayne. He may have a perfectly *gut* explanation."

Miriam pushed away her plate. "I think I will fast and die by evening. I'll never be well again. Not if *another Swartz* girl steals my boyfriend." Miriam stood up and grabbed the edge of the table for balance.

Aunt Fannie was by her side at once. "You have to eat, Miriam, even if I have to spoon-feed you. You need your strength."

Miriam resisted for another moment before she gave in. Grudgingly, she took a bite with Aunt Fannie watching closely. Miriam whimpered between each bite.

Aunt Fannie stayed beside her. "We should get Wayne and William in right now and straighten this thing out."

Miriam shook her head.

"But the problem has to be gotten to the bottom of," Aunt Fannie insisted.

"It's already solved, and I've lost," Miriam managed. "There's nothing more to say."

Aunt Fannie took a deep breath. "Are you giving up that easy? Surely not!"

Miriam groaned again. "All is lost. That's the reality. Twice now, all is lost."

Aunt Fannie ignored her. "It's exhaustion from your trip to talk like that. I should have kept my big mouth shut. At least you should talk with Wayne before you go off the deep end. There's always hope."

"I'll deal with this in my own way." Miriam choked down one last bite before she got to her feet. "I haven't even shared any news from home with you."

Aunt Fannie waved the comment away. "The news can be told later. There are more important things going on right now."

"You should have told me last night already, so I could have wept for hours." Miriam paused by the kitchen table as the first gush of tears came. She held them up as she rushed up the stairs. Once there, Miriam collapsed on her bed. With her head in the pillow she muffled her sobs. She heard her aunt's footsteps come up the stairs and stop by the bedroom door, only to leave again. Miriam knew she needed to work through this herself. But how? She had no idea where to begin. She didn't want to speak with Wayne. She couldn't bear the pain. She had given her whole heart to him and trusted him. How could he do this to her? He could at least have told her he wanted the relationship to cease, that he preferred Esther over her. Those things did happen to people. But instead he'd led her on—and probably still would. But why would he do that? What would it accomplish? And they had specific wedding plans now, although Wayne didn't know about all of them.

Miriam stopped her thoughts. This reaction was way out of proportion. She must control her emotions. Just because Ivan had reminded her of the past didn't mean she should arrive back at her Oklahoma home and fly off the handle at the first sign of trouble. Hadn't she expected Esther to increase her attentions toward Wayne once she was gone from the community? So what if Wayne had spoken with Esther beside his buggy. That might have happened, but it wasn't the end of the world. What she should do is act as if Aunt Fannie had told her nothing and see what Wayne said when she met him. Wouldn't that be the best course of action? Things never turned out well when a woman had suspicions—even if those suspicions were correct.

Miriam sat up on the bed and dried her tears. She would do that. Where the strength would come from, she had no idea. Perhaps the Lord would have mercy and compassion on her and pour out further grace. Nothing else made much sense. She got off the bed and took the stairs with care, her hands on both sides of the wall for steadiness. Her head still swam, but Aunt Fannie had been wise to make her eat. She needed her strength.

Aunt Fannie's concerned face met her at the kitchen doorway. "Are you okay?"

Miriam nodded. "Well enough to go out. I'm going on with the day, and I'll start by helping you with the dishes."

Aunt Fannie touched her shoulder. "They're done, dear. You can go to the schoolhouse if you want to. I'll have William harness Sally for you."

Miriam shook her head. "Thank you, but I need the exercise."

Aunt Fannie hesitated. "If you say so."

Miriam moved on to find her coat in the closet.

Aunt Fannie's voice followed her. "I'll have a lunch packed for you by the time you have Sally hitched to the buggy."

She really didn't care, Miriam thought, but Aunt Fannie's gesture was kind. And Aunt Fannie had been right about breakfast. Maybe she would need food at lunch time...even if it probably would taste like plastic.

She slipped out the washroom door and ran across the yard in a quick dash. The conversation with Wayne would come eventually, but she'd have more strength tomorrow. Maybe if Wayne didn't see her until she was out the lane, he wouldn't attempt to have words with her. And surely she had his guilty conscience on her side. The man must feel shame over whatever he'd done.

Sally neighed when she walked in. Miriam stroked her face as tears stung her eyes again. At least her horse welcomed her home with an honest heart. But what terrible thoughts those were. She needed to contain herself until Wayne had his say, and even then she had to forgive him. From somewhere the grace would come. It had to. She couldn't live with bitterness in her heart, whether it was against Wayne or Ivan or both. They had a right to choose the *fraus* they wanted to spend their lives with.

"*Gut* morning. I see you're finally up."

Miriam jumped and whirled around when Wayne's voice greeted her from the barn door. She didn't say anything.

Wayne sounded cheerful. "I couldn't wait to speak with you."

"Aren't you needed at the greenhouse?" Miriam said steadily.

"Your Uncle William understands." Wayne chuckled.

"I've not been gone that long," Miriam managed to squeak out. She clung to Sally's halter for a moment before she led the horse out of the stall. She had to act normally. But how? Wayne seemed his usual self. Surely he couldn't pretend this well?

"Surely you missed me?" His teasing voice was closer now.

"I missed you a lot." Miriam forced herself to face him. She didn't have to make that emotion up. She had missed him terribly.

"Same here. I couldn't wait until each day had turned into the next one. They couldn't go by fast enough. I love you a lot, Miriam. I want you to know that."

"Really?"

"Of course." He touched her face briefly. "Still beautiful as ever. I see no one stole that away in Possum Valley. Here, let me take Sally. I'll get the harness on for you."

The man was guilty. Miriam was sure of it. Why didn't he just say so? He had to notice how unresponsive she was. He had to notice she'd been weeping.

"I'll hold Sally," she said instead.

Wayne moved toward the harnesses on the wall and then had Sally's on the horse's back in no time. "How was the trip?" His smile was back.

"Okay, I guess. I never like the bus, but *Mamm* and *Daett* were doing well when I arrived. Shirley, of course, is very troubled from the accident."

"I would expect so." His voice sounded genuinely concerned.

How could Wayne fake his emotions to this extent? Or were they faked? They felt like they always had…before. He was a little overeager, but what boyfriend wouldn't be on the first morning his girlfriend returned from an extended trip?

Miriam forced her thoughts back to Shirley. "She'll have scars on her face for the rest of her life, probably. That's difficult for Shirley to accept because she always thought her beauty was her best asset. But who can argue with the Lord's will?"

"That's true," Wayne concurred. "One must accept what is." He gave her a gentle smile and led Sally out toward the buggy. "I'm so sorry about your family's trial. I'm sure it's difficult for everyone."

"*Yah*, it is," Miriam agreed. She helped him fasten the tugs and climbed into the buggy.

Wayne patted Sally on the neck before he gave Miriam the lines. "See you later," he said. "I hope we have more time to talk soon."

Miriam tried to smile as she drove Sally out of the driveway. Wayne hadn't asked about the wedding plans, but maybe he'd forgotten that was one of the reasons she went home. Yet what man would forget that kind of thing?

Chapter Sixteen

⸺ ◆◆◆ ⸺

The early afternoon sunlight filtered in through the school-house windows. Miriam pushed aside the lunch pail Aunt Fannie had packed and walked across the floor. Had a buggy driven in or had she imagined it? She paused when she caught sight of one in the schoolyard. She pulled in a sharp breath as Sarah Mullet, the substitute teacher for the time she'd been in Possum Valley, climbed out. Miriam went out and greeted her. "*Gut* afternoon! What a surprise for you to show up. And after you put in all that time taking care of things while I was gone."

"Did you find everything okay?" Sarah stepped inside. "I thought I'd come by and check."

"Of course." Miriam didn't hesitate. "You're a teacher. I'm sure things were a much greater mess when you came than when you left."

"Thanks. You are more than kind." A concerned look crossed Sarah's face. "That's not the only reason I came over."

Miriam let go of the door, and it swung shut. "Did you have

to spank one of the children? I know I'm not the best disciplinarian in the world."

A trace of a smile filled Sarah's face. "No. They all behaved themselves quite well. It's about you and Wayne, or rather how Wayne and Esther acted while you were gone. I thought you should know."

Miriam put her hand against the wall for support. "I think I'd better sit down before you tell me more."

Sarah followed Miriam over to a student's desk and watched as she sat down. "You don't seem surprised. Do you already know?"

Miriam tried to breathe evenly. "I know less than you do, I'm sure. Aunt Fannie told me this morning that she saw Wayne and Esther smiling at each other a lot. I'm so embarrassed, Sarah. Was there an awful display?"

Sarah wrinkled her face. "I wouldn't say it was awful, but Esther clearly has her intention set on Wayne. She spent all day at the services smiling at him and teasing him whenever they crossed paths, which she made sure was quite often."

"Did everyone else see it?"

Sarah shook her head. "I don't think so. But I did catch them alone behind the buggies after the hymn singing. Esther was in his arms, and…"

Miriam's voice trembled, "Were they kissing?"

Sarah shrugged. "Maybe. I didn't want to think that, and I was the only one who saw them. Which I wouldn't have if our buggy hadn't been parked right beside Wayne's. He took her deeper into the shadows after he noticed me. Anyway, I felt you should know so you could at least ask Wayne about it. Maybe it's all much ado about nothing."

"Maybe…" Miriam said, but tears were threatening to fall again.

Sarah gave Miriam a quick hug. "I wish you the best. I just thought you should know. *I* would want to know if Wayne was my boyfriend. Wayne always turned down Esther's attentions when the Swartz family lived here, so I don't know why he would be showing any interest now. Wayne made an excellent choice when he began dating you. I wanted to tell you that and hopefully encourage you."

"Thank you, Sarah." Miriam tried to smile. "And thank you too for teaching for me while I was gone."

Sarah nodded. "You're welcome. And how is your sister doing—the one in the accident?"

Miriam forced herself to think of faraway Possum Valley. The place seemed unreal right now. "Shirley's going to go through a lot, I'm afraid. She was a beautiful girl—unlike me—and now she has a permanently scarred face."

"Don't knock yourself." Sarah patted Miriam's arm. "You've captured Wayne's heart. Take courage. You can keep his affections, I'm sure."

"Do you really think so?" Miriam half rose from the small desk.

"All things are possible with the Lord. I'll help you pray, okay?"

"Oh, would you? That's so kind of you."

"But you can't pray well if you don't know the truth." Sarah smiled as if that settled it. She moved to leave. "I'll help out again with the teaching anytime you need me."

"Oh, that's so nice of you to offer." Miriam followed Sarah to the door and watched while she left in her buggy. With a final wave, Sarah turned the buggy and headed up the road. Miriam sank to the floor and sobbed until her strength was gone.

Finally, she rose to notice her half-eaten lunch still on her desk. Numbly she gathered up what was left, tucked it inside, and closed the lid on the pail. She wouldn't be eating any more today. She just couldn't. With another sob, she dropped to her knees. Choked words found their way out of her mouth. "Help me, dear Lord! How can this be happening? What am I supposed to do? How can I not ask Wayne if he still loves me? And why was Esther in his arms? And what if Wayne kissed her? Esther wouldn't have missed an opportunity like that. And what does this mean for Wayne and me? Please answer, Lord! Otherwise, I don't know if I can bear this. Not after Ivan…"

Miriam lifted her head to look toward the window and the patch of sky that lay visible outside. How did the Lord speak to His people? Today God didn't talk with a voice like He did with Abraham and Jacob. Then how? Her gaze lighted on the Bible sitting on her desk. With a trembling hand, Miriam reached up, grabbed it, and opened it. She read the first words she came across, which happened to be in Psalm 31: "I will be glad and rejoice in thy mercy: for thou hast considered my trouble; thou hast known my soul in adversities."

Miriam's breathing slowed. The Lord thought of her. He knew the pain of her heart. Was that not enough? And if the Lord knew, then His mercies would not fail. She had His promise right here regardless of how her relationship with Wayne turned out. That she would lose Wayne was almost too much to contemplate, but the Lord's mercies would not fail!

Slowly she rose to her feet and determined to fix her hope on a positive outcome to all this. Perhaps by Monday Wayne would say something that would comfort her heart. He might apologize and promise he'd never smile at Esther again. Miriam's heart would soar again and hope would return. Couldn't this just be a bump in the road like many couples went through? And Sarah must have thought there was hope. Otherwise she wouldn't have made the trip over to the schoolhouse. Sarah hadn't come to spread gossip. Here the community people prayed more intensely and responded quicker, it seemed, than those in Possum Valley.

Miriam gathered up her lunch pail and locked the front door on the way out. Sally neighed when Miriam opened the small horse shelter. She embraced the horse's neck for a long moment as tears threatened again. She wiped them away, and hitched Sally to the buggy. On the drive home, the steady beat of hooves against pavement quieted Miriam's spirit. She breathed another quick prayer as she approached her uncle and aunt's greenhouse. "Please let Wayne be gone for the day, dear Lord. I can't stand another 'fake talk' with him right now. And let Wayne tell me the truth tomorrow so we can grow beyond this."

Miriam pulled into the driveway and parked by the barn. Sally looked back at her as she was climbing out of the buggy. Miriam's quick glance around revealed no one coming to help her unhitch. She breathed easier, and soon Sally was in the barn with the harness pulled off. A small bucket of oats was Sally's reward for the trip to the schoolhouse, and the horse munched away with a look of contentment on her face as Miriam gave her a quick rub down and currycombed her coat.

Oh, to be as free from worries of the world as the animals are, Miriam thought. Didn't Jesus say He took care of the sparrows? Not one of them fell to the ground without Him knowing it. The Lord knew how much she loved Wayne. The Lord knew the devastating pain she'd feel if their love was destroyed.

Miriam left the barn as anger rose up inside her against Esther Swartz. What was wrong with the Swartz family that they produced such heartless females? Laura hadn't hesitated to win Ivan's heart when he was showing an interest in her. And now Laura's sister was on the same path. Miriam steeled herself. Esther had lived in the community before she did, and she obviously knew her way around Wayne's heart. She must not think ill of Esther or Laura, but neither would she allow Esther to take Wayne away from her— if it wasn't already too late.

Aunt Fannie opened the front door with a worried smile. "So how was your day? I hope better than this morning?"

Miriam tried to look strong, but the tears came without her

permission. Her resolutions didn't last much longer at the moment than Shirley's did.

"Oh, you poor thing." Aunt Fannie took Miriam's hand and led her niece to the couch. "Sit down and recover yourself. Maybe I can think of something to cheer you up."

"I'd hoped your suspicions were only dark thoughts like mine were," Miriam muttered. "But Sarah Mullet stopped by and told me she saw Wayne and Esther holding each other behind the buggies after the hymn singing. If Sarah saw them, who else did?"

"Were they kissing?" Aunt Fannie's eyes were wide.

"Sarah didn't think so, but I doubt Esther would pass up such an opportunity."

"Now let's not imagine." Aunt Fannie reversed her viewpoint. "We don't know what really happened until Wayne tells you. I saw him go into the barn after you did this morning. I take it the conversation didn't get serious this morning."

"It didn't." Miriam wiped her eyes. "He didn't even ask how the wedding plans had progressed in Possum Valley."

Aunt Sarah wrinkled her forehead. "That doesn't sound *gut*, but still…"

"I'm trying to keep up my courage." Miriam pocketed her handkerchief. "But it's so hard! I'm not going to just leave it be, either."

"That's the spirit! We'll have supper soon. I've made soup, and I hope it will help you feel better." Aunt Fannie bounced to her feet. "We'll eat once William comes in, which shouldn't be long."

"You won't tell him, will you?"

"Not in front of you, but he is my husband." Aunt Fannie smiled sympathetically. "One shouldn't keep secrets from one's husband, but I will be discreet, and so will he. But come, I can serve you a little soup to tide you over."

Miriam shook her head just as the outside washroom door slammed shut.

"There's William now." Aunt Fannie disappeared. Moments later she was back with Uncle William by her side.

Miriam glanced up at her uncle, but he didn't appear troubled. Aunt Fannie hadn't told him yet. She almost wished Uncle William already knew. He might offer her words of comfort or direction. Back in Possum Valley, *Daett* would have something to say about the situation.

"Long day at the schoolhouse?" Uncle William regarded her with a steady gaze.

"Just the usual." Miriam forced a smile. "I enjoy my job, and it's *gut* to be back."

"You look upset. Did you and Wayne have a tiff this morning?" Uncle William appeared puzzled. "He did speak with you in the barn, didn't he?"

Aunt Fannie interrupted before Miriam could answer. "We'll talk about this later, William. Supper is waiting, and Miriam is starving."

"So am I." The puzzlement hadn't left Uncle William's voice. "I declare, Wayne was distracted all day."

"Don't mention Wayne!" Aunt Fannie ordered. "Not now— later after we've eaten!"

"Why? What's happened?" Uncle William wasn't dissuaded so easily.

"Later, I said!" Aunt Fannie pulled on his arm. "Come and eat, please."

Uncle William gave in with a grudging smile. "I'm sorry, Miriam, if I was interfering."

They all took their seats at the kitchen table. To Miriam's surprise, the soup looked good. She hadn't thought she could eat a thing, but hunger stirred in her stomach. Maybe this was the Lord strengthening her so she could go on?

Miriam bowed her head as Uncle William prayed:

Thank You, dear Lord, for Your grace and mercy today. Thank You that we had customers at the greenhouse and can make a living. Thank You for this *wunderbah* food that Fannie has prepared. Bless the work of her hands and her willing heart. Bless also our home. And remember Wayne and Miriam tonight. Amen.

"Amen," Aunt Fannie echoed.

Miriam bit her lip to keep back the tears.

Chapter Seventeen

———✦✦———

The Sunday noon meal had been over for some time, and the press of women cleaning the dishes in Deacon Phillips's kitchen was intense. Miriam slipped into the washroom to catch her breath. No one would notice, as there were plenty of hands to help with the work. The truth was, she wanted to get away from Esther Swartz's smiling face. The young woman had been practically glowing all day, which had confirmed Miriam's worst fears. She hadn't dared look at Wayne during the service, and he had to have noticed. That is, if he still cared about her. His brief words from yesterday held little comfort today.

Oh, why was this happening all over again? She couldn't believe it. Was it the money's fault? That seemed like a likely explanation. Was she being punished by God? She ought to go to the bank and ask for the whole amount in cash, and then tear every dollar bill to shreds. But no, that would be foolish. There must be another way.

Miriam straightened her *kapp* as the knob to the outside door turned. Had some woman forgotten her shawl? A gasp escaped her when Wayne appeared in the doorway.

"Did I startle you?" His grin was nervous.

"Well, I..." The rest of the words stuck in her throat.

Wayne tilted his head. "I thought maybe I could see you this afternoon instead of after the hymn singing. Or both times maybe? Unless your uncle might object, of course."

"He wouldn't," Miriam said. Her thoughts were spinning.

"Shall I take you home then?" Wayne asked, still at the doorway.

"*Yah*, if you want to." The words tumbled out.

Wayne nodded and vanished into the house. How had he known she was in the washroom? The thought whirled through Miriam's mind. In the crowded kitchen she would have been almost invisible. He must have kept close track of her movements to have seen her enter here. Warmth spread into her cheeks. Maybe he does still care. Maybe there is a perfect explanation for what had happened between Wayne and Esther while she'd been gone. This trouble might go away like a bad dream. Perhaps she'd awaken from this nightmare to find Esther back in Possum Valley and life going on like it had been.

"Fat chance," Miriam muttered. She slipped back into the kitchen and leaned against the counter. The first of the women appeared ready to leave as the kitchen was spotless by now. Every dish had been washed and returned to its place. Deacon Phillips's *frau*, Katie, could relax this afternoon after everyone had left. Miriam frowned. Now, if only she could relax, but wild and conflicting thoughts kept racing through her head. She needed to get answers out of Wayne this afternoon or she'd lose her sanity for sure.

Miriam caught a glimpse of Wayne through the kitchen window as he left through the front door on his way to the barn to get his horse. She should tell Aunt Fannie so they would know she had a ride.

Miriam moved away from the window and glanced around the kitchen. Aunt Fannie was seated near the living-room doorway. Miriam made her way over to her and whispered, "Wayne will be taking me home."

Aunt Fannie raised her eyebrows.

Miriam continued. "He also wants to take me home after the hymn singing tonight."

"Then he's still..." Aunt Fannie left the rest of the thought unspoken.

Miriam nodded, and hope rose in her heart. She tentatively smiled. She stepped into the washroom. If Aunt Fannie had arrived at the same conclusion she had, then she couldn't be wrong. Wayne wants to continue their relationship! They would work this out.

"Hi, Miriam." Esther's cheery voice made her jump. "I haven't had a chance to welcome you home yet."

Miriam gathered her courage and put on a smile. "Thank you. I'm glad to be back."

"Did you have a chance to see Ivan and Laura while you were back in Holmes County?"

Esther's cheer and smile hadn't dimmed. "I saw Ivan at the church services," Miriam replied. "Laura wasn't well that Sunday so she stayed home."

"Oh, I hadn't heard that. Well, anyway, I just wanted to say hello. I'll see you again soon." And with that, Esther wrapped her shawl tightly around her shoulders and left.

Miriam drew in a deep breath. She had handled that well, hadn't she? She hoped so. She stepped outside the washroom door in time to see Esther give Wayne's buggy a quick wave as she climbed into the back of the Swartz family's surrey. Esther's Uncle Troy was in the front with their smaller children. His *frau*, Lavina, must have stayed home with Mabel today. Why hadn't Esther stayed home to care for her grandmother? The bitter thought raced through

Miriam's consciousness, and she quickly dismissed it as unworthy of her. She approached Wayne's buggy. After he pushed open the door for her, she climbed in and settled on the buggy seat. Wayne drove out of the lane and onto the main thoroughfare. Miriam stole a quick glance at his face. He didn't appear the least bit guilty, which was a small comfort at least.

Wayne smiled. "It was sure *gut* to look over and see you in the service today. It seems like years since you left. Are you glad to be back?"

"I'm very glad to be back." Miriam kept her voice steady.

Wayne appeared pleased. "So tell me more about the trip. We only had a brief moment in the barn the other day, and I'd love to hear all about it."

Miriam opened her mouth, but the words stuck in her throat. How could she chatter about innocent things when the weight of uncertainty hung over her head? And why hadn't Wayne noticed her discomfort?

Silence enveloped them as Wayne drove down the dirt road. She still hadn't said anything, and Wayne was staring straight ahead. She would say nothing until Wayne spoke again.

"The bus ride must have been rough." Wayne glanced at her. "I never liked bus trips myself."

Miriam couldn't think of a response. Why was he so clueless about the situation?

Finally, keeping his eyes on the road, Wayne asked, "There's something wrong, isn't there?"

She felt awful to force the issue. This was so awkward! But at least it was a beginning. She plunged ahead. "Aunt Fannie told me about seeing Esther and you together. So did Sarah Mullet."

His back stiffened. "And what did they say?"

"I'm not going to go into details." Her voice was way too sharp, but she couldn't help it.

"You're not a jealous woman, are you?" He tried to smile but failed.

Miriam sighed. "Did you give me cause to be? Did you spend time with Esther behind the buggies after the hymn singing last week? Were you in each other's arms?"

"Oh, that." Wayne laughed without mirth. "Why are you letting the community's busybodies scare you? You know that tongues wag at the slightest provocation."

"In Oklahoma? I doubt that. Maybe in Possum Valley."

"What has Oklahoma got to do with it?" Surprise was written on his face.

"Tongues don't wag around here, Wayne, like they do back home. This community's different from Possum Valley."

"I see." Wayne didn't look at her. "Esther and I were just talking, that's all. She's weighed down with the care of her grandmother, and she needs a friend. Her burden gets heavy at times."

A sharp retort rose inside her, but Miriam squashed it. She asked the question that burned on her heart instead. "So you didn't kiss her?"

"Why would I kiss Esther?" His voice caught a little.

"Because she's beautiful, and charming…and after you." The words burst out.

Wayne didn't answer as he slowed down for the Byler's driveway and turned in. He stopped beside the barn, but didn't move or climb down.

Miriam's voice choked on the words. "Well, did you? Did you kiss Esther?"

Wayne held the reins tightly. "Okay. Maybe I did. But it wasn't planned. It was more she kissed me. We have a past together, you know."

A sob strangled Miriam for a second. "How could you, Wayne? It doesn't sound very 'past' to me. Why else would you kiss Esther where people could see you?"

Wayne had a pained look on his face. "Doesn't that show you I didn't plan to…well, kiss her? It was an accident, and I'd forgotten all about it already. Esther and I used to pay each other some attention while she lived here, but it never worked out. Esther understands that—both back then and now. She's not like you."

Miriam said nothing, her mind reeling at the image of Esther and Wayne kissing both now and then.

"Look…" Wayne glanced behind the buggy. "Your uncle and aunt will be home soon, and we can't sit out here as if something is wrong."

"Something *is* wrong," Miriam choked. "Aunt Fannie already knows. Uncle William probably too by now."

"You told her?" Wayne's glance accused her. "Before you asked me for the full story?"

"Wayne, she knew something was wrong already. People aren't blind. Remember, she saw you and Esther together. And what full story is there besides the one about kissing another woman when you're promised to someone else?" Miriam held back the tears as Uncle William's buggy drove past theirs and stopped closer to the barn.

Aunt Fannie climbed down with baby Jonathon in her arms and hurried toward the house without a backward glance. Uncle William didn't look their way either. He unhitched Sally and led her into the barn.

"I'm sorry, Miriam," Wayne whispered. "I'm really sorry. I shouldn't even have talked with Esther while you were gone, but I gave in. One thing led to another, and we kissed like we did a long time ago. But that was it. It'll never happen again. I promise, Miriam. I really do. Will you please forgive me? Can we go on like we were before? Surely you can see that I'm sorry. Why else would I be here with you?"

"My money maybe?" The words slipped out.

Wayne forced a laugh. "Now that's a funny one. You know your money means nothing to me. My family isn't exactly poor. Miriam, your character far exceeds Esther's charm any day. That's the real reason I love you."

"You should have remembered that before you kissed Esther."

"Okay, I'm stupid. I'll give you that. But I said I'm sorry."

"Esther's not going away. You know that." Miriam met his gaze. "She was waving to you again today."

"Don't worry about her." Wayne took Miriam's hand. "Esther will be Esther, but we can patch this up. Things like this happen in life. Don't you think there will be other Esthers around after we've said the marriage vows? We have to be bigger than these temptations, Miriam. I love you, and you love me. Nothing has changed that."

Slowly her fingers moved in his. Could she believe him? And forgive him? She wanted to. Wasn't that what love did? And Wayne was here with her, not with Esther. Shouldn't she count that as a victory?

"Can we?" Wayne's gaze searched her face. "I really am sorry."

He looked sorry, Miriam could see that. And she so desperately wanted to feel his arms around her.

"I guess," she whispered.

Wayne wrapped her in a tight hug. "It'll be okay," he said. "Esther is in my past. I promise."

Miriam said nothing but nestled tightly against him

Chapter Eighteen

———◆•◆———

Ivan glared at the pile of dirty dishes. Laura was obviously not feeling well again, but a man ought to come home to a clean house—to say nothing of a prepared supper. But not a dish of food was steaming on the kitchen stove. He could never remember in all the years of his youth when his *mamm* had failed to have supper on the table, and she'd borne a dozen children.

"Laura!" he called out. His voice echoed through the house.

"Ivan!"

Her voice came from the bedroom. He headed that way and pushed open the door.

"Ivan, I'm so weak. I think you'd better take me to the emergency room." She struggled to sit.

"The emergency room?" Ivan made no attempt to hide the horror in his voice. "But the clinic in Millersburg was open all day. You could have gone there."

Her face fell. "And how was I to harness Beauty to the buggy in my condition? I could barely get about the house today."

"We're not going to the emergency room." His voice was firm. "I can't afford it. And you could have called me at work from the phone shack. I would have come home and taken you to the clinic."

"How was I to walk to the phone booth?" The tone of her voice revealed her attitude. "I guess you don't care if I die in bed tonight."

He hesitated. "You don't look that sickly. I'll fix you something to eat. You'll feel better then."

"I haven't had anything since last night. I don't think I can get and keep anything down."

Ivan tried to feel sympathetic. "Come sit at the kitchen table, and I'll fix something. Perhaps you can keep me from burning the house down."

A trace of a smile played on her lips.

Ivan took Laura's arm. *Yah*, she was weak. He could see and feel it as she leaned on him. Regardless, he wasn't going to the emergency room. He'd go for the midwife first. The nerve of the woman—to entertain such fancy *Englisha* thoughts. As if they could afford such luxuries.

Laura groaned. "Maybe some cottage cheese and red beets. That's what would sit well on my stomach."

"I'll get some from the basement." He helped her to a kitchen chair.

Laura's voice stopped him halfway to the basement door. "There aren't any red beets down there, and all the cottage cheese is gone since last night."

He stopped midstride as visions of his *mamm*'s well-laden basement shelves formed in his mind. Red beets were a staple of any Amish home. How could the woman not have any? Hadn't she canned last summer?

"I didn't bring any along from *Mamm*'s," Laura said, as if she'd read his thoughts. "And store-bought ones aren't the same. Haven't you noticed I've been making do without?"

A retort died in his mouth. What was the use? This conversation would go in circles all night. Laura would no doubt want credit for the money she'd saved him by not buying store-bought red beets by the time it ended. She knew of his obsession with expenses, but she only played that card at her convenience. The emergency room! The nerve of the woman.

Laura looked up at him. "You can run over to my parents' place. They'll have both items, and *Mamm* will understand. She's borne many children herself."

"At this hour of the evening?"

"You don't want to take me to the emergency room," she pouted.

"Not when red beets and cottage cheese take care of the problem," Ivan agreed. "I'll be right back."

"Hurry," she said, her voice following him out the door.

Billy's whinny greeted Ivan inside the barn, but he went to Beauty's stall instead. After he'd wed Laura, he'd bought her this spirited buggy horse. She bobbed her head in protest when Ivan led her out of the stall. "I don't want to go out on the road again," he muttered. "But I have to, so you might as well get some exercise too. And I'm starved. At least you've had oats tonight."

With the harness on, he hitched Beauty to the buggy and urged her out of the driveway. Ten minutes later he pulled into the Swartz family driveway and stopped by the hitching post. He'd come here often during his short courtship time with Laura. The months seemed years ago now. Thoughts of Miriam entered his mind. He wondered if she'd arrived safely back in Oklahoma, and whether Esther's plans to derail the courtship had succeeded. Laura hadn't said anything since Miriam had left, and she would have if Esther had been successful. Such news would have been shared, he was sure.

Ivan tied up Beauty and approached the front door. He knocked, not that he would have to—he was family now—but it felt like the right thing to do.

Laura's *mamm*, Rachel answered the door with a smile. "Why, Ivan! What a surprise."

"Laura isn't feeling well tonight," he mumbled.

"Oh?" Concern flashed on Rachel's face. "The pre-baby blues?"

Ivan nodded. "Something like that. She wants red beets and cottage cheese." A deep blush rushed up his neck, and Ivan rubbed his stubbly beard. Hopefully his facial hair had grown enough to hide his embarrassment. A man shouldn't show his feelings like this.

Comprehension dawned on Rachel's face. "Oh, I see. I went through that all the time myself. Why, with Esther I ate cabbage every night for two months—and that in the middle of the winter! Drove poor Peter to distraction, to say nothing of the money the stuff cost him at the grocery store." Rachel waved Ivan on inside. "Do have a seat while I get the items. We're eating supper right now. Do you, perhaps, want some?"

"No, I'd better hurry back," Ivan said. Rich aromas drifted out from the kitchen while Ivan waited. His stomach growled, but he kept his seat. He wouldn't humiliate himself further by the acceptance of a meal, but the thought of food left him weak.

Rachel reappeared moments later and handed him a heavy paper bag. "There, that will tide Laura over for a while."

"Thanks." Ivan hesitated as fresh odors drifted from the kitchen. Rachel must be serving fresh bread and pecan pies for supper. His mouth watered.

Rachel's gaze followed his. "Do you want to say hi to the rest of the family at least? If you can't stay for supper?"

"Just tell them to eat well." Ivan forced a smile and hurried out the door. Back at the buggy, he glanced over his shoulder before he loosened the tie rope and tossed it under the buggy seat. He climbed in as visions of Rachel with her hands holding a plate of hot food, fresh bread, and pecan pie rushed through his mind. He should have accepted her offer that he stay for supper, but pride had prevented him.

Ivan drove Beauty out of the Swartz's driveway and toward home. He was thinking that now he'd have to fix his own supper. With such bitter thoughts on his mind, Ivan pulled into his driveway, unhitched the horse, and led her to her stall. Beauty nickered, but Ivan didn't offer her any oats. There was plenty of hay in the manger, and since he wasn't eating that well himself, he had no sympathy for a horse's appetite. Ivan had never mastered the art of cooking, so the evening wasn't going to get any better. No man should have to acquire kitchen skills, he groused.

Laura was still sitting at the kitchen table when he walked in. She glanced at the bulging paper bag and a smile spread across her face. "I see *Mamm* set you up."

"Of course." The bitterness slipped out. "She's not going to let her little girl starve."

A pout spread over Laura's face. "It's not my fault I'm pregnant, you know."

"Children are a blessing from the Lord," he scolded. "You need to adjust your attitude, and perhaps you'd feel better."

Laura ignored him and pulled out the red beets and cottage cheese, placing the jars on the table. "Can we pray, so I can eat?"

"Someone around here should pray!" he shot back.

"You don't have to be so snippy, Ivan. I really am sick."

"Morning sickness," he snapped. "All women deal with that, and they don't stay in bed all day."

A scowl crossed her face. "That's very unkind of you. I'm not feeling well."

Ivan hesitated, and then he reached over and gave Laura a quick hug. "I'm sorry, dear. It's just that I'm hungry, and it's late."

"Then we should pray, and you can make yourself something." Her face brightened. "I'll be having supper ready for you again once I feel better."

That didn't sound like the near future, Ivan thought, but he bit back a response. Children *were* a blessing from the Lord, and one should expect trouble to arrive with them. But they would be worth every moment of sorrow, Ivan reminded himself. He should be ashamed of himself. He had no excuse to treat his *frau* like this even if he was hungry. Ivan sat down and bowed in head in silent prayer. He couldn't find the strength for words tonight, and he figured the Lord would understand.

When he lifted his head, Laura said, "I could use a plate and two forks, please. If you don't mind?"

Moments later Ivan forced cheerfulness into his voice as he set down the requested items. "Here they are. Can I get you something else?"

"The mail perhaps?" she said.

Ivan wished he hadn't asked, but here was a chance to straighten up his own attitude. He obviously needed the practice. "I'll be right back." Ivan hastened out the door and down the lane. He should have retrieved the mail on his trip back from the Swartz place, but he'd been too distracted. At the mailbox Ivan pulled out several advertisements from the feed company and a letter. *Me, Esther,* was written on the left-hand corner, along with an Oklahoma address. Ivan sighed. Esther's capers were all he needed tonight. This couldn't be helped either, unless he wanted to destroy the letter. The thought lingered in his mind. No, that wouldn't be wise. Esther and Laura would eventually get their heads together and figure out the letter had been lost at his hand. He'd hear no end of the matter then.

When he walked into the house, Laura looked much better. Bits of cottage cheese still lay on her plate, and she'd just opened a red beet jar. His stomach turned at the combination, but he reminded himself he wasn't the one who was pregnant.

He held out the letter. "From your sister."

Laura gave a little yelp of excitement. "Just what I need to cheer me up at the end of a horrible day."

Ivan puttered around the kitchen while Laura ate her red beets and read the letter. Supper would have to be eggs, he decided. Fried with toast. He couldn't think of anything easier. He needed basic nourishment until better times arrived. The pan sizzled on the open flame.

Laura giggled. "This is so *gut*, Ivan. I have to read it to you."

"Not that!" Ivan groaned. He didn't want to think of Miriam again tonight.

Laura ignored him. "Esther got a kiss out of Wayne. Can you believe my sister? What a charmer. I do declare, she can outdo even me."

"Esther kissed Wayne while Miriam was here in Possum Valley?" Shocked, Ivan held an egg in midair.

"That's what I said." Laura glowed. "Listen to this."

Ivan's protest died as Laura continued.

"I did my best, Laura, while I had the opportunity. And you know we discussed this before—how great a catch the man would be. I always thought so even while we lived out here. And it's not my fault we weren't dating when we left. In fact, we'd be married already if the matter was up to me. Look at me. My younger sister is married and expecting before I am. How did that happen?"

Ivan attempted a smile. "Really sweet, I'd say."

Laura went back to the letter. "I turned on the charm all day at the church services, and I could see Wayne was weakening. Not that I expected him not to, but you don't want too easy a victory. That would make the conquest of lesser value, don't you think?" Laura paused for another glance at Ivan. He kept his attention on his four eggs now cooking in the pan. Laura went on. "After the hymn singing, I asked him a question and told him some of my troubles with Grandma. I followed Wayne out to his buggy. He didn't protest, and I knew I was well on my way. We kissed by the time things were over. Oh, it was delightful, Laura! I always knew the man was a keeper and well worth the hard work. And get this, his conscience kicked in right away. He said he was sorry, and that this could never happen again. Now isn't that a testimony to the man's character? I told him I understood, but you know how it will go. I'll have him in a few months, and Miriam will be history. Oh, if only there had been another week to work on the man. Miriam would have returned to find herself without a boyfriend." Laura glanced up at Ivan. "Now isn't that a lovely story? That was what I needed. An inspirational shot in the arm."

What about Miriam? Ivan wanted to ask. But that was a question a little late for him. He hoped that Miriam would win the match this time. The girl didn't deserve to have her heart broken twice.

Chapter Nineteen

———◆◆◆———

Lee glanced at Shirley. "Are you going with us tonight?"

For a moment Shirley didn't answer. When she'd gone with Lee and Mark the last time, it had been hard on her—staying in the shadows, listening to all the others having the fun she used to enjoy before...before the accident. But then she'd met that kind man, Glen Weaver. Would he be there again? Would he speak with her? Or was he just being polite last time and would avoid her at all costs if he saw her again?

"I think I'll stay home." Shirley kept the tremble out of her voice.

"You'd better come." Lee's voice was resolute. "The last time did you a lot of *gut*."

Yah, it had, she supposed, shadows and all. And *yah*, she should venture out of the house more often—even with the embarrassment that someone might see her and comment about her face. With her low spirits, *Daett* wouldn't object to her continuing to venture into a more normal *rumspringa* time. Anything was better to *Daett* than Jonas Beachy.

"We're leaving, so you'd better decide quick," Lee said. He left by the washroom door without a backward glance. Mark was already outside, so Shirley hurried toward the stair door to go to her room to make a quick change of clothes. *Yah*, she would go.

"Be nice to your brothers." *Mamm* looked up from her rocker. "That was really decent of Lee to offer."

"*Yah*, I know." Shirley held back the sting of tears as she went up the steps. What a change this was from even a few weeks ago. Her family now huddled over her like a warm quilt. They meant well, and she was grateful, but the extra attention was hard. Perhaps this was part of the lesson she was supposed to learn from the accident—how to accept the kindness of others.

Shirley changed quickly and avoided glancing in the mirror. Her face was the last thing she wished to see right now. She pulled off her *kapp*, and covered her head with a handkerchief. On evenings like this…not that long ago…she wouldn't have been able to wait to uncover her head when she got into Jonas's convertible and let her hair down. But there would be none of that tonight. Her wild side seemed to have flown far away. She didn't want Lee or Mark to see her with her hair blown over her face. They agreed with such actions during *rumspringa*—at least in principle. And they saw their sisters around the house with their hair down all the time. But not in public. She didn't need to experience their shocked expressions or exclamations with her bruised feelings so near the surface. Shirley tightened the handkerchief ends before she hurried back down the stairs. *Mamm* gave her a warm smile but said nothing as Shirley dashed past her and went outside.

A misty rain greeted her, and Shirley retreated into the washroom for her coat. She'd been too wrapped up in her own world to notice the change in weather. The rain suited her spirits. She'd cry right along with the skies. Her whole world lay in ruins, so this was appropriate.

"You don't have to hurry so much," Mark told Shirley when she reached the buggy. "We would have waited for you."

"I know you would have." Shirley didn't look at Mark as she climbed up and squeezed into the buggy seat between them. "Thanks though."

"Anything for my sister," Mark commented.

Lee drove Sandy out of the lane.

Mark asked, "Where is the gathering tonight?"

"In the Brinkman's barn," Lee grunted out.

"So there's dancing?" Mark's voice lifted a notch higher.

"Don't know."

Lee couldn't hide the interest in his voice, and even Mark noticed. "You can't learn how to dance if you don't stay off the Pepsi cans."

"Ha! You're one to talk. You'll be falling all over your own two feet." Lee glared at Mark. "And I can drink all the Pepsi I want to."

"Suit yourself." Mark shrugged.

Pepsi. Daett would have things to say if this ever came out at home, Shirley thought. But what did *Daett* expect? *Rumspringa* was a time to sample forbidden things, and Lee was only taking the opportunities offered him. At least Lee seemed to sample his forbidden things in moderation. And Pepsi wasn't so bad. It could be worse. As for dancing, Shirley wouldn't be tempted in that direction at all. That would expose her face to the light of the lanterns hanging overhead. She would stay in the shadows instead and dream of her evenings with Jonas.

"Almost there," Lee said as he pulled Sandy to a stop at State Route 39. He guided the horse toward Berlin. They rode in silence to the steady beat of the hooves striking pavement. Several other buggies joined them, and the motorized traffic was soon backed up.

Lee glanced in the mirror. "I'm not pulling over. We're almost there."

Mark didn't object, and moments later Lee turned off 39. They drove through a parking lot and into an open field behind a barn. He drove to a board fence with a line of buggies and horses already tied up. Lee swung his buggy into place. Mark had jumped down with the tie rope in his hand before Lee came to a halt. Shirley made a more dignified descent. Lee climbed out and waited for her. Together the three of them approached the barn.

They entered to find a small crowd had already gathered. A stage made out of straw was set up on the barn floor. Various musical instruments lay on the bales. Mark had been right—there would be dancing tonight. Neither of her brothers seemed to have any fear, but perhaps this was old hat to them. They had, after all, been on *rumspringa* without her for some time. And it wasn't like they'd speak of such things at home around *Mamm* and *Daett*.

Shirley stopped short when she caught sight of Glen Weaver. So he was here. He hadn't seen her, and she slunk deeper into the shadows. She had no reason to think there would be a repeat performance of his attentions tonight. How needy had she been that an unknown man's smiles made her breath come up short? The truth was Glen didn't have to say what he did. He'd insinuated she still was interesting—even with the scars. She could tell by his expression more than his words. But that was all her vanity, she was sure. She needed to move beyond that. Maybe that was the greatest lesson the Lord wished to teach her. As Shirley watched, a boy stood on a hay bale and hollered out, "We're about ready to begin. This here is Holmes County's down-home country music band!"

Laughter filled the air as more young people came into the barn.

The boy continued. "We aren't the best, of course, but we're *gut* enough."

More laughter followed as the boy grabbed a guitar and began to strum a tune.

Shirley didn't recognize the song, but that wasn't a surprise. Lee and Mark seemed to know the words, and they sang along. A few couples made tentative ventures onto the barn "dance" floor, their hands held lightly together. At the end of the song, another boy joined the one on the stage, and they did a duet. More couples took the floor.

Shirley gasped when a calloused hand touched her arm. "You want to take a turn?"

She searched the darkness with a quick glance, but she could make out only the outlines of a male figure. "I don't think so. I don't know how to dance very well. Thanks for asking."

"Ah, come on. You can learn."

He was obviously not persuaded easily. *You haven't seen me*, she wanted to warn.

The man had his hand on her arm again. "Come, please. It's easy."

Shirley gave in, but kept her head low. Perhaps no one would notice. It seemed the easier course to escape further argument with this unknown man. His shirt smelled of hay and cologne. She did her best to follow his lead, and he appeared pleased as they moved across the floor. She had no idea what she was supposed to do, but her feet seemed to have a mind of their own. At least she hadn't tripped him.

"See, it's easy," he murmured.

He didn't seem bothered by her silence. Perhaps he thought she was shy. What a strange description that would be of her. If he only knew just how not shy she used to be.

The song ended, and Shirley moved with the man toward the shadows before she lifted her face. Here the gas lantern light didn't quite reach. A sigh escaped her lips.

"You were very *gut*."

Admiration was obvious in his voice. Shirley touched his arm. "Thanks for teaching me. Um...I think I'll move on."

He called after her as the music began again. "I'll take another one."

That wouldn't happen, Shirley told herself. She would have to show her face if she stayed around much longer, and that would end the dance invitations she was sure. How could it not? Thankfully the man didn't pursue her. Shirley shielded her face as she approached a wagon where drinks had been set out. This had to stop somewhere. She couldn't go around in the shadows for the rest of her life. But for now this seemed the simplest answer to her problem.

Shirley reached for and popped open a Pepsi can. The sweetness soothed her throat. She jumped when a familiar voice spoke at her elbow.

"Shirley? I've been waiting for you since I saw you out on the dance floor. I didn't know you could dance so well."

"I can't." Shirley choked on her drink.

"You seem to hide your charms quite well." Glen's voice sobered. "Was that someone you knew?"

"No." Shirley glanced at Glen. "Why?"

"You seemed cozy with him, that's all."

A bitter laugh escaped her. "I was hiding my face."

"You need to get over that," Glen said. "You have a beautiful face."

This time the words burst out. "*Had*," she said. "Not anymore."

"Come." Glen's voice was gentle. "Let's dance. You shouldn't let such talent go to waste."

"Out there again?" Her gaze went toward the lantern-lit dance floor. She set down the Pepsi. The song was a slow one. If she hid her face on his shoulder, maybe it would be okay.

"Where else?" Glen answered her question with a tug on her arm.

She yielded. His gaze was on her face, and she was transfixed as the light fell on him.

His eyes twinkled as their feet moved together. "Forget about everything tonight, Shirley Yoder. There's just you and me and some *wunderbah* music."

A tear slipped down her face as she looked up at him. "Why are you so nice to me, Glen?"

"Because you're beautiful," he whispered in her ear.

She lay her head back on his shoulder, savoring Glen's words—the best music of all. The Lord must still have mercy on her to send such a man to soothe her spirit, she decided. Either that or Glen Weaver was an angel. There could be no other logical explanation.

Chapter Twenty

———◆◆◆———

"What did Wayne say again?" Aunt Fannie asked while she and Miriam washed the Saturday-night supper dishes.

Miriam frowned. Her aunt wouldn't leave the subject alone. "Wayne's sorry for what happened, and I believe him. He has a history with Esther, but it's in the past…like my history with Ivan. Wayne doesn't hold that against me."

"But Wayne kissed someone else while he was dating you, not just before!" The words exploded out of Aunt Fannie's mouth.

Miriam sighed. "I thought you supported us working things out."

"I do, but this is a serious matter that needs time. You should at least postpone the wedding. The few months you have until this fall isn't enough to work this out properly."

"Postpone?" Miriam's mouth dropped open. "And give Esther more time to get her foot in the door again?"

Aunt Fannie studied her. "So this is what it's come to—a competition between Esther and you? You don't want to go into marriage like that, Miriam. It's not worth living with a man when love isn't the foundation."

"I *do* love Wayne," Miriam protested. "And he loves me."

"He has a fine way of showing it! I still say you need to work this through with Wayne—and properly. Do you want to ask Uncle William for a second opinion?"

Miriam shook her head. She was sure Uncle William would side with Aunt Fannie.

"And another thing. I don't want you to go blaming yourself about this. You did nothing wrong."

Miriam wiped her eyes. It felt *gut* that her aunt understood how she felt.

"I have a good mind to have William speak with Wayne about his shameful actions," Aunt Fannie offered.

"No, don't. Please!" Miriam finished the last of the dishes. "We have to work this through ourselves. And I've forgiven Wayne. That's the first step. And Wayne *is* sorry."

Aunt Fannie appeared doubtful. "And what about trusting him and his feelings for you? That's just as important as forgiveness right now. Can you really trust him?"

Miriam hesitated before she answered. "You trust Uncle William. Did he ever kiss a girl before he married you?"

Aunt Fannie's face colored. "We'd better leave that one alone."

When Miriam said nothing, Aunt Fannie finally said, "It wasn't Uncle William who did the kissing. It was me. To this day your Uncle William doesn't know what I did."

A small gasp escaped from Miriam's lips.

Aunt Fannie found a kitchen chair and sat down. "See? I acted like Esther did, only it was with an *Englisha* boyfriend from my *rumspringa* days. I saw him in town a month or so before I married William. I took what I told myself was 'just a short ride' with him, and we ended our time together with a goodbye kiss. For old-time's sake, he said. My heart struggled with that for a very long time. Kissing a man is no light thing, Miriam. I wasn't fair to William when I married him the next month."

Miriam sat down beside her aunt. She hadn't expected this confession from her pious aunt.

Aunt Fannie rubbed her forehead. "I'm sorry if I've disappointed you with this news. But you see, we all make mistakes. It takes time to heal them."

"Then you of all people should know there's hope for Wayne and me. Just like there was for you and Uncle William."

Aunt Fannie shook her head. "I never said there wasn't hope. I just said you need to slow down and make sure this is fully worked out. And you need to not blame yourself."

Miriam rose to give her aunt a hug. "I'll try not to. Now I suppose I should get to bed. It's still early, but Sunday morning and the services will come soon enough."

Baby Jonathon whimpered in the living room.

"Fannie!" Uncle William called out. "Baby's getting fussy, and he doesn't like me."

Normally Aunt Fannie would have chuckled at the joke and rushed off to help, but her face remained serious. She didn't move.

Miriam waited while Aunt Fannie gathered herself together and finally led the way into the living room. Miriam sent a quick smile toward the fussing baby Jonathon on his blanket at Uncle William's feet, and then she went upstairs to her room. She'd been sitting on her bed for just a few minutes when she heard the rattle of buggy wheels in the driveway. Who would be coming at this late hour? She pushed back the curtain to peek out. Miriam caught her breath as Esther parked her buggy at the hitching rack and climbed out. Miriam froze as the front door slammed. That would be Uncle William on his way to see what Esther wanted. But Miriam already knew. Esther was here to speak with her. Her heart pounded at the thought. What mischief was Esther up to now? But one thing was of comfort. If Esther thought she'd conquered Wayne's heart already, she wouldn't have shown up here on a Saturday evening.

She might as well prepare for the unwelcome visitor, Miriam told herself. The meeting would have to take place in her room. Whatever Esther had to say, Miriam didn't want Aunt Fannie or Uncle William to hear. Miriam tiptoed down the stairs.

Aunt Fannie was rocking Jonathon with a worried look on her face. When she saw Miriam, she asked, "What do you think that girl wants?"

"She wants to speak with me, I'm sure. What for, I can't imagine."

"Wayne, of course." Aunt Fannie sighed. "It couldn't be anything else."

With courage, Miriam walked to the front door and stepped out on the porch where Uncle William and Esther were standing.

Uncle William cleared his throat. "Esther is here to speak with you."

"I see." Miriam attempted a smile. "We can speak upstairs."

Esther had remained silent, but now she burst forth with a gush. "Thank you so much for understanding, Miriam. This will only take a moment of your time because I know it's Saturday night, and tomorrow's the Lord's special day. I wouldn't think of keeping you long."

"Come on in." Miriam motioned toward the door. Once inside, she went to the stair door, and Esther followed her.

"*Gut* evening," Aunt Fannie greeted Esther as they passed through the living room.

Esther returned the greeting and then closed the stair door behind her. Before they reached the bedroom, Esther was chattering away. "Like I said, I'm sorry about this, but I wanted you to hear it from my own lips instead of secondhand. After Wayne came by this morning and spoke at length with me, I told myself that I had to come by and speak with you. I told him I was sorry about...about what happened. He said he would convey my apology, but I couldn't let such an important apology be delivered by someone else. I really am sorry about what happened when you were in Possum Valley. I really am."

Miriam closed the bedroom door behind her. She motioned for Esther to seat herself on the bed, and she took the chair.

Esther continued as if she'd never paused. "Apparently I've conducted myself in a much worse fashion than even I could have imagined. I told myself that's not how I act, but it seems I went too far. I'm quite sorry things have come to this, and I promise it won't happen again."

Miriam sighed. "You're referring to the kisses you shared again with Wayne while I was gone? Is that what you're sorry about?"

Esther glanced out the window. "Well, I wouldn't call it exactly a kiss. We did get a little close in conversation, and we might have..."

"You don't have to excuse Wayne or yourself. I already know, and I've forgiven both of you."

Esther paused for a moment. She smiled thinly. "Wayne came by this morning and apologized for our alleged kiss—or his part in it. He says the community is quite upset over what happened, not that I think it's anyone's business. Here in Oklahoma things are handled a bit differently than in Possum Valley. That's why Wayne always insisted on keeping our relationship such a secret when my family lived here."

Miriam leaned forward. "Wayne went to your house to speak with you this morning?"

Esther frowned. "*Yah.* He's the most decent fellow you could imagine, and he really is sorry. I can't be blamed that I adore the man, but I do understand that he's promised to you. What's done is done. I want you to know that I'll try to stay away from Wayne—act like I'm expected to under the circumstances...unless, of course..."

Miriam sat back in her chair. "Unless what?" she asked warily.

"Well, the truth is, you and Wayne aren't married yet and…well, if he should still have fond feelings for me…"

Miriam stood. "If he has fond feelings for you, I'll release him from his promise immediately."

Esther stood too. "I'm sure that won't be necessary. Wayne is a man of his word. He feels committed to you. If he promised to marry you, I'm sure he will."

"Esther, I think it's time you left. My best advice to you is to stay away from Wayne altogether. Do you think you can do that?"

Esther shrugged. "I can try."

"And if you kiss Wayne again…" Miriam felt heat flame into her face as she stopped herself. A threat wasn't right. She wasn't in competition with Esther.

"Things will go better from now on, I promise." Esther reached over to squeeze Miriam's hand. "Wayne doesn't have feelings for me like he does for you. I'll *try* to behave myself. Thank you for taking the time to speak with me."

Esther turned and slipped out of the bedroom door. Miriam didn't move as she listened to Esther's footsteps descend the stairs. Uncle William and Aunt Fannie would think what they wanted when they saw Esther exit the house by herself.

Chapter Twenty-One

———◆•◆———

The next evening, after the hymn singing, Miriam pulled herself into Wayne's buggy and tucked her shawl around her as she settled in the seat.

"Hi," Wayne said, apparently in a *gut* mood like he was earlier in the day at the services and tonight at the hymn singing.

Miriam had noticed that Esther had the decency to sit in the second row and keep her smiles in Wayne's direction to a minimum. But they'd still been there. Aunt Fannie and Uncle William had been sober-faced all day, but not a question had been asked about Esther's visit last night. Miriam hadn't offered any explanation. She wanted to speak with Wayne first.

Wayne glanced over at her as they drove out of the driveway. "Did I say something wrong? You don't even have a *gut* evening for me?"

Miriam glanced at him. "You've said nothing wrong. But I guess I haven't gotten over Esther's visit last night and that you went over to talk with her yesterday morning."

Wayne groaned. "Do we have to speak of Esther? That's behind me now—behind *us*. And her smiles—that's only Esther. She can't help it."

"And I suppose you couldn't help paying her a visit?" Now she sounded bitter, but she couldn't help it.

"I'm sorry for everything, Miriam. I really am. I thought it best if I cleared things up with Esther in person."

"And you've cleared things up?"

"Of course." He sounded surprised. "And she did speak with you like she said she would."

"So you knew Esther was going to visit me?"

"Esther suggested it, and I thought it might help."

"So she was trying to please you."

"Miriam, you're not making a bit of sense." Wayne slowed down on the paved road. State Route 48 was quiet this time of night. Only a few headlights on the horizon were visible.

Miriam composed herself. "I'm sorry. I don't like this conversation myself, but are you sure this hasn't got something to do with the money and the farm we plan to buy after the wedding? What if I didn't have two million dollars?"

Wayne stiffened on the buggy seat beside her. "That's an awful thing to say. I haven't thought about the money in a long time— if I ever really did beyond how it could benefit *us*. It means nothing to me, and you mean an awful lot to me. I don't know what I would do if I would ever lose you. Owning a farm would be *wunderbah*, of course, but I don't let it cloud my thinking. I love *you*, Miriam. I do!"

"And I love you," Miriam affirmed.

Wayne didn't respond for a moment. Then he continued. "I don't know what I can do to prove myself. That's why I went over to see Esther. It was probably a crazy move, but it shows how desperate I am."

"It's okay." Miriam said, but the vast Oklahoma countryside

seemed to swallow her words. She wanted to understand, yet she felt insignificant and very alone. Why had she come out West to escape her problems? Oklahoma had seemed like a land of promise, but everyone knew a person couldn't run away from things. Troubles only followed. And that was proving to be the point exactly.

"Miriam, please." Wayne's voice broke into her thoughts. "I know I made a big mistake, but let's work through it."

Miriam glanced at him. "I want to trust you, Wayne, but my heart hurts like it will break apart."

Wayne pulled back on the reins even though there was no stop sign in sight. The buggy bounced as he turned into a farmer's field. "There's no reason we can't straighten this out right now."

Miriam forced herself to take a deep breath. She had to get through this.

"Can't we?" Wayne tried again.

Miriam clasped her hands in silence. Finally she said, "The farm and the money—they really mean nothing to you?"

"Nothing." Wayne's voice was firm. "Absolutely nothing."

"You'd not give in to Esther's attentions if I didn't come with such wealth?"

Wayne didn't hesitate. "I wouldn't."

Miriam took a deep breath, but the next words stuck in her throat.

Wayne's fingers touched her arm. "I'd do anything to prove myself to you, Miriam. I really would."

"I guess it's not really you, Wayne. It's just the memory of Ivan's attentions that were based on what I'd inherited."

Comprehension dawned on Wayne's face. "Ivan Mast. You don't think I'm like Ivan, do you?"

Miriam gulped hard. "I know you're not, Wayne. I just don't want to be hurt again, that's all. And it was Esther's sister, Laura, who helped hasten my broken heart."

Wayne held her, but his gaze was fixed on the horizon.

Miriam reached for his hand and squeezed it. "I'm sorry, Wayne. I should be able to leave the past behind. All these fears are bringing me torment and heartache. I want them gone."

"Trust me, Miriam, and the fears will disappear," Wayne said, squeezing her shoulder.

Miriam nodded in the darkness. "I'm trying, but you didn't make it easy."

Wayne said nothing for the longest time. His voice trembled when he spoke again. "I thought I'd lost you for a moment."

"Oh, Wayne!" Miriam whispered. "Our wedding is this fall. We should be planning it instead of quarrelling." She glanced up at him. Wayne looked so exceedingly handsome in the starlight. How quickly emotions could change when lovers quarreled. And they were lovers. She had what Esther Swartz didn't have—Wayne with her in the buggy on this beautiful night. Why was she wasting the moment? A kiss? Wouldn't that be a perfect ending to this evening?

Wayne gazed at her in silence before he whispered, "You're so beautiful."

Miriam reached for his face with both hands and waited while he slowly came closer.

"I love you, Wayne," she whispered.

He hesitated. He held the buggy lines in one hand, and the other one tightened around her shoulders. His head lowered further, and his lips met hers. Wayne lingered for a long moment with his cheek close to hers. "You're as sweet as ever, dear. Thanks for forgiving me."

Tears stung her eyes. Miriam leaned against Wayne's shoulder as he took the lines in both hands. He chuckled. "I guess we'd better get on back before your aunt and uncle wonder what's become of us."

Miriam clung to Wayne's arm as they bounced back onto State Route 48. "They'll be in bed by now," she ventured. If they weren't,

Aunt Fannie would see her glowing face because happiness filled her all the way to her toes. How *wunderbah* it was not to quarrel with Wayne. She would trust him again.

Wayne seemed pensive as they drove north.

Miriam leaned against him, glad he was driving the buggy slowly. He could drive on forever and she wouldn't mind. In what seemed only minutes, Wayne turned into her driveway.

"Here we are," Wayne said quietly as he pulled his horse to a halt.

The gas lantern was still burning in the living room. "I guess you were right," Miriam said. "They're still up."

"Must be worried about us." Wayne smiled as he climbed down. "I think we can ease their minds in no time."

Miriam climbed out and waited as Wayne tied his horse. They walked together toward the house. When they stepped inside, Uncle William was seated in his rocker, but there was no sign of Aunt Fannie or baby Jonathon. Uncle William appeared quite stern, which seemed unlike him.

Miriam pulled the front door shut behind her and faced him. "I know we're late, but we had some things to discuss."

Wayne was all smiles. "And they are solved, thank the Lord."

Uncle William's gaze drilled into Wayne. "Would this be about you kissing Esther Swartz while Miriam was gone?"

Wayne's *gut* mood fell. "*Yah*, but that's between Miriam and me. And we…"

Uncle William cut him off. "I'm not her *daett*, but she is staying with us at our house so she is under my umbrella. I don't think this should be swept under the rug as you seem more than willing to do."

"But I didn't." Wayne tried again. "As I was saying, we've worked it all out on the way home tonight."

"I'm afraid something else has come up." Uncle William's words were clipped. "Something that changes things."

Aunt Fannie appeared at their bedroom door with her face tear-stained. Uncle William glanced at her before he continued. "This whole thing didn't strike home for me until last night, but now it has. I think you need to take some time off from your relationship with Miriam until you show some real repentance. From what I understand, you didn't confess to this transgression until you were caught. And you wouldn't have, either, I hear, if someone from the community hadn't seen you behind the buggies with Esther."

"Please, William," Aunt Fannie begged. "Don't be so hard on him because of my faults. It's not the same."

Miriam reached for the couch and sat down. So Aunt Fannie had told Uncle William about her past regret. Uncle William had obviously not reacted the way Aunt Fannie had expected him to. Who would have thought he would take this tack?

Wayne stood still with puzzlement on his face.

Miriam found her voice. "I know what you're talking about, Uncle William, because Aunt Fannie confided in me. Wayne and I have spoken at length tonight. He's not hiding anything, and he's sorry. I've forgiven him and agreed to continue our relationship."

"You're young, and you don't understand everything, Miriam." Uncle William didn't back down. "In this case, I'm going to step in and interfere because I think it's necessary. Wayne needs to stop seeing you for a month or so—for his own sake and for yours. It will be for the best. You can see then how both of you feel about the matter."

"Would someone please explain what's going on?" Wayne still hadn't moved from where he'd been standing when he came in.

Uncle William stood. "We're going to retire now, and Miriam can explain further. I will hide my face from the shame, and I pray the Lord will help all of us through this problem."

Aunt Fannie had a steady stream of tears on her face as she turned to follow Uncle William. The two entered their bedroom, and the door closed with a soft click.

Miriam's mind reeled. Where had all this come from? And seemingly so suddenly? What had gotten into Uncle William? Wasn't she right to have made up with Wayne so quickly? Doubts raced through her mind. She hadn't thought to wonder what *Daett* would say, but he'd likely side with Uncle William—even if *Mamm* had never done what Aunt Fannie had.

"Can you tell me what's going on?" Wayne moved closer to the couch.

The story of Aunt Fannie's *Englisha* boyfriend spilled out in spurts as Wayne sat beside her.

When Miriam finished, he hung his head. "I guess we'd best do what your uncle wants. It's not like we have much choice. It's only going to make things worse if we don't."

"Oh, Wayne…" was all Miriam could say. She leaned into his hug for a long moment. He kissed her lightly on her *kapp* and then rose. He said good night, opened the door, slipped out into the darkness, and closed the door behind him. Miriam stood by the window and watched his buggy leave. Tears trickled down her cheeks. They would make it through this, Miriam assured herself. The Lord would help them.

Chapter Twenty-Two

The next day, when Miriam drove her buggy into the driveway of her uncle and aunt's place after school, she noticed several of Uncle William's shirts were still gently flapping in the breeze on the clothesline. Aunt Fanny must be feeling quite low to have her work fall so far behind. Miriam had realized how bad things were when Aunt Fannie and Uncle William hadn't spoken a word at breakfast. Uncle William had even skipped their regular devotion time in God's Word.

Determined to keep her courage up and think on the *gut* side of things, Miriam prayed her aunt and uncle would work things out…just as she and Wayne had done. After all, hadn't she and Wayne gained a great victory in their relationship? The memory of Wayne's kiss last night lingered in her mind. The Lord must have known she needed the encouragement for what lay ahead—the separation Uncle William insisted on. They certainly couldn't continue to see each other in secret. Uncle William would find out, and she didn't wish to defy her uncle.

Miriam had noticed Wayne's buggy pulling into the greenhouse at the usual time this morning, so he must have smoothed things over enough with Uncle William that they could work together in peace. Wayne wouldn't convince Uncle William to change his mind about the month-long separation though. From what she knew of her uncle, he rarely backed down once he'd taken a position. Since she had forgiven Wayne, she figured the month would go by quickly. And she wasn't going to worry about Esther either. The Lord had given her the grace she needed not to fight that battle again.

Miriam unhitched Sally from the buggy and glanced toward the greenhouse. Maybe Wayne would stick his head out of the door and wave. Several cars were parked at the greenhouse. Wayne didn't appear as Miriam led Sally into the barn. She pulled the horse's harness off and put it away. She fed her hay and a small bucket of oats. After a quick rubdown and curry, Miriam headed outside. She retrieved her schoolbag from the buggy and entered the house. Aunt Fannie was sitting in her rocker with baby Jonathon asleep in her arms. Her face was haggard.

Miriam rushed to her aunt's side.

"*Shhh.* Don't say a word," Aunt Fannie whispered. "I'm so sorry, Miriam. I never thought things would come to this. Now Wayne and you are affected because of me."

"It's not your fault," Miriam protested. "You didn't know Uncle William would react like this."

"I said don't say anything." Aunt Fannie stared out the window.

Miriam ignored her. "I don't understand why Uncle William is reacting like this over a kiss. I forgave Wayne, and Uncle William should forgive you."

Aunt Fannie pulled in a sharp breath. "Oh, he says he's forgiven me. It's just that all things have consequences, he says. He wants me to do a church confession."

"About something like that so long ago?" Miriam made no attempt to keep the horror out of her voice. "But you confessed to him freely. Oh, Aunt Fannie! This is all my fault. I was the one who dug it out of you when you were trying to help me."

Aunt Fannie shook her head. "This is way past blame time, and it wasn't your fault. I'm just sorry you have to suffer for my sins."

"Then Wayne sinned too—if you did."

Aunt Fannie shrugged. "I guess I shouldn't get off any easier than Wayne."

Miriam stood. "What Uncle William is demanding of Wayne and me is bad enough, but punishing you so long after the fact doesn't seem right. I'm going out to speak with him."

"No! Please don't," Aunt Fannie begged. "That will only make things worse."

Anger stirred inside of Miriam, and she marched out the door without a backward glance. To humiliate Aunt Fannie in front of the ministers and the whole church was completely out of order. This was an intimate and private matter that Aunt Fannie had revealed to her and later to Uncle William. He might not listen, but she would speak her mind.

Two cars were still in the parking lot. Miriam slowed down. How was she to speak with Uncle William with customers present? She wouldn't create a scene. Perhaps Uncle William would be alone. It was worth checking. If he wasn't, she'd smile at Wayne and leave. Surely they were allowed smiles to each other!

Miriam slipped inside the greenhouse door and glanced around. Uncle William's straw hat wasn't visible, which was *gut*. That meant he was probably out back. Wayne was at the checkout counter with a customer. He caught sight of Miriam and waved. She returned the wave but moved away from him.

Miriam saw another customer ahead of her. Uncle William was standing beside the woman and helping her load several baskets of plants into her cart. He was also giving her instructions on their care. Miriam stepped behind a large plant until the customer left for the counter. She approached Uncle William and cleared her throat.

He whirled about startled. "Oh, it's you." Relief flooded his voice.

"*Yah.*"

"Did you come out to speak with Wayne?" Uncle William gave Miriam a direct look.

Miriam steadied her hands. "No, I came to speak with you. Specifically about how you're being unfair to Aunt Fannie. It isn't right."

Uncle William stared at Miriam. "And how is that your business?"

"Because you wouldn't know about this if Aunt Fannie hadn't shared it with me while comforting me. She meant you no disrespect. And she's made it right all these years with you."

"Your aunt married me with conflict in her heart," Uncle William said. "She had her mind still on…" Uncle William paused and looked away.

Miriam spoke up. "Aunt Fannie's heart is broken. Now why would that be, if she didn't care about you?"

"Are you the expert now?" Uncle William gave Miriam a quick glance. "You'd best stay out of this."

"You should forgive her like I forgave Wayne."

Uncle William hesitated. "I have forgiven her, but sin has consequences. Do you think you can just forgive and that kind of problem goes away? I don't think so. I want you to take this month to ponder the problem you have with Wayne so you'll see if I'm not right. The man is conflicted over you and Esther, and you shouldn't marry him until he gets his mind straightened out."

Miriam forced herself to focus on Aunt Fannie's situation. "You shouldn't make Aunt Fannie confess in church. She's not conflicted about you. She loves you. She bore your child."

Uncle William nodded. "I know that, and we'll be okay. I want this problem solved just as much as you want your problem with Wayne solved."

"But *we did* solve it!"

Uncle William met her gaze. "Trust me. A kiss or two while making up doesn't eliminate the root problem."

Miriam felt heat rise up her neck. Had she been that obvious last night? No doubt her face had still glowed when they'd walked into the house, but she hadn't expected Uncle William to notice.

A soft smile played on his face. "I don't blame you, Miriam. Wayne's a decent man and a *gut* catch, but some things can't be swept under the rug. And this is one of them. Aunt Fannie will make her confession in church, and you'd best make sure Wayne has all of his interest in Esther out of his mind before you marry him this fall."

"What you're asking of Aunt Fannie is cruel. Surely you know that."

Uncle William shook his head. "On that you would be wrong. I love Fannie. If I didn't, I wouldn't require this of her."

"That's a strange way to show your love."

"Covering up things isn't the way to show love." Uncle William gave Miriam a nod. "I'm not your *daett*, but I think he'd say and do the same thing. Write and ask him if you don't believe me."

Miriam held her focus. "What would I have to do to make you change your mind about Aunt Fannie's confession? This is, after all, partly my fault that it got brought up all these years later."

"Sin always comes to the surface." Uncle William picked up a potted plant and stared at it. Clearly this conversation was over on his part.

Miriam wasn't done yet. "You haven't answered my question, Uncle William."

He looked up but didn't say anything.

Miriam continued. "Your *frau's* heart is ripped open. Whatever repentance *you* think is *gut* for her might not be. This step isn't necessary. The shame is too much, and Aunt Fannie shouldn't have to bear it all these years later. She's proven her love for you."

Uncle William hesitated. He then said, "I'll decide that, not you. Now go. Help your aunt with her housework if you want to be of aid." Uncle William moved away.

Miriam waited a few minutes before she retreated back to the house. Aunt Fannie was no longer on the couch. There were noises coming from the kitchen. Miriam found her there.

Hope flickered on Aunt Fannie's face. "What did he say?"

Tears sprang to Miriam's eyes. "This is so wrong. I still hope he'll back down eventually, but he wouldn't now."

"Don't give me hope where there is none, Miriam." Aunt Fannie's eyes filled with tears. "This is a shame I must bear."

"But you only kissed the man goodbye!"

Aunt Fannie hung her head. "I suppose I did love that *Englisha*—at one time, at least. But I didn't want his world. Was I wrong to make that choice?"

"Of course you weren't!" Miriam wrapped her aunt in a hug. "This severity is so unlike Uncle William. What has gotten into him?"

"I don't know." Aunt Fannie wiped her eyes. "It's like I don't know the man anymore."

"We must pray then—that he'll change his mind."

"Or that God will give me the strength to bear this shame."

Miriam shook her head. "That's not an option. I'll vote against the confession if it comes to that. I am the schoolteacher and have some standing, after all. I also have access to Deacon Phillips and his *frau*, Katie. That's what I should have told Uncle William."

"No, you mustn't," Aunt Fannie said. "Threatening does no *gut*. You were right about praying. Something is bothering William—more than my kissing my *Englisha* boyfriend so long ago. He's never acted like this before. I know the Lord can heal his heart—and mine—if we ask."

"Then we must." Miriam didn't wait before she knelt by one of the kitchen chairs.

Aunt Fannie followed her and lifted her face toward the ceiling. She prayed,

Dear Lord, we pray that you be with us during this difficult time. I'm sorry for the mistakes I've made in my life.

Aunt Fannie's voice caught and she hesitated before continuing.

But You've forgiven me, and I ask Your forgiveness in not foreseeing William's hurt. I was so caught in my own concerns that I was blind to his. Please minister to William's pain, whatever it is. And help me bear with him, even if it takes a confession at church. Thank You for bringing Miriam into our lives. Thank You for the blessing she is. And we ask that her troubles with Wayne also be brought to an end. We ask all this in Your name, amen.

"Amen," Miriam echoed. She'd planned to pray aloud also, but the words had flown away. Aunt Fannie seemed to understand as they rose to their feet. She glanced at her aunt. "Do you really think something else is bothering Uncle William? More than what happened before you were married?"

"I know there is," Aunt Fannie replied without hesitation.

Her aunt was mighty confident, Miriam thought. But the truth was that this behavior was completely out of character for Uncle William—at least from what she knew of him.

Chapter Twenty-Three

———◆◆◆———

Shirley pulled Mindy to a stop at the hitching rack in the Berlin Shopping Plaza. She paused for a moment before she climbed down. *Mamm* had allowed her to drive into town for the shopping, but that wasn't why she'd decided to appear so openly in public for the first time. Nor was the cause the hopeful words the plastic surgeon had spoken last week when she'd visited his office in Canton. Rather it was Glen Weaver's kindness at the *rumspringa* gatherings that had lifted her spirits. Her courage had returned, even if she didn't fully understand why.

With an inward groan, Shirley stepped to the ground and tied Mindy to the long steel bar. Several other buggies were already parked there, and one of the horses neighed in their direction. Mindy lifted her head briefly, ears forward, but didn't respond.

"I wouldn't talk to him either." Shirley patted Mindy on the neck and glanced around the parking lot. She made a quick dash for the plaza doors with her head down. No one gave her a second glance. The memories of her times here with Jonas rushed through her mind. She could hear the roar of his convertible and feel the wind fly over her face and through her hair as they sped down the road. Jonas hadn't been by to see her again, but she was to blame for that. She didn't want attention given out of pity, so she'd asked him not to visit.

Shirley stiffened her shoulders and walked even faster. There was little that could be done about her face. The scars wouldn't go away anytime soon, even with the surgeon's assurances last week that he would do his best. The reconstructive surgery could be scheduled whenever she was ready...but she wasn't ready.

Shirley grabbed a cart and made her way down the grocery aisles. She clutched her list in one hand and kept her head down. Glen's kindness had helped, but she still knew life would never be the same. *Yah*, she admitted she still wanted to feel the love and excitement that filled her heart when she was around Jonas. Glen Weaver was kind and decent and manly, but he wasn't Jonas. She was being unfair to even compare Glen to Jonas.

Shirley jumped when a woman's voice said, "*Gut* morning, Shirley. It's nice to see you out and about."

Shirley whirled around to see Rachel Swartz's smiling face in front of her. She said a quick, "*Gut* morning." She didn't know Rachel that well, so surely this conversation wouldn't last too long.

Rachel continued. "We were so sorry to hear about your accident. I haven't had a chance at the Sunday services to express my regrets to you, what with all the work the women have to put in to feed the men lunch." Rachel gave a short laugh at her own joke. "So what a coincidence to meet you now. I hope things are going well with you." Rachel peered at Shirley's face. "I hope there's more they can do to help you."

Ugh. So it was that bad? Shirley thought. *Yah*, she knew it was, which was exactly the reason she'd kept herself out of sight whenever possible. Rachel could have found her after Sunday services if she'd been that interested. The woman probably had other things on her mind.

Shirley just nodded and waited. Rachel seemed to want to say something more.

Rachel looked away and tapped her shopping cart handle. "I hope there are no hard feelings between our two families. I know things haven't been going that well between Esther and Miriam in Oklahoma. Well, actually between Wayne and Esther and Miriam. I thought I should say something because I'm so sorry for that situation. Esther told me she apologized to Miriam, so that was good."

Shirley's face showed her puzzlement. "I have no idea what you're talking about."

Rachel stared at her for a moment. "Surely Miriam would have told your *mamm* by now."

"Told her what?"

Rachel gasped. "Oh my, I should have kept my big mouth shut. I was afraid there would be hard feelings. I told myself, doesn't a daughter tell her *mamm* such things? I know my children do." Rebuke crept across Rachel's face. "Miriam shouldn't keep such things from her *mamm*."

Shirley returned her stare. "Maybe you should tell me this important news so I can tell *Mamm*."

Rachel appeared doubtful. "Such a thing should be heard directly from the source. That's what I always say."

"Miriam's not here, and I am. And you brought it up."

"It's just that…" Rachel hesitated. "Oh, well. Why not? I guess you'll find out anyway. And the sooner such things are taken care of the better. At least that's what I always tried to teach my girls."

Shirley waited as Rachel caught her breath. "And Esther did go over to apologize to Miriam, so I'm not telling secrets that shouldn't be told. Something happened between Esther and Wayne while Miriam was here visiting."

"Go on," Shirley encouraged when Rachel hesitated again.

Rachel seemed to make up her mind and continued. "Well, Esther apologized because she and Wayne got a little too close while Miriam was out visiting you after your accident. One thing led to another, and the two kissed. Nothing serious, of course. They were both overcome by the moment. It just sort of happened, what with their past relationship and all. Esther admits this was wrong."

Shirley shook her head. "Esther is interested in Wayne?"

Rachel's face lit up. "Oh, yes. To be honest, I think Esther had high hopes Wayne would return her attentions someday, even after we moved here. But that still doesn't mean she isn't sorry she kissed someone else's boyfriend. That was out of the line, and Esther knows it."

"Miriam and Wayne have plans to wed this fall."

"I know." Rachel frowned. "That's what makes this so uncomfortable."

"Okay." Shirley held up her hand. "Thank you for telling me and expressing your regrets. I'll be sure and tell *Mamm* everything you've told me."

"You do that." Rachel moved down the aisle. She cast a last mournful glance over her shoulder. "And maybe your *mamm* and Miriam should talk more or write more." Rachel then disappeared around a corner.

Shirley took in a long breath. Now that had been weird. Did *Mamm* know anything about this and hadn't told her? That was possible. If Miriam's heart was broken by her boyfriend's betrayal with Esther, that was serious. And how like Miriam not to tell them of her struggles. Shirley kept her feelings out in the open, but Miriam didn't.

Shirley considered the problem. Perhaps she should do something about this herself. It wouldn't hurt to think of other people's problems instead of her own for a change. But what could she do?

Miriam wasn't here, so she couldn't offer a sisterly hug or a comforting word. Knowing her sister, she could imagine that Miriam had forgiven Wayne by now. Still, kindness helped heal wounds. Look how much Glen's attentions had helped her.

Shirley found the last item on the shopping list and paid at the register. She pushed the cart across the parking lot, and Mindy turned her head to watch her approach. While Shirley loaded the items into the back of the buggy, a car the color of Jonas's convertible eased past the parked buggies. It sparked another painful memory. At least Jonas had never kissed another girl while he dated her. He might be doing so now, and the thought hurt terribly. But Jonas had a right to do whatever he wanted. She'd sent him away because their relationship had been a fantasy on her part from the start. *Mamm* and *Daett* had warned her, but she hadn't listened. If she had, these scars wouldn't be on her face now.

Shirley wiped away a tear and untied Mindy. She climbed into the buggy, lifted the reins, and clucked. Mindy took off at a moderate pace when Shirley let out the reins. She held Mindy back until they were out of town, then Mindy shifted into a faster clip. They both were in a hurry to get home, Shirley decided. The thought of Miriam in trouble with her boyfriend was disturbing.

Shirley turned Mindy into their driveway and unhitched beside the barn. Lee would have come out to help her if he'd been around, but she'd seen the distant forms of her brothers and *Daett* at work in a field. Shirley led Mindy into the barn and put her into her stall. With her arms full of groceries, she entered the house.

Mamm called from the kitchen, "That was a quick shopping trip. No Jonas, I hope."

Shirley took in a deep breath. *Mamm* had remembered, and she'd been worried. Jonas, though, was no longer a danger.

Mamm seemed to read her silence correctly. She came over to give Shirley a quick hug. "I'm sorry for your heartache, but you knew deep down that you and Jonas could never be a couple. Besides, isn't there a nice, young Amish man paying you attention at the gatherings?"

"Glen Weaver," Shirley admitted. "We're just friends." No way would she admit the scope of what Glen had done for her. Not to her family, at least. He was the reason she'd felt brave enough to venture out today. She changed the subject. "Is there something going on with Miriam and Wayne that I don't know about?"

Mamm was puzzled. "Not that I know of. Why?"

Shirley shrugged. "Rachel Swartz spoke with me at the store. It sounds like Esther is trying to steal Wayne from Miriam. She even kissed him while Miriam was out here visiting me and planning her wedding."

Mamm stopped in midstride. "And why was Rachel telling you this? If it's even true, which sounds perfectly awful."

"She said something about not wanting trouble between our families. Rachel thought we already knew."

Mamm shook her head. "Thank the Lord that Miriam has the sense not to write such gossip home."

"I might write Miriam a letter just to encourage her," Shirley said.

Mamm hesitated for a moment. "I guess that would be nice, but I think Miriam can take care of herself."

"I suppose she can," Shirley agreed as *Mamm* left the room. She would still write. Shirley knew she would want a letter of sympathy from Miriam if Jonas had done such a thing.

Chapter Twenty-Four

———— •◦• ————

Shirley settled into the seat of Glen's buggy. She wasn't sure how he had talked her into leaving the *rumspringa* gathering north of Berlin, but here she was headed with him for the Mount Hope Auction. She was going to a horse sale! Maybe it was just as well. What trouble could she get into on a buggy ride with Glen? She'd risked far worse with Jonas, so there was no reason she shouldn't enjoy time with Glen.

"You sure about this?" Glen gave Shirley a quick sideways glance.

"Sure. Happy as can be." Shirley smiled. "I like horses."

"So do I, and I like to spend time with you too."

"Thank you. And you're pleasant enough yourself."

Glen looked ready to say more, but he was distracted by traffic as they pulled up to a stop sign.

"What do you call your horse?" Shirley steered the conversation in a safer direction.

"Buster," he said with a straight face.

Shirley laughed. "Come on, don't tease me."

He pretended a hurt look. "Why? Don't you like Buster?"

"No one calls their horse Buster."

"Okay, so what do you suggest?"

"I'm not going to name your horse when he already has one."

Glen chuckled. "How about Duke?"

"That's better, but you're still teasing."

"No, I'm not. That was his name when I purchased him at the Mount Hope Auction."

"I like it." Shirley leaned forward to study the horse's back. "He trots like a duke."

Glen laughed. "Now how would that be?"

"I don't know. It's just how I imagine a duke would move, I suppose."

Their laughter filled the evening air and blended in with the horse's steady hoofbeats on pavement.

After the comfortable silence that followed, Glen glanced at Shirley. "How's your sister in Oklahoma getting on?"

"Okay, I guess. I meant to write her a letter this week, but I haven't gotten around to it."

Interest showed in Glen's face. "I like letter writing, though I've never had much chance to practice. I've heard of dating couples who lived apart and filled their courtship with letters. Wouldn't that be romantic?"

Shirley thought of Jonas and his kisses. She stared straight ahead. *That* had been romantic. "I think I'd rather spend time together than write letters. I'm not *gut* at such things."

"You would be with practice." Glen gave her a warm smile. "You have a talent for writing."

Shirley laughed. "And you can divine that how?"

"Your hands." Glen ran his fingers lightly over hers. "See? They're just made for writing."

"You're such a tease." Shirley moved her hand closer to Glen's.

She didn't want to flirt with him, but she was in his buggy...and if he wanted to hold her hand...well, who was she to stifle romance?

Instead, Glen appeared lost in thought. "So, let's see. I can imagine how this would go, so why don't you compose your letter to Miriam while we drive. I'll give you correction as needed."

"Out loud?" Shirley asked, startled.

"Of course. You don't have secrets, do you? I'm expecting you say only sisterly things."

"Well..." Shirley's mind whirled. "Maybe we do have secrets."

Glen laughed. "You don't tease well, you know."

Shirley made a face at him. "I'm not teasing, and I don't think it would be appropriate to share what I have to say, even if I could write it down right now."

"Come on try," he begged. "That's why you never write. You put things off at the slightest excuse."

Shirley gave him a quick glare. Maybe he needed a *gut* lesson. And surely he could handle the information.

"Please?" Glen begged again.

"Okay, here goes." Shirley took a deep breath and cleared her throat. "My dear sister, Miriam..."

"That's *gut*," Glen interrupted.

Shirley ignored him. "Greetings in the name of the Lord. I hope all is well, but from what I'm hearing, I'm guessing there might be trouble in Oklahoma. This week Rachel Swartz spoke with me at the..."

Glen help up a hand. "You should do a little more breezy talk first, I think, instead of leaping right into the trouble subject."

Shirley ignored him and kept on. "From what Rachel said, it sounds like Esther is trying to steal your boyfriend. I'm sorry to hear that. I know from my time out in Oklahoma that Wayne is a nice man, and I know you must love him if you plan to..."

"What are you saying?" Glen cut in.

Shirley gave him a fake smile. "See, I said we shouldn't do this."

"Someone is making a move on your sister's boyfriend?"

"That's what Rachel said. Well, not exactly like that. She said Esther, her daughter, was sorry for making a move on Miriam's boyfriend while Miriam was visiting out here."

"That is bad. And from the sound of things, Miriam hasn't written you or your *mamm* yet if you had to get this information from another source."

"Miriam's a godly woman who bears her sorrows well," Shirley said. "Better than I do."

Glen didn't say anything for a moment. "Do you think your sister will end the relationship?"

"I doubt it. Miriam's probably already forgiven him."

"And why don't you sound happy about that? Forgiveness is a right Christian thing."

"Would you kiss a girl while you dated someone else?"

Glen didn't hesitate. "No, of course not. But everyone has a weakness."

Shirley glared at Glen. "If it were me, I'd bonk his head."

Glen chuckled. "I like your spirit."

Shirley ignored the compliment. "Lee and Mark wouldn't act like that, and I know *Daett* wouldn't. And I can't imagine Uncle William kissing another girl while he dated Aunt Fannie."

"Uncle William?"

"William Byler. Why? Do you know him?"

"*Daett* does." Glen grinned. "They were *gut* friends in their *rumspringa* years. Small world, huh?"

"I guess," Shirley agreed.

Glen rattled on. "As I remember it from *Daett*, William almost married an *Englisha* girl. They were secretly engaged until she broke off the relationship. *Daett* said William took it so hard he went to the bishop and wanted to make a church confession. Of course he couldn't since he wasn't a member yet. The bishop said coming back to the church was a *gut* enough sign of repentance, and that the years of *rumspringa* time were there for a reason. He said he was thankful William had found his way back."

"I think I've heard enough secrets for one night," Shirley murmured, in shock at Glen's revelation.

Glen acted like he hadn't heard. "So that's the end of the story—and not a very pretty one at that. But I suppose we all have our faults."

"Do you have faults?"

Glen laughed. "I suppose so, but not serious ones like that."

Shirley held still on the buggy seat. Would Glen ask her if she had secrets? She didn't really—unless kissing Jonas counted.

Glen didn't say anything as Duke slowed on the climb up a long hill.

When they reached the top, Glen still hadn't spoken, and Shirley sighed in relief. Her thoughts turned to Glen's story. Did Uncle William still miss his lost *Englisha* girlfriend? She had a similar situation in her life. Jonas Beachy wasn't *Englisha*—in fact, worse perhaps, but he was still forbidden. Maybe she should go to Bishop Wagler and confess. She could see why Uncle William would seek such a thing. Jonas would stay in her heart for a long time if something wasn't done. Did Uncle William wish things could have been different? Like she did with Jonas? A relationship with Jonas wasn't possible, but still…A tear slipped down Shirley's cheek.

Glen gave Shirley a sideways glance. "Did I say something to disturb you? I'm sorry if I did."

Shirley shook her head. "It's not that. I was just thinking."

"I see," Glen said. Silence fell again, and he broke it a few minutes later. "I'm sure your Uncle William found peace with your Aunt Fannie. *Daett* said William was so happy when he began dating his Amish girlfriend. *Daett* even introduced us at a wedding once. She's a very nice woman. No man who married her would have regrets."

"That's nice of you to say." Shirley smiled. Her problem wasn't Uncle William. She was worried about her own heart—and that was something she wasn't ready to share with Glen.

The man seemed to read her thoughts though. "Has Jonas Beachy—that boy in whose car you wrecked—been in touch with you?"

"Jealous?" Shirley forced herself to tease.

Glen smiled. "I hope not. I have no claim on you, though if I were him, I'd sure make contact."

Shirley looked away. "Jonas stopped by, but I told him not to come back anymore. We are worlds apart—have always been, really. Jonas understands that. He and his family aren't part of the Amish community." Shirley kept her voice steady. "I don't want his attention because of pity for the way I look."

Glen looked like he wanted to say something but kept silent.

The noises of a crowd of people and horses rose in the distance. "That's the stockyards," Glen said. "Where the auction is held."

"Okay." Shirley forced herself to chatter cheerfully as they approached the site. "It's exciting, these auctions. At least the few times I've been to one with Lee and Mark. Especially when horses are involved. They are such beautiful animals. I like to think they'll find homes where they're wanted and loved. Makes you want to buy all of them yourself and fill up the barn."

Glen didn't appear scornful at her impracticality. He nodded as if he agreed and brought Duke to stop. Leaping down, he grabbed the tie rope. Shirley followed and stood by his side while he tied Duke securely to a hitching rack. All around them the roar of the auctioneer's voice through loudspeakers could be heard. Glen grinned as he shouted above the din. "Want to get something to eat first?"

"*Yah*," she hollered back. Now that she thought about food, she was starved.

"This way," he gestured. "The best-made sandwiches are at the Troyer's stand."

Shirley kept close to him as the crush of people increased. True to Glen's statement, the Amish selection of meats and cheeses was extensive. A cheerful, young girl waited on her. Shirley selected pan-roasted turkey, German bologna, and corned beef. To this she added butter cheese and lacey Swiss.

"That should be *gut*," the young girl said with a bright smile.

Glen ordered after her, and Shirley waited for him. Together they walked to the bleachers and found comfortable seats near the ringside.

"These spots aren't open often," Glen hollered to Shirley.

"Maybe someone just left," she said.

He nodded and settled in. In front of them horses were being led back and forth in a corral by young boys, while the auctioneer blared away from his stand high on the other side.

Shirley didn't know much about auctioneering, but the man sounded like an expert. And he was Amish, which didn't surprise her. The *Ordnung* among all the districts left that career field open to Amish men with the talent.

Glen sent a warm smile toward Shirley.

They had so many things in common, Shirley thought. They both love horses, and auctions, and Troyer's sandwiches. That wasn't much, of course, but it was a start. Could she fall in love with Glen? Shirley glanced his way, and Glen smiled again. There was definitely a warm feeling that filled her when she was around him. That much she knew. But love was another matter. And if she were honest, her heart still pined for Jonas. She didn't want to admit that fact, but it was true. How Uncle William had dealt with his love for an *Englisha* girl was something she wished she could ask him. Maybe Aunt Fannie could tell her sometime. As his *frau*, Aunt Fannie would surely know Uncle William's secrets. Married couples lived that way—intimate in spirit and fact.

Shirley could easily imagine a no-secrets life with Glen, but this wasn't the time to think of such things. She was here to enjoy the evening, and her relationship with Glen was still at the friendship stage. That was *gut* enough for now. She would be thankful for what the Lord gave and not ask for more. Jonas had been a once-in-a-lifetime experience. And, truthfully, it was one she wasn't sure the Lord had sent her way. She took another bite of her delicious sandwich and gave Glen a gentle nudge with her shoulder.

He grinned but said nothing as the auction excitement continued around them.

Chapter Twenty-Five

———◆◆———

Ivan pushed open the barn door and led Beauty outside. Laura's *mamm* had stopped by right after they'd finished supper and was still in the house. Her horse neighed at the sight of Beauty, and Ivan kept a tight grip on her bridle. The two horses shook their heads at each other, but they soon settled down. Ivan stroked Beauty's neck and led her toward their buggy. He'd finished his chores while he waited on Rachel to leave. What the two women spoke of, he didn't have to think long to imagine.

Esther's situation in Oklahoma occupied a large portion of Laura's waking hours. Rachel thought Esther should ease up on her advances toward Miriam's boyfriend, Wayne. That surprised Ivan. Laura was of a contrary opinion, and Wayne had thought the two sisters had received their attitudes from their *mamm*. That thought hadn't comforted him in a way. It also supported his own feelings against Laura's viewpoint. He'd have to take up the issue with Laura once Rachel left. From what he'd heard, Esther had apologized to Miriam and might be persuaded to stick with her attempt at repentance—if Laura didn't encourage Esther in the other direction.

Laura hadn't shown him the letters she'd written Esther this week, but he could guess what they'd contained. He'd bring that issue up too. Laura had a right to private letters to her sister, but not if they contained instructions he didn't agree with. He was the head of their home. He would stand his ground. He assumed Rachel was attempting to do the same at the moment. From the length of the conversation in the house, he figured the matter wasn't settled. Laura wouldn't back down easily from her position. She had too much invested already.

Ivan backed Beauty between the buggy shafts and fastened the tugs. Laura had wanted to accompany him into town for the grocery items they needed. But if they wished to reach town before dark, they'd have to leave soon. Perhaps he should interfere and take up the matter about Esther with Rachel present for support. Ivan glanced toward the house. He shook his head. Let Rachel speak her mind, and he would stand on his own two feet later. He would have done so a long time ago if his own standing hadn't been so shaky. But that was in the past now. He was married to Laura, and he must let go of his need to justify his choices…and so must Laura.

The front door opened. Rachel came out with her shawl wrapped tightly around her shoulders.

Ivan untied Rachel's horse from the hitching post and turned the buggy toward the lane. Rachel gave him a grateful smile. "Thanks, Ivan."

"Tough conversation with Laura?" he asked.

"You could say that." Rachel's smile vanished. "What I did wrong raising my girls, I can't imagine."

"Esther's not the first girl who has kissed someone else's boyfriend." Ivan chuckled to lighten the mood.

Rachel gave him a sharp glance. "Did you steal Laura from someone?"

Ivan laughed. "Not that I know of."

"But Laura stole you from someone—that I do know."

The laughter died in Ivan's throat.

Rachel shook her head. "It's such a disgrace, that's all I can say. But, thank the Lord, Laura at least got a decent husband."

"Thank you," Ivan responded. "You have a *gut* evening now."

"And you too." Rachel climbed into her buggy and drove off down the lane.

Ivan watched for a few moments before he walked toward the house. Laura had been in her work dress when he'd seen her last. She hadn't changed yet, he was sure. They wouldn't leave for town until she had. He might as well wait in the house. Maybe she'd take the hint and hurry.

Ivan opened the front door. Faint noises came from the bedroom, so he settled on the couch. Laura stuck her head out moments later. "You can clean the kitchen while you wait."

A retort rose to his lips but he stifled it.

Laura smiled and disappeared into the bedroom again.

He should take up reading *The Budget*, Ivan told himself. He glanced into the kitchen. Laura had moved the dirty dishes to the counter, and the table was clean. He'd help Laura finish after they returned from town, he decided. He returned to the living room. "Laura, hurry up! We need to leave."

A loud protest came from the bedroom, but Ivan couldn't make out the words. He squared his shoulders. It was time he was the man of the house. This would be a little practice for the conversation that lay ahead of them. He took a deep breath and said, "I'm leaving in five minutes. I'm waiting by the buggy."

Hurried sounds came from the bedroom as he walked out of the house. Now what would he do? Did he have enough nerve to leave without Laura? *Yah*, he would. He'd get into the buggy and drive out the lane. He usually shopped by himself anyway…at least ever since Laura became pregnant.

Just as Ivan was untying Beauty, Laura rushed out of the house, sputtering. "In my condition, Ivan! How dare you!"

"It's time to go." He calmly climbed into the buggy and waited for her.

"You could have done the dishes." She came to a stop by the buggy step. "And am I getting no help to climb in?"

Ivan didn't move. "You're not that far along, and you need the exercise."

Her face puckered and tears threatened. "How cruel is that, Ivan? And after *Mamm* already gave me a lecture tonight."

"I'm sure you needed it," he said. "Now climb in."

Laura did so—rather carefully. She cast a nasty look Ivan's way. "What has gotten into you? And *Mamm*'s no better. You're both on the warpath."

"Maybe someone needs to put their foot down," Ivan said, as he drove Beauty out to the main street.

"If this is about Esther, you have no room to talk. You certainly didn't seem to mind my attentions when everyone knew you and Miriam were sweet on each other. What's wrong with Esther doing the same thing?"

"Is that what you told your *mamm*?"

Laura sniffed. "No, of course not. But so what?"

"You normally tell your *mamm* everything. You didn't tell her because you knew it wasn't right."

Her silence was answer enough, but it didn't last long. "You liked my attentions, Ivan, and that's that. I'm sure Wayne will feel the same way once he and Esther are wed and settled in."

"So you think you can persuade Esther to go back on her apology and try for Wayne's affections?"

"*Yah*, but she doesn't need my encouragement. She'll do it because it's what she wants."

Ivan had no answer for that. Laura was probably right.

Sensing her advantage, Laura turned to another subject. "Why didn't you do the supper dishes while you were waiting?"

Ivan pulled up to a stop sign. "We'll take care of that when we get back." In the silence that followed, Ivan gathered his courage. "You will write Esther and tell her that your opinion has changed."

"But it hasn't." Laura's voice was sharp.

"Then it will!"

"Now you're the one who's making no sense."

"I'm making perfect sense. This has gone on long enough, and I'll not have you be involved in Miriam losing a boyfriend she's engaged to."

Icy silence filled the buggy.

"I won't," he repeated. "And you will listen and obey."

She titled her head. "So you think our marriage was a mistake? Is that what you're saying? That you wish you were wed to Miriam instead?"

Ivan kept his gaze on the road. "That's avoiding the subject, and you know it. We're married now, and it's time we act like it."

She glanced down at her midsection. "I think there's plenty of signs already that we're married. I also think Esther should get the man of her dreams. After all, I did."

His protest died in his throat, but he rallied quickly. "I wasn't dating Miriam, so that was different. And you will write Esther and say what your *mamm* and I think…and that you're withdrawing your support. That's the least you can do."

Laura took a deep breath. "What's happening to you, Ivan? What's happening to us?"

"Nothing. But this situation with Esther isn't right."

He tightened the reins as they approached the busy State Route

39. He leaned out of the buggy to turn on the extra flasher. Dusk was the most dangerous time to travel, but the tourists were usually careful. The locals were used to buggy traffic. But not far from here he'd witnessed the wreck involving Jonas and his convertible. At least jumping deer didn't harm buggies. Ivan grinned at the thought. No deer in history had ever attacked a buggy that he knew of.

Laura glared at him. "It's not funny, and I don't like it when we quarrel."

"Sorry," he said easily. "I was thinking of something else."

She didn't ask what, and the sounds of busy traffic settled around them as they drove north toward Berlin. He'd be happy once they were off the main road. This quarrel had made him nervous. He ought to apologize to Laura, but how could he do that? Still, he should try. Ivan cleared his throat. "I'm sorry about tonight. I wasn't trying to be harsh and all that, but something must be done about how you're encouraging Esther. Your *mamm* is right on that subject."

Laura didn't move for a moment, but she soon slipped her hand around his arm. She nestled her head against his shoulder. "Are you trying to be the man of the house now?"

Warmth crept up his shoulder. "Maybe."

"I like it," she whispered. "But I can't write the letter you want. *Mamm* will write Esther. I'll say nothing. That's the best I can do."

He couldn't force her, Ivan figured. So why push the fight further?

"Thank you," she whispered, "for being understanding."

Laura knew him too well, Ivan told himself. That was what he'd always liked about her. She touched his heart even when she did things he didn't approve of. He was right to take this stand. Even Laura could see this was no reflection on their situation. He was a happily married man with a child on the way.

Ivan slipped Laura's hand off his arm and then pulled her closer.

"Are you happy you married me?" Her face was turned up toward him.

"Of course." He smiled down at her. "You're a *wunderbah* woman."

"Even when I'm headstrong?"

He chuckled. "*Yah*, even then. I like spunk."

"Oh, Ivan!" She leaned against his shoulder. "I'm still not writing Esther…"

Her words were interrupted by a sudden screech of brakes. Ivan sat up straight and grasped the reins. Beauty had drifted across the yellow center line! He yanked on the reins, but it was too late. With the buggy halfway turned on the road, the oncoming car hit his side of the buggy.

Weightlessness hit Ivan, and he blacked out for a moment. His body smacking the pavement when he landed sent a surge of pain through him. He cried out as something huge catapulted by him. There was a loud crunch of steel. Ivan groped with both hands in the darkness, but he found only rough stones. He tried to focus. Where was Laura? He tried to stand, but he fell flat on his face. He lifted his head again to see the heavy mass of Beauty illuminated in front of him. Must be headlights on, he thought. Laura's horse didn't move. Ivan passed his hand over his eyes to clear them. Blood stuck to his fingers, and he could feel it smear across his face. His head throbbed with severe intensity.

"Laura!" he called out.

A man's voice answered. "Hold still, please. You've been injured. Help's on the way."

"Laura," he tried again. "Laura, where are you?"

"He's calling for a woman!" The man seemed to be speaking to someone else. "Look around, will you?"

"She's over here in the ditch," a voice soon called. "She seems to be badly injured."

"Don't touch her until help arrives," the man ordered.

"Laura!" Ivan shouted. He tried to move, but nothing seemed to work in his body. Laura will be okay, he told himself. The car had hit his side of the buggy. If he was alive, Laura should have fared even better. Blackness threatened and then overwhelmed him. He drifted into nothingness.

Chapter Twenty-Six

———◆◆◆———

Miriam drove Sally home from the schoolhouse. She glanced toward the west. The sky was dark with clouds seemingly as low as the horizon. She wasn't used to such displays in the sky. The weather this afternoon had been as stormy as the news had been in the community this week.

Esther Swartz had rushed home to attend her sister's funeral after the tragic car and buggy accident late Friday night. Miriam wouldn't wish anything bad on Esther, let alone her sister's death. But the Lord made His choices, and they often weren't easily explained.

Now Ivan was a widower. A tremble ran through Miriam at the thought. She could have been the one in Ivan's buggy instead of Laura. Would she have been prepared to cross over to the other side on such short notice? Likely neither Ivan nor Laura had been aware of the soon-to-happen disaster. From what she'd heard, the two had been on the way to Berlin for some shopping. They may not have had any warning at all.

Miriam turned into her driveway and pulled up to the barn. Wayne's buggy was still parked near the greenhouse, but he didn't come out to help unhitch. His help was forbidden since Uncle William's enforced month-long suspension of their relationship had begun. She could barely wait until the time was over. So far, at the Sunday services and at the youth gatherings, Wayne had behaved himself around Esther and stuck to Uncle William's rules.

Miriam noticed that Esther had managed to smile a little less at him. That was probably difficult to accomplish because Esther smiled at everyone. But from all appearances, she was making a serious effort to mend her ways since the apology. Miriam chose to trust Esther. There was really no other choice, Miriam decided.

Wayne and Miriam were to be wed this fall. They had parted on *gut* terms, and Wayne had given no indication that he blamed her in any way for Uncle William's separation order. Perhaps she should have resisted Uncle William's decree, Miriam thought as she unhitched Sally. Wayne would have followed her lead, she suspected. But that would have caused a rift between them and her relatives. Tension was something they needed less of, not more.

This morning was the first time she'd seen a break in Aunt Fannie's sorrowful attitude. She had even hummed the tune "What a Mighty God We Serve" as she prepared breakfast. Had Aunt Fannie and Uncle William finally settled their quarrel? The church confession hadn't come about yet, and the thought of Aunt Fannie's humiliation in front of the whole church was almost too much for Miriam to bear. With great effort she managed to keep quiet. Aunt Fannie had said Uncle William must have a hidden motivation for his severe reaction.

Miriam glanced again at the sky before she entered the house. Deep, dark storm clouds were gathering on the horizon. She shouldn't be so wrapped up in her own troubles. Rather, she should pray for protection. There was obviously rough weather ahead this evening from the looks of things. With a firm push, Miriam closed the front door against a sudden gust of wind.

"You're home!" Aunt Fannie's cheerful voice called from the kitchen.

"*Yah,* and just in time. The weather doesn't look *gut.*" Miriam peeked in the kitchen, and baby Jonathon cooed to her from his blanket on the floor by the stove.

"He likes you." Aunt Fannie looked up from the kitchen sink with a smile.

Miriam took baby Jonathon into her arms. His arm reached up to touch her face, and Miriam blew kisses into his hand. The baby giggled.

Aunt Fannie watched them for a moment before a concerned look crossed her face. "I noticed the weather too, but it's normal for around here this time of year."

"That's *gut* to hear," Miriam said as she returned baby Jonathon to his blanket. From her attitude, Aunt Fannie had *gut* news to share so Miriam waited patiently. Perhaps Aunt Fannie would soon volunteer the information.

Aunt Fannie didn't wait long. "I suppose you're wondering why I seem so happy?"

"*Yah,* I noticed," Miriam said with a wondering smile.

Aunt Fannie nodded. "Well, William finally opened up to me, and…"

Miriam interrupted. "You don't have to tell me the details, you know."

"It's okay," Aunt Fannie said. "I figure you'll think it's worse than what it is if I don't…" Aunt Fannie pulled out a kitchen chair. "Sit, Miriam. We shouldn't stand for this conversation."

"Really, Aunt Fannie," Miriam protested again. "I'm just glad things are going well between the two of you again."

Aunt Fannie smiled. "I want to tell you, Miriam. You've been honest and open with us about everything, and I want this out in the open too. William no longer asks that I do a church confession." Aunt Fannie clasped her hands on the kitchen tabletop. "But there's a reason. It seems William was engaged to an *Englisha* girl before we met! It was during his *rumspringa* time. I didn't know until he told me this week. William planned to marry her and jump the fence, but the girl broke off the engagement." Aunt Fannie's breath caught, and she choked.

Miriam reached across the table to hold her aunt's hand. "Are you okay?" When her aunt nodded, Miriam continued. "This isn't necessary, please. I've gotten you into enough trouble already."

A faint smile played on Aunt Fannie's face. "This was all a blessing, Miriam. I know it didn't seem so, but it's true. These things aren't meant to be kept secret. Look at the bitterness that lay beneath the surface of William's life. As a result of our confessions to each other, our relationship has deepened in the past few days—more than I can tell you. I have you to thank that everything is out in the open."

"I don't know about that..." Miriam demurred.

Aunt Fannie's hand clutched hers. "And I have the Lord to thank that the scales fell off William's eyes when his heart was broken by his *Englisha* girlfriend. He saw how close he'd come to joining the *Englisha* world and changing his whole life. After the wedding to the *Englisha* girl, he probably never would have come back to the faith, Miriam."

Aunt Fannie paused as a shudder shook her. "William told me that in his shame he went to the bishop and offered to confess the whole thing in front of the church, even though he wasn't yet a member. The bishop told him that wasn't possible, and this was what *rumspringa* was for. The bishop said he was glad the Lord had opened William's eyes."

"So it's better now—your relationship?" Miriam asked.

Aunt Fannie nodded and rushed on. "William wanted me to

confess in church because he thinks he could have forgotten his *Englisha* girlfriend completely if the bishop had allowed his confession. But he realizes now that confession to each other was all that we needed."

"I'm still sorry I ever brought this up." Miriam reached over to hold both of Aunt Fannie's hands.

"Stop saying that." Aunt Fannie gave Miriam a quick hug. "On the other side of the pain lies a great blessing. Like I said, things are much better now. Already the Lord has placed a new song in my heart. William loves me as I love him. Our love has deepened now that he has shared this with me. Neither of us should have kept secrets from each other to begin with. Regrets aside, we have much we can be thankful for—and so do you, Miriam."

"I agree. And that's kind of you to say," Miriam said.

Aunt Fannie rose. "So that's over. Now, we'd better get busy with supper. Here I am all wrapped up in my own problems when the poor Swartz family is dealing with much worse. And your friend Ivan is still in a coma. He'll wake up to find his *frau* already in the grave with his unborn child. How awful is that?"

"Sometimes I just don't understand the Lord's ways," Miriam said as she stood. She glanced toward the window as a gust of wind shook the house and rattled the panes. "And the weather outside...I'm still worried."

Aunt Fannie followed her glance out the kitchen window. "Oh, it'll storm, but that's normal. Still, maybe we should pray. Would that make you feel better?"

"*Yah*, I think so," Miriam said as she bowed her head. Aunt Fannie did likewise. Aunt Fannie's lips moved silently as Miriam spoke her prayer:

> Protect the people in the path of the storm tonight,
> dear Lord. Give them warning of what's coming and
> time to get out of the way. Keep the children safe from

harm, and let no awful nightmares enter their lives because of this. Help us all—and especially the Swartz family as they bury their dear loved ones. And Ivan too as he lies in an unconscious state. Be with his soul, Lord.

Aunt Fannie had already lifted her head when Miriam finished with amen.

Aunt Fannie smiled. "It's so *gut* to have a Father in heaven we can trust even when life looks dark."

"*Yah*," Miriam agreed as she glanced again out the window.

Aunt Fannie opened the breadbox on the counter. "Will you change clothes and help me with supper? I expect William will be in soon."

As if in confirmation, Wayne's buggy went past the living room window and out the driveway.

"Of course I will. I'm in my own daze." Miriam smiled and hurried upstairs to her bedroom. She peeked out past the drapes. Wayne's buggy was a dark dot on the road. With a quick rush around the room, Miriam changed and made a dash down the stairs.

"Slow down!" Aunt Fannie lectured when she ran into the kitchen.

Her aunt was definitely more herself again, Miriam thought as she joined in the supper preparations. They were still at work when Uncle William entered the utility room with a loud bang of the outside door.

"Storm's brewing tonight!" he hollered.

"We know," Aunt Fannie answered. "We've been talking and praying."

"That's a *gut* idea." Uncle William stuck his head into the kitchen. His worried face broke into a smile at the sight of baby Jonathon. "Hi!" He waved to the baby and glanced toward Miriam.

"I've told Miriam the story," Aunt Fannie said.

Uncle William dropped his head for a moment. "I suppose that was okay. One's sins always come out in the end. I'm sorry I wasn't more open to your suggestions, Miriam—the evening you spoke with me in the greenhouse. I was blinded by the reminder of my own sins."

"I understand." Miriam gave him a weak smile.

"And now on to a more urgent subject," Uncle William said. "I've spoken with Wayne and told him my objections to your relationship are in the past. I was a little hasty, what with my own problems and all. I explained to Wayne, and he forgave me. I hope you will do the same, Miriam. I am sorry. Wayne said he'll talk with you tomorrow. And I won't be surprised if he brings you home on Sunday evening."

A thrill ran through Miriam. "Thanks for the *gut* word," she told her uncle. "It was for the best, I suppose. I do forgive you, Uncle William."

Uncle William nodded with a sober face. "You are a very understanding girl, Miriam. Wayne will be getting a *gut frau*. I need to check on the horses in the barn, and then I'll be right back for supper."

"He's a *gut* man," Aunt Fannie said with a smile after Uncle William vanished through the washroom door. Outside rain was lashing against the kitchen window, and a roll of thunder pealed across the open prairie.

Chapter Twenty-Seven

Miriam climbed into Wayne's buggy Sunday evening after the hymn singing. "*Gut* evening," she greeted Wayne, giving his face a quick glance and a smile before she settled into the seat.

Wayne grinned. "I guess it's legal to be seen with you again. I almost forgot there for a minute."

"Oh, Wayne!" Miriam leaned against him. "It's so *gut* to see you and sit next to you."

Wayne's smile was broad as he drove out of the driveway into the gathering dusk.

Out of habit, Miriam had almost gone to the barn after the singing ended to hitch Sally to the buggy. The separation from Wayne had seemed to last for months…but, thankfully, that was behind them now. She relived the joyful memory when the ban from each other was lifted.

Wayne had stopped by the house Friday after his work ended in the greenhouse, and they had spoken at length for the first time in almost a month. She'd expected his arrival, and the knock on the front door that evening had sounded through the whole house.

"Go see who it is!" Aunt Fannie motioned toward the door with her hand.

Miriam set down the plates and forks. Her hands were trembling. Wayne was at the door. She knew it, and so did Aunt Fannie. Her aunt's gentle smile was all the confirmation the young woman needed. She drew in a long breath as she opened the door to reveal the familiar form on the front steps.

"*Gut* evening!" Wayne's smile was soft.

"*Gut* evening!" Miriam replied. She tried to quiet the beating of her heart. Other than smiles exchanged at the community meetings, she hadn't stood this close to Wayne since the separation.

"I wanted to see you, and to speak with you." Wayne's smile broadened. "Your uncle told me…"

Miriam didn't allow him to continue any further. She wrapped her arms around Wayne in a huge hug. They clung to each other for long minutes, until Wayne whispered into her ear. "This is kind of public, I think."

Miriam had chuckled and let him go. Just like that their separation was over; they were together again.

The buggy wheels rattling beneath them brought Miriam back to the present.

Wayne glanced at her. "Are you cold?" he asked with concern.

"A little—but I'm warm on the inside. Oh, Wayne! We're together again after those long weeks."

Wayne wrapped his arm around Miriam's shoulders for a quick squeeze. He let her go to pull a buggy blanket out from under the seat. He handed it to her.

Wayne was still a gentleman, of course. The thought brought a fresh smile to Miriam's face. "So what were you doing with yourself during all that time?" she asked.

"Waiting till I could speak with you again." Wayne's arm crept around Miriam's shoulders again. He pulled her tightly against his side. "I'm so sorry for my part in this, Miriam. I know Uncle William insisted that we spend the time apart, but that wouldn't have been necessary if I'd…"

"Shhh…" Miriam silenced him. "We will speak no more about this. Couples quarrel—even married ones. But, please, I don't want another fight like this for the rest of my life."

Wayne laughed. "You'll get no disagreement from me on that point."

Miriam looked up into his face. "With this storm in the past, we should be ready to go on with life together. Have you been past the farm north of the community lately? The one we're looking into buying?"

Wayne shook his head. "I haven't thought of the farm, Miriam. I was too busy thinking of you. You're such a dear. I can't express my appreciation enough for how you've taken all of this."

She hesitated for a moment. "I have my faults, you know. One of them is that I never told *Daett* and *Mamm* about the inherited money. They'll have to be told sometime."

"We'll tell them together." Wayne's voice was resolute. "We'll do everything together now, Miriam. And I'll have nothing but the best words to speak to your *daett* if he questions your handling of the money."

"Wayne," Miriam sighed as she leaned against his shoulder again, "you have no idea what a great weight that takes off my mind. I should have told *Daett* from the beginning, but I couldn't. He was always so focused on the evils of money. You've changed my life for the better. Why the Lord has sent me such a *wunderbah* man, I'll never know."

"I think you were sent to me, not the other way around," Wayne teased. He changed the subject. "Are your parents coming to Oklahoma anytime soon?"

Miriam shrugged. "Not that I know of. Shirley has another operation soon. *Mamm* mentioned it in her last letter. It's with a plastic surgeon. There's been no crisis that would require a trip all the way out here. I guess that means you'll be traveling with me to Possum Valley to meet them after school is out for the summer. They'll be so happy to see you. I know they will."

"I hope I pass their inspection." Wayne hung onto the reins as they approached State Route 48. He pulled to a stop. "Did you tell them about our forced separation?"

Miriam shook her head.

"Thank you." Wayne smiled down at her. "Even if you had, I could still sit in your halo when I'm around them. The light would drive away all my shortcomings."

Miriam laughed, and Wayne laughed along with her.

When silence settled in the buggy, Wayne said, "I know you're still worried about the money, but you shouldn't. You ought to accept what the Lord has given you, Miriam. Look how well you've done with the money so far. You haven't indulged yourself at all, like many people would have. I love you for that."

Miriam bit her lip and pressed back the tears. "I've had plenty of fears about the money, you know that."

"You have done well." Wayne's arm tightened around Miriam's shoulders. "The Lord gave you the money, and that's now part of your life story. Don't run down the gift or think less of it. Maybe we can do something *wunderbah* with the gift, such as helping other people."

Miriam studied his face. "I'll be so glad when this is all over and we're married. Then you'll be responsible for the money. After we buy our farm, you can do what you want with the rest."

Wayne fell silent for a few moments before he spoke again. "Thanks for the confidence, Miriam. Right now I'm focused on counting the days until our wedding day arrives."

"Oh, Wayne," she breathed. She steadied herself with one hand on the buggy door as Wayne drove the buggy into her driveway. "I do have to say this yet. *Daett* always taught us that money corrupts so we should stay away from it. I didn't listen for a while, and then I was afraid of spending the money and falling into a trap set by the devil. That was what kept me out of trouble more than any virtue on my part."

Wayne reached for Miriam's hand as he pulled the buggy to a stop. "That's all behind us now. We've weathered the worst of the storm. I'll be by your side when you break the news to your parents. It'll be okay, Miriam. You are a blessing to me and to so many in the community. You and I will pray that the Lord will guide our hands as we make decisions on what should be done with the money."

Miriam gave Wayne a quick hug before she hopped down from the buggy and helped unhitch his horse. She waited while he put the horse in the barn and then returned. She smiled up at him and took his hand. Together they walked toward the house.

When they entered the living room, Miriam motioned for Wayne to seat himself on the couch. "I'll make popcorn and squeeze some orange juice. You can wait here."

A look of mock horror filled Wayne's face. "After all these weeks apart you expect me to twiddle my thumbs in the living room while you work in the kitchen? I'll squeeze the oranges, if nothing else."

A warm glow filled Miriam. She'd hoped for such a reaction, but she still teased, "Think you know how to squeeze oranges?"

Wayne's response was to jump up from the couch and rush toward her. Miriam allowed a delighted squeal to escape her lips as she ran into the kitchen. They were acting like teenagers, but it felt good. They needed relief from the tension of the separation.

Wayne collapsed in a kitchen chair as if exhausted. Miriam stifled a giggle and reached into the cupboard for the bag of oranges.

"There," she said, plopping them down in front of him. "Let's see what you can do. We only have a small hand press."

"I'll be looking at you," he teased, "so what does it matter how hard I work?"

Miriam hid her blush with a quick turn of her back. She took her time searching through the drawer even though the hand press was in plain sight. Wayne wasn't fooled. He had a big grin on his face when she turned back to him.

"What?" Miriam demanded.

"Nothing!" He chuckled. "I'd better get to work."

"*Yah*, you should," she chided. She glanced out of the kitchen window as lightning lit the southwestern sky. The strike was distant and filled only the horizon. She'd been too wrapped up with Wayne all evening to notice the weather. Would it storm tonight? On this, their first evening back together? She hoped not.

Wayne had followed her glance. "Awful stormy of late, it seems. Maybe it mirrors our lives right now."

"I hope not," Miriam protested. "Besides, in that case it should calm down now."

Wayne chuckled. "I'm not superstitious in the least. Don't get me wrong. This is normal for this season in Oklahoma. Spring weather can be quite unpredictable."

"That's what I'm learning," Miriam allowed. "Aunt Fannie says the same thing."

Wayne appeared pensive. "This year, though, our horses have taken to breaking out of their stalls when the evening storms come through. I don't know what's gotten into them. We couldn't figure out for the longest time how they did it, but my sister, Joy, finally discovered the problem. One of the younger work mares lifted the stall latch with her nose and then let the others out. Now we have to tie her latch down unless we want horses dashing all over the barnyard in these lightning storms."

"Smart horse." Miriam grinned and shook the popcorn pan. "But, of course, she's female so how can she help it?"

Wayne roared with laughter. "You are full of razor blades tonight!"

"I'm just happy," Miriam said, sending him a gentle look. "Popcorn will be ready soon, so you'd better get busy."

"You are the limit!" Wayne chided, but he vigorously set to work with the hand press. He had two glasses of orange juice finished when Miriam dumped the still-snapping popcorn into a large bowl. Together they grabbed some small bowls and carried the orange juice and popcorn into the living room.

Wayne settled onto the couch with a sigh. "Now this is living. Popcorn and orange juice on a Sunday evening—with you on the couch beside me."

"You have your sights set quite low," Miriam said as she sat close to him. Close enough to touch his arm lightly with her shoulder.

Wayne calmly filled his popcorn bowl, but his racing heart and flushed face revealed he was as overcome by the moment as she was. "Penny for your thoughts," he teased.

Miriam felt a deep blush spread over her face. "I will not speak my thoughts right now!" she declared.

Wayne laughed heartily. "I'll take that as a compliment."

"You may," Miriam assured him. "But I'm still not talking."

"The sound of your voice saying anything is sweet enough for me." Wayne took a long sip of orange juice before he glanced at her with a twinkle in his eye. "And I'm having a little gift prepared for you, after our separation."

Miriam giggled. "Stop now, Wayne. It's enough teasing for this evening. You are enough of a gift. Now, let me gather my wits around myself. You have me at a disadvantage."

Wayne's pleased look showed plainly that he had no regrets over the situation. Miriam kept her gaze on the front door until the beat of her heart slowed down. Thankfully Wayne changed the conversation, and she listened as he told a story of chasing horses all over the barnyard in the middle of the last storm. "We could leave them outside, I suppose," Wayne concluded. "But *Daett* doesn't think horses do well getting soaked in storms, and I agree. Hopefully Joy's discovery will solve the problem, and we'll have no more breakouts from here on out. *Mamm* and *Daett* are leaving for a trip soon to Possum Hollow, and we can use peace around the place."

"*Daett* would agree with you," Miriam said once Wayne lapsed into silence. Wayne's thoughts were obviously elsewhere, as were hers. This conversation had never been about horses or storms. They spoke to enjoy each other's company, and silence would do just as well now that things had relaxed between them. Miriam reached for Wayne's left hand, and they finished their bowls of popcorn with their fingers intertwined.

Chapter Twenty-Eight

---◆◆◆---

Ivan fought the darkness as great waves of fear crashed over him. This must be a dream! he told himself. He couldn't breathe. One could always breathe in dreams. He gasped for air and pushed upward with both hands. Suddenly he realized a tender hand was stroking his forehead.

"It's okay. You're awake now."

Ivan recognized the voice of his sister Marjorie whispering above him. He forced his eyes open, but he couldn't focus. His parched lips worked slowly. "Am I in a dream?"

"Not now, but you might have been." Marjorie held Ivan's hand. "But you've come to now. The nurse who stops by to check on you should be here soon."

"Where's Laura?"

Marjorie hesitated. "We'd best not speak of that now."

Ivan tried to sit up. The throbbing in his head drove him back. "Is she hurt badly?"

"Perhaps *Daett* or *Mamm* should talk to you about the accident." Marjorie's voice trembled.

Ivan groaned and moved his head on the pillow. "You might as well tell me, Marjorie." Another low moan escaped his lips. "Or maybe you're telling me I don't want to know?"

Marjorie didn't say anything for a moment. "We have you at home but in a hospital bed. You've been unconscious ever since the accident, which happened a little over a week and a half ago."

"Where's Laura?" Ivan repeated. Marjorie's frightened face appeared through a dull haze in front of his eyes. When she didn't answer, he said, "I want to know, Marjorie. Right now."

With a sigh of resignation, Marjorie said, "Ivan, Laura's dead and buried."

"No!" His cry was deep. "She can't be. We were just talking, and I…"

"Ivan, please." Marjorie had both of his hands in hers. "It's the Lord's will, and we must all submit."

"She's gone? But I didn't get to…" Ivan turned his face sideways on the pillow.

"She couldn't be helped, Ivan." Marjorie stroked his forehead. "Don't blame yourself."

"It was my fault. We had an argument. I insisted…"

Marjorie shushed him. "No one is blaming you, Ivan. These things happen."

"Leave me alone," he said, his voice hollow.

She didn't move from his bedside. "I'm here to help you; I'm not leaving."

Ivan whispered, "The best thing you can do is give me some time…alone." When she still didn't move he lapsed into silence. After several minutes, he finally said, "All right, then tell me what you know about the accident."

Marjorie stroked his arm. "You were on Highway 39 near Berlin on a Friday night. We assume you were on the way to the shopping plaza because Laura had her shopping bags along. You were struck from the front by a car. You were thrown from the buggy." Marjorie's voice dropped. "Laura was also thrown, and she died where she fell. We buried her three days later."

"Who was the *Englisha* driver?"

"That's not important, Ivan. You know that."

"Did the police say why the accident happened?"

"They'd don't know for sure."

"I know." His voice was a groan. "Beauty drifted across the yellow line because I wasn't paying attention to her." Marjorie's silence told him that his answer was one she'd heard. He half-closed his eyes. "You'd best leave me alone now." Marjorie's form stayed beside the bed for a moment longer before seeming to drift away. Darkness threatened again, but Ivan fought hard to stay conscious. There would be no gain if he avoided facing this nightmare. Laura was dead. He couldn't get his mind around that apparent fact. How could that be? Marjorie wouldn't tell him something that wasn't true, especially something so big. She said they'd buried Laura. That meant the baby was gone too. The baby wasn't old enough to survive outside the womb, even if the doctors had tried to save it. He'd lost them both.

Ivan moved his hand across his face. Laura would never be back, and he hadn't even had a chance to tell her goodbye. And the accident was his fault. Marjorie seemed to have known, so the rest of the world probably did too. People might not blame him outright because accidents did happen, but still…

Moaning again, Ivan moved his legs to the right. Here he was in bed when he should be at his job. He could do nothing about Laura or the baby. The agony in his soul might lessen if he could work with his hands. With care Ivan flexed his fingers. They seemed to work. Slowly Ivan moved his legs more and then sat up. The world swam before his eyes, but he managed to stay upright.

A cry came from the doorway, followed by the sounds of quick footsteps.

"You can't get up, Ivan. You can't!" Marjorie insisted.

Stubbornness was strong in his voice. "I'm no *gut* lying around. And after what I've done…"

"But what if you injure yourself again?" Marjorie wrung her hands. "I'm responsible for you until *Mamm* or *Daett* get here."

Ivan groaned but lowered himself back on the bed.

Marjorie stepped closer. "Pushing yourself will not bring Laura back."

"I want to speak with Laura's *mamm*. Will you go get her for me?"

"Right now?"

"*Yah*, now! Why should it wait? It's already been too long. I need to face this, and putting it off will just make it more difficult."

"You don't have to speak to her right now, Ivan. The Swartz family holds nothing against you."

"Maybe I hold something against myself." Ivan looked up at Marjorie. "Please get her."

Marjorie hesitated but soon left. She came back with her shawl. She pulled the blankets back over Ivan and then draped the shawl over her own shoulders. "Are you still sure about this, Ivan?"

"*Yah*, please. I'm very sure."

Marjorie nodded and left.

Through the window, Ivan saw Marjorie reach the barn and go in. A few minutes later, he watched as she led her harnessed horse out of the building and over to a buggy. She hitched the horse to the buggy. Ivan was reminded of Laura's horse. No doubt Beauty was dead or had to be put down. He had a vague memory of a large shape lying still on the blacktop. He hadn't thought to ask about the horse, but what did it matter? Compared to the loss of Laura and the baby, Beauty was a small matter. Still, the ache in his heart increased.

Laura…if they only hadn't argued before the accident…His thoughts paused as he heard Marjorie drive quickly down the lane. No doubt she wanted this deed over and done with. He was

thankful she respected his wishes, especially because she'd probably been told not to leave him alone. The idea to speak with Rachel
had sprang into his mind, but he was sure he was right. He needed
to see someone from the Swartz family at once. They might understand if he waited a few days after waking up, but they would
respect him more this way. Now, if he could stay awake and alert
until Rachel arrived.

A chill settled in, and Ivan wrapped the blankets more tightly
around his body. His teeth chattered, and a hazy whiteness floated
around his head. With a long sigh, he settled back and closed his
eyes. He just needed to drift off a bit. Maybe he'd never come back
to this world. What a relief that would be. But obviously the Lord
wanted him to remain. His injuries must not be life threatening;
they wouldn't result in death regardless of how long he slept. And
sleep wasn't really what he wanted right now. He needed to mourn
for what had happened. But how did a man do such a thing? Especially when the accident was his fault? Tears filled his eyes, and the
pain in his heart didn't lessen. Perhaps when Rachel arrived and he
spoke with her...

Ivan covered his face with both hands. *Laura was buried.* He
still couldn't believe it. She'd been in this house with him only
moments ago...or so it seemed. How could this have happened?
Ivan stared at the ceiling and willed the moments to speed by
quickly. They crept along instead. Ivan counted them off for forty-
five minutes before he heard the sound of a buggy rattling down
the driveway. The noise stopped short of the barn, and soon he
heard rapid steps run up the walk. Ivan lifted his head as the front
door burst open. Marjorie appeared, one hand on her chest.

"I'm still here," Ivan managed to whisper. "Just weak...very weak."

Relief spread over Marjorie's face. "I'll go take care of my horse,
and I'll send Rachel in."

Ivan settled back into the bed. Moments later the front door
opened again, but this time he didn't look up.

"*Gut* morning," Rachel greeted him as she appeared in the doorway to his room.

"*Gut* morning," Ivan replied, turning to face her. "Thanks for coming. I'm so sorry about everything."

Rachel took the chair beside the bed and ignored his apology. "I'm glad to see you're awake. You had us worried."

Ivan shook his head. "Let's not speak of me. Laura and the baby are gone. I allowed Beauty to drift across the yellow line. Laura and I were talking…"

Rachel wiped away a quick tear. "I know. Marjorie told me you told her that. That could happen to anyone."

"But it happened to me…to Laura and me…and our baby." Ivan stared at the ceiling.

"Tell me about her last moments," Rachel asked, interrupting Ivan's agonized thoughts.

Ivan swallowed hard. "I'd made a fuss about her writing letters to Esther and encouraging her to…well, you know about what. We argued before we started out on our shopping trip, and it continued for some time on the road. I wanted her to write to Esther and tell her not to…to interfere with…" Ivan's voice drifted off.

"Did you settle the argument, before…"

"*Yah*," Ivan interrupted. He nodded. "She was leaning against my shoulder and agreeing to stop encouraging Esther. She was going to leave it up to you to correct Esther. You had a *wunderbah* daughter in Laura, Rachel."

Rachel blinked a few times. "I know. I'm glad to hear your last moments together weren't spent on a quarrel. Laura could be a little headstrong, but I'm sure you knew that."

"I'm sorry she's gone," Ivan whispered. "I'll never be able to make it right to you."

Rachel reached over to squeeze his hand. "I'm thankful you loved my daughter, Ivan. I was always glad you married her. Laura and you were good together."

Ivan turned his head away from Rachel for a second. "I don't know about that, but thank you."

"You must go on with life now." Rachel regarded him with intensity. "Whatever lies ahead of you, don't ever think that I hold any of this against you. I'll always miss Laura, of course. I do wish I could have held my newest grandchild, but the Lord knows best."

"I'm sorry I couldn't be there," Ivan tried to sit up. "At the funeral and all, I mean."

Rachel rose to her feet. "I know you must have felt you needed to tell me this, but I want you to know I wasn't holding a grudge against you in my heart. And neither does anyone of our family. We are glad you are part of our family. We know it was an accident. In the end, we all have to say that the Lord allows what He wishes."

"I'm sorry, just the same." Ivan rested his head on the pillow again. "I should have paid better attention."

"You loved Laura. That's *gut* enough for me." Rachel wiped her eyes. "Rest now, Ivan. And get well. And may the Lord bless the rest of your life. We wish you well, and will always think of you as part of our family."

He tried to protest, but deep weariness swept over him. Rachel's face was starting to float in front of him. Just before he drifted off he realized Marjorie was standing next to Rachel. "I'm sleeping now," he murmured.

Chapter Twenty-Nine

Shirley felt the bandages on her face and then pressed them gently with her fingers. Dull pain erupted, and she winced. How well had the surgery gone? she wondered again. The nurse she'd asked earlier hadn't been too forthcoming other than to say, "The doctor will be in to see you in the morning."

Mamm, sitting in a chair beside her bed, broke into a warm smile when she saw Shirley looking at her. "How are you feeling?"

"Okay, I guess. I want to go home."

Mamm's smile lingered. "Tomorrow we'll take you home."

"Will I be beautiful again?" Shirley couldn't stop herself.

Mamm sighed. "You really shouldn't be thinking like that, Shirley. Your obsession with beauty isn't right before the eyes of the Lord. *Daett* wasn't even sure if this operation was right to begin with, but he allowed it because you wanted it so badly. Think about what happened to Ivan and Laura. That is real trouble. Thanking God for your survival and praying for Ivan would be a better use of your time."

Shirley nodded. "I am thankful, and I'm sorry…" She paused as a figure appeared in the hospital doorway. "Glen!" Shirley cried out. "You've come to visit me!"

A gentle laugh escaped the man's lips. "Is that okay? I can leave if I'm a bother."

"No, of course not!" Shirley half rose from the hospital bed.

Mamm reached over and gently pressed down on her shoulder. "Don't move, Shirley." She turned to Glen with a soft smile. "So you're Glen. Shirley has mentioned you." *Mamm* stood. "Please take my chair. I'm stepping outside so you two can chat."

"Thank you." Glen sat down and fidgeted for a moment.

Mamm gave them both another quick glance from the doorway before she left.

Shirley took a deep breath, and gently put her hands on her bandages again. "I can't smile at you, or I'd give you a big one, Glen. It's so nice of you to come. I hadn't expected you to."

Glen grinned. "I got off from work and came right up. I know we're not…well, you know, we're not seeing each other. But I wanted to stop by and encourage you."

"Thank you. I need a strengthening of my spirits. I'm feeling pretty blue. How did you know?"

"I didn't." He looked sympathetically at her. "But I know operations are difficult, and the pain medication afterward doesn't always make a person feel too well. I know it was pretty rough for me when I had my appendix out a few years ago."

"You did? I didn't know that."

Glen shrugged. "*Mamm* caught it in time, even when I thought I could outlast the stomachache."

"Men!" Shirley scolded. "It could have burst, and then…"

"I know, but it didn't, so all's well that ends well," he said, gently interrupting her.

Shirley touched her bandages again. "I hope this ends well, and that my vanity doesn't get the best of me. What if the Lord decides to make me even uglier than I was?"

Glen scolded, "You know better than that, Shirley."

"I wish I did, but…"

"You'll feel better soon." He reached over to squeeze her hand. "Has that Beachy boy been by yet to see you?"

Shirley giggled. "Now you're being jealous."

"I would be jealous…" Glen faked a glare, "…but I take it he hasn't been here."

"No. I'm glad *you* came."

Glen wrinkled his brow. "Will you go home tomorrow?"

"I guess that's what one of the nurses told *Mamm*."

A grin filled his face. "See? The operation went fine. They wouldn't let you go so soon if it hadn't."

"You're so full of cheer and goodwill."

"I try to be."

Silence hung between them for a moment. Glen was no Jonas Beachy when it came to having money, Shirley told herself. But he was here for her. That counted for a lot—maybe more than having money. Maybe that was the lesson the Lord wanted to teach her through the accident. She certainly hadn't learned any other way.

Glen cleared his throat. "There's something else I want to ask you, Shirley, *before* the bandages are taken off."

"Yah?" Shirley turned her head to face him.

"Would you be interested in us seeing each other more often? Once you're well, of course. Maybe even dating me? I hesitate to ask that right now, but I wanted to say something before you know the results of the surgery. I want to make sure you know that I'd ask the same question even if you'd never had this last operation. I'm hoping you know that."

Shirley drew in a sharp breath. "Glen…really? You're so sweet. You're going to make me cry."

His face lit up. "Then you'd consider it?"

"Maybe." She reached out for his hand. "Would you really have asked even without this…?" She pointed toward her bandaged face.

He nodded solemnly. "Even then. I would have asked before, but we hadn't known each other that long. You are so…so…"

She interrupted him. "Don't say it, Glen. I'm not that good of a catch. *Daett* is a poor farmer. We make do because of Miriam's farm, and that's about the only reason."

Glen ignored the comment. "At least you said you'd consider it."

She didn't answer for a while. "Are you sure you want to date me? I mean, is it really fair to you? You could probably have any girl you want."

"I'm sure," he said, a tease in his voice. "But I'd like to know if you still have feelings for…for that Beachy boy. Jonas, wasn't it?"

Shirley looked away. "Maybe a little. But like you said, he hasn't been here today or this evening."

"He paid for your operation."

"That's because it was his responsibility," Shirley said at once. "Plus he probably had insurance for car accidents."

Glen let out a faint groan. "*Yah*, but even then I could never have arranged for this kind of care. I don't have that kind of money."

She reached over and took his hand. "Glen, you've become a *gut* friend. More than I deserve. But you don't know me very well. I'm not very *gut* with promises. And I always seem to do things I shouldn't."

"Like seeing Jonas Beachy." Glen gave Shirley a sideways glance.

Shirley looked away. "*Yah*, that for one. But you're here to see me and he isn't. That says a lot. I do appreciate our friendship. Can we keep it like that for now?"

Glen was silent for a moment. "That's *gut* enough for me, Shirley. And if you never want to be more than just friends, I'll consider it a privilege to know you."

"Glen," Shirley moaned under her breath, "you need to have your sights raised when it comes to dating women."

"You have more to offer a man than you think," Glen said, looking at her intently.

"I'm going to turn the color of a beet if you don't quit," Shirley said.

"It's the truth," he insisted. "And don't you dare think otherwise."

Shirley took a deep breath. "Your wish is my command."

He chuckled. "Enough of that. So tell me about Oklahoma. Have you had a letter from your sister lately?"

Shirley shook her head. "We had one last week from Aunt Fannie. She said everything is going well. Miriam is awful busy with the schoolwork, and they've been having plenty of storms this spring. Nothing unusual for Oklahoma, Aunt Fannie assured us, but it still makes me glad I'm here and not there."

"I want to travel someday." Longing showed in Glen's face.

"Maybe you can visit Oklahoma someday—when you can afford to take off from work." Shirley reached over to pat his arm.

"Perhaps you should go visit Miriam when you're up to it."

Shirley sighed. "It would be *gut* to see Miriam again…but Oklahoma? I'm afraid I have too many failures out there to face up to."

Glen shifted on his seat to face Shirley. "You must be mistaken about your failures wherever you say they happened."

Shirley snorted. "I'm afraid not. I tried to straighten up my life while I was out there, but I failed miserably. I wouldn't be in this mess today if I'd behaved myself and taken the medicine the Lord had given me."

Glen looked away for a moment. "Regret is a strange thing. We see so clearly looking back—or think we do. It might not have been that way at all."

Shirley reached out to touch his arm. "You say such kind things, Glen. Thank you. But life is what it is."

"You must have faith," he said.

Shirley's laugh was curt before she said, "That's another area where I seem to be lacking."

Glen stood. "I doubt that. But now I really should be going or your *Mamm* will chase me out. You need to rest."

Shirley nodded.

Glen retreated with a quick goodbye wave at the door.

Mamm appeared moments later. "Are you up to more visitors?"

"Who is it?"

"Lee and Mark." *Mamm* beamed. "They even brought Naomi along."

"Oh," Shirley cooed as the three came in, "you came to visit your wicked sister."

The three laughed as *Mamm* reprimanded her. "That's not necessary, Shirley. Words mean things."

"Don't scold her," Lee objected. "We all knew she was teasing."

"Maybe so," *Mamm* allowed. "I still don't like it. I don't want her to believe such a thing."

"Are you coming home tomorrow?" Mark asked.

Shirley nodded. "If the plans hold."

"Will your face be all fixed up?" Naomi asked.

Before Shirley could answer, there was a soft knock at the door. They all turned and Shirley had to stifle a gasp at seeing Jonas in the doorway.

"Anybody home?" he asked.

Before Shirley could find her voice, *Mamm* jumped up and held out her hand. "Welcome, Jonas. Have my seat."

Jonas shook *Mamm*'s hand, solemn-faced now. "I came to see how Shirley is doing. I just spoke with the doctor, and he has high hopes this operation repaired a lot of the damage." Jonas's face softened as he approached the bed. "You're looking good, bandages and all."

She wanted to cry and laugh at the same time, but still no words came. Jonas seemed to understand.

"I thought I'd stop by and say, hi. I see you have plenty of company, so I won't stay long."

No one said anything. As Jonas turned to leave, Shirley finally managed to say, "Wait."

He paused, turned, and looked at her with a smile.

"Thank you for coming, Jonas. I really mean it," Shirley said.

"Sure thing," he said.

Mamm followed him out the door, and the murmur of their voices could be heard in the hall for a few minutes.

"That is one handsome dude!" Naomi whispered. "I've never seen him up close before."

"Don't be getting any ideas," Lee teased.

"That goes for Shirley too," Mark added with a direct look at his bandaged sister.

"I know," Shirley agreed. "He's just being nice by stopping by. It's his duty."

Before her brothers could add anything, *Mamm* reappeared. Words rushed out of her. "We're thankful for what the Beachy family is doing, Shirley. And Jonas is being very nice to you, but I hope you won't read more into this than what you should. Glen is the man you should be setting your affections on. He's one of us, Shirley, in so many ways. And your *daett* approves of him, remember that."

"I wish you wouldn't say that," Shirley said, resistance rising inside of her.

Alarm showed in *Mamm*'s face. "Surely you don't plan to…"

Shirley shook her head. "No, *Mamm*, it's just that…" The words stuck in her mouth again, and she decided it wouldn't be good for Naomi to hear her twisted logic anyway.

After a moment's awkward silence, Lee began to chat about their work on the farm, and Mark joined in.

She would stay on the straight and narrow, Shirley told herself. This time she would heed her lesson. Besides, she'd always have the scars on her face to help her remember. Maybe that was the Lord's grace, hard as the idea was to accept. And Glen wanted to date her no matter what she looked like. He was such a decent man, and she should be very thankful.

Chapter Thirty

The following Wednesday evening, Miriam glanced out the kitchen window as she set the last of the supper dishes on the table. Storm clouds were gathering again. She shivered. She knew she should be used to these Oklahoma spring cloudbursts by now, but she wasn't. Even Aunt Fannie held baby Jonathon a little tighter tonight as the wind picked up to a dull roar that came through the walls.

Miriam forced herself to think about *Mamm*'s letter today from Possum Valley:

> Shirley had her bandages taken off at the doctor's office today. I expected the worst and insisted I stay in the room as comfort for Shirley. Thank the Lord, the scars are only little red traces across her face now. Even those will eventually fade from sight, the doctor assured us. Shirley must learn to place less weight on her looks, but we are still thankful the Lord saw fit to make things

easier on her rather than harder. This is the grace of the
Lord we all need, I am sure.

So Shirley's operation had been a success. *Mamm* was happy
about something else too. That was evident from the tone throughout the letter, although *Mamm* hadn't explained further. Shirley's recovery must be going well in more than the physical realm.
Maybe other *gut* things were also happening in Shirley's life. But
what? "Thank You, dear Lord, anyway," Miriam whispered. Then
her thoughts returned to the sounds of the storm drawing closer.

Aunt Fannie stood up to glance into the living room. "It sounds
awful, I know, but it's not unusual for this time of the year."

Her aunt was trying once more to settle her nerves, Miriam
realized. This was, after all, her first spring in Oklahoma. Miriam
tried to trust that all would be well. Her last look out the living-
room window had revealed banks of clouds rolling ever closer in
from the southwest. Uncle William still hadn't come in from the
greenhouse, so he must be busy preparing for the storm. She would
comfort herself with that thought. And in the Lord's goodness, He
would surely not allow anything to happen that did not meet with
His approval.

"Just sit down," Aunt Fannie said. "If you'll hold baby Jonathon,
I'll go see where William is and if he needs help."

Miriam glanced at the look on her aunt's face. She was clearly
more worried than she wanted to admit.

Before Aunt Fannie could move, a loud bang at the washroom
door announced Uncle William's presence. From the violence of
the sound, the wind must have knocked the door against the side
of the house.

Aunt Fannie fastened her gaze on Uncle William as he walked
in from the utility room, a wild gust of wind following behind
him. The blast was strong enough to blow part of the tablecloth
over the food dishes. She gasped and shooed Uncle William in and

hurriedly closed the door behind him. Miriam leaped to her feet to rescue the food. A washrag was needed, and she retrieved one from the kitchen sink. Carefully Miriam pulled the edge of the table-cloth away from the gravy and cleaned the mess as best she could. When she glanced up, both Aunt Fannie and Uncle William had disappeared into the living room. She laid the rag on the kitchen table and peeked in. They stood in front of the living-room win-dow watching the approaching storm.

Uncle William had baby Jonathon in his arms. He turned around first. "I think we'd better take shelter in the basement. That's no ordinary storm. That's a tornado!"

Aunt Fannie gasped and grabbed Uncle William's arm.

"What about the food?" Miriam asked.

Uncle William shook his head and led them toward the base-ment door. "There are more important things right now than sup-per. We have to pray for protection—for us and our neighbors. Only the Lord can still the wrath of tornadoes. I've not seen such a dark funnel build up in a long time. Miriam, make sure you bolt the door behind us."

Miriam glanced at the heated dishes on the kitchen table before she followed Aunt Fannie. It seemed a shame to leave all the food, even if fear was gripping her heart. The danger must be great for Uncle William and Aunt Fannie to flee to the basement so quickly. They knew what actions to take and when. They were used to life on the prairie.

Uncle William was already on his knees near the washtub when Miriam arrived at the bottom of the stairs. He cradled baby Jona-thon in his arms and had his eyes closed. Aunt Fannie knelt beside him, and Miriam joined them. Uncle William led out in prayer:

> Dear Lord in heaven, be with us. If it be Your will, pro-
> tect us and our neighbors this evening. We ask not for
> the things of this world that pass away, but for our

loved ones that they would be safe. Comfort the hearts of the children tonight as this tornado rages around us. Let no memory of its terror linger long in their hearts. Let the sweet presence of Your Spirit dwell over us, and let Your grace encamp around us. Give us humble hearts to accept Your will—whatever that might be tonight. Let not our hearts blame You for the wrath that is released upon this world of sin. It's only by the mercy of Your great hand that we are not all-consumed even this very day. Help us...

Miriam listened as the sounds of the winds increased and intruded through the basement walls. Uncle William continued to pray, and Miriam heard a deep rumble that seemed to shake the very air. She sensed it was coming from the direction of Clarita. Her schoolhouse was near there. Would the building stand up to this wind? What if she arrived tomorrow and found the roof gone or the windows blown out? They couldn't have classes with the schoolhouse in such a condition. Surely the Lord would protect the community from such extreme trouble! Miriam brought her thoughts to the present when Uncle William rose to his feet.

He listened intently, and then motioned with his hand. "We should go to the other side of the basement. The storm is coming this way."

Miriam followed her trembling aunt, wishing she had Wayne's arm to cling to just as Aunt Fannie was clinging to Uncle William. Instead, all she could do was pray as the roar outside increased. No wonder Uncle William had left supper to grow cold. In just minutes the storm had intensified. She pictured the food taking flight in the wind. Then she imagined the entire house being lifted. Surely that wouldn't happen! Uncle William and Aunt Fannie couldn't lose their house. Miriam had thought the weather looked threatening this afternoon, but this was more than a threat. This was actual danger.

They sat down as close together as possible.

Aunt Fannie whimpered as booms and crashes sounded above them and around them.

"It's the greenhouse," Uncle William said matter-of-factly. "We can build it again."

Aunt Fannie's eyes were wide as they stared at the far wall.

"The Lord gives grace even when He chooses to take away," Uncle William said with a steady voice.

"Our dear Lord in heaven," Aunt Fannie whispered, "forgive us our sins. Forgive me for where I've not been the wife, or the mother, or the aunt I should have been. I know I fail You so many times."

"It's okay." Uncle William wrapped the arm not holding baby Jonathon around Aunt Fannie's shoulders and pulled her close.

Miriam leaned against Aunt Fannie, and they huddled together as the sounds of wrath continued outside. If the house should suddenly lift off, she wouldn't be able to breathe from the terror, Miriam told herself. The house disappearing into the night seemed totally possible with the sounds the storm was making. She must trust the Lord!

Long moments passed, and no light appeared above them. Uncle William looked up at the basement ceiling as silence slowly fell outside. He withdrew himself from Aunt Fannie's embrace and handed her baby Jonathon, who wrinkled up his face but no wails came.

After several minutes of quiet, Uncle William said, "We'd better go up and see what's left." He moved toward the stairs. "Prepare yourselves though. I'm sure it won't be pretty."

Miriam's knees were still trembling as they approached the door. Uncle William unbolted it, and they stepped into the kitchen. Oddly, the first thing Miriam noticed were the supper dishes sitting undisturbed where they'd left them. She glanced out the kitchen window and gasped. Debris lay everywhere. The greenhouse was entirely gone. Ripped greenery and broken pots were everywhere. The mess extended out to the road and into the field beyond.

"Yep, looks like we lost the greenhouse," Uncle William said stoically.

Aunt Fannie slipped her arm around Uncle William's waist and leaned against him as they stared where their business once stood. Neither of them said anything more as they gazed out over the scene. In Aunt Fannie's arms, baby Jonathon also remained silent.

Miriam pushed open the front door. The shock of the destruction settled deeply in her heart. She couldn't imagine how Uncle William and Aunt Fannie must feel. There was no insurance or extra money to fix the damage. Surely the community would rally to their aid. Still...She looked up at the roofline of the house. Shingles had been torn off, but no other damage was evident. The house had been spared. The Lord had been with them even with the loss of the greenhouse. Uncle William's barn still stood, and only a few of the windows were smashed from what she could see.

Miriam searched the distance. The trees to the south and west were flattened to the ground. It was as if the prairie had reclaimed its own, opening up the countryside right into Clarita. Where houses and streets should have been, there was a path of debris tossed and thrown about. The metal water tower once in the center of the town lay to the north, twisted into a massive steel pretzel. Miriam's head spun when she realized that her schoolhouse lay directly beyond the horizon on a straight path of devastation. Had it been destroyed? "It can't be," the cry escaped Miriam's lips. "And what of the people in Clarita? And what of Wayne?" She wanted to know immediately!

Miriam's hands trembled as she reentered the house. Uncle William passed her on his way outside. Aunt Fannie sat at the kitchen table with little Jonathon in her lap. Her eyes were bright with tears, but her face showed courage and resolve. "We will make it through this, Miriam. We will."

Miriam nodded, afraid to trust her voice at the moment.

"Were our neighbors hit?" Aunt Fannie asked.

Miriam tried to keep her voice steady. "I think so. The town looks pretty bad. I'm worried about the schoolhouse. I'd like to go see if it's still standing."

"You should," Aunt Fannie agreed. "I will go with you, and we can swing by the town afterward to see if anyone needs help."

"That's not necessary," Miriam protested. "You and Uncle William have enough on your minds right here."

Aunt Fannie stood and touched Miriam's arm. "There's not much I can do here now. I too want to know how your schoolhouse fared."

"I'll get Sally ready then," Miriam said. She turned and left the house. She entered the barn to the wild whinny of the horses. How had Wayne fared with his family's horses? Miriam wondered. His parents were gone on a trip. Surely Wayne had been able to handle things well. Miriam approached Sally's stall and quieted her with soft strokes on her neck. "It's over now and nothing happened that the Lord can't take care of," she said soothingly. Her words calmed the horse, and Miriam led Sally out of her stall. At the barn door, Sally balked. Miriam whispered in the horse's ear, "We need to see about my schoolhouse before it's totally dark. And some townspeople might need our help." After a loud whinny, Sally settled down.

Together Miriam and Aunt Fannie hitched the horse to the buggy and climbed in. As they drove out of the lane, Miriam saw Uncle William's form among the ruins of the greenhouse. He stood, his hands in his pockets, gazing over the damage.

"The poor man," Aunt Fannie's voice choked. "He's lost so much."

"Shouldn't you be with him?" Miriam asked. "I can run over to the schoolhouse alone. I can check on the town too."

"William needs to be by himself for a bit," Aunt Fannie said.

Miriam nodded and drove slowly out of the lane. She had to

concentrate because Sally threw her head up and sidestepped a few times in fright at the debris scattered along the way. Miriam kept a firm grip on the lines as they turned onto State Route 48. In the distance, the wail of sirens hung in the air. Red and blue lights appeared from the direction of Coalgate. Aunt Fannie clutched baby Jonathon tightly to her chest. "Do you think there were any deaths tonight?"

"I hope not," Miriam said, shuddering but keeping her eyes fixed on the road. She soon turned Sally toward the schoolhouse and tried to see across the branch-strewn fields. Uncle William had prayed for the safety of people's lives, but he hadn't asked for the protection of buildings or trees. Perhaps that would have been too much to ask? The Lord's wrath displayed in the weather could not be totally contained, and the destruction of Clarita lay in plain sight before them. They both stared but said nothing.

There was another turn of the road as they approached the schoolhouse lot. Miriam kept her eyes averted. She wanted to see, but now that she was here, her courage had fled away. Aunt Fannie's gasp made Miriam look up. The schoolhouse was gone. Not a piece of wall stood upright in the tangled mess. Where the playground had been, glass was scattered. Pieces of the swing set and wood fragments stuck out of the ground across a neighbor's field. It was as if a giant had crushed the building in his hands and then torn the pieces apart in his fury.

A moan escaped her mouth as Miriam pulled Sally to a stop. Only hours ago, she had left this place. The children had played here today and studied. Now the building was gone. The play equipment was gone.

"We can build again." Aunt Fannie's hand touched Miriam's arm. "The community will rally. We can be thankful that no one was at the school. That would have happened if the storm had come earlier."

"There's a shelter in the basement," Miriam whispered, realizing that would have been scant protection. Obviously the schoolhouse had been in the direct path of the tornado. How like Aunt Fannie to point out the hand of protection from the Lord even in this tragedy and to find a reason to give thanks.

They sat in silence in the buggy for a long time. Finally Aunt Fannie's hand tugged on Miriam's arm. "We should go back now."

Aunt Fannie was right. They should get back. Life had to go on. That was the way the Lord made things, and they must accept His power and grace. Miriam had always looked on this land as a place of promise, a place where her heart might find rest and peace. The storm today hadn't been part of that promise, but there would still be God's grace even when one's expectations remained unfulfilled. In the end, the Lord's hand would serve only what was best.

Twenty minutes later, Miriam pulled into their driveway. Uncle William came out of the greenhouse ruins at a fast pace, his face shadowed by grief. Miriam knew she could do little to comfort her uncle's heart. The family's tragedy was great, and from the intense activity of the rescue vehicles in Clarita, their neighbors may well have suffered even greater losses. The memory of her demolished schoolhouse appeared dim now when compared to the thoughts of people trapped in their homes. Some may have even died.

"Dear Lord, comfort all our hearts tonight," Aunt Fannie whispered a quick prayer beside Miriam on the buggy seat.

Uncle William met them near the barn door. "Don't unhitch," he ordered in a weary voice. "We must go see if we can help our neighbors."

Aunt Fannie didn't hesitate. "I was thinking the same thing. We should take food perhaps. We still have supper on the table."

"Can it be taken?" Uncle William glanced toward the back of the buggy.

"*Yah*," Aunt Fannie answered. "Some of the food at least. We'll go get it ready."

"Let us leave soon. People will need help," Uncle William said. "I'll get a shovel and pry bar from the barn."

Miriam shuddered at the images in her mind—twisted timbers, fallen masonry walls, people trapped in the debris. Uncle William was right, she was sure. They had prayed for safety, but the Lord did what He thought best. She must not question His ways, regardless of how wrong or destructive His choices seemed. The Lord often chose a direction mankind could not understand. In the end, though, He always gave a blessing.

Miriam hurried after Aunt Fannie.

Uncle William tied Sally to the hitching post and disappeared into the barn.

"Let's see, how shall we do this?" Aunt Fannie placed Baby Jonathon on a blanket beside the stove and rubbed her forehead.

"We can take the bowls of food. Someone among the *Englisha* will surely have a portable gas stove we can heat it with."

"They'll have disposable plates and utensils to eat with too," Miriam suggested.

"*Yah*, that would be right." Aunt Fannie began to move with quick motions. "And we must take coffee. They will have pots and cups, but we will need some grounds to make it. This will be a long night unless I miss my guess."

Miriam loaded up with the bowls of food and made a trip to the buggy. Uncle William had placed tools in the back, but he was nowhere around. Sally turned her head to stare at her, as if she couldn't understand all the fuss. "There is much trouble afoot," Miriam told her.

Sally nickered softly.

"Don't be frightened with all the noise and lights in town." Miriam patted Sally's neck. "People are just trying to help, and that's how the *Englisha* do things."

Miriam turned as Aunt Fannie came from the house with her

arms filled. "There's one more load," Aunt Fannie said. "Then I'll get the baby."

The two were on the way to the house moments later. A wave of weakness swept over Miriam as they neared the front steps. Aunt Fannie stumbled on the way up. They were both near collapse from stress and tiredness, yet the night was still ahead of them. A night filled with labor and tragedy, to say nothing of further shocks. At least all at the Byler house had survived without bodily harm.

"Thank You, dear Lord, for Your grace," Miriam whispered as she gathered up the last of the food bowls and a bag of ground coffee.

Aunt Fannie had baby Jonathan wrapped in a blanket and was already at the front door. Miriam followed her aunt outside and loaded her bowls into the back of the buggy. When she finished, Aunt Fannie had climbed in while Uncle William held baby Jonathon.

"Lord, protect his eyes and ears from the destruction all around him," Uncle William prayed as he handed Jonathon up to Aunt Fannie.

"Amen!" Aunt Fannie agreed.

Miriam hopped into the back of the buggy and held on as Uncle William climbed in and urged Sally out the lane at a fast clip. Her hooves beat a steady rhythm on the pavement as they headed south on 48 and turned west at the first dirt road. The lights of emergency vehicles stabbed the darkness ahead of them. A soft glow filled the horizon as they approached Clarita.

"So how was the schoolhouse?" Uncle William asked Miriam.

"Nothing is left," Miriam said.

"I'm glad school wasn't in session," Aunt Fannie said. "No one would have survived, I'm sure."

Uncle William was about to respond when a buggy appeared on a side road. "That would be Deacon Phillips," he commented.

"There must not be too much damage to the community people if he has time to arrive and help the *Englisha*."

"Be thankful for that," Aunt Fannie said. "I have a feeling that not all our people were spared damage. We couldn't be the only ones."

"It wouldn't be the Lord's judgment if we were," Uncle William chided. "Surely you were not thinking so." He slowed Sally so the deacon's buggy could pull in front of them.

Aunt Fannie hung her head for a moment. "I will think on the Lord's grace and not His judgment tonight."

"That would be wise," Uncle William agreed.

Moments later a firefighter appeared on the road ahead of them and directed them into a nearby field. Deacon Phillips's buggy turned in to park, but Uncle William continued forward.

"Ask him about the food," Aunt Fannie spoke up.

Uncle William called out, "Whoa there, Sally," and brought the horse a quick stop.

The firefighter waved his hands and shouted. "Move on, mister."

Uncle William ignored the order. "We've brought food along… and coffee. Where should we take it?"

A pleased expression flooded the firefighter's face. "In that case, keep going another block. They have a command tent set up there. Come back here to park."

"Will do, and thank you." Uncle William clucked to encourage Sally to move forward.

Deacon Phillips hollered from the darkness, "Wait a minute!"

Uncle William pulled Sally to the side of the road, crossing a shallow ditch.

Miriam opened her buggy door as Deacon Phillips hurried toward them.

"Sorry," he said. "I don't mean to hold you up, but how are things at your house?"

Uncle William leaned out of his buggy door. "The greenhouse is completely gone, but we're all here, so the Lord be praised."

"*Yah*, that is true." Deacon Phillips caught his breath from his quick rush. "Your house is okay?"

"A few shingles are gone. The barn was spared for the most part. How is everyone at your place?" Uncle William inquired.

Deacon Phillips said, "We thought we were in danger, but the storm passed to the west of us. The town got the worse of it…and you apparently. We are not worthy to be spared, but we were."

"Miriam said the schoolhouse has been completely demolished. However, it's not a night for condemnation or judgment," Uncle William said. "We must do what we can."

"*Yah*," Deacon Phillips agreed. "Good to know about the school. Just doing what we can, that's why I came. And there are others coming behind me." Horses hooves beating pavement could be heard in the distance as if supporting Deacon Phillips's claim.

"How is everyone else in the community?" Uncle William asked.

"I don't know. I came past Bishop Wengerd's place on the way over here. They suffered quite a bit of damage to their house, but the family survived in the basement. They'll be spending the rest of the night with extended family. I suppose we'll know when the morning comes how everyone else fared."

"May the Lord give us all grace for what lies ahead," Uncle William stated. "We've got food that we best get down to the command center. Then we're coming back here to park. After that we'll see if we can find a place to help."

"Sounds good," Deacon Phillips said. "I have my tools along. I'm sure they'll have some place for us to help. The town looks pretty torn up from here."

Uncle William clucked to Sally, and they pulled back onto the road. On the street ahead of them, bright lights surrounding a tent lit up the night sky. Uncle William stopped near the front.

Miriam climbed down and reached up to take baby Jonathon.

Aunt Fannie came out of the buggy and looked around. *Englisha* were rushing about all over the place. Most of them were firefighters and police. No one paid them any attention. Aunt Fannie peered into the tent for a moment. "I guess we'll have to take care of ourselves," she said. "They do have a food table set up at the far end, but there's not much offered."

"We should have left baby Jonathon with someone," Miriam said. "I suppose that would have taken too much time."

"Food isn't the main event tonight," Uncle William told them. "However, let's put out what we have. While you do that, I'll go see where they need the most help."

While they transferred the food items inside the tent, Deacon Phillips passed them with a shovel over his shoulder and a toolbox dangling from his left hand. After they were done, Uncle William climbed back into the buggy and drove toward the parking area. Miriam followed Aunt Fannie back into the tent. Two *Englisha* ladies appeared with smiles on their grim faces.

"This is so kind of you," one of them said as they took in the food bowls. "I'm Margaret and this is Leslie. We're trying to set up for the rescue workers, but we haven't gotten very far. I know they'll be hungry soon."

Aunt Fannie smiled. "I'm Fannie Byler, and this is Miriam. That's my baby boy, Jonathon. How bad is the damage in town?"

"Bad enough," Leslie said. "I've heard about one fatality. There are no doubt more. Clarita got hit straight on."

"We're so sorry to hear that." Aunt Fannie clasped and unclasped her hands. "Should we perhaps go help search for people?"

Margaret shook her head. "There's plenty of help pouring in, and I see that more Amish are arriving. We're so grateful for the aid. Right now food is the one thing we lack. There's a utility trailer out back they brought in ten minutes ago, but I haven't had time to check what it contains. Perhaps you can help there?"

Aunt Fannie nodded.

"Do you need someone to look after the baby?" Leslie asked, concern on her face.

Aunt Fannie chuckled. "He'll be fine on a blanket in a corner that's out of the way. It's way past his bedtime, I'm thinking, so he shouldn't be any trouble."

Leslie and Margaret appeared skeptical, but they waited while Fannie set up a blanket in a nearby corner. Baby Jonathon kicked his legs but didn't protest when Aunt Fannie set him down. Miriam left the three women watching baby Jonathon and went to explore the utility trailer. Shelves of packaged food lined the walls, along with gas stoves and other small appliances she didn't know the use of. Miriam returned to the tent with several gas stoves. She set them up on the table.

Margaret and Leslie had disappeared.

"You'd best eat something," Aunt Fannie said, coming to stand by Miriam. "Crackers maybe?" Aunt Fannie followed her own suggestion, and Miriam did likewise while they heated bowls of food.

Strength slowly returned to her body as Miriam chewed on crackers spread with peanut butter. They were a poor substitute for the supper they'd anticipated hours ago, but that food must go to the rescue workers. Even then, from the looks of things, there wouldn't be enough to go around for long.

"We'll mix in ours with theirs," Aunt Fannie mused. "That should make a good start." She made a quick trip out to the trailer and returned with bags of corn chips and slices of plastic-wrapped meat. These she laid out on the table beside the bowls of food from home.

The offerings wouldn't go far, but they could ration things for a while, Miriam figured. Already she heard footsteps shuffling about outside. Soon a line of emergency response personnel was formed at the table. Miriam dipped out of the bowls in small quantities, while Fannie made coffee. People served themselves from the rest of what was available. The food was gulped down while the men and women stood. They washed down the quick meal with coffee and bottled water that Fannie brought from the trailer.

"Excellent stuff," one gruff firefighter told them. "Thanks."

"You're welcome," Aunt Fannie said. "And thank you for your help tonight."

A tear glistened in the man's eyes for a moment. "These things are hard to understand, but I'm glad to see people of faith here tonight. It comforts our hearts."

"We can all believe in the Lord," Aunt Fannie assured him as he took another gulp of water.

"How did your place fare?" the man inquired. "I assume it's outside town?"

Aunt Fannie's smile was strained. "The Lord was with us, and our lives were spared. All that was lost was our business—our greenhouse. We will rebuild if the Lord allows."

"I'm sorry to hear that," the man said. "Thanks for coming out even with your own losses."

"We wouldn't have it any other way," Aunt Fannie said.

Fifteen minutes later Miriam watched the man leave as she dipped the last of the mashed potatoes from one of the bowls. She added a dash of gravy to the plate and closed the lid. Their supper had helped, but greater things were on people's minds tonight than food. Uncle William had been right. When lives are at risk, all else dims in comparison.

Miriam stepped out of the tent to take a look out over the town's horizon. The bright lights had moved further south, so the search of the north side of town must have concluded. Uncle William and Deacon Phillips were out there somewhere. Had Wayne arrived too? He would have come if he could. She hoped the Yutzy farm hadn't suffered too much damage. She figured Wayne was safe or she would have felt it in her heart. She trusted the Lord had watched over them as He had the Byler household.

Miriam took another look at the lights over the town before she slipped back into the tent. The food line had grown longer. She hurried back to the trailer for more food to prepare. At least she was of use tonight. That was a comfort to her heart.

Chapter Thirty-One

———◆◆◆———

The morning sun had just risen above the horizon when Miriam peeked out her bedroom window. Even in the shadows of the dawn the destruction from the tornado was obvious. The heartache from last night returned with a vengeance. There would be no school today, and many in town would be in sorrow over the passing of their loved ones. The damage to hearts would take time to repair, and plenty of money would be needed to rebuild the destroyed properties. She would have to trust the Lord again this morning. She sent a quick prayer upward. "Help us all, dear Lord, and be with those who suffered the loss of loved ones last night. I know I can't begin to understand their pain, but You can." Miriam hesitated as that sober thought filled her. "Be with the hurting families," she whispered as she dressed.

She hadn't seen Wayne in town, but no doubt he'd been helping out someone…if his parents' place didn't need work. Today he'd probably stop by to check on her and to let her know how he'd fared. She figured he'd probably heard that the greenhouse had been destroyed.

Aunt Fannie was already in the kitchen, she was sure. Her aunt usually would have awakened her, but Aunt Fannie probably thought she needed the sleep after their late night. They hadn't gotten back to the house until after two o'clock in the morning. Even then sleep hadn't come easily for Miriam. The extent of the tragedy had weighed too heavily on her spirit.

Miriam paused by the bedroom window as the clip-clops of hooves sounded in the still, morning air. She strained her eyes to catch the faint outline of a buggy in the distance. Was it Wayne? She studied the buggy as it approached. The familiar gait of the horse caught her attention first. It wasn't Wayne's horse, it was Deacon Phillips's. She couldn't be mistaken. Had the deacon come to help Uncle William clean up his property? At this time of the morning after such a late night? Probably not. He must have come with other news from the community. Miriam's heart pounded at the thought. She hurried down the stairs. As she'd surmised, Aunt Fannie was busy in the kitchen.

"You should have called me," Miriam scolded gently.

Aunt Fannie smiled wearily. "There'll be plenty to do today, don't worry."

"The deacon's here," Miriam said. "He must have news."

Aunt Fannie shook her head. "Deacon Phillips is probably checking up on us. Even with what we told him last night, he would wish to check in, especially with the loss of the greenhouse. William's outside already. They can talk, and we'll hear later if there's anything we need to know."

"I suppose so," Miriam allowed as she set out the breakfast plates. Deacon Phillips must be deep in conversation with Uncle William. Maybe Aunt Fannie was right, and the deacon wanted nothing more than to check up on their well-being. That wouldn't be out of character for him. Both the deacon and his wife, Katie, had gentle hearts, and the duty of a deacon was to care for the community's people. Miriam's face fell as her thoughts turned to the destruction that lay just outside the house. Uncle William and Aunt Fannie's greenhouse was gone. Their livelihood was gone. Her aunt and uncle would struggle to make ends meet and rebuild. And there might not be as much help available from the community with other homes and barns damaged. Miriam glanced at her aunt. "I'm sorry about the greenhouse. I'd almost forgotten for a moment."

Aunt Fannie's glance was grim. "It was a tragedy, but we'll come through. We always do."

Miriam stopped in the middle of the kitchen floor as the thought raced through her mind. Why hadn't she thought of this before? The money! She could spend some of her money to help her aunt and uncle. Wayne and she wouldn't need all of the money to purchase the cattle farm. The rest could go to help with the storm damage. Wayne would agree, wouldn't he? How could he object? He said the money didn't matter to him in the first place.

Aunt Fannie was staring at Miriam when she came out of her daze. "The money! I can give you and Uncle William enough money to help rebuild the greenhouse. Then I can help other people too if they need it."

"What money?" Aunt Fannie asked, puzzled.

"The two million dollars."

Comprehension dawned on Aunt Fannie's face, which was quickly followed by doubt. "You can't do that. We can't take your money."

Miriam clasped her hands tightly. "After I help you and Uncle William, I can give some funds to Deacon Phillips to divide up for anyone else that needs help in the community. And if he needs help figuring it out, the other ministers can assist. Wayne will have no objections, I'm sure."

Aunt Fannie didn't look convinced. "You should still speak to him first."

Miriam paused. "I will, but he won't object." Joy filled her heart. "Wayne and I planned to use the money to buy a cattle farm, but there will be a lot leftover. We can use that to help people hurt by this tornado."

Aunt Fannie continued with her work. "That's an awful lot of money to let go of. An awful lot."

"I know, but it's for the best. Wayne will be right with me on that." Relief swept over Miriam.

"You're a brave woman to let go of that security," Aunt Fannie said. "But it would be a helpful decision. That much I do admit."

The clink of pots and pans filled the kitchen for the next few minutes. Aunt Fannie finally said, "I think we're ready. Call Uncle William. If Deacon Phillips is still here, call him too. He's welcome to our table."

Miriam moved toward the front door. Should she tell Deacon Phillips her plan right now before she discussed it with Wayne? Surely Wayne would join her in rejoicing that the funds would be put to such *gut* use. Perhaps this was even why the Lord had allowed her to receive the money in the first place!

Miriam opened the door and stepped out on the porch. Deacon Phillips and Uncle William were standing beside the buggy with bowed heads. Miriam stopped short. Deacon Phillips must have brought sad news. How else could the sorrow on their faces be explained? They looked up and both of them turned her way for a moment. Then they bowed their heads again.

Whatever news Deacon Phillips brought must be born with faith and hope in the Lord. This she knew, but the weight from tragedy again pressed hard on her shoulders. Miriam sagged and sat on the porch.

Uncle William took a step toward her, followed by Deacon Phillips. The two men stopped in front of her.

Miriam looked up. "You'd best tell me." Miriam's voice cracked. "I know something terrible has happened by the looks on your faces."

Deacon Phillips cleared his throat. "I wish I were not the one to bring you such news, Miriam."

"Please tell me." Miriam searched the deacon's face.

"The Yutzy place was hit hard, Miriam. As you know, only Wayne and Joy were at home. They were found this morning. Their *Englisha* neighbors went over and discovered their bodies several hundred yards from the house. Wayne was still alive, but he passed to the next life on the ride to the hospital in the ambulance. Joy was already gone when they found her." Deacon Phillips paused for a moment. "I am so sorry, Miriam. My heart is too broken for words, and yet I had to come to tell you."

"You did no wrong." Miriam's head and heart were spinning as she clutched the edge of the step for balance. "He's gone? Wayne is gone?" Miriam sobbed. She tried to collect herself. "They must have been trying to bring in the horses."

"No one will ever know what happened, Miriam." Deacon Phillips hesitated. "You must not trouble yourself with the whys of this tragedy."

"He is right," Uncle William said. Then he walked past Miriam and went into the house.

The deacon cleared his throat several times as Miriam's sobs increased. He finally reached out and touched her hand.

Miriam let go of the step and grasped his hand. They were in this awkward position when Aunt Fannie ran through the front doorway and wrapped Miriam in her arms.

"He's gone," Miriam wailed. "He's gone, Aunt Fannie!"

"I'm so sorry." Aunt Fannie held Miriam tightly. "Oh, you poor dear."

Miriam took a deep breath. "I want to go see him. I want to go to him right now."

"You can't," Deacon Phillip protested.

"Why not?" Miriam searched the deacon's face again.

Deacon Phillips stared at the ground before finally looking up. "Miriam, the funeral will be closed caskets for both of them. They were severely injured in the storm. Do not see him like this. You want to remember him as you do now. The Lord has done what He thought best, and we won't always be able to understand."

"*I will see Wayne.*" Miriam stood. She placed a trembling hand on Aunt Fannie's shoulder. "I was promised to him."

"She shouldn't do this, William." Deacon Phillips glanced at Uncle William for support.

Uncle William shrugged. "You are the deacon, but if Miriam wishes, I won't disallow it."

"I agree," Aunt Fannie said.

Deacon Phillips hesitated before he said, "The bodies were taken to a mortuary in Coalgate. They'll probably be taken to Raymond Yutzy's house. That is where the funeral will be held. Wayne and Joy's parents are on their way back from Possum Valley this morning. Your parents are coming with them, Miriam. They will be driving straight through the night, I'm thinking. The van driver will have to sleep sometime, but they should be here in less than forty-eight hours."

Uncle William nodded.

Silence fell over the four of them. Miriam's sobs had ceased, though her heart still screamed. Numbness was creeping through her body. How could this be? How could the Lord have taken Wayne? After all they'd been through? The man who had loved her despite her faults. The man who didn't care that she'd inherited a farm and money. Despair rose in her throat, and this time Miriam couldn't hold it back. The mournful sound traveled across the lawn and over the mangled forms of the timber that had once been Uncle William's greenhouse. It could be rebuilt, but Wayne's torn body would never be repaired. Miriam sobbed and allowed her body to sag. Aunt Fannie caught her before she hit the floor.

Deacon Phillips and Uncle William waited until she had calmed before they turned to walk toward the deacon's buggy. Aunt Fannie sat down on the porch and gently rocked Miriam in her arms as if she were baby Jonathon. Miriam didn't object as the now-quiet sobs moved through her body in slow convulsions. Deeper emotions than she could express tore at her spirit. Wayne was gone. This she would never understand or comprehend. Why had the Lord done this to her? Had she sinned?

Aunt Fannie seemed to read her thoughts. She whispered in Miriam's ear, "This is not a time for condemnation or judgment, dear. Remember what William said last night."

Miriam remained silent, but Aunt Fannie's words did bring some relief. If Miriam searched her heart and heaped on blame on top of everything else this morning, she would go mad. Then a thought niggled at Miriam. She waited for a few moments getting used to the idea. "*Mamm* never got to see Wayne like he was—alive, vibrant, loving. I'm glad in a way, I guess, about the closed casket. I wouldn't want *Mamm* to see him in any other way."

Aunt Fannie pulled Miriam close for another tight hug. "I'm so sorry. You should eat something before you go. You'll need your strength."

Miriam stifled her protest. She couldn't possibly stand to eat at the moment, even though she knew Aunt Fannie was right. Life did go on, and she must travel with it. "Maybe later," Miriam promised.

Aunt Fannie took Miriam's hand and led her inside. Uncle William and Deacon Phillips came in through the washroom door and seated themselves.

Miriam didn't remember Aunt Fannie calling them to breakfast, but maybe that wasn't so surprising. Her ears buzzed with each step, and the usually quiet house seemed to drone on and on and on.

Aunt Fannie helped Miriam into a kitchen chair and seated herself next to her. Across the table, Uncle William and Deacon

Phillips bowed their heads. Miriam followed their example. She couldn't eat, but prayer was needed…desperately needed. Her sobs came again as Uncle William prayed aloud:

> Oh, God, the great Ruler of heaven and earth. Our hearts cry out to You this morning in our great sorrow. We do not understand Your ways or the choices You have made. Be with us. Let not bitterness take root in our hearts. Give strength to Miriam this morning and in the days ahead. Quiet the pain in her heart as she lives through these next few hours and days. Carry her in Your loving arms. You have given us so much good in life, and now that evil has come, let us not question the mercy of Your hand.

> Oh Mighty One, You've given us Jesus, Your only begotten Son, for our redemption and for our peace. We shall never know the sorrow You felt when Christ cried out on that cruel cross, "My God, my God, why hast thou forsaken me?" We shall never be forsaken, regardless of the dark valleys we walk through or the depths to which our human spirits plunge. For this we give You thanks for the hollow of Your hand that hides us in these troubled times.

Miriam pressed Aunt Fannie's handkerchief against her face as Uncle William continued with his prayer of thanksgiving for the food. She couldn't listen any longer or hear the words even if she wanted to. The noise in her head was too loud. The Lord would understand. Was He not the God of compassion and mercy? Had He not given her Wayne's love in the first place? She would trust Him. The One who gave also had the right to take away.

"Come, you must eat," Aunt Fannie's voice whispered in Miriam's ear. The prayer had finished apparently. Uncle William and

Deacon Phillips's voices were hushed as they made plans for the day. A spoon touched her lips, and Miriam automatically opened her mouth. She was like baby Jonathon right now, helpless and unable to fend for herself. No one seemed to think this strange. She swallowed.

After a few more bites, Aunt Fannie pressed the spoon into Miriam's hand. "I'm sorry, but you must eat."

Miriam obeyed until the bowl was empty. It seemed so wrong. How could her body accept nourishment when Wayne was gone? Yet life stirred around her. The Lord still lived, and so did she. She would have to face the world.

"That's a good girl," Aunt Fannie said quietly. "Are you ready to go now?"

Miriam didn't answer, but stood up from the table. Uncle William and Deacon Phillips had gone. She hadn't noticed their departure. Baby Jonathon was in Aunt Fannie's arms, and he smiled at her.

"The breakfast dishes…" Miriam said. "We can't leave them."

Aunt Fannie didn't answer, but she gripped Miriam's arm to steer her outside. Uncle William waited with Sally and the buggy. Aunt Fannie handed baby Jonathon up to him, and then she turned to help Miriam into the back. Miriam didn't resist. She settled into the buggy seat with slow motions. Her whole body ached. The drive over to the Yutzy place was a blur of motion outside the buggy door and the soft beats of Sally's hooves on dirt roads. Aunt Fannie helped Miriam out again when they arrived, and from there into the house.

"She would see him," Aunt Fannie told Bishop Wengerd, who was standing at the front door.

"Have you not heard the condition of his body?" the bishop protested.

"She would see him," Aunt Fannie repeated firmly.

Bishop Wengerd shrugged and led them into the front bedroom

on the first floor. Miriam waited near the door, listening to the sounds of screws being turned in wood. It seemed a long time before Bishop Wengerd stepped aside. Aunt Fannie stayed by the bedroom door as Miriam approached the casket on her own. Another casket sat on the other side, and Miriam reached over briefly to touch its rough-sawn lumber. Then she gazed into the opened casket. He didn't look like her Wayne. Maybe it was best if things were this way. She would remember him as he had been—alive and in love with her.

"It is enough," Miriam said to no one particular. She turned from the casket. Aunt Fannie caught her just before she slipped to the floor.

Miriam struggled to stay aware, barely realizing Aunt Fannie was holding her up. She didn't say anything as Aunt Fannie guided her into the living room and into a chair. She would stay here until the funeral was over. That would be the day after tomorrow perhaps. She would not move from the house or from Wayne's side until they lowered him into the ground. She'd lost him and would say goodbye, depending on God and on memories of Wayne to get her through. That she would always have. Memories. That would have to be enough apparently. The Lord had so willed it, and one did not argue with Him.

Chapter Thirty-Two

———◆◆◆———

Miriam awoke with a start in the upstairs bedroom of the strange house. The faint light of dawn was on the horizon, but the rays of sunlight had yet to penetrate past the drapes across the window. She remembered she was at Wayne's Uncle Raymond's house, and today was Wayne's funeral. She hadn't wanted to sleep, but Raymond's wife, Louise, had insisted that she climb the stairs in the wee hours of the morning.

"Try to shut your eyes at least," Louise had begged. "You need your strength for tomorrow."

Like she needed food, Miriam told herself, the thought bitter. But Louise was right. *Mamm* and *Daett* would be here this morning, along with Wayne and Joy's parents, Eugene and Rosemary. The traveling party all the way from Possum Valley would be more exhausted than she was, even if her whole body ached to the bone. They should be here soon. Miriam stood and pushed aside the drapes on the window. A van was parked below, and several figures had climbed out. The familiar forms of *Mamm* and *Daett* brought a sharp intake of breath. The arrival of the van must have been what had awakened her. Miriam pinned her *kapp* on her head and hurried down the dark stairwell.

"They're here!" Louise whispered from near the kitchen doorway. "I was ready to come up and awaken you."

Miriam nodded and followed Louise outside. The crisp coolness of the morning air flooded over her face and dried the tears that had formed on her cheeks. *Mamm* came toward her with her arms opened wide, and Miriam ran the last few steps to meet her. With a loud sob, she let herself be wrapped in her *mamm*'s arms. "He's gone, *Mamm*! He's gone!" Miriam wailed. "And you never got to meet him."

"I know," *Mamm* comforted. "But we must not question the will of the Lord even as we sorrow in our hearts."

"I'm not." Miriam choked back another sob. "But Wayne is still gone."

Mamm said nothing more but continued to hold Miriam tightly.

Moments later *Daett* cleared his throat loudly beside them. "Eugene and Rosemary also mourn," he reminded. "They have gone into the house, and you should be with them."

Miriam pushed away from *Mamm* with a start, but *Mamm* held on to her arm. They walked together toward the front porch. Miriam had meant no disrespect by running straight to *Mamm* instead of greeting Wayne's parents. They would understand, she was sure. She'd been Wayne's promised one, but that was now in the past. Still, until the funeral was completed, she would function in that role. She must act like the life they'd planned was still real. *Mamm* had been right, though. The Lord could change anyone's plans without any prior consultation. She would have to submit her will afresh today as final goodbyes were made. It would not be easy.

Miriam leaned into *Mamm* as *Daett* held open the front door for them. Wayne and Joy's parents had disappeared into a back bedroom. Soft sobs drifted from behind the closed door. They would also want to see what she had seen—and see Joy too. Miriam knew it wouldn't be any easier for them than it had been for her. Likely they would feel the pain even harder than she did. Had they not birthed and loved both of their children into adulthood? She had only known Wayne for a short time, yet in that time a great love had grown between them. A love that had already weathered a fierce storm. Death was one storm that didn't give back what it took. The sobs from beneath the bedroom door increased. Miriam glanced at *Mamm*. "Should I go in?"

Daett cleared his throat, but *Mamm* spoke first. "Let them have a time alone. You can be with them soon enough."

Miriam didn't press the point. She wouldn't be much comfort to Eugene and Rosemary anyway. Not with the pain still ablaze in her own heart.

"Why not tell us about him?" *Mamm* whispered while they waited.

Tears stung Miriam's eyes again. The last thing she wanted right now was to think of the *gut* times she used to spend with Wayne…or Wayne's *wunderbah* qualities that *Mamm* would never get to experience.

Mamm pressed a handkerchief into Miriam's hands. "Please tell us. I know it's hard, but it won't get any easier later. And it will help us."

Mamm was probably right, Miriam told herself. The memories of the life she used to live with Wayne could easily turn into bitterness if she held it all inside with the hope the pain would decrease on its own.

"I loved him," Miriam began. "But you already know that."

"*Yah.*" *Mamm*'s hand touched Miriam's gently. "You told us that much when you came home after Shirley's accident. Can you share a special time you had with him? If it's not too personal, of course."

Miriam swallowed twice, but her voice still came out a whisper. "There's a little place down by a creek not far from here, down near the schoolhouse. Wayne took me there that first fall when he asked me to be his *frau*. He took me there again this spring when things were a little rough for me." Miriam's voice caught. She paused as the downstairs bedroom door opened. Wayne's *Daett* came out first, Rosemary right behind, hanging onto his arm. Their faces were tear-stained. *Mamm* helped Miriam to stand, and Miriam was thankful because she couldn't have done so on her own. Not right after she'd spoken such personal memories about Wayne. *Daett* had also stood, and he led the two of them forward.

Rosemary let go of Eugene's arm and hurried toward Miriam, taking her into her arms for a tight hug. "You've been so brave," Rosemary whispered in Miriam's ear. "I didn't mean to ignore you when we came in, but I wished to see my son and daughter."

"I understand." Miriam assured her. "And I'm so sorry for your loss."

"We're in this together." Rosemary gave Miriam another long hug before she moved on to the kitchen.

Daett had been in a whispered conversation with Eugene and now turned to Miriam. "Come, daughter," he said. "We must pray before the funeral begins. My heart is much troubled about this matter."

"This matter?" What had Eugene told *Daett*? Miriam wondered. No doubt the conditions of the bodies spoke of the great wrath of the storm. That likely reflected the Lord's wrath. *Daett* would think so at least. Uncle William had assured her that such thoughts of blame should not be entertained. She would not protest, Miriam decided, but her heart would stand firm in the conviction that the Lord had His reasons for the tragedy. The fault did not lie with any-one in the community. *Daett* would have to find the answers to such questions on his own. She would pray. That she could always do whatever the reason.

Mamm's arm slipped around Miriam's shoulders as they knelt by the couch beside *Daett*. Miriam saw Rosemary glance out the kitchen doorway with a look of understanding on her face. Miriam forced herself to bow her head and focus on *Daett's* prayer as his voice rose and fell quietly in the living room:

> Dear God in heaven, You who ride the winds of the storm and speak with Your fierce wrath. Have mercy upon Your children today. Forgive us our trespasses as we have forgiven those who trespassed against us. Hold not our iniquities to our account, and look kindly on Your children here in Oklahoma. Thank You for a safe journey these last forty-eight hours when so many things could have gone wrong. We have arrived safely by the grace of Your hand. Be with us now as we face this new day and say our last goodbyes to a brother and a sister who have been much loved this side of eternity. We believe You hold them in Your arms even now and lay before them all the glories of heaven as befits Your will. Have compassion on us who remain behind. Comfort the hearts that grieve. Amen.

Miriam stood and wiped her eyes, as did *Mamm*. *Daett's* prayer comforted her. At least he hadn't laid blame on anyone, and had only asked for forgiveness. Who didn't need forgiveness? That was a daily prayer they all prayed. Hadn't Wayne shown her that they both needed to walk in understanding and tenderness toward any weaknesses found in the other? At the thought, a quiet sob rose in Miriam's throat again. She leaned against *Mamm*, who helped her to the couch. *Daett* had gone outside, so only the two of them were in the living room.

More people would arrive soon. Breakfast would be brought in by the community's women, and benches would be brought and set up in the living room for the funeral. She didn't want to see any of that. She didn't want to say the goodbyes that lay ahead. Yet the moment would come.

As if someone was reading her thoughts, a buggy drove into the lane. Two others soon followed. Deacon Phillips's wife, Katie, was the first of the other guests to enter the front door. She carried a large, covered plate in her hands.

"*Gut* morning," Katie's soft voice greeted gently even as her face remained sober. "This must be your *mamm*, Miriam."

"*Yah*, it is." Miriam was on her feet and belatedly made the introductions.

Mamm shook hands with Katie.

"You have a *wunderbah* daughter," Katie said, a slight smile playing on her face for a moment. "She is much-loved in the community. We all mourn with her."

"I can't thank you enough." *Mamm* wiped away a tear. "It's such a comfort to arrive after a long drive and find that your daughter has been in such *gut* hands. You have been a great blessing to Miriam. Why the Lord chose to take away so much, we will never understand."

Katie nodded. "Yet we will comfort ourselves that the Lord loves those He chastens. We have been chastened greatly these last days, and we humble our hearts to accept both the *gut* and the difficult from His hands."

"I agree," *Mamm* said. "Let me take your plate," she offered.

Katie held fast the plate. "No, others are coming to help, and you're not to move a finger as our guest. Other than to eat and prepare for the service, of course. You must be exhausted after all those hours on the road. I see your driver has fallen asleep in the van already. The poor man must have been exhausted."

"*Yah*, the driver did *gut*," *Mamm* agreed. "The Lord was with us.

We sang and prayed when sleep became a problem. And he'd stop and nap when necessary.

"Should we awaken him for breakfast?" Katie asked.

"He will probably be hungry." *Mamm* glanced out the window. "Let me go and ask once the food is ready."

"It'll only be a few minutes." Katie turned and opened the front door for several other community women. They greeted Miriam, and she introduced *Mamm*. Then the women hurried on to the kitchen.

Miriam took a seat on the couch again, and *Mamm* went to speak with the van driver. Miriam felt a wave of weariness sweep over her, and things became a blur. The plate of eggs, bacon, and toast that Katie brought her ten minutes later never came into focus, and Miriam managed to eat. She moved upstairs when the men brought in the benches and began to set up for the service. The noises downstairs continued for a long time.

Mamm found Miriam in the upstairs bedroom an hour later. "Come, it's time to change," *Mamm* told her.

Miriam managed to stand on her own. She lifted a black dress from the closet rod. Aunt Fannie had brought her the mourning clothes the day before. Tears flooded Miriam's eyes again. *Mamm* quietly helped her change as if she were a small girl. In some ways she was, Miriam thought.

Dressed and as ready as she ever would be, Miriam followed *Mamm* downstairs. The benches for the family were set up near the back bedroom. Miriam took her place beside Rosemary. The extended Yutzy family, including children, gathered on benches behind them.

The ministers filed in, and the service began. Miriam tried to listen, but the words pushed themselves together in her mind until the voices were soft buzzes. Time slipped by quickly, as if the Lord was revealing His mercy by the tears that fell to the hardwood floor under Miriam's feet. The usual viewing of the bodies didn't happen. Instead, the family stood and led the way outside.

Miriam drove with *Daett* and *Mamm* in a buggy Deacon Phillips had supplied for them, but at the graveyard she took her place beside Rosemary.

Bishop Wengerd stepped forward and with bowed head and clasped hands led out in the final prayer. The wind moved across the prairie, but this time Miriam could make sense of most of the words. When he was finished, both caskets were lowered into the ground and dirt was thrown on them. Miriam kept her sobs quiet, and Rosemary leaned into her.

When the graveside service was done, the people walked together back to the buggies. *Mamm* appeared in front of Miriam, slowed down, and took her daughter's hand. Miriam sank against *Mamm*, who waited until Miriam could continue. *Daett* walked up on the other side of Miriam, and between the two of them they helped her into the borrowed buggy. The long line of buggies began to move. Miriam thought she saw Wayne's buggy ahead of them. Who would be driving his buggy today? she wondered. Likely she would see Wayne in everything for a long time— unless the Lord healed her heart quickly.

"Help me, Lord, please," Miriam begged as *Daett* drove.

Mamm, sitting beside her, held her hand until they arrived back at the Yutzy home. Miriam whispered, "I have to go on with life now."

"I want you to," *Mamm* assured her. "We just have to help each other through the rough spots."

"The Lord will help us," *Daett* said as he brought the buggy to a stop by the barn. "We'll continue to pray for you, Miriam, and to seek the Lord's guidance."

"Thank you," Miriam told him. "And thank you for coming to Oklahoma."

"I wouldn't have it any other way," *Daett* said. "The Lord will be with you, Miriam. As I know He already has in mind whatever lies on the road of life ahead of you."

Miriam lowered her head and hurried toward the house. *Mamm* walked closely beside her. *Daett's* kind words brought fresh tears to her eyes, but Miriam had cried enough for one day.

Chapter Thirty-Three

———◆◆◆———

The late-evening shadows were creeping across the lawn when Miriam stepped out of Deacon Phillips's walkout basement door. A weary smile spread across her face at the sight of her horse, Sally, tied to the hitching post. Deacon Phillips's *frau*, Katie, had gone out of her way all week to make sure everyone was comfortable and felt welcome for the last week of school—including Miriam. School was being held in temporary quarters in their basement.

Wayne's funeral was in the past, and Miriam had struggled to gather herself together these past days. Life must go on. That Sally should be hitched up and ready when she was done working late this Friday night didn't surprise her. Katie must have encouraged Deacon Phillips to do the task. Miriam decided Katie deserved a moment of her time and a hearty thanks. She walked up the incline to the house and knocked on the front door.

"Come in!" a cheery voice called out.

Miriam opened the door and stuck her head in. "You didn't have to arrange to hitch-up Sally, but thanks! And also thank you for the help and encouragement all week. You and Deacon Phillips have been so kind."

Katie appeared in the kitchen doorway. "You know we wouldn't have it any other way after your great losses—Wayne, Joy, and the schoolhouse."

"But it's still so nice of you."

Katie smiled. "Well, you have a *gut* evening now. I'm sure you're enjoying having your *mamm* and *daett* around. The Lord must have gone out of His way to comfort your heart."

"*Yah*, He has. Thanks again!" Miriam closed the door and walked toward her buggy. She untied the rope, tossed it under the buggy seat, and climbed in. Once inside, Miriam settled in and drove out of the lane toward Route 48. The low profiles of the few homes and buildings left undamaged in Clarita appeared on the horizon. *Daett* and other men from the Amish community had worked in town the past few days to help the *Englisha*. They'd also been working on the wrecked schoolhouse site. Just last night Uncle William had told her the basement walls should be up today.

She should drive past and see for herself. The jaunt might help buoy her spirit, which was still reeling with the pain of losing Wayne. A cloud crossed Miriam's face, and, instead, she headed Sally toward home. Maybe she would make the trip tomorrow. Tonight she would stay home and rest. A weary body didn't help a weary and sorrow-filled mind recover any sooner.

There was also the matter of the upcoming conversation with *Mamm* and *Daett*. She still needed to reveal her secret. She'd pushed the subject to the back of her mind all week, using the extra work on her shoulders at school as an excuse. But she needed to settle the matter of giving to the relief effort. She wanted to get their opinion on what to do about the money, but first they had to be told about it. Aunt Fannie or Uncle William hadn't told them because *Daett* would have brought up the subject himself. The shock when *Daett* was told could be considerable, and she hated to have him know she'd been hiding such a secret so soon after the funeral, but there seemed no other way. She'd already waited too long.

What a mess. *Daett* had spoken so kindly to her after the funeral, but he had strong feelings about money, and he might not easily overlook her keeping this knowledge from him. What a relief it would be once he'd been told. He'd decide what to do with it after that. Wasn't giving to help rebuild the community a chance of a lifetime? And for such a decent cause, the Lord must have played a part in the matter. Help was desperately needed in this time of sorrow.

Miriam sighed and turned her thoughts elsewhere. *Daett* and *Mamm* had told her some *gut* news this week. *Mamm* claimed Shirley was doing much better lately, and that a nice, young, Amish man by the name of Glen Weaver had started paying her attention at the *rumspringa* gatherings. That was *gut* news indeed.

Miriam pulled Sally to a stop at Highway 48. She looked both ways before she guided Sally north. *Daett* would have to be faced tonight. She would always have regrets if she didn't speak with him while he was in Oklahoma. He'd be busy again tomorrow, and there was a potluck supper in Clarita for everyone in the evening. That had also been Katie's idea—to show appreciation for the help with the cleanup everyone had given, but especially for the men from the community. The *Englisha* people would also participate. Due to the entire ruckus, the picnic for the last day of school had been postponed until next week. Hopefully things would calm down a bit by then.

Through it all, Katie had been a jewel. If someday she could only be half the *frau* that Katie was…But why think about that now? Wayne was gone. Miriam bit her lower lip. Perhaps she would never be a *frau*. It was in the Lord's hands, and she would trust Him. That she could do.

Miriam pulled into her driveway and drove past the empty space where the greenhouse had been. The few sections still standing would be pulled down. Uncle William thought that was the best plan, and the other workers had agreed. The whole building would be rebuilt soon—once most of the immediately needed cleanups in the area had been addressed.

Miriam stopped by the barn and climbed out of the buggy. She unhitched as another thought raced through her mind. Uncle William would have to raise the money for his greenhouse by some other means if she didn't contribute what he needed. He probably hadn't even considered that she had money available. He was too decent a man to let his personal needs influence her financial decisions. She pushed open the barn door and led Sally inside. With a groan, Miriam pulled off the harness and put it on its hooks. She placed Sally in her stall. A quick glance around showed her that Uncle William had left the outside door open where fresh grass was available. Uncle William didn't want the horses fed oats, he'd told her again this week. There were nutrients enough in the open fields. Sally, though, waited by the grain box and nickered.

Miriam reached in to pat her neck. "You'll be okay. Just go outside to eat."

Sally tossed her head and looked out the open door, as if she understood.

With a final pat, Miriam left the horse and walked to the house. Aunt Fannie and *Mamm* had most of the supper dishes on the table. They greeted Miriam with smiles tinged with sorrow.

"Working late, I see," Aunt Fannie said.

"*Yah*, but I'm here now." Miriam returned their smiles. "What can I do to help?"

"We're almost finished." *Mamm* glanced out of the kitchen window. "And here come the men now. Sit down and fill us in on school news."

Miriam did so and straightened the edge of the tablecloth with one hand. "I can do something and talk at the same time. Besides there's not much news—just the same stuff under more difficult circumstances. You both know how things are in school. Katie goes out of her way to make everyone feel welcome. I'm very thankful for her help. She even had her husband get Sally hitched-up for me tonight."

"Everyone is trying to help," Aunt Fannie agreed. She placed the last dish on the table and sat down.

Mamm joined them. "Something's troubling you, Miriam," *Mamm* said matter-of-factly. "Are you still thinking of Wayne?"

"*Yah*." Miriam produced a crooked smile. "But I also need to speak with *Daett* and you about something important tonight. I need to confess to something I should have brought up a long time ago."

Aunt Fannie sighed but nodded approvingly.

Mamm looked at Miriam with alarm. "What is it, Miriam?"

"I want to wait until *Daett* is here so I only have to explain once. I've done something wrong," Miriam said.

"I wouldn't say it quite like that." Aunt Fannie reached over to squeeze Miriam's arm. "It's not life-threatening, you know. I do agree you need to let your *mamm* and *daett* know."

There was a rattle at the washroom door and then came the sounds the men made as they cleaned up. Miriam took the next few moments to ponder how best to tell her parents. She still hadn't decided when the men came in and sat at the table. They looked weary.

"So much damage," Uncle William admitted. "But the Lord has given us the strength to work, and we are grateful for that."

"I agree," *Daett* added. "We have much we can be thankful for, even when tragedy strikes."

"Let us pray now." Uncle William bowed his head and led out in prayer.

When the "Amen" came, everyone raised their heads. Silence settled over the table as the food was passed around. Even Aunt

Fannie, who usually had something to say, was quiet. Aunt Fannie nodded to Miriam.

She took a deep breath. Now was the time to speak up. With food in front of him, perhaps *Daett*'s reaction might be less severe. And the presence of Uncle William and Aunt Fannie wouldn't hurt either. Miriam passed the mashed potatoes and took another deep breath. "I have something I want to speak with you about, *Daett* and *Mamm*."

"Oh?" *Daett* said without looking up.

Miriam spoke quickly. "*Yah*. It's something I should have told you a long time ago." She paused. That was an understatement, but she had to begin her confession somewhere.

Daett dipped out two big scoops of mashed potatoes onto his plate. "You have done something wrong?"

"Not really," Aunt Fannie interjected. She fell silent after *Daett*'s quick glance toward her.

Miriam forced the words out. "I'm afraid I didn't tell you everything back when Mr. Bland died and left me the farm. He also left me money. Lots of it, in fact. I really should have told you both sooner, but it seemed like...like..." Her voice trailed off.

Daett's gaze was stern. "Mr. Bland left you the farm *and* money?"

Miriam nodded.

"A few thousand dollars or what?" *Daett* asked, his spoonful of food suspended mid-air.

"Two million dollars," Miriam said, relieved that secret keeping was over.

"Two million!" *Daett*'s spoon clattered to his plate. "I don't believe this!" He stared at his daughter.

"It's true," Uncle William confirmed. "Miriam told us about it soon after she came out here."

"But I was not told?" A stunned, hurt look spread across *Daett*'s face.

Miriam's words came out in a burst. "I wasn't trying to do

wrong by you, *Daett*. I really wasn't. It all happened so fast, and you've always said money can ruin people. It seemed best to break the news to people a bit at a time. After all, inheriting the farm itself was a huge thing in the community. And then Ivan Mast made enough problems for me just knowing about the farm. I can't imagine what would've happened if he and everyone else found out about the money too."

Daett shook his head. "You possess two million dollars? My daughter has that much money?"

"*Yah*, I do." Miriam reached across the table to grasp his arm. "In fact, with the interest it's earning, the amount is probably quite a bit more. I still think of it as 'the two million' though. I'm sorry I didn't tell you and *Mamm* sooner. It's been a horrible burden for me to bear because I know how you feel about money. Will you forgive me? I'm so sorry I waited so long. I really am."

"You have sinned with this money?" *Daett* asked as he studied her face closely.

"No!" Miriam gasped. "No! I haven't done anything with it. It's sitting in the bank."

"She wants to give some of the money away," Aunt Fannie put in.

Daett was still facing Miriam. "Did Wayne know about the money? Is that why he was marrying you?"

"Of course not," Miriam said at once. "He did know, but he didn't care. He loved me before he knew about it."

"I think we'd better finish supper and let the news sink in," Uncle William interrupted. "We can talk about this later in the living room."

Daett thought about that for a moment before picking up his spoon. "I think those are wise words."

Silence fell as they ate. Miriam kept her gaze on the table and took deep breaths several times to keep back the tears. She knew her parents were in shock, and it was her fault. She should have told them from the beginning. Knowing how *Daett* felt about money had made it difficult. And now he was thinking the worst about Wayne. How could she have messed things up like this?

"Let us give thanks for the food," Uncle William finally said when everyone was finished. They all bowed their heads. With the prayer finished, Miriam stood and went with everyone into the living room. She sank onto the couch between *Mamm* and Aunt Fannie.

"You've not done wrong with this money," *Mamm* whispered into Miriam's ear. "*Daett* knows that, and I know that."

Miriam held still as *Daett* cleared his throat. "To say this is a great shock to me is an understatement. I cannot believe this kind of deception was going on right under my nose. My daughter is given two million dollars. She moves to Oklahoma and tells my sister-in-law and brother-in-law about it. Then she becomes engaged to a man whom she tells also. All this, and still I am not told."

"I'm so sorry," Miriam said again. "I should have told you, but my heart was much troubled. I knew how you felt about money, and I knew how Ivan had reacted to the news about just the farm. When I came out here, I met Wayne…Wayne loved *me*, *Daett*. I'm sure of that."

Daett didn't appear convinced, but he nodded. "I wouldn't wish to speak ill of the man. I never met him, after all. We will leave that for now. What the Lord has done cannot be undone. The future lies before us, and in it we must make the right choices. So Fannie said you want to give some of this money away now that Wayne is gone?"

"Wayne and I talked about what to do with it. And after the tornado I immediately thought of helping people rebuild. I didn't have time to tell Wayne before I found out he'd been killed." Miriam paused. "With Wayne gone, I'd like your help in deciding what to do. I wasn't sure before, but now I know what I'd like to do."

"Then let us decide now, and turn this potential evil into a *gut* thing." *Daett* leaned forward. "What is your idea?"

"I want to give the money to the community to rebuild after the tornado," Miriam said.

Daett sat back and considered the proposal.

Miriam continued. "Perhaps this was the very reason the Lord allowed this to happen. As Mordecai said to Esther, 'Who knoweth whether thou art come to the kingdom for such a time as this?'"

"All of the money or just some?" *Daett* asked.

"All of it, I think. If that's what you suggest."

"Then you will be rid of the money," *Daett* said. "And there will be no more secrets?"

"No more secrets," Miriam assured him.

Uncle William spoke up. "We can drive over right now and speak with Deacon Phillips."

"This can wait," *Mamm* protested. "Miriam is tired and heartsick..."

Miriam kept her voice steady. "I'll go. It needs to be done. And *Daett* and you are here to go with me. That will make things much easier."

Mamm didn't appear convinced, but *Daett* gave her a sharp nod. Any further words from *Mamm* died in her mouth.

Miriam forced herself to stand up. Her legs wobbled a bit. "I'll change then. My dress collar is wet from my tears, I'm sure."

Daett shook his head. "That's not necessary. A few tear stains in this situation are nothing to be ashamed of. Deacon Phillips will understand after we explain."

The thought of the coming conversation made the tears come again, but Miriam held them back. Deacon Phillips's *frau* would be there. Katie would bring comfort.

Aunt Fannie had risen to her feet and now spoke up. "We should also go with them, William. They are our guests. I don't want Miriam and her parents to drive over there alone at night."

Uncle William didn't object to his *frau*'s suggestion. "If that's all right with everyone?" He looked at Miriam and her parents.

When they gave their agreement, he continued. "I'll get Sally harnessed to the spring wagon so we can all ride together. There will be room enough."

Daett nodded and followed Uncle William out the door. Aunt Fannie pulled Miriam tightly against her body. She let go when baby Jonathon wailed from the bedroom. She smiled. "He's awakened from his nap just in time to go along."

"All this fuss woke him." Miriam groaned. "I'm sorry to cause such a disturbance."

Aunt Fannie silenced Miriam with a quick look. "Let's not hear any more of that talk. You have plenty of reasons to cry, and that was quite a serious discussion. I'd be bawling my eyes out myself if I were in your shoes."

Miriam held back the tears as Aunt Fannie left for the bedroom. Her aunt returned in moments with a diaper bag in one hand and the sleepy-eyed baby nestled in her arm.

"I'll take him!" Miriam said. She reached for him, and he immediately snuggled against her shoulder.

Aunt Fannie steered everyone out the front door. Uncle William had Sally hitched to the large spring wagon when they arrived. *Daett* was already in the front seat. Miriam waited until Aunt Fannie had climbed into the back before she handed baby Jonathon up to her. *Mamm* climbed up next. With a glance at *Daett's* sober face, Miriam pulled herself up and sat on a wagon seat that faced Aunt Fannie and *Mamm*.

"I'm glad you've made this choice, Miriam." *Daett* had partially turned around to speak as Uncle William drove out of the lane and south on Highway 48.

"Wayne would want this too," she responded.

Daett didn't say anything for a moment. Then he chided, "You must never again come close to money, Miriam. Never! It corrupts the soul and everything it touches. I'm going to get rid of that farm

Mr. Bland gave you once you get home. I believe I've been corrupted myself by all this."

Miriam clasped her hands together in desperation. "I don't think that's a good idea, *Daett*. We need the income. You can't sell the farm on your own anyway. It's set up as a trust for the family."

Daett regarded Miriam with a troubled look. "That it is, but I can no longer excuse the situation on technicalities. You must sell the place, Miriam, and give the money to those who are in desperate need. There's a Haiti mission near Berlin that can place the funds to *gut* use if you have no other thoughts."

"But our family…" she tried again.

"We must trust the Lord." *Daett*'s face was resolute.

"Mr. Bland did nothing wrong by leaving me the money," Miriam protested.

"Perhaps not." *Daett* studied Miriam for a moment. "But look at all that has happened to you." *Daett* waved his hand about. "And there's the matter of Ivan Mast. Once we've taken care of the money and farm problems, I'll speak to him once we get back. If he has repented of his love of money, perhaps there can yet come *gut* out of this situation. Perhaps a blessing for you, Miriam. I do not understand the mind of the Lord, but clearly you and Ivan have another chance at a relationship. That might be the way the Lord has opened up for you. Now that Ivan's *frau* is gone and your Wayne too, Ivan might be a proper husband for you."

"*Daett*, please!" Miriam objected. Horror gripped her heart. She could not, would not marry Ivan, much less love him!

Daett ignored Miriam and continued with his lecture. "And with the farm gone, this would further clear up the way between the two of you."

Miriam gasped. No words would come out. Surely *Daett* didn't mean what he said! But she knew him well. He did. And nothing she could say would change his mind. *Mamm* would support

Daett too. A quick glance at *Mamm*'s face was all the confirmation she needed. *Mamm* gave her a kind-but-firm smile. She was in full agreement with *Daett*. *Ivan!* Miriam prayed that Ivan had the good sense to not attempt a renewal of their relationship. That idea was long dead and gone.

Daett went on as if Miriam hadn't protested. "I will find out more about Ivan. I'll ask around about him once we get back. I know he works for the Beachy family. I won't allow Shirley's past connection with Jonas to cloud my judgment. A job is a job, and I've heard Ivan is a hard worker."

Miriam struggled to speak. Finally a squeak came out followed by words from her heart. "Please don't mention Ivan right now, *Daett*. My heart can't take it."

Daett shrugged. "Ignoring the obvious is not the answer, Miriam. After I fully understand your history with Ivan and the money is taken care of, it only makes sense for the two of you to consider saying vows. I know how men think. I'm sure the man must be troubled in his conscience about the matter if it is as you say it is. After I speak with him, I'm sure he will be calling…when the trouble is cleared up between the two of you."

"I can't even think about dating someone right now, *Daett*," Miriam tried again.

"You must not be bitter." *Daett*'s voice was firm but gentle. "King David wrote, 'I have not seen the righteous forsaken, nor the seed of the Lord begging bread.'"

"I don't feel so righteous." Tears stung Miriam's cheeks again.

"But you are laying up treasures in heaven. And you will do that even more with the sale of the farm and the giving of the money to the Lord's work." A smile crept across *Daett*'s face.

Uncle William guided Sally into Deacon Phillips's driveway. He pulled her to a stop and got out to tie the horse to the hitching rail.

Miriam took a deep breath and climbed down from the spring

wagon. She turned to take baby Jonathon from Aunt Fannie. *Mamm* squeezed her hand and offered another kind smile. The two men led the way to the house.

Deacon Phillips opened the front door. "Well, what a surprise! Come in, come in."

Miriam bit her lower lip as they were shown to seats in the living room.

Katie said, "I think this calls for popcorn!"

Aunt Fannie reached over to touch Katie's arm. "No, don't bother. We're fine. Just come and sit down with us."

"I wouldn't think of it," Katie insisted. "And I have oranges in the basement. Does anyone want orange juice?"

"Then I'll come help," Aunt Fannie said, giving in. The two vanished into the kitchen.

Miriam remained seated with *Mamm* beside her. This was the perfect time to spill the news to Deacon Phillips as to why they'd come, Miriam decided. Then everyone could enjoy the rest of the evening the best they could. She'd smile on the outside and weep on the inside, but that couldn't be helped.

Daett must have had the same idea because he cleared his throat and said, "I don't know how best to break this news, but I thought we'd come along to better explain things." *Daett* glanced at Uncle William, who nodded his agreement.

Deacon Phillips smiled and waited.

"Miriam was given a fairly large inheritance by an *Englisha* man some time ago," *Daett* said. "A farm first of all…" *Daett* paused, and Deacon Phillips nodded. That was old news to him. "She was also given a large sum of money." *Daett* added, "Two million dollars, in fact."

Deacon Phillips leaned forward, a concerned look on his face.

Daett hurried on. "I myself only learned of this tonight. Miriam kept this matter a secret from us for her own reasons, but she sees her mistake now. She wishes to give the money to relief efforts in this area to help the community rebuild." *Daett* cleared his throat again.

"All of it?" Deacon Phillips found his voice. "All two million dollars?"

"*All* of it—two million plus whatever interest has accumulated," *Daett* told him. "And if you would keep the source of this money quiet, we would really appreciate it."

"Of course." Deacon Phillips seemed to struggle to breathe. "That's a large sum of money. I'll have to involve the other ministry people for integrity purposes. I won't have to disclose the source."

"That would be *gut*," *Daett* said. "And may I suggest you use the funds to help the community people first and then the *Englisha*?"

"Of course," Deacon Phillips said.

Sounds of popcorn popping came from the kitchen, and a peaceful silence settled over the living room. Miriam was glad she hadn't come by herself. Things would not have gone as well without *Daett* and Uncle William taking charge. The still-startled look on Deacon Phillips's face showed her that plainly enough. The deed was done. She'd cry more tonight over Wayne, but for the spending of the money, she'd shed not one tear.

Chapter Thirty-Four

———◆◆◆———

M iriam pulled Sally to a stop in the schoolyard on Saturday. For two days this week crews had worked at the site. Lunch could now be served inside for the school picnic. Miriam climbed out of the buggy and unhitched. Others should be here soon, but she'd wanted to arrive early. The basement might still be cluttered by tools and construction debris. The truth was that she wanted a few minutes alone at the schoolhouse before the bustle of the day began. The days behind her weren't nearly enough to heal from the loss of Wayne, but she'd made a start. Here at the place of so many *gut* memories more of her heart might be comforted. She'd be leaving the Clarita Amish community next week. The decision weighed heavily on her. *Daett* had insisted it was for the best that she come home for a while, and *Mamm* had agreed. What else, then, could Miriam do?

"Possum Valley, here I come again," Miriam muttered. Great sadness crept over her, but she pushed it away. Deep down she wanted to stay here, but now that seemed impossible. *Mamm* and

Daett had made it clear enough before they left for Possum Valley. *Daett* was going to speak with Ivan like he'd promised. Miriam frowned. She didn't want to think about that man. Still, she couldn't defy *Mamm* and *Daett*, could she? No, she'd go home—at least for the summer.

The thought of returning at the end of summer seemed like a possibility. Unfortunately she hadn't been invited to teach next year by the school board. She wasn't sure how she felt about that. For all she knew, the board might already have a new teacher lined up. If she came back she could work at the greenhouse. It should be rebuilt by then.

Miriam shook herself. She was going to cry if she didn't stop these thoughts. With an effort she turned to more pleasant things—memories of the school year, including the games she'd played with the children. Right here little Adam Yoder had pulled a new trick while they played prisoner's base—rolling several times toward safety. The maneuver had so astonished Verna—one of the eighth-grade girls who had been assigned to guard him—that Adam had arrived untagged.

Miriam smiled. There were also more pleasant memories. That of being called "teacher," for one. The feeling of belonging, of being needed and appreciated by the students. They had liked her. Miriam let the joy fill her heart.

She entered the newly framed school building. No drywall or insulation was up yet. That would happen this summer before the start of another school term. She imagined the voices of the students when they would again recite their lessons and sing cheerful songs about the glories of God. She could see the light in their eyes as one and then another caught on to the lessons. *Yah*, she would miss this—more than she wanted to admit. That sorrow must also be overcome. She couldn't expect the school board to rehire her.

Horse hooves beat on pavement, and Miriam moved to the

window. She looked out to see Deacon Phillips and Katie driving up. They were very early. Why would they arrive before everyone else? Did he wish to speak with her in private?

Miriam had been to Coalgate and the bank on Thursday. Then she'd driven over that evening with a cashier's check for almost two million fifty thousand dollars just as Deacon Phillips had requested. The check was made out to the relief fund that had been created for this purpose. Had she made a mistake? She took a deep breath. She would not assume she'd made an error. If there was a problem, it would be handled. At least Katie was along to soften any criticism. She was one of the kindest people Miriam had ever met.

Miriam waited in the schoolhouse until Deacon Phillips had unhitched his horse. She walked over to meet the two of them at the schoolhouse door.

"Good morning, teacher!" Katie greeted her. "Early on the job, I see."

Deacon Phillips smiled and nodded his greeting.

"Did I do something wrong with the check?" Miriam blurted out, ignoring her decision to not assume fault.

"Oh no!" Deacon Phillips assured her. "The relief board had nothing but *gut* things to say about such a large donation. They wanted to meet the person and thank him themselves, but I said that wasn't possible." Deacon Phillips smiled again. "Of course, I didn't breathe a word about you. Your secret stays with me. I do want to tell you that I agree totally with your *daett*. You couldn't have done a wiser thing than laying up treasure in heaven through your gift."

Miriam blushed and looked away. "Let's not talk about me. I do hope Uncle William will be given enough for his greenhouse."

Deacon Phillips didn't hesitate. "That's up to the relief board, but I'm sure your uncle will be dealt with fairly because no one knows the source of the money."

"I'm sorry. I probably shouldn't have asked." Miriam lowered her head in contrition.

Deacon Phillips cleared his throat. "Katie, we'd better hurry and ask our question before the crowd begins to gather for the picnic."

Miriam felt her body stiffen from the sudden chill in her heart.

Deacon Phillips continued. "You probably don't know all our customs around here regarding school, Miriam. The school board doesn't usually ask the current teacher to stay another year until the last day of school. Now with you, we could have asked a long time ago because we knew what we wanted, but then those of us on the board decided to stick with our tradition." Deacon Phillips appeared apologetic. "We've had bad experiences in the past with other teachers, so we're never sure what might come up. Miriam, we'd like you to be our teacher next year. If you'll consider it, of course."

Miriam took a deep breath. "I wasn't sure if my failure to tell my parents about the full inheritance would disqualify me. It didn't reflect well on my character. And a teacher must be of the highest character."

Deacon Philips nodded. "*Yah*, I do wish you had told your parents about that from the beginning. But mistakes like that happen to the best of us. And with the gift you've given, that's all behind you. I can't think of a better teacher to ask to come back for next year. I understand your parents want you back in Possum Valley. Hopefully that's just for the summer. You wouldn't need to be back here until the week before the new term starts."

"We would like to have you back very much," Katie hastened to add.

Miriam's mind spun. She hadn't dared hope for such an offer so liberally given. Tears filled her eyes. Now that the moment of decision had arrived, she had to consider if she could live in the land where she'd lost Wayne.

"Of course you can think about it for a week or so," Deacon Phillips said, interrupting her thoughts. "Or you could even write from Possum Valley. We hope you don't wait too long to give us a positive answer." His smile was back full force. "Our children have certainly enjoyed you as their teacher this year."

"I'll do it!" Miriam stood tall and smiled. "I'll come back and teach next year."

"Are you sure?" Katie reached out to squeeze Miriam's arm. "I know this has been a hard season for you."

"I'm okay," Miriam said. And she really would be by then.

Deacon Phillips and Katie glanced at each other. Deep smiles filled their faces with joy. "I'm glad to hear that!" Deacon Phillips told Miriam. "I think you'll be in a much better state by then. And I know the Lord will be with you this summer."

"*Yah*, and many blessings to you during your time off," Katie added.

Miriam glanced toward the schoolyard. She'd heard several buggies pulling in while they'd been speaking, but she hadn't taken much notice.

"Thank you both so much," she told them.

As representatives on the school board, Deacon Phillips and Katie were already greeting the other arrivals.

Miriam took her place at the schoolhouse door, a smile on her face for the first time in weeks. Her heart still pounded at this sudden turn of events. She'd been the teacher last year and now she was asked to be the teacher for next term. She should act like she'd received a great gift—because she had. The loss of Wayne and the misstep with the money hadn't carried over and taken her job away.

"Heal, heart, heal," she whispered to herself and sent a prayer heavenward. "Help me, dear Lord. I need all the grace I can get to move forward with Your joy."

And as if to test such a prayer, the next buggy to arrive belonged to Wayne's *mamm* and *daett*. She could handle this, Miriam encouraged herself. She'd smile and act normal, and no one would see the huge hole in her heart. Miriam kept up the smiles and shook hands with the parents and students who came past. Apparently most of them assumed she'd accepted the school board's job offer for the next term.

"It's so *gut* for you to come back next year."

"We really enjoyed the time you've been in the community."

"We love to have Shirley around as well," a woman added. "She was such as sweet girl. I heard she had another operation."

"*Yah*," Miriam replied. "She's doing much better."

"That's so *gut* to hear!" the mother said, turning to her young daughter who was pulling on her dress sleeve.

Miriam watched as a softball game was beginning on the playground, and recruits were being called for among the men. Reluctantly a few joined. They pretended to limp onto the field with exaggerated gestures. Deacon Phillips hauled himself to the field as if every muscle in his body had been pulled out of shape.

Miriam grinned. The truth wasn't that far away. Some of the older men only played at community picnics, so strained muscles and sprains weren't unusual. The steady, strenuous farm work most of them performed, for the most part, didn't involve sudden moves and hard jolts.

Miriam jumped when a familiar voice came from beside her. "Enjoying the game?"

"*Yah*," Miriam responded, giving Katie a quick smile.

"There will be a lot of men with sore muscles tonight," Katie commented with a chuckle.

Miriam laughed too. Although her heart still hurt for Wayne, there was also joy in this day. And for that she would give much thanks.

Chapter Thirty-Five

Shirley rocked gently in her chair on the front porch. Miriam would soon arrive from the bus station. *Mamm* and *Daett* had left right after lunch with their neighbor Mrs. Faulkner to pick up Miriam from her long trip from Oklahoma. Shirley had considered going along to welcome Miriam home but decided not to. Miriam's return was joyfully anticipated by the whole family, and she was sure everyone in Possum Valley would be happy to see her sister back. Miriam would take center stage again, but Shirley could deal with that. She was selfish to even think of such a thing, she told herself. Especially since Miriam's heart must still be bleeding from all that had happened.

Shirley glanced up as Naomi approached. "I'll wait out here with you if you don't mind," the girl said. "It's so exciting that Miriam's home again—and for the whole summer."

Shirley motioned toward the other porch rocker. "*Yah*, I know. I thought I would be out here to welcome her."

Naomi nodded. "Miriam will appreciate the effort. She's such a saint. I can't believe that awful thing happened with Wayne. And I never got to meet him. What kind of man was he anyway? You saw him once, didn't you?"

"I did," Shirley said. "Wayne was nice enough from what I could see. I guess the Lord had other plans for Miriam."

Naomi stared into space. "I sure hope the man I love doesn't up and die on me. What a heartbreak poor Miriam has gone through!"

"I was thinking the same thing," Shirley agreed.

Naomi glanced at her older sister. "How are you and Glen getting along? I must say, he seems much more suited for you than that Jonas Beachy ever was."

Shirley bit back a quick retort. There was no need to antagonize Naomi. And Glen was *gut* for her.

Naomi appeared quite concerned since her sister hadn't responded. "Surely Glen hasn't broken off your relationship?"

Shirley laughed. "No, I'm more like the one who would do that. Glen is a jewel."

"Life is sad sometimes, isn't it?" Naomi asked. "I'm sorry for Miriam and you. You've had a rough time this year, and Miriam had been planning her wedding for this fall."

Shirley reached over to touch Naomi's hand. "Sometimes it seems that way. And I appreciate Glen's attentions. He's helped me get over the accident. He's coming by this evening to help us celebrate Miriam's homecoming."

"He is *gut* for you," Naomi said. "He's considerate, kind, and compassionate. You should marry the man."

"Now that's going too far yet," Shirley gently countered.

Naomi appeared ready to say something, but her response was interrupted by Mrs. Faulkner driving her car down the driveway. Both girls rose and were standing at the end of the sidewalk when the car came to a stop. *Daett* climbed out first, followed by Miriam.

Mamm was right behind them, having exited via the front passenger door. Naomi rushed forward to wrap Miriam in a tight hug, but Shirley held back now that the moment had arrived.

Miriam didn't seem to notice her hesitation. After hugging Naomi, she turned and opened her arms wide. "Shirley! It's so *gut* to see you."

"And you," Shirley whispered as the two embraced. They stood for a moment afterward taking in each other, their hands clasping.

Daett plunked two suitcases near the sidewalk and called out, "I could use some help here. Miriam has a bag you can get, Shirley."

Shirley hurried to respond, but Miriam intercepted her. "I'll get the bag."

"You will not!" Shirley said. "You're a visitor now."

Miriam laughed. "Not for long, I hope."

"You are never a visitor," *Mamm* assured Miriam. "I'm glad you're home. But come, we'd better get these things inside."

Everyone's hands were full, and they all headed toward the house. Shirley hung back from the others to whisper to Miriam, "I'm so sorry about everything that happened in Oklahoma. Are you okay?"

Miriam took a moment to respond. "The Lord is helping me. But let's not talk about that right now. I'm home and life goes on. How are you doing?"

"Okay, I guess." Shirley wrinkled up her face.

Miriam set her suitcase down to gently trace the faint scars on Shirley's face with one hand. "I'd say things are doing quite well. This looks so much better from the last time I saw you. There is much to be thankful for."

"There is," Shirley agreed. "And Glen thinks I'm...well..." Shirley looked at the ground.

Miriam smiled. "I'm glad to hear it. You deserve the blessing of the Lord."

How could Miriam be so cheerful after what she'd gone through? Shirley wondered. The two picked up their loads and hurried to catch up with *Mamm* and Naomi. After going into the house, *Mamm* put a suitcase down and slipped an arm around Miriam's shoulders. The two spoke together in low tones.

Shirley couldn't keep tears from trickling down her cheeks. Already Miriam was the shining beacon in the Yoder home. But that was how it should be, and she mustn't be jealous.

Naomi must have noticed Shirley's distress because she dropped back a step. "Miriam sure seems happy, but you'd be happy too if you'd just come home from that wild and terrible Oklahoma."

Shirley grimaced. "I liked it in Oklahoma, and so did Miriam."

Naomi didn't look convinced. "There are tornados like oceans out there. They get almost three times the number of tornadoes we do! That's what *Mamm* and Miriam are talking about right now. With so many tornadoes there must be very little land that doesn't get hit."

"Miles are different from oceans," Shirley corrected. "I guess I'm a little emotional right now. Miriam's the one who should be crying."

"Miriam's come home," Naomi said, as if that explained everything. "And Glen's coming this evening. You'll feel better soon."

A smile crept across Shirley's face.

Naomi grinned and left to give Miriam another hug.

Done talking with *Mamm*, Miriam lifted her head high to take in a deep breath. "Home at last—and off that horrible bus. I declare, they get noisier every time I ride in one."

Mamm ignored the remark and ushered Miriam to the couch. "Sit down and tell us all about little Jonathon and more about your trip…if you want to."

"Well, as I said," Miriam began, "the bus ride wasn't that great. Uncle William and Aunt Fannie took me to the bus station in

Coalgate with their faithful driver, Mr. Whitehorse. That was on Monday morning, and…"

The front door opened. *Daett* came in and plunked two more suitcases on the floor. He regarded Miriam for a moment. "My eldest daughter back home and safe. We have much to be thankful for."

"Thanks, *Daett*, for everything," Miriam murmured.

Daett went on, a smile on his face. "I want to say again how glad *Mamm* and I are over the choices you've made lately, Miriam. I know you took the loss of Wayne deeply to heart, but in the end it will all be for the best."

Miriam frowned slightly.

Daett glanced at the suitcases on the floor for a moment. His face sobered. "I need to tell you, Miriam, that I spoke at length with Ivan last Sunday after the service. I've been wanting to tell you this since I picked you up at the bus station, but with Mrs. Faulkner in the car it didn't seem…"

Mamm spoke up. "*Daett*, not now. This can wait until we speak with Miriam in private."

Daett swallowed hard but nodded. "I suppose so. I know I don't always wait for the proper moment."

"You spoke with Ivan?" Miriam's face was pale.

Naomi leaped to her feet. "I think I'm leaving about right now."

Shirley stayed rooted in her seat as Naomi vanished up the stairs. If they wanted her gone they could say so. This conversation was obviously going to continue now, even over *Mamm*'s objections.

Daett waited until Naomi's footsteps had died away. "Let me explain. You were doing so well with your recent decisions, Miriam, that I thought I should follow my promise to you and speak with Ivan. I'm sure he's had thoughts about you, after everything you told me out in Oklahoma and since his *frau* passed. I wanted to clear the air with him. I was also upset over how things went between the two of you—back when. So I wanted to know his heart on the matter—on the farm, that is—and let him know we're getting rid of that problem."

"You didn't, *Daett*." Miriam's voice was pained.

Mamm kept quiet, but she reached over to hold Miriam's hand.

Shirley hadn't expected this. Was this what *Mamm* had meant earlier when she referenced a wedding this fall? Her parents had apparently given their approval to Ivan renewing his interest in Miriam. And obviously they expected Miriam to follow their lead. Shirley gripped the edge of her seat with both hands. She couldn't have gotten a word out of her mouth if she'd tried. Some welcome home *Mamm* and *Daett* had planned for Miriam.

Daett stared at the suitcases and then looked at his eldest daughter. "Ivan has changed much since Laura's gone, Miriam. Sorrow does that to the human heart. And so have you, but you're back now. Ivan would make a decent husband for you. I know your heart may need time to heal from the loss of Wayne, and so does Ivan's from the loss of Laura. He loved his *frau*, but the Lord obviously had other plans for him. For the two of you."

"But I *can't* do this," Miriam whispered. "I'm just back, and…" Her voice died away.

Shirley forced herself to stand and go sit beside Miriam on the couch. She slipped her arm around Miriam's shoulders. What she should say, she still had no idea. Hopefully Miriam would know that she wasn't in on this scheme.

Miriam turned to study Shirley's face for a moment. "Do you support this?"

Shirley's thoughts tumbled over each other. First of all, there was no way she wanted to contradict *Mamm* and *Daett* in front of them. Second, she'd been wrong when it came to love before. She'd resisted Miriam's initial interest in Wayne because she'd wanted her to accept Ivan's attentions despite Ivan's faulty reasons.

Miriam looked away when her sister didn't answer.

Shirley tightened her hand around Miriam's shoulders, trying to send a message. That she could do. She would supply moral support for whatever decision Miriam made in the end. Miriam would have something to say about this, even if *Mamm* and *Daett* thought the matter a closed subject.

"*Daett* is right on this," *Mamm* interjected. "Like he was right in Oklahoma about the money. Think for a moment, Miriam. Doesn't it feel like a great burden is off your shoulders now that you've given away that money? When we sell the farm, you'll be rid of the last of this awful mistake."

"Mr. Bland's decision was not a mistake!" Miriam seemed to gather strength. "I was the one who was too weak to handle the gift correctly. And *Daett* will not be selling the farm. I've given it to him, but legally it can't be sold by you. And that's that."

Daett's lips pressed together. "Now we're back to the same old argument, Miriam. I will sell the place after you sign the deed over to me."

"Possession of the farm was set up as a trust for our family. You might be able to break the trust with lawyers, I suppose," Miriam said softly.

Daett sighed. "And here I thought you'd been making such wise decisions lately. Was I wrong?"

Miriam sat up straighter. "*Daett*, you can't possibly know how I feel right now. About marrying, my heart hasn't healed yet. I can't even think about loving someone else again. And certainly not Ivan."

"We do understand." *Mamm* moved closer. "But won't you at least consider what *Daett* has said? Don't write off Ivan so easily. Take your time, Miriam, and let the Lord heal both of your hearts."

Miriam forced a smile. "I appreciate your concern. I just can't talk about Ivan now. On the farm issue, *Daett* must accept that the farm was a gift from me with a plan in place so that it couldn't be sold without the entire family agreeing. And I do not agree."

Daett shook his head. "I can't keep the farm. My conscience won't allow it."

Miriam stood and faced *Daett*. "Maybe your conscience is too tender in some areas. Look at how our family has suffered because of your convictions. You refuse to deal with the tourists that everyone else caters too. That's why I had to take the job to help Mr. Bland to begin with. And that's why I stuck with it—because it paid so well. And that's why I received the farm and the money. Because I did my work conscientiously. I think you should consider that you're not right about everything."

Shirley felt her head nod as she whispered, "That I *can* agree with." She glanced at *Daett's* face. How was he reacting to his daughters' obvious defiance?

Daett studied the two of them but refused to say anything.

Mamm broke the ice by standing and saying, "Let's not pursue this now. Go unpack, Miriam, and then rest a while. We have a nice supper planned especially for you tonight. Shirley's Glen is stopping by. You'll get to meet him."

Miriam nodded. After *Mamm* and *Daett* left for the kitchen, Miriam whispered to Shirley, "Thank you for the support."

"I'm glad you're home!" Shirley whispered back. She stood and pulled Miriam close for a long hug.

Chapter Thirty-Six

◆◆◆

As the sun set that evening, Shirley helped *Mamm* lay out the supper dishes. Upstairs Miriam finished unpacking and laid down to rest. She could hear her school-aged brothers and sisters playing outside.

Shirley glanced out the kitchen window to check on the kids, and they were all racing around the yard in the best of spirits. Baby Anna had awakened from her nap and was cooing on her blanket in front of the stove. Thankfully things had calmed down after *Daett* and *Mamm*'s startling disclosure about talking with Ivan Mast. Miriam had taken the revelation quite well, Shirley thought. But Miriam was that kind of person. It did sound like *Daett* had talked to her about Ivan before...perhaps in Oklahoma. Miriam had always been an example for the rest of the family in obedience. Now she appeared to be headed for a renewed relationship with Ivan whether she wanted to or not, whether she liked him or not. Perhaps even wedding him this fall. Would Miriam even consider such a thing? This was, after all, *marriage*. Could Miriam ever really love Ivan? Could she vow to live with him in obedience the rest of her life? One thing Shirley was sure of, if *Mamm* and *Daett* thought their second daughter should marry a man she didn't love, there wasn't a chance she'd comply.

But she was no Miriam, who seemed able to change direction as the Lord changed her circumstances. Shirley sighed. She was still struggling with having good memories of Jonas and their heady relationship. The thought of fast car rides and fancy restaurants lingered in her mind. No man would ever be able to kiss her like Jonas. That was simply not possible. Dazzling fire filled Shirley's heart at the memory of his passionate kisses.

"Is Glen still coming tonight?" *Mamm* asked, interrupting Shirley's thoughts.

"*Yah*." Shirley quickly returned to the present.

"How are you and Glen getting along?"

"Okay, I guess," Shirley said with a shrug.

"It's nice that he's coming over for supper tonight." *Mamm's* voice revealed hopefulness.

A warm feeling did fill Shirley's heart at the thought of Glen's kindness. He'd been the first one who made her feel good despite her scarred face. And he'd come to see her in the hospital after her most recent surgery. The man was a treasure. There was no doubt on that point. He just wasn't Jonas.

Before *Mamm* could press her point, footsteps came down the stairs. Miriam appeared in the kitchen doorway.

After looking over all their food preparations, Miriam exclaimed, "This wasn't necessary. Why, look at all this food you've made!"

Mamm practically glowed. "It's not much, and I didn't invite any visitors other than Glen, who sort of invited himself. You don't even have to dress up. We wanted to do some little thing at least to welcome you home."

Miriam looked ready to protest further, but instead she said,

"That's awful nice of you, that's all I can say." She quickly washed her hands in the kitchen sink and turned her attention to baby Anna. "Hi, little one!" she cooed. "Are you awake from your nap?" Miriam leaned over and tickled Anna on the cheek. The child waved her arms and smiled. After a few minutes of murmured endearments, Miriam stood up. "So, what can I do to help, *Mamm*?"

"Sit right there and talk to us some more about Oklahoma," *Mamm* ordered, pointing to a kitchen chair. "We were interrupted earlier, and I'm sure there's more to tell, isn't there?"

Miriam nodded and picked up baby Anna before she pulled out a chair. "Well, for one thing, the school board asked me back for another year. I accepted."

Shirley gasped. "You're going back there with Wayne gone?"

Miriam's face clouded for a moment. "I know—it may be hard at times. But life goes on, and I have to go on with it. I like the community there, and they like me. I really enjoy teaching too."

Mamm stared at Miriam. "What about Ivan?"

"I don't really want to talk about him," Miriam replied. "Instead, why don't you tell me about Glen, Shirley? Start at the beginning. Where did he come from? Men like that don't drop in out of the blue."

"You're supposed to be telling us about Oklahoma," Shirley reminded her.

Miriam laughed softly. "Touchy subject, is it? Well, that must mean there's something to it. And he's coming tonight? *Daett* must like him to allow that."

Shirley said nothing even though *Mamm* smiled. The answer was obvious, Shirley thought. And she did like the man, just not the way her family and Glen wanted her to. But she would try. Glen was a decent man. She couldn't go wrong with him.

"You still haven't told us about Aunt Fannie and baby Jonathon," *Mamm* pressed.

A smile flew across Miriam's face. "He's growing like a weed the last few weeks. Fat and chubby for a little boy. Just adorable! We all love him."

Mamm appeared wistful. "I'd love to see him again. I guess one of you girls has to hurry up with a wedding so your Aunt Fannie and Uncle William have an excuse to visit."

Miriam ignored the comment, and Shirley did the same.

"Then there is all the rebuilding going on," Miriam said.

The sound of buggy wheels came from the driveway, and Shirley glanced out the kitchen window. She was on her way to the utility room seconds later.

Miriam's words followed her. "I'd say there is something to this Glen fellow."

Which was true, Shirley supposed. Glen had arrived, and her feelings had perked up for the moment. She wanted to welcome him since he'd been nice enough to come. The younger children had already gathered around the buggy, and Shirley shooed them aside. "Move back and let the man get out."

Glen grinned as he climbed down. "What a welcome! I think I'll come more often. Shall I tie up or unhitch?"

"Tie up is fine. Supper won't last that long."

His face fell, but Glen didn't say anything as he pulled the tie rope out from under the buggy seat.

"Come to think of it," Shirley rushed on to say after noticing his look, "why don't you unhitch? The evening is…" She left the rest unsaid. She saw Glen's face light up. He clearly wanted to stay past suppertime to spend time with her.

"How's Miriam after the long bus trip?" Glen asked. He walked around the buggy to undo the tugs, while Shirley took care of the side closest to her.

"Rough ride as usual." Shirley gave him a friendly smile.

Glen led his horse forward. The children returned to the yard to continue their play.

Shirley followed Glen to the barn. "You can use the empty stall in the back."

Glen put his horse inside and was pleased when he returned. "Thanks for letting me stay the evening, Shirley."

"Maybe we can take a stroll before suppertime," she offered. "I think *Mamm* has things under control without me. It'll be dark soon, so now is a good time."

His face lit up even more. "I'd enjoy that."

"Then here we go!" Shirley led the way outside and around the side of the barn.

Glen gave her a quick sideways glance. "You're looking *gut*."

Heat rushed up her face, and Shirley looked away. "That's kind of you to say."

"I'm not just *saying* so," he protested. "You've always been beautiful. From the first time I saw you. But now you're…"

"We're taking a walk, Glen, and enjoying the late afternoon." Shirley tried to look stern. "And you've always been too kind." She reached for his hand even though they were still in sight of the house. Her fingers lingered in his for a few moments before she let go. "Thank you for all you've done for me, Glen. I don't deserve your kindness."

"I beg to differ." His gaze searched her face when they stopped momentarily at a pasture gate.

She opened it for him. She could still feel the flush of embarrassment on her neck.

"Is something wrong?" Glen asked with concern as they walked further and further from the house.

Shirley shook her head. "Not really, I'm just thinking about things."

Glen fell silent for a few minutes. "I've been thinking too, Shirley. I was wondering if we couldn't…" He didn't want to waste words. "The truth is, Shirley, I'm ready to settle down. I know *rumspringa* is a time to find out where your heart is and taste a few

things of the world. I've done that now. There's nothing out there
for me. And now I've found you. I..." Glen's voice drifted off.

He was waiting for an answer, and Shirley wanted to say something, but she couldn't think of what. "I'm glad for you," she finally
managed to get out.

He studied her face. "Where are you at, Shirley? You know, with
your *rumspringa* time."

"I guess I've not had too much of it yet." Shirley knew that was
a lame answer, and Glen's face showed his disappointment.

"I'm sorry to push the subject. I know I told you I'd wait for you
to decide, but I'd really like to be bringing you home regular on
Sunday evenings."

I thought we could just be friends. The words almost slipped
out, but Shirley caught them just in time. Although true, they
felt unkind. Glen wanted more out of the relationship. He'd never
made that a secret. He wouldn't be here tonight if he didn't want to
know her family better...because of knowing her. Marriage would
eventually be on his mind, that was certain.

"Well, maybe we can." The words came out easier than she
expected.

"Like when?"

Shirley laughed. Glen appeared to not believe his own ears. "I
don't know. You're the one to do the asking."

"Are you sure you're ready?" He saw a stone in the path and
kicked it to the side. "I didn't mean you had to answer tonight. I
can wait longer if need be, Shirley."

"It's okay." She took his arm in hers. "You can bring me home
this Sunday evening if you wish. Is that soon enough?"

The glow on his face was all the answer he gave until they
reached the edge of the woods. "You make me very happy, Shirley.
Do you know that?"

She looked at the ground and then confessed, "I'm afraid you don't know everything about me yet, Glen. I tend to be unstable and flighty. I don't keep promises very well. And I've been known to break a few rules. I can be quite stubborn and headstrong."

He laughed and squeezed her arm.

He didn't believe a word she said, Shirley realized. Well, he would find out soon enough. At the moment she wanted only to feel the comfort of his presence and the warmth he stirred in her heart. There was none of the wild giddiness Jonas provoked, but that was *gut*, was it not?

Glen reached over and traced his fingers across the disappearing scars on Shirley's face. "You grow more beautiful each day. I can't believe I get to drive you home on Sunday evening."

Shirley lowered her head, afraid he might want to kiss her. "Just hold my hand as we walk along. We'd better get back now. Supper will be ready."

He took her hand in his and led the way across the pasture. They were still holding hands when they approached the barn. Several of the younger siblings noticed, stopping their play to point and giggle.

Glen grinned.

"Come!" Shirley tugged on his hand. "The rest of the family will be happy to see that you've come tonight. Lee and Mark, *Mamm* and *Daett*, and Miriam and Naomi." Shirley didn't add that her family's greatest happiness was in the fact that, by all appearances, she finally planned to settle down with a decent Amish man. She did in fact intend that. And she couldn't find anyone better than Glen in that regard. She grew more sure of that every day, it seemed.

Chapter Thirty-Seven

Ivan stirred his bowl of oatmeal at the breakfast table for a few seconds before he added milk. He took a bite and chewed slowly. The emptiness of the house rang in his ears, and he shook his head for a moment. Was this another aftereffect of the accident? The hollow feeling in his chest certainly was. The fact that Laura was gone forever and there was nothing he could do about it was a hurdle he couldn't seem to jump.

He shook his head again. Was the Lord already making a way through this wilderness for him? Why else had Eli, Miriam's *daett*, shown up to speak with him after the service on Sunday? Maybe he did need to find a new *frau* sooner than later. Mostly though, the man had given him a lecture for the way he'd used Miriam before his marriage to Laura. From what he could tell, Eli didn't know everything. Miriam must not have told her parents all the details of their exchange, which showed the strength of Miriam's character.

Ivan groaned. His marriage to Laura couldn't have been a mistake. He'd loved her. Besides, regrets did a man little *gut*. He would trust the Lord to guide him through this dark time. Apparently the first direction had arrived with Eli Yoder. *Yah*, repentance was in order. Ivan had agreed with Eli and apologized. The man seemed satisfied. He'd even suggested that Ivan approach Miriam for a renewal of their relationship now that Miriam had also lost the one she loved.

"I didn't know about Wayne," he'd admitted to Eli.

With another groan, Ivan pushed aside his partially eaten oatmeal and stood. Most of the muscles throughout his body still ached, even after these many weeks since the accident. Thankfully, he could do his chores again, but he hadn't been back to his job. He needed to move about more. Maybe he should harness his old horse, Billy, to the buggy and go for a ride.

Ivan heaved a sigh and walked out of the washroom. He crossed the front yard as questions whirled in his mind. Did he dare visit Miriam today? She'd only been home a few days, and he would see her at the Sunday service. How uncomfortable that might be since Eli would have told Miriam by now about their conversation. No, it would be better to speak with her in private or among family. Since she'd expect him to speak with her, why not do it today? Eli was right. With the money given away and the farm Mr. Bland had given Miriam sold off, he could begin anew with Miriam. The woman wouldn't doubt his intentions again.

Yah, he had best go visit Miriam. He rubbed his head and entered the barn. After easing the harness on Billy's back, he led the old horse outside and hitched him to the buggy. He climbed in, and pain shot up his back. Ivan ignored the continuing stabs and drove out his lane. Before long he'd feel young again, he told himself. Once his body and heart healed. That was why he planned to stop at the graveyard before he visited Miriam. His sisters had taken him there last week, but he needed to go alone. He knew Laura wasn't there, but he wanted to show his respect for the love and attention she'd shown him in their brief marriage. She had been a *gut frau*. If she had lived, he would have grown to love her even more deeply. There was no doubt in his mind about that.

He let his mind wander as the steady beat of Billy's hooves on pavement filled his ears. He pictured Laura on their wedding day, her face aglow with happiness. *Yah*, she'd put a lot of effort into their relationship and had won his heart. He hadn't deserved such love, Ivan acknowledged. Just as he didn't deserve this second chance with Miriam that came with the visit from her *daett*. Why the Lord continued to give him both direction and rebuke, he couldn't imagine. And added to that, Eli's approval if he should seek Miriam's hand in marriage.

A tear crept into his eye, and Ivan wiped it away. There had been enough of those shed on his pillow since he'd come out of the coma. A man must move on, even with deep regret in his heart for his actions. He'd wronged both Laura and Miriam. Darkness swirled in his mind as he pulled up to the graveyard and climbed out of the buggy. He left Billy standing along the fencerow without a tie rope. The old horse would go nowhere.

He found his way through the tombstones with names both familiar and unfamiliar: Yoders, Bylers, Troyers…Ivan forced himself to look ahead to the freshly dug grave on the far edge of the cemetery. Small blades of grass had begun to spring up on the mound of dirt. The tombstone the Swartz family had set in place glistened from the recent rains.

Ivan read out loud, "Laura Mast and child, beloved wife and daughter…" He knelt next to the dirt and lifted his head to the heavens. He found himself whispering, "I'm so sorry for what happened, Laura. I know you're with the angels and much happier than any of us on this earth can imagine. But still, the accident was my fault. I should have paid attention to where we were going. Please forgive me."

Ivan bowed his head and waited. There was no voice from heaven, but he didn't expect one. Peace was enough of an answer. He kept his head down and spoke again. "Thank you, Laura, for the love you gave me. Thank you for our times together. You were much more than I deserved. Thank you for our...our..." Ivan's voice broke. "I'll never see our child's face on this earth, but I'm sure the baby is sweet like you are."

Silence settled around him, and Ivan didn't move for a long time. Then slowly he rose and made his way back to his buggy. Billy lifted his head and looked at him. "*Yah*, she's gone," Ivan said out loud. Billy wouldn't understand the words, but Ivan wanted to say them. He wanted to face what had happened and to move on. He was in no shape to visit Miriam, but perhaps she should see him in his broken condition. If he ever wanted to ask her to be his *frau*, there should be nothing hidden between them—even his sorrow over what had happened. Miriam was a woman of character. She would understand.

Ivan climbed into the buggy and turned toward the Yoder place. Billy objected to the direction with a jerk of his head, but he soon settled into his slow, steady gait. Ivan turned to look back at the graveyard until they took a side road north. Another buggy approached, and Ivan leaned forward to wave. Bishop Wagler stuck his head out and then pulled his horse to a stop. Billy had already begun to slow down, so the two buggies ended up side-by-side.

"*Gut* morning, Ivan." Bishop Wagler's concerned face peered at him. "How are you doing?"

"Out and about by myself, I guess." Ivan managed a chuckle.

Bishop Wagler's gaze went back down the road from where Ivan had come. A look of understanding crossed the bishop's face. "It must be a difficult time for you."

"*Yah*." Ivan nodded. "I visited Laura by myself for the first time. Sort of saying goodbye, I guess. But how does one do that?"

The bishop was all sympathy. "None of us can carry or understand another's sorrow fully, Ivan, and yet we can try. That's what the community is here for, and you must ask us if you have needs. Are your chores being taken care of?"

Ivan nodded again. "*Yah*, my family helped, but I'm well enough now."

"And your field work? Has Deacon Hochstetler been by to see you about that?"

"I don't think that's necessary," Ivan replied. "But thank you anyway. Laura only had a garden."

The bishop chuckled. "I guess that's right. You don't farm. Well, it's a little difficult to keep track of what everyone does. I'm getting old, you know." The bishop sobered. "I've never lost a *frau*, yet the Lord has seen fit to take you through such dark waters at a young age. May the Lord's grace be with you."

"Thank you," Ivan said.

The bishop regarded Ivan steadily again. "I know this might not seem like the time to speak of the matter, but keep your heart open to the Lord's leading on another *frau*, Ivan. It's not *gut* that a man should be alone, especially someone so young. We have at least one young widow in the community. I wanted to remind you of that. Some of our men feel guilty about such thoughts, but the Lord has made man to move on with his life. So surely there will be among our sisters an unmarried one who would be open to your attentions."

Ivan swallowed twice. "I have thought of such a thing, but my heart still sorrows."

"As it should." The bishop clucked to his horse. "Don't be forgetting what I said now."

Billy turned his head to watch the bishop's buggy leave, and Ivan had to slap the lines to make him move. "Come on, old boy, let's get going. That's another sign for me, I would say." The bishop spoke of Mary Troyer, Ivan told himself. Mary was hazy in his mind. He hadn't paid that much attention to the women of the community while Laura was alive. He thought Mary had two small children from her short marriage with Mark Troyer.

Ivan let his mind turn to Miriam as he drove the final miles to the Yoder place. She would be heartbroken over her loss of Wayne, as he was over Laura. Ivan pushed that dark thought away. Miriam had once been convinced he tried to win her hand because of the farm she'd been given by the *Englisha* man she worked for. He'd always insisted there had been nothing to the accusation, but now that sorrow had ripped his heart open he saw a little more clearly. Perhaps Miriam had been right—at least in part.

Still, he was here, Ivan told himself, as he drove into the Yoder lane, and he wished to speak with Miriam. This relationship might go nowhere or Miriam could say no to his advances. After that, the bishop's suggestion was the next thing to look into. It didn't really matter to him right now. His heart hurt too much.

The barnyard was empty when Ivan pulled up to the hitching post. He climbed out of the buggy and left Billy untied again. He walked up the sidewalk, and Miriam's *mamm* came to the door with a smile on her face. "*Gut* morning, Ivan."

"*Gut* morning." He was expected, Ivan told himself. He stood tall. "May I speak with Miriam?"

"She's in the kitchen." The smile still hadn't faded. "I'll tell her you're here."

"I'll stay out here," Ivan said. He waited on the porch. Miriam must already know he'd arrived, so the wait didn't speak well for his chances of a happy outcome from this visit. Still, what did he expect? Miriam wouldn't be easily won over, even under the most ideal of circumstances, which these were not. The door opened, and Miriam stepped outside. "Hello, Ivan." Her face was unreadable.

He cleared his throat. "Sorry for the unexpected visit, but may I speak with you for a moment?"

She studied him. "That depends, I guess. Couldn't you wait until Sunday?"

"So you do know what this is about?" The words came out quickly and awkwardly.

"*Daett* told me, *yah*, about your conversation." She pointed toward the front porch rockers. "Shall we sit?"

He didn't answer but led the way over to the rockers. He waited until Miriam had seated herself. "I'm sorry again about all of this. And your loss of Wayne."

She looked at him. "I suppose you expect a wedding next month already?" Her voice was bitter.

Ivan drew in a long breath. "I'm sorry, Miriam, about what happened in Oklahoma. I really am. But I also have suffered my own great loss."

She dropped her head and wiped her eyes. "*Yah*, I'm sorry for the way I sounded. There's still some hurt. You must know that."

Ivan hesitated for a moment. "*Yah*, I know." This wasn't the right time, but here he was. He began again. "You and I, Miriam, we go back a long way. I guess to our schooldays. You know I used to have affections for you. And now that Laura's gone..." Ivan reached for Miriam's hand, and she didn't pull back. "I'm truly sorry about Wayne. I know the pain must be awful. You wouldn't give your affections to a man halfway. But remember that I also loved Laura. She was close to my heart, and she loved me. She was bearing our child." Tears welled up in his eyes again.

She nodded. "I'm sorry for your loss too, Ivan."

He attempted to smile, but the lump in his throat wouldn't let more words out.

"Maybe this is all too soon." Her words were tender.

"Maybe," Ivan conceded. "But I wanted to at least speak with you after your *daett* came over. I wouldn't even have dared come otherwise."

Her gaze was fixed on his face.

"Look." Ivan stood. "I appreciate that you even came out of the house to speak with me. That's how low I feel about everything. I know you didn't have to, but you did. My head is still swimming about all that is happening. I–I–I, well, I visited Laura's grave on the way over…"

Miriam's hand reached over to touch his. "I understand. I wouldn't refuse to visit with you, Ivan. Though a visit is hardly a promise to pursue a relationship. It's way too soon for me, regardless of what *Daett* says."

He squeezed her arm. "*Yah*, I was wrong to think it could be anything more this soon. But I had to come. Perhaps then sometime in the future we might speak more on this?"

"Maybe." Her voice was soft. "But know this is *Daett*'s idea and not mine. I still sorrow deeply."

"I understand," Ivan said. "I'll leave you then." Miriam's hand left his arm, and he found his way back down the porch steps. He walked across the lawn and climbed into the buggy. Only then did he look back and wave. Miriam was still standing on the porch, and her hand came up in response to his. She is a decent woman, Ivan thought as he drove out of the lane. But he'd felt nothing like what he used to. Still, they should try to see if Eli was right. Maybe the Lord would bring a blessing from their common great trial. They would have to see, that's all he knew for now. This time the effort was honorable and aboveboard at least. For that he was thankful.

Chapter Thirty-Eight

Miriam washed the dishes with a slow motion, her gaze fixed out the kitchen window. The yard was flooded with the dusty light of the late-Friday evening. Several of her younger siblings were playing prisoner's base, the game her schoolchildren had enjoyed during recess. Likely they were missing school too. A tear crept into her eye at the thought. She missed her students…and Oklahoma, if the truth be told. Much more than she'd imagined. Baby Jonathon would have put on weight by the time she saw him again, and no doubt he'd be cuter than when she'd left him. Uncle William's greenhouse would be rebuilt by then. But how lonely it would seem without Wayne working there. Could she bear it? She would have to heal more before she returned to Oklahoma this fall, that was certain.

"Please help me, dear Lord," Miriam breathed as she washed another dish.

Footsteps came down the stairs, and Miriam looked up with a smile to greet Shirley. Her sister was dressed for an outing with

Glen, no doubt. The two were officially dating now. Miriam was glad.

"I hate to go out and leave you here hard at work," Shirley said with a concerned look.

"I'm almost finished," Miriam replied, lowering her head lest the tears come back again. Any sympathy from her family had that effect right now. "I'm so glad things are going well for Glen and you."

Shirley smiled thinly. "I like the man, so perhaps it will work out. He's being so kind to me."

"The Lord will guide you," Miriam offered.

A look of pain crossed Shirley's face. "Sometimes my heart still mourns at what I've lost, but *Mamm* and *Daett* both think I'm on the right path. So maybe they know more than I do."

"So you're not dating Glen because you might be in love with him?"

Shirley shook her head. "Not yet anyway. I like the man though. What about Ivan and you? Can you even say you like him?"

Miriam bit her lower lip. "No, I can't really. We both just have similar sorrows we're working through."

"Then you might be right for each other." Shirley's voice was guarded. "I hate to see you forced into something, Miriam."

"I won't be." Miriam glanced out the kitchen window. "Here comes Glen. You'd better go out to him."

Shirley followed her sister's glance and then rushed for the front door.

Miriam couldn't help but smile at her sister's thinly veiled enthusiasm. Shirley liked Glen more than she cared to admit. And the two were suited for each other in more ways than either of them were aware. Perhaps as she and Ivan might be. The thought popped up from nowhere, and Miriam didn't push it away. At the moment she felt too weak to fight or reason the matter through. For the moment she would go with the flow and see where she ended up. Maybe life with Ivan wouldn't be such a bad thing. Laura had loved him, and *Daett* and *Mamm* approved of the match. Was there not safety in that?

Doors slammed upstairs, and seconds later Lee and Mark burst into the kitchen. Both skidded to a stop at the sight of her.

Lee spoke first. "This is not *gut*."

"I agree," Mark seconded his brother.

"We need to take her with us," Lee said as if Miriam wasn't there.

Miriam chuckled. "I'm not going out with the two of you. My *rumspringa* days are long over."

"Oh, come on!" Mark urged. "You need to stop moping and get out of the house."

"I'm not moping," Miriam protested.

"Have it your way," Mark said.

The boys turned and raced out the door. Lee called over his shoulder, "Have fun then!"

Miriam smiled and waved from the kitchen window. Their joy did lift her spirits. They were young yet and hadn't been through many sorrows. She didn't wish suffering on either of them. That would come soon enough. But maybe they were right. Maybe she should go somewhere. But where? Well, there was one place where she would be welcome, and where her presence would make perfect sense. Ivan's place. Maybe she could cook supper for him. They could see if their relationship could grow again—even return to what it once had been. She'd never been this bold with a man, but *Daett* and *Mamm* would likely approve. If they didn't, Naomi might agree to accompany her. Miriam finished the last dish and entered the living room. *Mamm* looked up from the rocker where she was knitting.

Miriam came right out with it. "What would you think about me going over to Ivan's place to make supper for him?"

A pleased look crossed *Mamm*'s face. Even *Daett* looked up. "I like that idea."

Mamm hesitated for a moment. "Did Ivan invite you?"

Miriam shrugged. "No. He's being patient with me—and with himself. Let's put it that way. And I can ask Naomi if she wants to go along, if…"

Mamm seemed to ponder the question, but *Daett* spoke first. "You can go by yourself. Just be back before ten or so."

"Okay." Miriam turned to go.

Daett's voice stopped her. "I'll get Mindy ready while you change."

She'd planned to go in her everyday dress, but perhaps *Daett*'s idea was better. Without protest Miriam went upstairs to change. She was outside before *Daett* had Mindy out of the barn. Miriam waited beside the buggy and lifted the shafts when *Daett* brought Mindy up. Once the hitching was done, Miriam climbed into the buggy. *Daett* patted Mindy's neck and she was off.

"Cook him a big supper now!" *Daett* called after her.

She didn't love Ivan, Miriam told herself. Those long-ago feelings from her schooldays had been lost in the love she'd felt for Wayne. But that marriage was not to be. Maybe love could come again—it its own time. After all, she didn't find Ivan disagreeable. He was a decent man, and *Daett* liked him. Her heart might come around. And if not, what would be wrong with a relationship based on what was right—with or without fuzzy feelings? Miriam guided Mindy at the correct turns, and the miles passed quickly beneath the buggy. All the while, Miriam tried to conceive why it might work out with Ivan. If he still hurt as much as she did, then they had that much in common. They could be two hurting hearts clinging together through their pain. Would such a thing not be right?

Yah, it could be right, Miriam decided as she approached Ivan's small house. An equally small garden choked with weeds filled the backyard. Ivan must not be able to care for the plot or he didn't have the interest with Laura gone. Would she be able to fill Laura's shoes…if something came of this? Miriam pushed the thought away as she pulled Mindy to a stop by the hitching post.

Ivan came out of the barn. "Miriam!" he exclaimed. "I didn't expect you. What brings you here?"

Miriam climbed down to meet him. She allowed a smile to spread over her face. "You could use a good supper, could you not?"

"Supper?" His face lit up. "You can say that again. Did you bring supper with you?"

She wrinkled her nose. "No, I thought I'd make supper here. Is that all right?"

"Oh, of course." He grinned. "My, I'm still trying to get over my shock that you're really here. You are so welcome anytime."

"My horse?" She pointed toward Mindy. "Should I put her in the barn?"

"Oh, *yah*." Ivan moved quickly as he unhitched. "Sorry, I'm a little slow catching on here. I'll take care of her."

"*Daett* said I have to be back by ten," Miriam offered. "That should leave plenty of time to cook a little supper and have a good visit."

"I can help with supper," Ivan offered as he took the reins from Miriam.

Miriam smiled skeptically. "We'll have to see about that."

He grinned. "Wait right here. I'll be back in a minute."

Ivan was all smiles when he returned from the barn. He began chattering away. "You have no idea how a man suffers who has to make his own meals. Of course *Mamm* and my sisters help out, but they have only so much time, what with all their other duties back home."

They reached the front door, and Ivan held it open for her. The inside was surprisingly clean, which was like Ivan, now that Miriam thought about it. When he'd eaten lunch at his school desk, he'd always brushed the crumbs carefully back into his lunch bucket. Most boys left them alone or pushed the particles over the side onto the floor.

Ivan followed her gaze. "It doesn't have a woman's touch, but I try."

"It looks fine," Miriam assured him.

"So," Ivan waved his hand toward the kitchen, "what can I do to help?"

"I don't know yet." She entered the kitchen. Here things were also clean and neat. She looked around for a moment. "What shall I make? Soup maybe? Would that be okay?"

"Sure." Ivan's face glowed as he moved toward the cellar door. "What vegetables do you want?"

"I'm not really sure yet. Mind if I look around?"

"Come with me then." Ivan lit a small lantern and led the way downstairs.

A small shelf of jars awaited them at the bottom—all the food Laura had prepared earlier in the spring or that had been brought in as wedding gifts.

"Not much here," Ivan said apologetically. He was ready to say something more but changed his mind.

"Oh, there's plenty here," Miriam said. She lifted a jar of tomatoes and carrots from the shelf, followed by a jar of green beans. Ivan took them from her as Miriam bent down to pick up a smaller jar of beef from a bottom shelf.

With a smile, Ivan led the way upstairs. He shut the lantern off and hung it on a nail. He moved to the counter and opened all the lids. As he worked, he asked, "So tell me the truth. Does your *Daett* and *Mamm* approve of this outing?"

"*Yah*, of course," Miriam said with a warm smile.

"That's nice of them, and it's nice of you to come."

Miriam found the measuring cups in the cupboard. Breaking the silence, she said, "Tell me about Laura, Ivan. I'd like to know about her."

A sigh escaped Ivan's lips. "I miss her, that's for sure. Who would have thought that something so sudden would happen? And that I'd be spared?"

She stopped him with a quick shake of her head. "Do not our people believe that the Lord does all things well?"

"*Yah*," he agreed. "But it's still hard to understand. Surely you know what I mean, what with the loss of Wayne."

Pain ran through her. "*Yah*, of course. But no matter how we feel about it, we have to get our thinking in line with what's right."

"I guess so." Ivan sighed again. "I think I needed to hear that. You've come apparently to feed the soul as well as the body."

Miriam didn't look at Ivan. "I don't know about that. Maybe my soul needs feeding too."

"We all need it from time to time." Ivan stood again and came closer to her. "Are you sure I can't help with the food?"

Miriam thought for a moment. "Let's see. Measure this into the larger pot, while I look for what spices I can find." Miriam ticked off the amounts by memory.

Ivan followed her instructions. When the last ingredient was added, he looked with satisfaction at the large pot. "So how'd I do?"

Miriam looked inside the pot. "I'm impressed."

"Ah, I've done well." Ivan patted himself on the back.

Miriam laughed and added the spices. As Ivan took his seat at the kitchen table, she turned on the stove and set the pot over the open flame. A comfortable silence settled over them as she stirred the liquid. She glanced at Ivan and saw a smile creep over his face. She was glad she'd come. This was one small step, but a right one. Where the Lord might lead, she wasn't sure, but her heart would heal eventually. Already faith bubbled up inside of her.

She stopped stirring and moved to the cupboard, getting down two bowls. She set them on the table. "I'm not sure where everything else is. The soup will take a while."

"We could talk then," Ivan said. "You can sit down, and I'll finish setting the table. The house gets mighty quiet these days. Too quiet."

Miriam sat at the table while the soup simmered and Ivan bustled about. Soon he too sat down. He looked happy—and she felt a small tingle of joy herself. Was this not a woman's place? Why should she complain if the Lord should supply the needs of her heart in a way she hadn't expected—even if the feelings of love weren't there?

Chapter Thirty-Nine

———◆◆◆———

Miriam was upstairs cleaning her room when she heard the sound of a buggy approaching. She peered out her window and caught a glimpse of a buggy that looked like Ivan's. Was it? She set down her cleaning supplies and hurried downstairs. Saturday afternoons didn't bring many visitors, so who else could it be but Ivan…or maybe Glen? Another look out the living room window confirmed her hunch. *Yah*, it was Ivan. She rushed out on the porch, aware that she looked like an overeager teenager.

Even Shirley noticed. She stuck her head out of an upstairs window and teased, "You sure have fallen for the man."

Protest died on Miriam's lips. She was teetering on the edge about Ivan and their informal relationship, but she certainly wasn't in love yet. Shirley wouldn't believe her though, which was just as *gut*. Shirley thought she'd given in completely to *Daett*'s approval of Ivan, and she'd taken that as direction for her relationship with Glen. As always, Miriam was the example for the family.

After she'd ventured over that night to make supper for him, Miriam had returned once more—at Ivan's request—to make supper again. But Ivan had said nothing about where their relationship would go from there. He'd helped her hitch Mindy into the buggy shafts and given her a simple goodbye and a smile as a send-off.

She would not go over again, Miriam had decided on the way home, until Ivan made some move other than give her invitations to cook for him. Not that she minded the work or his company, but a woman had her dignity. She'd be the laughingstock of the community if this continued for long.

Miriam stayed on the porch as Ivan tied his horse to the hitching post. Not until he was halfway across the lawn did she step off the porch to greet him.

"What brings you this way?" she asked, knowing she was the answer to the question.

"I came to ask 'when's supper'?" he said with a grin.

"Well," Miriam motioned toward the front porch, "not yet, but do you want to sit until then?"

"I was kidding, of course," Ivan said, taking a chair facing Miriam. "I hope this isn't an intrusion. I didn't plan the visit until the last minute."

"I have some time to visit," Miriam said. "We're almost done with the Saturday cleaning. The girls and *Mamm* can handle supper. You can stay if you want. We have enough."

Ivan settled back into the chair. "I really want to thank you for the two times you've already provided my supper. It's been a great comfort to my heart."

"I didn't mind. I understand you still miss Laura." Miriam reached over to touch Ivan's hand.

Ivan seemed lost in thought for a moment before he asked, "Have you heard anything from Oklahoma lately?"

Miriam nodded. "Aunt Fannie wrote a nice, breezy letter last week. Baby Jonathon's growing fat and chubby, and the green-house is up and operating the best Uncle William can with most of his stock damaged—and without Wayne." At the mention of Wayne, Miriam looked down.

Silence settled on the porch.

Ivan finally grunted. He leaned forward. "I shouldn't have brought up the subject. It's just that you've been so kind to me, and I wish there was something I could do for you."

"There's not much that can be done." Miriam smile tiredly.

"I guess not." Ivan settled in his chair again. Seconds later he sat up again. "But maybe this was all the Lord's will—what happened to Laura and Wayne? Do you think so?"

Miriam took a deep breath. "I wouldn't argue with the Lord, although it does hurt."

Ivan didn't look satisfied. "But, I mean, the Lord must have wanted this to happen. All of it."

Miriam met his gaze. "I don't know the answer. Isn't it enough that we deal with what the Lord gives us? Must we must speak of what He wants? Who can know His mind?"

"I suppose so." Ivan rubbed his hand over his eyes. "I guess I shouldn't try to think so deeply, but since Laura's gone…"

"You can talk all you want about your loss." Miriam gave him an encouraging smile.

Ivan's gaze was steady on Miriam's face. "You're a *wunderbah* person. Do you know that?"

Miriam searched her thoughts but could find nothing to say.

Ivan didn't seem to notice her silence. "We need to talk about us," he said.

"*Yah*," Miriam allowed. "I suppose we do."

Ivan straightened in his chair. "You've been over to my house for supper twice now, which I really appreciate. And your *daett* has given his permission to…" Ivan waved his hand around. "At least to seeing you, and you seem agreeable. But perhaps we should speak more…" Ivan stopped as if he didn't know how to continue.

Miriam broke in. "It's okay, Ivan. I understand. Maybe we don't have to decide anything now. Maybe we can just go on like this."

"I don't know about that." He glanced at her. "We used to be sweet on each other—once upon a time."

"But a lot has changed since then."

"*Yah*." He hesitated. "I want to tell you something, Miriam. I admit now that I shouldn't have allowed the news of your inheritance to make me uncertain after I was already seeing Laura. Thankfully Laura wasn't offended, and she loved me through that time. She was who I needed her to be. I guess what I'm saying is that my marriage to Laura was no mistake."

"I never thought it was." Miriam kept her gaze away from him.

"Nor was your engagement to Wayne." Ivan hurried on. "We just weren't meant to be. The Lord had other plans at that time."

Miriam looked at him, her eyes tear-filled. "I wish I could understand the Lord's ways, but I can't. *Daett* thinks a blessing could yet be made out of the tragedy we've suffered. Do you agree with him?"

"I don't know." Ivan looked away. "That's too deep for me, but isn't it enough that we're here now and have another chance at love?"

"Do you love me?" Miriam studied his face.

Ivan met her gaze. "I'm not going to lie, Miriam. I admire you greatly, and you'll make a *wunderbah frau*. But I haven't forgotten Laura yet."

"Nor have I forgotten Wayne."

"Thanks for understanding." Ivan's gaze settled over the fields where the shadows had begun to lengthen.

After a few moments of silence, Miriam said, "On a lighter note, now how about that supper? Will you stay?"

Ivan appeared grateful as he nodded. "A man's own cooking gets awful dreary. My family can only help out so much."

Miriam stood. "I'll check on the progress and be right back."

A broad smile spread over Ivan's face.

Shirley and Naomi's questioning gaze greeted Miriam in the kitchen. "What's up with the two of you? It looked like a heavy discussion you were having," Naomi asked.

Miriam smiled. "Never mind that. He would like to stay for supper. How long till it's ready?"

"Half an hour if you'll help us," Shirley said. "*Mamm*'s in the bedroom with baby Anna at the moment. That slowed supper down."

"I'll tell Ivan," Naomi offered, her face a tease. "He can entertain himself with *Daett* and the boys in the barn until then."

"You do that," Miriam agreed.

"You just want to flirt with him." Shirley made a face at her sister.

Naomi giggled and dashed out of the kitchen.

"How's it going *really*?" Shirley asked once Naomi was gone.

"Okay, I think. We're getting there slowly."

Shirley gave Miriam a quick hug before she turned back to the stove. "But you're trying to do the right thing. That's *gut*."

And that was *gut*, Miriam told herself. She took the bread out of the cupboard and began to slice it. They would take things a day at a time until both of their hearts had begun to heal. Love would come when the Lord willed it.

Chapter Forty

Shirley slipped out of the washroom door and into the darkness of the summer night. Behind her the chatter of girls in the living room after the Sunday-evening hymn singing died away. She was now one of the dating girls, Shirley told herself as she searched the darkness for Glen's buggy. She felt downright old and ready to settle down—a thought that made her giggle behind her hand. To be truthful, this was more fun than she'd imagined. Not as thrilling as a ride in Jonas Beachy's convertible or an evening spent in a fancy restaurant, but certainly more wholesome. She might actually get to like this. And she'd almost forgotten about the scars on her face. She thought less about them with each hour she spent with Glen.

Shirley walked past two waiting buggies and pulled herself up to settle on the buggy seat beside Glen.

"I see you know how to find buggies in the dark."

"Didn't think I could?" Shirley gave Glen a fake glare and then laughed. "Just because I used to ride in—" Shirley bit off the words. She didn't want to offend Glen and revealing bitterness wasn't necessary. "Actually, I like your buggy," she finished.

"Glad to hear that." Glen smiled as his horse took up a steady gait.

Shirley took a deep breath and rushed out the words she'd been thinking. "Glen, don't you think we should both take the baptismal instruction classes this fall?"

Glen appeared startled at the sudden change in conversation. "What brings that up?"

"Well, we're…" Shirley reached for his hand. "We're both getting *old*, you know."

They laughed together.

"You're serious, aren't you?" Glen regarded Shirley with a steady gaze.

"*Yah.*"

"I guess I've been thinking about it," Glen admitted. "How did you know?"

"I didn't. It was my own thought."

"I like that." Glen squeezed Shirley's hand. "We think alike."

Shirley looked up at him. "I feel all old and decrepit, but it feels okay."

Glen made a face. "That's not *gut.*"

"Oh, it is for me." Shirley didn't hesitate. "Believe it."

"You? Old and decrepit?" Glen shook his head. "You'll always be young and beautiful to me."

Shirley clung to Glen's hand. "Why do you say such *wunderbah* things to me?"

"Because they're true!"

They traveled in silence for a while, and then Glen asked, "How's Miriam doing with Ivan?"

Shirley leaned against Glen before she answered. "Okay, I think. She's a great example to me. I know that."

"They're not dating though," Glen said. "At least they weren't last Sunday."

"No," Shirley admitted. "Miriam is coming home with Lee and Mark tonight as usual. Apparently Ivan wants a more informal approach. Not that Miriam has complained, but they do things a little differently. I do think they'll be getting married, but not this fall since Miriam has her teaching job in Oklahoma. I don't know how they'll work that out. All I know is that Ivan needs a *frau*, and Miriam is the most decent woman available for him."

"I wouldn't disagree," Glen allowed. "But I don't understand the no dating part."

"Miriam knows what she's doing," Shirley assured him.

Glen tilted his head. "I saw Mary Troyer making eyes at Ivan today. She's been widowed for a year or so and has two small children. I'm sure she could use a husband and, unlike Miriam, quick like."

Shirley groaned. "I hope not. I'd hate to see Miriam lose another prospect. Miriam is trying to follow *Daett's* instructions since Wayne passed. I think it'll work out this time."

"*Yah*, I heard through the grapevine that your *daett's* behind the whole thing. That he's trying to set up Miriam to heal her heart and bring a blessing out of the tragedy."

Shirley shrugged. "*Daett* did interfere at first, and I didn't like that. But Miriam seems to think *Daett* was correct, and who am I to second-guess my eldest sister? And I'm tired of running my own life. Look where that got me! But then again, here I am…"

"With me," Glen finished. "So I guess your logic must be right. I wasn't trying to say I disagreed. I hope Miriam does find happiness with Ivan."

"She will." Shirley sat up as he turned into the Yoder driveway. "And here we are—home!"

"Yep." Glen agreed. He pulled to a stop by the hitching post. Lee's buggy pulled in behind them with Mark and Miriam. Glen tied his horse and waited beside Shirley while Lee and Mark unhitched.

"Howdy there, stranger!" Lee hollered over to them.

"And to you," Glen hollered back.

Miriam approached them with a smile. "It's *gut* to see you here tonight, Glen. I'm happy for the two of you."

"Thank you." Glen grinned in the soft buggy light. "And the best to you and Ivan."

Miriam lowered her head. "The Lord will guide us. And thank you for the concern. I'm going inside. Are you two coming in?"

Shirley stepped forward but Glen touched her arm. "The moon's coming up. I thought Shirley and I could go for a little midnight stroll."

Miriam chuckled. "Not till midnight, I hope."

"Figuratively speaking, of course," Glen said with a laugh.

"You enjoy yourself then." Miriam moved on toward the house.

Once Miriam had left, Glen whispered, "She's burdened about something."

"She's suffered a lot," Shirley whispered back. "Suffering can do that to you."

Lee's booming voice interrupted them. "How's the happy couple tonight?"

"Going for a moonlight walk," Shirley chirped.

"Can't get more romantic than that," Mark smirked.

"I didn't know the moon was up!" Lee peered around teasingly.

"Shows how romantic you are!" Mark pointed at the horizon. "Just coming up."

"I have other sterling qualities," Lee protested as the two moved on.

"He's just teasing." Shirley glanced at Glen. "Don't take him seriously. Lee's the kindest and humblest fellow around."

"*Yah*, I thought so." Glen's gaze followed the two men as they entered the house. "I like your family a lot."

"That's *gut*, but come, let's go." Shirley pulled on Glen's hand. "You were going on a romantic stroll with me, remember?"

"Oh, I remember." Glen moved ahead of Shirley and pulled them both into a run.

At the pasture gate they paused, and Shirley undid the latch. On the other side, they walked hand-in-hand, pausing moments later to watch the moon rise. The globe inched upward and soon hung inches above the horizon.

"It's so peaceful," Shirley said softly as she leaned into Glen's shoulder.

"I know," he said. "But time moves on, and I guess our *rumspringa* time is about over if we join the baptismal class."

Shirley pulled her head away. "Now what brought that up?"

"I guess the night and the seriousness of this."

"Romance is serious," Shirley mused. "I never thought of that before."

"It's the Lord's way of pointing us in the right direction. Family, home, children, responsibility, hard work. He makes the way as pleasant as He can."

"Now you're going to make me cry. Stop it!" Shirley ordered.

Glen dug in his pocket and came out with his handkerchief. "Sorry, I didn't mean to." He touched her cheek lightly. "I think the Lord is leading the two of us together, Shirley. To spend our lives with each other."

"Is this a proposal of marriage, Glen?"

"No," he chuckled. "That would be a little rushed, but I can't imagine myself with anyone else as my *frau*."

"Hush, Glen. You've said enough."

"I know. Scratch my denial and take this as a statement of my intentions."

Shirley leaned against Glen's shoulder again.

Why she always hesitated when Glen tried to deepen their relationship, she had no idea. But he was patient with her, and she usually gave in. That meant they would likely be engaged before long. A thrill ran through her at the thought. Glen would be her husband someday! Not this wedding season, of course, but perhaps the next or the following. The possibility seemed very real and close. Like the moon in the sky. The large, glimmering globe felt like a person could touch it even though it remained far in the distance.

"Penny for your thoughts?" Glen teased.

Shirley felt heat rise up her neck, but she would be honest. "I was thinking about our wedding someday."

He pulled in a long breath. "That's nice to hear. I needed that encouragement."

"You're always so patient and kind."

He shrugged. "With you, it's not difficult."

"You can kiss me, you know." Shirley lifted her face to him.

Now Glen hesitated. "Don't couples usually save kissing for their engagement?"

He was quite innocent, Shirley thought, and then the words blurted out of her mouth. "Jonas and I didn't."

"And see where that ended up?" Glen regarded her skeptically.

"You're not Jonas. Kiss me, Glen, please."

"I'm not like Jonas," he protested.

"I know." Shirley pulled him close, and Glen's hands tightened around her shoulders. "Kiss me, Glen."

"I'm not sure about this, Shirley."

"Stop talking, Glen, please."

He still hesitated.

Shirley reached for his face with both hands. The moon hung beside him and illuminated part of his handsome face.

Glen's hands gently gripped Shirley's shoulders as he gave in. The slight bristles of his shaven face brushed her cheek before his lips met hers.

Shirley slipped her hands into his hair and wouldn't let go.

Glen pulled back after a moment, but lowered his head and his lips met hers again.

Shirley shivered. Glen's kisses were better than Jonas's! Glen's kisses had something Jonas's didn't. With Jonas, *yah*, her heart had pounded, but tonight there was a soft throb in her throat and Glen's solid character all around her. This man would always be here for her. He was steadier than a massive rock in midstream. Pleasure in his presence hadn't come in a hurry, but it had built until it enveloped her whole heart. That had never been in any of Jonas's kisses.

Glen lifted his head and appeared dazed.

Shirley held his hand and waited for his response.

"You are very *wunderbah*, Shirley," he finally whispered. He pulled her close, and his lips brushed the hair on top of her head.

Shirley looked up at him. "What did you really think when you saw me the first time—back at the gathering when I had all those ugly scars?"

Glen shushed her with a touch of his finger on her lips. "You kept your face hidden for a while. Remember?"

She nodded and his finger found her cheek and traced it gently. "You were more beautiful than I could ever imagine, Shirley. As you will be when I kiss you in the light of day."

She buried her face in his chest. "I'm going to write down and sell your beautiful words someday, Glen. They're worth their weight in gold."

"No, they're not," he whispered into her ear.

Shirley embraced him again. She let go when the tears had ceased to sting her eyes. "Should we go home now?"

"*Yah.*" He led the way slowly back across the pasture. "This is where you agreed to date me, remember?"

She nodded.

"It's a magical meadow."

He let go of her hand to open the pasture gate, and invited her to lead the way.

Glen was sent from the Lord, Shirley told herself. Certainty grew, and she figured it would continue to grow the longer she knew him. She took his hand again as they walked to the house.

Chapter Forty-One

———◆◆◆———

Ivan tossed in his sleep as he dreamed of great waves and crashing breakers lashing a rocky seashore. He was trying repeatedly to place a small boat in the water, only to have it cast back before he could climb in. He could hear voices calling him from the distance, but he couldn't make out the words. Ivan strained to listen and finally answered, only to awaken with a start.

He sat bolt upright and peered around the early morning darkness in his bedroom. This was the second dream he'd had that night, and it was the same as earlier. It was odd because he didn't often have nightmares. Was this a warning of some sort? But of what? He had only been to the ocean once in his life—with a group of young people during his *rumspringa* time. The experience hadn't been unpleasant, and certainly there had been no storms...and no bad dreams at the time. Even the accident when Laura passed hadn't produced nightmares. *Yah*, great sorrow, but not bad dreams. He rubbed his head. Miriam had been along on that *rumspringa* trip to the ocean, and he had enjoyed her presence. They had smiled and spoken to each other every chance they had. Miriam didn't give him nightmares.

Ivan groaned and got out of bed, dressing in the darkness. Next week he had to go back to work—a fact he didn't look forward to. He couldn't allow his relationship with Miriam to lurch on like this, though he knew his heart hadn't healed yet—nor had Miriam's. Ivan found the kitchen and lit a kerosene lamp. He paused to gaze at the flickering flame. This time the truth must be faced. That was what his dream was about. He'd have to face this issue head on. Laura might be alive today if he'd spoken his mind sooner instead of when they were on their way to town for a shopping trip.

Ivan set the lamp on the kitchen table. He had to be honest and admit that his heart was not drawn to Miriam again like he'd hoped and even prayed. Instead, he was being oddly drawn to the widow Mary Troyer. He'd noticed this at the last two Sunday services but hadn't wanted to admit the feelings. Likely the bishop's words that morning after Ivan left the graveyard had focused his attention on Mary, but he'd avoided the matter, as usual. The widow Mary's smiles reminded him a lot of Laura's. How Mary had remained a widow for almost two years, he couldn't imagine. Maybe Mary's two children were a drawback to some men, but he didn't mind. They were cute little girls, and he could easily imagine them as his own.

Ivan poured milk over his cereal and sat down to eat. Mary would heal his heart in ways that Miriam couldn't. How, he wasn't sure. Maybe because Mary was further from the pain of her loss than either Miriam or he was. Things worked that way, didn't they? And Mary attracted him in ways that Miriam didn't. He admired Miriam, but it wasn't the same as attraction. He'd thought this time things would be different, and they might have been if Mary hadn't appeared. Then the question had come into his mind: Would Mary welcome his attentions?

Yah, she would. He was sure of that. Mary's shy smiles in his direction were all the evidence he needed. In the meantime, Miriam must be told. He would have to face her with the truth this time. And sooner rather than later. She must not be hurt again.

The thought straightened his back. He finished his cereal and set the bowl in the sink. With his chin set, he slipped out into the dawning light and entered the barn. Old Billy was in the harness in no time, and Ivan was on his way. He would visit Miriam first. She needed to know. Then if Mary turned him down, he would be left with no prospects, but that would just have to be.

Sorrow gathered around his heart as he drove along the still, morning roads. Miriam would be surprised to see him, especially so early in the day. But would his words upset her? It was even likely Miriam had already picked up the uncertainty in his heart. Miriam was that kind of woman. She was a woman worthy of a decent husband, and that would not be him. Miriam would take his decision with the same grace she took all the sorrows life handed her. She might even be relieved. Their former attraction had not revived itself for her either. He would have known if it had.

"Hurry up there," Ivan urged Billy. He wanted this chore over and done with. The dread of it crept on him as the Yoder farm appeared in the distance. He could still drive on to Mary Troyer's place, which lay a few miles on the other side of Possum Valley. He could stop in to see Miriam on the way home. But his hands pulled the reins to the left, and Billy turned in the Yoder driveway and stopped in front of the hitching post.

Thankfully Miriam opened the front door and stepped out before he reached the porch. A slight smile played on her face. "*Gut* morning. What brings you out so early?"

"Well, I have to go back to work next week," he said haltingly. The words made no sense, but nothing did right now.

"I see. Are you feeling well?" Miriam regarded him with concern.

"I'm okay." Ivan stepped up on the porch and sat on a porch rocker without invitation.

Miriam obviously wasn't convinced and stepped closer to feel his forehead with her hand. "Are you sick or troubled?"

"Nightmares." Ivan looked up at her. "I'm sorry, Miriam, but will you sit down? I have something to say."

"*Yah.*" Miriam tucked her dress in and sat on the other chair. "Were they dreams about the accident and Laura?"

"No, this isn't about the accident...or Laura." Ivan let out a long breath. "It's you and me, Miriam. I can't go on like this, and you deserve to know."

Miriam was silent, her gaze fixed on the porch floor. The front door flew open before Ivan could continue, and Shirley stepped out.

"Oh, it's you, Ivan. I thought I heard someone drive in." Shirley smiled at them.

Miriam waved her away with a quick motion of her hand, before she turned to Ivan. "It's okay. I think I understand."

"*Yah*, I suppose you do. You're that kind of woman. Please don't think you're to blame for this. Your *daett* was well intentioned, but in my heart, Miriam, I just don't think we are meant to be."

Miriam sat back in her chair. At last she said, "Thank you for being honest this time."

He reached for her hand. "I've enjoyed our times together, Miriam. I really have. Like I did before when we were in our *rumspringa* time. Remember that trip to Virginia Beach?"

Miriam didn't answer.

Ivan hurried on. "You'll meet someone someday who will be just right for you, Miriam. I know that. You're decent and upright and..."

"It's okay, Ivan." Miriam smiled slightly. "You don't have to go on."

"I'm so sorry," he said again, rising to his feet. "I really am."

Miriam took a deep breath. "The Lord will give us both grace. He always has, it seems. Even in the darkest times of the night. Thank you again for being honest."

"Then we part in peace?"

"In peace." Miriam stood. "Goodbye, Ivan. I hope you find love again."

"And the same to you." Ivan turned to go. He stopped halfway across the lawn for a quick wave. Miriam, still standing on the porch, waved back.

With a final wave Ivan climbed into his buggy and drove Billy out of the Yoder lane. He turned toward his home. The visit to the widow Mary Troyer could wait. Miriam deserved that much respect. Mary would still be available on Sunday afternoon, and he would visit her then. They could be wed this fall, he was sure. Peace settled in his heart as Billy's hooves beat on the pavement.

"Comfort Miriam's heart, Lord," Ivan prayed out loud. "Give her a promise for tomorrow. Give her a future You bless, my Lord."

Chapter Forty-Two

———— ◆◆◆ ————

Two weeks had gone by since Ivan's early morning visit to the Yoder farm. Miriam sat quietly on the couch as *Daett* read the Scriptures for the morning devotions. She caught only snatches of his words as her mind spun with thoughts. First there was the pain as she recalled that soon after Ivan's visit he'd apparently turned to Mary Troyer for comfort. After their first date, Mary had still glowed with happiness at the next Sunday service. Once more Miriam had been passed over. *Daett* had refused to believe the news for a few days. He was ready to make a trip over to speak with Ivan until *Mamm* begged him to reconsider.

Second, there was her decision to schedule a meeting with Mr. Bland's sister, Rose, to end this whole affair about the inheritance. Mr. Bland had meant only the best when he'd left her the farm and the money, but she'd been unable to handle the matter properly. Perhaps Mr. Bland had misjudged her character. Well, at least the money had gone to good use after the tornado in Oklahoma. But the farm would forever be a source of contention in the Yoder family. Perhaps it was best that Rose take it.

Miriam forced herself to tune in to *Daett's* words: "…and being not weak in faith, he considered not his own body now dead, when he was about an hundred years old, neither yet the deadness of Sara's womb: he staggered not at the promise of God through unbelief; but was strong in faith, giving glory to God; and being fully persuaded…"

Miriam sat up straighter on the couch. That was what she needed! The promise of the Lord. She needed to believe that He would be with her always. Then she could be like Abraham, trusting that everything would turn out okay.

Miriam listened to *Daett's* words from the book of Romans again. "Now it was not written for his sake alone, that it was imputed to him; but for us also, to whom it shall be imputed, if we believe on him that raised up Jesus our Lord from the dead…" She did believe, Miriam told herself. But that seemed a little too easy. The last time she'd faced troubles, she had fled to Oklahoma to find a fresh promise for the future. Now she would return there this fall, but Oklahoma was no longer the land of promise she had once imagined it to be. Apparently wherever she lived could be the land of promise if she had faith. Christ was her Lord, and a lord took care of his subjects.

A faint stir of hope moved in her heart. Ivan had wished them both peace when he'd spoken that morning on the porch weeks ago. He likely found that easy in his new relationship with Mary Troyer. She, though, had to walk alone. And she would…by faith. By faith she would begin today by making the trip in to Sugarcreek and signing away the farm. The Yoder household income would be sparse as a result, but perhaps that was why *Daett* had read the Scripture on faith and promises. When Lee and Mark had been told last week that Mr. Bland's farm would no longer be in the family, they'd walked around with glum faces ever since. *Yah*, the Yoder family had difficult financial times ahead of them.

Daett closed the Bible. As he laid it down, he said, "May the Lord give us His promises, and may we believe."

Mamm reached for *Daett*'s arm. "Do you really think this is the right course about the farm? There's still time to change your mind, Eli."

Daett didn't hesitate. "There has been nothing but trouble for Miriam since that money came into our family. I'm ashamed of myself that I even let it happen to begin with."

Mamm fell silent, and Miriam didn't add anything. She couldn't agree completely with *Daett*. The Lord had made *gut* to come out of the money. Look how many people had been helped after the tornado damage in Oklahoma, including her own aunt and uncle. *Daett* might fail to see that, but she didn't.

"Let us pray." *Daett* got down on his knees and the others followed. Miriam prayed her own prayer while *Daett* prayed his: "Help us all, dear Lord, to believe and hear Your promises wherever we are." Long moments later *Daett* called out, "Amen."

Miriam quickly sent another short prayer heavenward. "Help me walk in faith both here in Possum Valley as well as Oklahoma when I return this fall."

When they all stood, Shirley slipped into the kitchen. Miriam followed her. "Are you okay?" Miriam asked.

Shirley shrugged. "I guess so. All this talk about the farm going back to the Blands doesn't really affect me. I'll be gone and married in a few years." A smile flashed across her face.

This too was also the grace of the Lord, Miriam thought. If her relationship with Ivan had ended a few weeks ago, Shirley might have despaired. But her love for Glen had grown in leaps and bounds of late. Just in time, as usual, to save the day. Bitterness could easily have overwhelmed Shirley over the failure of *daett*'s advice for Ivan and Miriam.

"How are *you* doing?" Shirley reached over to squeeze Miriam's arm. "I don't know how you hold up under all this."

"I don't know myself sometimes," Miriam admitted. "The Lord helps me, I guess."

"I'll be praying for you," Shirley whispered.

That was something new, Miriam thought. Shirley didn't often mention prayer. Tears stung Miriam's eyes. "Thank you. I appreciate that."

Shirley looked up as *Mamm* appeared in the kitchen and wrapped both of them in a tight hug. "My heart just breaks over this situation," *Mamm* whispered.

"We must pray about everything," Shirley said.

Miriam couldn't believe Shirley was the strong one this morning. What *wunderbah* things the Lord's grace had accomplished.

"We will make it with His help." *Mamm* let go of the girls and sat down on a kitchen chair. She sighed but hope was in her voice. "When I see how much faith Miriam has, I know anything is possible."

"That's not totally true," Miriam protested. "I'm faithless at times."

"You would say that," Shirley countered. "You have no idea how much of an example you are to me and to the rest of the family. Isn't that true, *Mamm*?"

Mamm nodded, her eyes now filled with tears.

"But—no, don't say that," Miriam struggled for words.

Mamm reached out to touch Miriam's arm. "The Lord's grace is best accepted with a thankful heart. And I know you do that."

"Mr. Bland's sister, Rose, is here!" Naomi called from the living room.

Miriam took a deep breath and left *Mamm* seated on the kitchen chair with her face still damp with tears—as was hers. Miriam smiled to think that Rose would ascribe her tears to the loss of the farm, but the tears were because of the Lord's grace to her in all that had happened. She'd come to understand she'd been given much more than she'd realized. That would explain how she had gone through the past weeks without a breakdown or some such thing. Ivan didn't have her heart like Wayne had, but the sight of Mary on her way out to Ivan's buggy on Sunday evening had still been humbling. Ivan had chosen another woman over her again. Yet she'd been able to continue the conversation with the other unmarried women until Lee had been ready to leave.

Miriam wiped her eyes as she walked out to Rose's car. "*Gut* morning," she greeted. "Thank you for coming to pick me up."

Rose regarded Miriam with skepticism. "Is everything okay, young woman?"

"*Yah*, it's fine." Miriam walked around to climb into the passenger side.

Rose still looked at her after Miriam had snapped on her seat belt. "Is your father behind this decision to not keep the farm?"

Miriam shrugged. "Some. But this was my choice in the end. I want to give the farm back to your family. It would be for the best."

Rose sighed. "Well, I assume you at least still have the money. That's something anyway."

Miriam felt blood rush into her cheeks. "Actually I gave that away…for tornado relief in Oklahoma."

Rose's hand paused on the steering wheel. "You did *what*?"

Miriam looked out the side window and remained silent.

"Well, that's nothing to be ashamed of, I guess," Rose finally stated. "Maybe we'd all be better off living that way. Is that why you did it? Because of your Amish beliefs?"

"It's a little more complicated than that," Miriam said. Thankfully Rose seemed to accept the explanation and didn't ask any more questions on the drive into Sugarcreek.

Rose was sober faced as she parked the car and led the way into Mr. Rosenberg's office.

The smell in the legal office was familiar from Miriam's previous visits. Here she had come as a scared, young Amish woman about to be told she'd been given a farm and two million dollars. How far the road had led since then. Miriam couldn't begin to put the experience into words. The grace of the Lord had been with her all the way. That was the only response that came to her mind.

When they were seated in Mr. Rosenberg's office, Rose said, "Miriam wants to give the farm to me."

Mr. Rosenberg appeared surprised, but he didn't protest. He glanced at Miriam and then at Rose. "Very well. I'll draw the papers up and have them ready to sign next week."

And that was that. The meeting was over quickly, and the two women left the office and headed back to Rose's car.

Once they were beyond the town limits, Rose glanced at Miriam, "I've made a decision, and I don't want any argument. You're surrendering the farm, but that leaves me with a farm that needs working. Do I look like a farmer? Of course not. I will need someone to manage the farm for me, and I'd like it to be your father. I want him to manage it and to keep the net profits."

"*Daett* will object," Miriam said.

"Then I will speak with him." Rose was firm. "I need someone to take care of the place for me. Besides, maybe I want to lay up some treasures myself in heaven. When I'm gone I'll leave the farm to your oldest brother, but don't tell your father. He doesn't need to know. I'll speak to the lawyer, and we'll settle that next week too."

"Okay," Miriam said. She settled back in the seat and didn't say anything for the rest of the ride home.

When Rose dropped her off and headed out of the lane, Miriam turned toward the barn. She had best tell this news to *Daett* at once. He wouldn't like it if she waited. The barn door was ajar, and Miriam pushed it open the rest of the way.

Daett looked up from his work near the hay. "*Yah*, you're back already."

"The papers will be ready for me to sign next week," Miriam said, moving closer.

Daett seemed intent on the harness he was mending. "That's okay. I understand."

Miriam waited a few seconds. "*Daett*, Rose wants you to continue farming the place like before and keep any profits."

Daett looked up and the harness slid from his hands. "How can this be? Did you beg, Miriam, for charity?"

Miriam shook her head. "I wouldn't do that, *Daett*. You know that. This was Rose's idea. She said she's not a farmer and can't manage a farm. She needs someone to do it for her. Besides, she said she wants to lay up treasures in heaven like we are."

Tears formed in *Daett's* eyes. After a moment, he surprised Miriam by saying, "Then I will humble myself and accept this gift when it is offered." He walked over to his daughter. "You are a woman of great virtue, Miriam. You influence the world around you for *gut*, even an *Englisha* woman like Rose. And who knows what would have happened after the accident if Shirley hadn't had your example to follow."

Miriam lowered her gaze to the floor. "You shouldn't say such things, *Daett*."

Daett's arms reached around Miriam's shoulders.

Not since she was a little girl had he hugged her like this. Miriam hugged him back, feeling his strength and smelling the leather on his hands.

Daett loosened his hug. His voice rumbled, "You are a woman among a thousand, Miriam, full of the grace and the glory of the Lord. Blessed may your days be on this earth, and may a thousand see the light of heaven in your life. May you live fully and walk the fruitful path that has been chosen for you. May you remember that your *mamm* and I will always love you."

"Oh, *Daett*," Miriam whispered, unable to move, "I am undeserving of such a blessing."

"Go now." *Daett* grinned and turned back to his work.

Miriam slipped away and closed the barn door behind her. On

the walk to the house the tears finally came—great floods of them. Miriam felt her way to a porch rocker. She let the sobs overwhelm her. *Mamm* must have heard because she came out to sit beside her. Shirley and Naomi stuck their heads out once but wisely retreated.

"It's okay," *Mamm* comforted, gently stroking Miriam's arm.

"I know," Miriam said once she could speak. "That's why I'm crying."

Mamm smiled and seemed to understand as she wrapped her eldest daughter in a tight hug.

"I have something for you," *Mamm* said after long moments of silence. She stood and disappeared into the house. The front door closed softly behind her but soon opened again. "This came a couple of weeks ago," *Mamm* said, when Miriam didn't look up. "Rosemary, Wayne's *mamm*, sent it. In her letter, she said they found this painting when the family cleaned out Wayne's room after his passing. At first, they couldn't figure out why he had a painting. Rosemary eventually visited the local *Englisha* artist whose name is written on the lower corner. He told them that Wayne had commissioned the work for his beloved. They think you should have it. Wayne meant it for you, Miriam."

Miriam looked up slowly and focused on the canvas *Mamm* was holding. There was a stream, a small bridge, a log, and water flowing, each ripple clearly seen. Miriam sat upright and gently took the painting from *Mamm's* hand.

"Do you know where this is?" *Mamm* asked.

Tears blinded Miriam.

"Do you?" *Mamm* repeated.

"*Yah*," Miriam choked. "It's the place where Wayne asked me to wed him. The place where I gave him my heart. He'd said something about having it painted, but I thought he was teasing."

Miriam clutched the canvas tightly to her. "Even from heaven Wayne has blessed me." She raised her eyes toward the heavens and whispered. "Thank you, Wayne. How I've loved you."

Discussion Questions

1. The story opens with a letter from Miriam's *mamm*. What advantage does this form of communication have over more modern forms? Does letter writing deepen relationships? Is slower better at times?

2. How well did Miriam handle Esther Swartz's return to Oklahoma and Esther's attempt to renew her relationship with Wayne Yutzy?

3. Do you think Miriam should have kept the secret of the two million dollar gift from her family?

4. Wayne Yutzy returns to the site of their engagement with Miriam where they renew their relationship and plan their wedding date. How does this choice illuminate Wayne's character?

5. What are your feelings on the insistence of Miriam's father that money is always evil and always corrupts? How well did Miriam deal with her father?

6. What advice would you have for Shirley? Should she have renewed her friendship with Jonas Beachy? Would their relationship have survived? Would you want Shirley to marry into the Beachy family?

7. How well is Ivan Mast adjusting to his marriage with Laura? Was Laura wise to marry him? Do you think their marriage would have been happy?

8. What are your feelings on Wayne's dalliance with Esther while Miriam visited in Possum Valley? Was the incident inevitable? Could Esther have succeeded if she'd handled the matter differently? Do you sympathize with Esther?

9. Does Miriam's choice to forgive Wayne for kissing Esther raise your opinion of her? What would you have done in a similar situation?

10. When Shirley ventured forth a new *rumspringa* adventure, she met Glen Weaver. What do you think of him? What do you think drew him to Shirley?

11. When Wayne and his sister, Joy, are taken in the tornado, what do you think of the Amish's unquestioning belief in the Lord's will? Do you think this prevents bitterness? How does it help with the grieving process? Would you make similar choices?

12. What do you think of the ending of the book? What do you think the future holds for Miriam?

About the Author

Jerry Eicher's Amish fiction has sold more than 700,000 books. After a traditional Amish childhood, Jerry taught for two terms in Amish and Mennonite schools in Ohio and Illinois. Since then he's been involved in church renewal, preaching, and teaching Bible studies. Jerry lives with his wife, Tina, and their four children in Virginia.

A Checklist of Jerry Eicher's
Harvest House Books

———— ••• ————

The Adams County Trilogy
Rebecca's Promise
Rebecca's Return
Rebecca's Choice

Hannah's Heart
A Dream for Hannah
A Hope for Hannah
A Baby for Hannah

Little Valley Series
A Wedding Quilt for Ella
Ella's Wish
Ella Finds Love Again

Fields of Home Series
Missing Your Smile
Following Your Heart
Where Love Grows

Emma Raber's Daughter
Katie Opens Her Heart
Katie's Journey to Love
Katie's Forever Promise

The Beiler Sisters
Holding a Tender Heart
Seeing Your Face Again
Finding Love at Home

Land of Promise Series
Miriam's Secret
A Blessing for Miriam
Miriam and the Stranger

My Dearest Naomi
Susanna's Christmas Wish

Nonfiction
The Amish Family Cookbook
 (with Tina Eicher)
My Amish Childhood

6-15

To learn more about Harvest House books and
to read sample chapters, visit our website:

www.harvesthousepublishers.com

HARVEST HOUSE PUBLISHERS
EUGENE, OREGON